# Shadow of a Doubt

## s. l. rottman

Ω
PEACHTREE
ATLANTA

*Also by S. L. Rottman*

HERO
ROUGH WATERS
HEAD ABOVE WATER
STETSON

Published by
PEACHTREE PUBLISHERS
1700 Chattahoochee Avenue
Atlanta, Georgia 30318-2112

*www.peachtree-online.com*

Text © 2003 by S. L. Rottman
Cover illustration © 2003 by Michelle Hinebrook

First trade paperback edition published July 2005

Cover design by Loraine M. Joyner
Book design by Melanie McMahon Ives

Manufactured in the United States of America
10 9 8 7 6 5 4 3 2 (hardcover)
10 9 8 7 6 5 4 3 2 1 (trade paperback)

Library of Congress Cataloging-in-Publication Data

Rottman, S. L.
  Shadow of a doubt / written by S. L. Rottman.-- 1st ed.
    p. cm.
Summary: As his sophomore year in high school begins, fifteen-year-old Shadow joins the forensics team, makes new friends, and struggles to cope with the return of his older brother, who ran away seven years earlier and now faces a murder trial.
    ISBN 1-56145-291-2 (hardcover)
    ISBN 1-56145-354-4 (trade paperback)
    [1. Brothers--Fiction. 2. Family problems--Fiction. 3. Forensics (Public speaking)--Fiction. 4. High schools--Fiction. 5. Schools--Fiction. 6. Runaways--Fiction.] I. Title.
PZ7.R7534 Sh 2003
[Fic]--dc21                                    2003004790

*With heartfelt thanks to all my family,
but especially to my son Paul,
for taking enough naps to allow me
to finish this book.*

∿

Special thanks goes to Carolyn Williamson,
for being a great forensics coach,
adviser, and GWHS Patriot.

And to my editor Vicky Holifield,
who has earned a week at a spa after all
the blood, sweat, and tears I put her through.

# Chapter One

**M**y fifteenth birthday marked the seventh year that Daniel had been gone. We didn't jump anymore every time the phone rang or someone knocked on our door. But there were times when the house got quiet, and I knew without asking what Mom and Dad were thinking about.

Even though I was a lot younger than my brother, we had been very close. He was my best friend. I guess he was my only friend. For nearly six months after Daniel left, I hadn't spoken to anyone, unless they spoke to me first. And then I only answered with one or two words. Mom took me to a psychologist after the first month of this behavior, but the shrink was convinced that I was mourning in my own way, and that I would get over it in time. He suggested my parents find a new activity to interest me.

They tried everything: model planes, drum lessons, even bird watching. Dad focused on sports, and I suffered through three days of karate, a week of swimming, two soccer practices, and almost two weeks of basketball before he finally gave up. Nothing worked. Without Daniel, nothing was interesting.

When I was ten, I found the library. We weren't supposed to be inside during recess, but the new librarian was a pushover for anyone who would sit quietly and read. I loved the peaceful and safe library much more than the chaotic noise of the playground. I almost ate fantasy books. The idea of different worlds and creatures fascinated me. Maybe I thought that in a different world trust and love could remain unbroken.

My fifteenth birthday also marked my first year of high school; I was finally a sophomore. I was eager to get to the new school. Junior high had been boring and predictable. In high school, I could pick some of my classes and get into subjects that actually required thought. Plus, two other junior high schools fed into the high school, so I'd be meeting new people. At Watson Junior High, I had stayed pretty much to myself, but I hoped to change and make new friends this year.

I showed up for high school registration dressed the way I normally did: black jeans and a black T-shirt. The new twist was the black leather jacket I had purchased with my birthday money. I had begun wearing nothing but black in the middle of the eighth grade. I liked the way it worked with my dark hair to make me look really pale. I was almost six-one, and the black accentuated my scrawny height. I had overheard some people say I looked like a vampire. I didn't really mind. I thought vampires were cool.

Dad had quit bugging me about the way I dressed, mostly because he was convinced I was following a trend. Mom, however, still hated it. A couple of weeks before school started, she bought me three new brightly colored shirts, some blue jeans, and a pair of khakis. She left a new outfit on my bed that first morning, hoping I'd wear it. She offered repeatedly to take the morning off and go with me to registration, but I kept telling her I'd be fine.

Even though my parents didn't like the fact that I wore all black, I knew they wouldn't do anything about it. They'd been like that ever since Daniel left. They'd tell me what they wanted me to do or not do, but they never told me I *had* to do anything. The only thing that they really insisted on was that I always tell them where I was going and when I would be home. If the plans changed or if I would be late, I was expected to call. I never really challenged their authority anyway. I sensed that it would be a terrible thing for all of us if I did.

Once, when I was ten, I was a few minutes late coming home from the library. When I got there, Mom was already on the phone with the police. She had called the library, and they had told her I wasn't there, so she'd panicked. For a long time after that, I had been afraid to be late. Now I figure being on time or calling if I'll be late is the better alternative to putting one or both of my parents in the hospital from a massive heart attack.

My fifteenth birthday wasn't any big party, but it was memorable for all of us. We were about to enter uncharted waters.

Daniel had been fifteen when he ran away.

A big banner above the door said, Palmer Panthers Welcome You! but the atmosphere at the school didn't seem overly friendly. I passed several tables where kids were signing up for clubs and activities. A bunch of cheerleaders in short skirts were selling T-shirts in one corner. I got in line in front of the registration table. The woman sitting behind it called "next," and I stepped up. Her neutral expression didn't change when I gave her my last name.

"Thompson...let's see. Oh yes, Thompson. Ernest—?"

"Shadow," I interrupted.

"Excuse me?"

"I go by Shadow."

She glanced down at my card and raised an eyebrow. She looked me up and down, studied the classes on my schedule, and began shaking her head. "Yes, well...um...Shadow, there appears to be a problem with your schedule. Step over to the line behind the next table, and they should be able to straighten it all out for you."

"What's wrong with my schedule?" I asked.

"They've put you in trigonometry and college prep chemistry."

I took my card and glanced at the rest of the classes. "My schedule's fine," I said. "Where do I go next?"

"Are you sure? You're—" She stopped and tried again. "We offer personal finance, auto shop, life science... That schedule is very..." She hesitated, as if she suddenly realized there wasn't a nice way to tell me it was a difficult schedule without making it obvious that she already thought I was an idiot.

"It's fine," I repeated. "Where do I go?"

She directed me over to the yearbook photographer. Although they assigned registration times alphabetically, everyone else seemed to have a group of friends to stand in line with. I saw a few people I recognized from Watson, but I didn't know any of their names, which was just as well. I wouldn't have known what to say to them anyway. I watched people watch me while I waited in line. I could tell the rest of the adults were forming the same opinion of me that the secretary had.

I'd been looking forward to a fresh start in high school, a chance to break out of the box I had put myself in. But it looked like nothing was going to change.

A guy wearing a black trench coat, combat boots, ragged jeans, and a Megadeath T-shirt came up and tapped me on the shoulder.

"Yo, you got a cigarette I could bum?"

"I don't smoke."

"Serious?" He seemed to be shocked. "Sorry, man." He turned around and walked off.

I sighed. Maybe someday I'd meet somebody who could actually wait until they knew me to form an opinion about me.

"Next," the photographer called, sounding incredibly bored.

I stepped up and sat on the little stool.

"Okay," he said, not looking up from the camera, "put your feet on the tape on the carpet, and turn your chin this way."

I complied.

"Good. Now take your sunglasses off."

"That's okay, I'll leave them on."

"I can't take your picture until you take your glasses off."

"Why?"

"Is there a problem here?" A very official-looking man dressed in a suit came up to see what was going on.

"I don't think so," I said.

The photographer made a face. "He won't take his sunglasses off."

"You have to take your sunglasses off," the man said.

"Why?" I asked again.

For a moment he seemed dumbfounded that I wasn't obeying immediately. "Because we don't allow students to take their pictures with their sunglasses on."

"Okay," I said, sliding off the stool, "Then I won't have my picture taken."

The man in the suit scowled. "You have to have your picture taken."

"Why? I'm not buying any."

"We need it for the yearbook."

I shrugged. "I probably won't buy one of those either," I said. I could tell the man in the suit was trying to control his anger.

"We need it for the school ID card."

"Fine," I said, getting on the stool again.

"Take your sunglasses off!" the photographer growled.

"Four people in front of me had their pictures taken with their glasses on."

"Those were corrective glasses, not decorative ones," the photographer said quickly.

"How do you know these aren't corrective?" I asked.

The man in the suit folded his arms across his chest. Without taking his eyes off me, he said, "Just take his picture."

Click. The camera flashed and I slid off the stool.

"Next," the photographer said in a relieved tone.

"Thanks," I said as I walked past him. "Now the rest of your day will seem easy!" He gave me an irritated look. I started toward the next line, the one to get my locker assignment.

"Just a moment." The man in the suit was still frowning.

"What?" I asked. I carefully kept my tone calm.

"What's your name?"

"Shadow."

"Shadow? Do you have a last name to go with that?"

"Thompson."

He stared at my face for a moment. "Daniel Thompson's brother?"

Embarrassed by the sudden tightening of my throat, I just nodded at him.

"Well, Shadow Thompson, my name is Mr. Barnett. I'm the Dean of Students. Do you know what the Dean of Students does?"

"You deal with discipline problems."

"Among other things, yes. So let me make this simple for you, Mr. Thompson. Classes start next week. If any teacher asks you to remove your sunglasses, or your leather jacket, or any other accessory you may have on, you will do so immediately. If you don't, you will begin the year serving detention for defiance. Is that clear?"

I nodded again.

"I have the feeling we'll be seeing a lot of each other this year," Mr. Barnett said.

"I doubt that'd be good for either of us," I muttered.

"What was that?" he said sharply.

Before repeating my remark, I took a good look at his face and decided that this was going the wrong way. "Nothing," I said. I went and stood in the next line.

"You are a dead man."

I turned around to find a short guy with big glasses and an even bigger nose standing behind me. His head came only halfway up my chest. I had to laugh.

"Is that a threat?" I asked.

"Not from me. From Mr. Barnett. He picks a target and he won't forget it. Your next three years here are going to be hell."

"How do you know?"

"My brother. He graduated a couple of years ago. He had a run-in with Barnett his first year, and Barnett never forgave him."

I shrugged. "I don't plan on talking to Barnett any more," I said simply.

"Good luck," he snorted. "I've heard it's not always that easy." After a few seconds' pause, the little guy asked, "What's your name?"

"Shadow. Shadow Thompson."

"Good to meetcha, Shadow," he said, pushing his glasses further up on his nose. "I'm Vernon Thomas."

"Next." The lady didn't even look up to see if I had stepped forward or not. "Name?"

"Thompson."

"Ernest Thompson?" Before I could reply, she was holding a card out for me. "Locker number 815. Next. Name?"

Vernon hustled up and gave his name. I stood off a few feet, looking around to make sure I had done everything I needed to do.

"Locker number 814. Next. Name?"

Vernon looked over at me. "Looks like we're neighbors," he said, grinning.

"Yeah, it does."

He looked at his watch. "I've got fifteen minutes to kill."

"Waiting for a ride?"

"No. I saw a sign saying that there's a meeting for the forensics team at ten-thirty in room 28. I'm going to check it out."

"Forensics?"

"Yeah, you know, speech and stuff."

"You like speaking in front of people?" I asked. I had gotten Cs in English class every semester we had to give a speech. I did not enjoy speaking in front of large groups.

"Not a lot," he admitted. "My cousin did it a couple of years ago and said it was really cool. Plus, I like to argue. Debate is part of the forensics team."

I raised my eyebrows. "A team that lets you argue? That could be interesting."

Vernon tilted his head toward the hallway. "Want to come? It's open to everyone."

"I don't know. I'm not good with speeches."

"I bet you could argue if you gave it a try. You sure didn't back down for the photographer or Barnett."

I shrugged. "All right." I wasn't going to join the team, but I had nothing else to do. I wanted to try to make a few friends this year. This was a good place to start.

As we walked to room 28, we checked our schedules and found out that although we had most of the same classes and teachers, we had them at different hours. We did have chemistry together, and the same lunch period. We also discovered that he lived just two streets away from me.

"How come I never saw you at Watson?" I asked.

"I went to a private school."

"St. Mary's?" I asked. The big Catholic school was the only private school I knew of in the area.

"Yep." He let out a long gusty sigh. "I fought with my parents every night last semester, trying to convince them to let me come to Palmer this year. I'm here strictly on a trial basis." He lowered his voice, presumably in an imitation of his father. "One screw-up and you're off to St. Mary's so fast that your butt won't feel the road rash till it's sitting in a desk in Sister Catherine's classroom."

I laughed. "Guess you don't want to screw up."

Vernon laughed back. "Well, I certainly don't want to get caught!"

There weren't many people in room 28. In fact, there were only three.

"Is this the room for forensics?" Vernon asked.

The two guys with their heads bent over a Gameboy ignored us, but the girl in the corner nodded before returning her full attention to her book. The room had a dull feeling about it. The desks were in rows and there were only one or two posters on the walls.

"Well, we are a little early," Vernon whispered, trying not to show his disappointment.

I raised my eyebrows but sat down at a desk next to him anyway.

For the next five minutes, the room was silent except for the occasional beeps from the Gameboy. Six more people stuck their heads in the door to take a peek, but only two of them came in, scuttling nervously to desks in the front row. We were all scattered around the room. It was obvious that this was not a meeting for the social butterflies.

I consulted my schedule again and realized that this was going to be my English room. From behind my sunglasses, I looked around, trying to get a feel for the teacher.

"What are you doing?" Vernon whispered.

"Why are you whispering?" I asked.

He shrugged and shook his head.

"I'm just checking out the room. Looks like it belongs to a pretty traditional teacher."

"You never can tell," Vernon said. "Sometimes people surprise you."

"True," I agreed, feeling hypocritical. Being classified as a stoner or a troublemaker simply because I wore all black was a pet peeve of mine. I resolved to give my English teacher a chance.

After another ten minutes, I was ready to leave. But just as I started to get up, four more guys and a cheerleader walked in. Even if the first guy hadn't been carrying a stack of papers and the second one wearing a Palmer Wrestling shirt, I could have picked them out as upperclassmen. They walked with a swagger and assurance that no one else in the room had.

"Okay." The one wearing the Palmer Wrestling shirt clapped his hands loudly to get our attention. When he turned and faced the room, he discovered how unnecessary that was. "Seven? Only seven of you?" The disappointment was plain on his face.

"You're all here for forensics, right?" the cheerleader said.

One of the newcomers shook his head. "I thought this was for the chess club."

"Nope," she said. "Wrong room."

"Oh," he said. He gathered up his stuff and left.

"Great," Palmer Wrestling said. "Now we're down to six new recruits." He sighed and pointed to the clipboard and papers the other guy had set on the desk. "Sign up, leave your address and phone number, and take a flyer. We'll see you next Wednesday after school."

The guys with the Gameboy stood up immediately and started for the desk. The girl in the corner picked up a purple backpack with a hot-pink fanged smiley face on the front and stuffed her book into a side pocket.

"We waited just for a sheet of paper?" Vernon complained. "Can't you tell us what this is all about?"

Palmer Wrestling looked at him. "That's what the flyer is for," he said, his tone adding the unspoken "moron."

"Then why have a meeting?" I asked. "Why not just pass out the flyers at registration?"

"What is it you want to know?" the cheerleader asked, cutting off Wrestling's reply.

The two guys finished filling in the information, grabbed a flyer, and left. The girl with the book stood and slung her backpack over her shoulder, listening intently. Another guy also stopped to hear what was going on.

"How often do we practice?" Vernon asked. "How long do we practice?"

"Come on, Tess, let's go," said Palmer Wrestling.

"Go ahead, Pat. I'll be there in a minute." Tess, the cheerleader, turned back to us, but Pat didn't leave. "You'll practice every Wednesday from three to four-thirty as a team," she said, "and on your own as often as you need to. Next year, if you're still serious about forensics, you can take the class as an elective, but for sophomores it's an after-school activity."

"Okay," said the girl with the purple backpack. "So what exactly are we practicing?"

"It depends on what you choose to compete in. You can do debate, either Cross Examination, which is with a partner, or Lincoln-Douglas, which is on your own. Or you can do different interpretive selections. There's original oratory, humor, drama, poetry, and extemporaneous."

"We compete? Even the beginners?" Vernon asked, sounding a little anxious. "When? How often?"

"About once a month," one of the other upperclassmen said. "On Saturdays usually, but sometimes there are weekend meets that go Friday and Saturday."

"But sophomores rarely get to compete," Pat said, "so you don't need to worry about it."

"Unless the team stays this small," Tess added. "We may end up using everyone."

"How do we decide what to compete in?" I asked.

"Look," Pat broke in, "all of that'll be figured out at practice, okay?"

I looked at him. "How are we supposed to know if we want to sign up for something when we don't know what it is?"

Tess laughed. "You guys should sign up. You've got the stubborn determination you need in debate, and you dig for information. Besides, if you don't like it, you can always quit." Her tone held a challenge.

Before we could say anything, the girl with the purple backpack spoke up again. "How many people do we speak in front of?"

"It depends on what's going on," Tess said. "Right

before a meet, you might run through your presentation in front of the whole team during practice. Otherwise, you might only do it in front of one or two people at a time. At some of the meets, only the judge and a couple of parents are there to watch; at others you can have an audience of up to fifty people."

"Any other questions?" Pat made it plain the answer had better be no. We were wasting his time. After a moment of awkward silence, he snapped, "Then sign up if you want to. Otherwise, go home."

Vernon and I looked at each other. I didn't really plan on staying with the team, but Vernon seemed to be waiting for me.

I shrugged and walked to the desk. "I thought we were supposed to be talking and debating," I said, signing my name with a flourish. "Isn't that what forensics is all about?" I grinned at Tess. She smiled back.

"You could use that killer dimple in interpretive readings too," she said. "Maybe you'll have to do both."

I didn't answer. The dimple was the reason I never smiled in pictures. I hated it.

Pat was looking at my name on the list. "Shadow? What, were you named after a favorite family pet?"

"I hope you don't write your own speeches," I told him, "because you're not very original." And then I walked out the door. It had been a long time since a comment about my name had gotten to me—turning fifteen had me thinking about Daniel too much.

Vernon caught up with me a few minutes later, just as I was leaving the building. "Hey, man, wait up."

"Sorry," I said.

He laughed. "You've got guts. Standing up not only to Barnett, but also to some senior who thinks he's tough. That girl was right, though. You should be on the team. You're good with words."

"I hardly said anything!"

"Yeah, but what you said and how you said it!"

I looked at him and snorted. "The whole time all I could think was, please, God, don't let my voice crack now."

Vernon laughed again. "It sure didn't show."

I shook my head and kept walking.

"Where're you going?"

"Home."

He stopped. "My mom's picking me up in front of the school in about ten minutes. We could give you a ride home."

Again I shook my head. "Thanks, but I'd rather walk."

"You sure?" Vernon looked a little hurt.

"Yeah."

"Okay. See you next week, I guess."

"See ya."

I knew Vernon was probably thinking I was brushing him off. I didn't mean to come across that way, but I didn't know how to tell him that without sounding really corny. No matter how often I tried to make myself act like the people I saw around me, I just couldn't get it right. I had hoped things would be different at a new school. But maybe I was wrong. Maybe there was just something wrong with me.

I didn't have to be home for another hour. I decided to stop at the library on the way home to see if they had the new Robert Jordan book. Along the way, I thought about the forensics team. Forensics sounded like it could be interesting, and having an after-school activity might get Dad off my back about getting involved in sports. At six foot three, he had always been a basketball junkie. He couldn't understand why I didn't want to play, especially since I was already so tall.

I wasn't sure I could speak to an audience at all, though, even a small one. Plus, it seemed clear to me that there was at least one complete jerk on the team. Did I really want to deal with that?

But it would be something new. And I was pretty sure Vernon and I could be friends.

Besides, if I wanted to change, joining the forensics team was almost the biggest leap I could make.

As I walked into the library, I took my sunglasses off, tucking them in the pocket of my jacket next to the forensics flyer. It was nice and cool in the library, an important detail when you dress in all black.

I browsed in the general fiction section, looking for something to catch my interest. They didn't have the new Jordan book yet. I prefer fantasy usually, but I'll read almost anything except romance or westerns. A couple of years ago I got into sci-fi. The first time a Star Trek conference came to our town, I was so excited I went all by myself. I didn't make it an hour. It was too depressing to see those geeky older guys walking around by themselves; it was even more depressing to think that could be me in a few years.

I pulled three books off the shelves, and went looking for a study carrel to use. I like to read a few pages of a book before deciding to check it out.

As I walked around, I realized I wasn't going to get a carrel. I finally spotted a small table in the back. Only one person was sitting there, facing the other way. On the table I saw a purple backpack with a pink vampirish smiley face on the front.

"Hi," I said. "Mind if I join you?"

She looked up, startled, and then shrugged. "That's fine," she muttered as she went back to reading.

I picked up the first book and leafed through a few pages.

"So where did your name come from?"

"What?" I looked up, confused.

"Your name. Is it a nickname?" A man at another table looked over, and she lowered her voice. "Where does it come from?"

"I believe you can find it in almost any dictionary."

She just stared at me for a second and then she went back to her book.

"No, wait, I'm sorry," I said. The man at the other table shushed us.

"I'm not trying to make fun of you," she muttered. "I was just curious."

"Yeah, well, I'm curious too," I whispered. "What's your name?"

"Robin."

"As in the first sign of spring?"

She made a face at me. "I wasn't trying to make fun of you," she repeated. "Sorry I bothered you." She turned away from me in her seat and looked back down at her book.

Twice in the last hour I had pushed people away without meaning to.

"Robin, wait a minute," I said. "I didn't mean it."

She looked at me doubtfully.

"When I was little, I always followed my br—I

always followed people around. So I got called Shadow and the name kind of stuck."

"And now you want to look like one." The man at the other table made a lot of noise as he packed up his stuff, giving us dirty looks the whole time.

"I guess," I said, surprised that she had made that connection. "So what do you think of the forensics team?" I asked.

"I was glad you and your friend spoke up," she said, sidestepping my question. "There sure wasn't much information on the flyer."

"You going to join?"

Looking down, she nodded. Her dark brown hair fell over her face. It was long and shiny, but the way it clung to her head made her look kind of shy and mousy.

"What do you know about this club that I don't?" I asked, trying to get her to look up and smile.

She glanced up at me, barely. "It'll be good for my career."

I blinked. "You have a career?"

She rolled her eyes at me.

I tried again. "I mean, you already know what you want to do? What?"

Robin shook her head. "Nothing. Forget I said anything." She tried to concentrate on her book. I wouldn't let her.

"Seriously. How can forensics help your career?"

"It makes you learn how to speak in public, and helps you learn how to use your voice and choose the right words to get your point across effectively. The way you say something is often more important than what you actually say. It can also give you poise and expand your vocabulary."

"Wow. You should have written the flyer." I raised my eyebrows. "Is joining forensics your choice or your parents'?"

"I changed my mind," she said suddenly. "I *do* mind if you sit here."

Grinning, I said, "It's too late. I'm already settled."

"Fine. Then *I'll* leave." She started to gather her stuff.

"Wait, wait, wait. I'm sorry, okay? I'll sit quietly and you'll never even know I'm here."

She glared at me but leaned back into her chair and opened her book.

I managed to keep my word…for about three minutes.

"Really, what career are you interested in?" I whispered.

She ignored me.

"Let's see. Public speaking…hmmm. A politician?" She didn't blink. "No, you couldn't be that slimy." Her eyes were still focused on her book, but they weren't moving across the page. "An actress? No, then you'd just take drama or be in the plays. What else? A TV anchor?" She was still trying to ignore me, but I thought her lips twitched with a suppressed smile. "Or maybe a lawyer? No, You don't look bloodthirsty enough to be a lawyer. Hmmm." I definitely saw a smile. "You know, this would be a lot easier if you would give me a clue."

"You're not supposed to be talking, remember?"

"Oh, yeah. Well, that's one of my faults, my poor memory. Do you think forensics can help with that?"

"I think you need more help than forensics or any other school activity can give you. I think you need professional help." She began to gather her stuff again.

"Okay, okay, I'm sorry. I'll be good this time."

"Too late," she said.

"Please!"

She took pity on me and smiled again. "I really do have to leave. See you next week."

"So you're definitely joining forensics?" I pressed.

"I'm definitely going to think about it." She took three steps from the table, but then stopped and looked back at me. "Will you be at practice next week?"

"Will you miss me if I'm not?"

She continued walking and said over her shoulder, "See you around—maybe."

"Bye!" I said as she walked away.

Yeah. I had to give forensics a try.

# Chapter Two

**M**y last days of summer vacation sped by. I was pleasantly surprised when Vernon called and suggested we go to a slasher movie the next Saturday. Of course, I had to tell my parents who Vernon was, where he lived, what his phone number was, where we were going, and when I'd be home before I could leave for the mall. I wasn't supposed to keep any part of my life from them, because they didn't want another surprise like Daniel had given them. I hated what he had done to us.

When we came out of the movie theater, I asked Vernon casually if he knew the other people who had been there to sign up for forensics.

He gave me a strange look. "No. If I had known any of them, I would have talked to them."

"No, I know you don't know any of them. I meant did you know who any of them are? Like their names or anything?"

"I don't think so. I might have seen that girl in the corner around somewhere before, but I'm not sure."

"Oh."

"Why?"

I shrugged. "Just wondering."

"Did you know any of them?"

I shook my head.

Vernon began to grin. "But I bet you want to get to know one of them."

"Whatever."

"It's that upperclassman, isn't it?"

"Who, the cheerleader?"

"Yeah!"

"You're crazy. And anyway, I'm pretty sure she has a boyfriend."

"How can you tell?"

"Look at her, Vernon. She's gorgeous. And smart. Of course she has a boyfriend."

"I knew it!" Vernon gloated.

"I'm not interested in her. She's probably dating that wrestling musclehead anyway."

"But you're going to join the forensics team, right?"

"Might as well," I said, trying to sound nonchalant.


Sunday night Mom, Dad, and I had hamburgers for dinner and then sat around the living room. The TV was on, but I was paying more attention to my book. The phone rang, and Dad got up to answer it. "Hello?... Yes, just a moment, please." He held the phone out to me, eyebrows raised in surprise. Getting two phone calls in a week was rare for me. I usually only got calls from relatives on my birthday.

"H-hello?" I winced. There went my voice, cracking again.

"Hey, Shadow. This is Vernon."

"Hey," I said. "What's up?"

"I was just calling to see how you're getting to school tomorrow."

"I was planning on walking. Why?"

"I couldn't decide if I should walk or ride the bus."

"Well, if you decide to walk, meet me in front of the Mini-Mart at 7:15." Even though it meant a twenty-minute walk, I wanted to avoid the bus.

"Cool," Vernon said. "I'll be there."

"See you tomorrow."

"Bye!"

I hung up the phone and went back to my chair.

Mom and Dad were watching me expectantly. I picked up my book.

"Shadow?" Mom said in a prompting tone.

"What?"

"Who was that?"

I sighed but explained as quickly as I could. "Vernon. He's the guy I met at registration, remember?"

"The one who you went to the movies with?" Mom clarified. "Didn't you say you met him during the speech meeting?"

"The what?" Dad stared at me in shock.

"He's joining the speech club," Mom said smugly.

"I'm just thinking about it, Mom—"

"That's...different," Dad interrupted.

"Shhh!" Mom said. "Don't discourage him!"

"But what about basketball, or soccer?"

I ignored him. We had had that discussion a hundred times.

"What were you and Vernon talking about?" Mom asked me.

"We're going to meet before school tomorrow and walk together."

"Would you like a ride?"

"No thanks."

Before she could ask any more questions, I escaped to my room. I glared at the empty room down the hall. Because Daniel had shut our parents out, they had always forced themselves in on me.

The first day proved that high school would be as boring as junior high. It was a bigger building with more kids in it, but the teachers still acted like they expected most of their students to be idiots. I made sure I had a good book with me at all times.

Most teachers gave us alphabetically assigned seats. I liked that because it often put me in the back of the classroom. I ended up sitting behind Vernon in chemistry. We were also assigned as lab partners for the entire year.

I looked, but I never saw Robin. She wasn't in any of my classes, and I didn't see her during passing periods, either. I hoped she had been serious about joining forensics. I was getting impatient for Wednesday's practice.

After school on Tuesday, Vernon invited me to his house to work on our first trig assignment. We had the class at different hours, but so far the teacher was giving the same pages for homework. I called Mom as soon as I got there, and then I stayed for almost an hour. The last three problems stumped us. We promised to call each other later when we figured them out.

I hadn't been home for ten minutes before the phone rang.

"I've got it!" I called, and picked up the phone. "H-hello?" My voice cracked again.

"You know, you've really got to fix that," Vernon said.

"Yeah, yeah, yeah," I said.

"Well, I've got number 23."

"Really? Cool." He walked me through it. Once he told me the step we had missed, it came together quickly. "Thanks, man."

"No big deal. But now *you* have to do number 24."

"I'll call you when I get it," I promised.

I sat down at my desk and started to work through the next problem.

"Shadow, dinner's almost ready!" Mom called.

"Be there in a minute," I hollered back.

The phone rang again. I couldn't believe Vernon had figured out number 24 so fast!

"Hello?" Thankfully my voice didn't crack this time.

"Shadow?"

"Yeah?" I didn't recognize the voice at all.

"Shadow, it's Dan."

"Dan who?" I asked.

It was quiet for a moment and then the voice said, "Daniel. Your brother, Daniel. I just…just… Look, I'm sorry… Tell Mom and Dad I'm sorry, okay? That's all I wanted to say… You still there, Shadow? Shad?"

I'm pretty sure that's when the whole world came to a stop. A low buzzing started in my ears.

"Shadow? You still there?"

My stomach began launch preparations.

"Man, don't hang up!"

I dropped the phone and backed away from it like it was radioactive. I tripped over my chair, knocking it to the floor with a loud crash. Mom came running to my room.

"Shadow? What's wrong?"

I couldn't say anything, couldn't take my eyes off the phone.

My mother's face was full of concern. "Shadow, are you okay?"

I shook my head, still staring at the phone. After what had just happened, I wouldn't have been surprised if it had flown away. Daniel's voice started squeaking through it and I flinched.

With a puzzled look, Mom picked up the receiver while still watching me. "Hello?" she said cautiously.

Slowly she raised her hand to her mouth. Her eyes welled up with tears. I had never seen anyone's face actually glow before, but at that moment, hers did.

Daniel must have been talking a mile a minute, because she didn't say anything. Finally she simply said, "Oh, Daniel!" and started crying.

I closed my eyes and opened them again. I was still on the floor, and Mom was still on the phone. Apparently it had really happened. Daniel had called. How often I had wished he would come back home! But instead of being happy, I felt strangely empty.

"Mark!" Mom screamed down the hall suddenly, making me jump. "What?" she said into the phone. "Why?... Where are you?" The joy in her face seemed to drain away. "You're where?... Why? What happ—?" Then she shook her head. "Never mind, never mind. You can tell us when we get there."

"Get where?" Dad asked from the door.

"Of course we're coming!" Mom said into the phone. "We'll be right there!"

"Where?" Dad asked again.

"I love you," Mom whispered into the receiver. "We'll see you soon." She hung up the phone gently, reluctantly.

It was quiet. Dad and I were staring at Mom, but she didn't take her eyes off the phone.

Suddenly I felt weird sitting on the floor. As I struggled to get up, Dad crossed my room quickly and reached down a hand to pull me up.

"You okay?" he asked, helping right the chair.

"Yeah."

"You sure?"

I nodded.

We both looked at Mom expectantly. Finally, Dad said, "Caroline? Mind telling me what's going on?"

His voice seemed to break the spell. She clapped her hands like a little girl. "Come on! We have to go!"

"Go? What's going on?"

"Daniel! Daniel's come back to us!" She was disappearing down the hall.

"Daniel?" Dad hurried after her. Their voices became indistinct murmurs in their bedroom.

In a daze, I walked into the living room and sank into the couch. Daniel was coming home. So many times, I had imagined the moment. But now that it was real, I didn't know how I felt. I tried to organize my thoughts, but they stayed jumbled in my head.

Where had he been all this time? What did he look like now? How long would he stay? He was twenty-two years old now—he couldn't be planning on staying here forever. Why hadn't he called before? Why was he calling now? What did he want?

Mom and Dad rushed through the living room and out the door to the garage, without ever glancing in my direction. I wasn't really surprised they had forgotten about me. After all, this was the moment they had been waiting for, ever since that horrible morning when my brother had disappeared.

"Shadow!" Dad bellowed, opening the door. "Hurry up!"

I slouched a little further into the cushions, wishing they really had forgotten me.

"Shadow!" he called again, striding back into the house. He was halfway across the living room before he spotted me, drawn as tightly into the couch cushions as I could get.

"Come on! We haven't got all day."

"No," I said. My voice sounded strange to me. "We've got years. That's how long he left us to wait."

My father's face became very stern. "I'll pretend you didn't say that. Now let's get moving. Visiting hours end soon."

"Visiting hours?" I felt my stomach clenching up, preparing for a blow. How many times had I imagined him hurt or sick or starving and all alone? How many times had I cried, thinking he must already be dead? "Is he in the hospital?" I asked weakly.

"No," Dad said curtly. "He's in jail."

I had thought there couldn't be any more surprises; I was wrong. "Why? What did he do?" I asked.

"We don't know. He didn't have time to explain everything to Mom."

"He didn't have time? Or he didn't want to because he was afraid you wouldn't come see him?"

Dad's face turned a little pink. "Let's go. We don't have time for this," he said, heading back to the door.

I still don't know if I didn't move because I couldn't or because I didn't want to.

He opened the door to the garage, barely pausing to ask, "Are you coming?" before slamming it shut behind him.

I listened to the car doors shut, and a few seconds later, the garage door. The house was silent except for the ticking of the clock. About ten minutes after they left, the phone rang. I let the machine answer. It was Vernon, bragging that not only had he been the first to solve number 23, he had also now solved 24 and 25. If I wanted the answers I was to leave $25,000 in unmarked bills in his mailbox and call him back. Just as everything got quiet again, the oven timer buzzed loudly. I tried to ignore it, but it got on my nerves. I finally got up and turned off the timer and the oven. The ticking clock seemed to get even louder in the silence. It was strange, because it felt like the world should have stopped. But it kept on going.

What did my brother want from us now? That was the thought I couldn't get out of my head.

What did he expect from us?

What could we expect of him?

I walked slowly down the hall, past my room into Daniel's. Without turning on the light, I stretched out on his old bed. Daniel had gone on a rampage the night before he left. Mom had insisted on putting everything back into place and leaving all his stuff in his room. She washed the sheets and comforter every month, and they smelled fresh. For years, I had sneaked into his room, imagining the day he would return, or sometimes even pretending that he had never run away. I knew his room by heart.

Even without looking, I knew the names of the bands on every poster on the wall. The stereo and speakers were back in place, and the CDs he hadn't destroyed or taken with him that night were arranged in a rack. I knew Daniel's skateboard was still propped against the wall inside his closet. His clothes were hanging neatly on the rod, a lot neater than he had ever hung them. I had never understood about the clothes. After a couple of years, my mother had to know that they wouldn't fit him even if he did return.

My parents had always talked about *when* Daniel would come home. I don't know when that phrase had changed in my mind, but it had never changed for my parents. I had talked about when Daniel would come home for a long time, but eventually it had become *if* Daniel would come home, and finally I had quit talking about it altogether.

My parents' *when* had become *now*. And I didn't know how to feel about it.

# Chapter Three

When I heard my parents come in, I was still lying on Daniel's bed. I blinked in surprise at my watch. It was nearly 11:30 P.M. I must've fallen sound asleep.

I heard their muted voices in the kitchen. Getting up crossed my mind, but I didn't have the strength. After a few minutes, the hall light clicked on. A triangle of light spilled into the room, just touching the corner of the bed.

I heard footsteps heading into my parents' room across the hall. Someone else walked to my room, paused in front, then came to Daniel's door and pushed it open. The sudden light was blinding, even with my arm over my face.

"Aaah!" I blinked hard a few times, trying to adjust to the light before I lowered my arm to see who was there.

My father was leaning against the door frame. "Your mother is very upset," he said.

"Why?" I asked. "What did Daniel do?"

Dad shook his head. "She's upset with you!"

"With me? What'd I do?"

"You made us lie to Daniel. We had to tell him you were too sick to come see him."

"You didn't have to lie to him."

"We didn't want him thinking his only brother didn't want to see him after seven years."

I snapped my mouth shut so hard my teeth hurt. Staring at the ceiling, I focused on keeping my teeth together. Silence was better than anything I might say to him. Daniel left us—never even called for seven years—and only decides he needs us after he gets arrested. But my parents were mad at *me* for not throwing my brother a welcome party.

"You were gone a long time."

"You know it takes a couple of hours to get to Denver," he said calmly.

"Denver? Is that where he's been all this time?"

"Yes."

Denver. So close and yet so far. Our local station and newspaper sometimes carried Denver info, but only big stuff.

"Talk to me, Shadow," Dad said, trying to sound encouraging. "What's going on?"

"Why did he call?" I blurted out.

"Because he missed us."

"Now? After seven years? It took seven years for him to miss us?"

"He's missed us for a long time. It took seven years to get the courage to call us again."

"I don't get it. What's he want?"

Dad hesitated. "He wants to come home."

"No, what does he *want?*" I insisted. "He must want something from us, or he wouldn't have called all of a sudden."

"He wants our family—" Dad began.

"But why *now*? What is it about now? Why not four years ago? Last year? Ten years from now? What's so special about now?"

"Shadow, we have to give him a chance," Dad tried again.

"What's he in jail for?" I demanded. "What did he do?"

"He's not really in jail. He's just being held until the arraignment. They'll do that tomorrow, and decide if they've got enough to hold him over for trial."

"How long have they been holding him?"

"He's been in custody for a few days now."

"Are you going to pay the bail for him?"

Dad nodded.

"What did he do?" I asked again.

"We don't think— He didn't do anything. He's accused of..." Dad's voice trailed off.

"Accused of what?"

Forcing the word out, Dad was barely able to say it loud enough for me to hear. "Murder."

My brain refused to process the word. My brother, who used to give me piggyback rides and always gave me half of his candy bars, was sitting in a jail cell.

While I was silent, Dad hurried on. "It can't be true. There's no way our Daniel could have killed someone. He was just in the wrong place at the wrong time. He's innocent."

"So that's why he calls now," I muttered. "He needs bail money." Then I asked, "What makes you so sure he didn't do it?"

"Shadow!"

"Well, what makes you so sure?" I repeated. "He

hasn't been 'our' Daniel for a long time. You say a trial date's going to be set and they're releasing him on bond, so somebody thinks he did it! How many other times has he been arrested?"

"This is his first arrest," Dad began, but I was on a roll.

"How do you know he hasn't killed lots of people? How do you know he hasn't been arrested before and there just wasn't enough evidence to convict him? Maybe someone on the jury just had a shadow of a doubt." I read John Grisham and watched *Law and Order*; I knew what I was talking about.

Dad's face tensed up and he took half a step toward me. "This is Daniel we're talking about," he ground out, his voice shaking. "He's your brother!"

I was quiet, staring at the comforter. I was ashamed of what I had said, but I wasn't going to take it back. Just because it was an uncomfortable thought didn't mean it was impossible.

I could feel Dad's eyes on me. Long seconds dragged out. Finally he sighed. "It's late."

"I know."

He hesitated for a minute, like he wanted to say something more, but then he turned and walked away. I stayed on Daniel's bed a little longer, and then I went to my room and closed the door. I never turned on any of the lights.


When I woke up, I was still on top of the covers, fully dressed. Sunshine was streaming in my window. I sat bolt upright and looked at the clock. Almost 9:00!

Frantic, I rushed to the bathroom, tore off my

clothes, and hopped into the shower. I finished in record time, wrapped the towel around me, and stepped into the hall.

Through their doorway I could see Mom and Dad sitting on the far side of their bed. They were talking quietly. It looked like they were arguing about something. I racked my brain. I was positive it was only Wednesday. What were they doing home?

Dad looked around. "It's about time you woke up. Another ten minutes and I was coming in to get you."

I walked a little closer.

"Don't you think you should apologize to your mother for last night?"

I chewed on my bottom lip for a minute, and then very carefully said, "I'm sorry you had a rough day yesterday, Mom."

She acknowledged my apology with a slight bow of her head. She was pale and tight-lipped. Dad glared at me.

"What's going on?" I asked in confusion. "Why aren't you guys at work?"

"We're bringing Daniel home today," Mom said simply.

I stared at her for a moment, waiting for more, but apparently she thought that explained everything.

"Why didn't you wake me up? I'm late for school."

"Daniel's coming home," Mom repeated. "You're not going to school. Now, get dressed. We've got a lot to do."

"Mom, I need to go to school. I've got three assignments due and forensics practice after school."

Dad shook his head. "You can turn the assignments in later."

"This is the first forensics meeting. I *have* to be there."

"You can go next week. I'm sure your friend will tell you about whatever you miss today."

"You don't understand," I said. "I don't want to miss school today."

"Shadow, I think your brother is a little more important than some club meeting," Mom said, sounding exasperated.

"It's the first meeting of the year!" I protested. When they didn't say anything, I exploded. "It's not fair! He messed everything up when he left! Why does he get to screw it up all over again?"

"Shadow!" Dad said sharply.

I went back to my room, trying not to stomp. I quickly got dressed and put my books into my backpack. Grabbing my jacket, I headed for the kitchen.

"Shadow!" Mom called from her room. "You and your father are going to get Daniel's room ready, while I run out to the store. I don't know if Daniel's going to want to go out to dinner tonight or stay home, so I want to be prepared."

I grabbed some breakfast bars from the pantry and slipped out the back door, closing it quietly.

I walked down our street quickly, nearly jogging. I kept expecting to hear one of them yelling at me. When I finally turned the corner, I took a deep breath and slowed down. A little.

At school, the halls were quiet. Third hour had already started. I thought about trying to go to Dr. Anderson's class without a pass, then dismissed the idea. He was too structured and by the book. He would insist on a pass.

Sighing, I switched directions and headed toward the attendance office. It just happened to be right next to Mr. Barnett's office.

I gave the secretary my name and explained that I needed a late pass.

"Is it excused?"

"I overslept," I said.

She raised her eyebrows. "Into third hour?"

I didn't say anything, just nodded.

"We don't consider oversleeping an excuse," she said primly. "I'll write the unexcused pass, and you'll have to arrange detention with your first and second period teachers." She began to write me a pass. Right then, the door behind her opened and a kid kind of slouched his way out of Mr. Barnett's office. Mr. Barnett followed him.

"Ms. Day," he said to the secretary, "Mr. Spencer needs to sign up for in-school suspension for the remainder of the week." The kid sat in one of the chairs against the wall.

Ms. Day finished writing my pass and started to hand it to me.

Mr. Barnett intercepted the pass. "Mr. Thompson? Why are you late?"

I hesitated, and Ms. Day answered for me. "He claims he overslept."

"I didn't *claim* to oversleep. I really did oversleep!" I suddenly realized I wasn't using the best tone. "I forgot to set my alarm last night," I added quietly. Mr. Barnett gave me a fatherly smile—the kind of smile my father gives me when he knows he's caught me doing something wrong.

"Why don't we step into my office, Mr. Thompson?"

he said, gesturing toward his door.

I sighed and tried not to roll my eyes as I walked into his office and stood in front of his desk. He shut the door and sat down in his chair. "You almost broke your brother's record," he said mildly.

"What?"

"He got detention on the first day of school," he said. "Why are you late, Mr. Thompson?" He gestured for me to sit down.

"Shadow."

"What?"

"I'd rather be called Shadow."

"I'm calling you Mr. Thompson to show you respect."

"Yeah, right," I mumbled. "It sounds more like you're patronizing me."

"That's not my intent."

"Please call me Shadow. If it will make you feel better, I'll even call you Arthur." His nameplate was sitting front and center on his desk, facing me.

"No need to get smart with me, young man."

"Why do adults always say that when a kid makes a point?" I asked.

Mr. Barnett actually smiled. A begrudging smile, but a smile. "Okay, Shadow, I get your point."

"Thank you, Mr. Barnett," I said, doing my best to keep the sarcasm out of my voice.

"Now, can we get back to our problem?"

"I overslept. It won't happen again." Then I added, "I don't think."

"You didn't just decide to cut class?"

"No. In fact, I have my trig homework from second hour and I'd like to go turn it in."

"If I call home, is there someone who could back you up?"

"Please don't do that," I said a little too quickly.

"Why not, Shadow?" Mr. Barnett asked innocently. "Would that get you into trouble? Were you someplace you shouldn't have been?"

"No, but I am now," I muttered.

"Excuse me?"

I slumped a little further down in the chair. "I got in a fight with my parents this morning," I began reluctantly.

There was a sudden knock at the door.

"Yes," Mr. Barnett snapped.

The door opened partway. Ms. Day smiled apologetically. "Mr. Barnett, I'm sorry to interrupt, but Mrs. Thompson is on line three right now, and she sounds a little agitated."

"Thank you, Ms. Day." The door closed softly. Mr. Barnett watched me thoughtfully for a moment before picking up the receiver. "Mrs. Thompson, this is Mr. Barnett, Dean of Students. How may I help you?... I see.... Yes.... Yes, he is here.... Uh-huh.... Okay, I'll be sure that he gets the message.... Certainly.... Thank you." He hung up the phone and considered me carefully before beginning. "Your mother said you left the house without permission to come to school this morning." He sounded a little confused.

I nodded, staring fixedly at his nameplate.

"She asked me to tell you that you're to come straight home after school today."

I grimaced.

"That bothers you?"

"I have forensics practice after school today."

"Would you like to call her back and let her know that?"

"She knows," I said bitterly.

"Would you like to tell me what's going on?"

I shook my head.

Mr. Barnett waited another minute, but when I didn't say anything else, he scribbled on my pass and then handed it to me. "You'd better get on to class," he said. His eyes almost looked sympathetic.

I stood up and took the pass from him. When I reached the door, he said, "Mr. Thompson...um... Shadow?"

I turned to go.

"If you need to talk, my door is open."

"Thanks," I said, and then left as quickly as I could.

On my way to class, I looked at the pass. He had changed it from an unexcused to an excused tardy.


"So where were you this morning?" Vernon asked as we were leaving chemistry.

I shook my head. "Long story. Long, boring, ugly story."

Vernon grinned. "Sounds like the kind I should ask about."

"I wish you wouldn't."

"Okay," Vernon said, shrugging agreeably.

We went to our lockers, and then split up again to go to different classes, planning to meet back at our lockers before lunch.

As I made my way through the crowded hallway, I collided with someone and several books fell to the floor.

"Hey, watch where you're going!" an angry voice exclaimed.

"Sorry," I muttered, stooping down to retrieve the books. I glanced up and then smiled. It was the cheerleader from the forensics meeting.

I stood and handed her the books.

"Slow down a little in the hallways," she advised. "It doesn't look cool to hurry. And it's really uncool to bump into people."

"Sorry," I said again. "Will you be at practice today?"

"Of course," she said, flashing me a grin. "I'm one of the co-captains, so I have to be there."

I stared after her for a second, admiring the way her denim skirt swung from side to side, then hurried to class. In spite of her advice to slow down, I didn't want to get an unexcused tardy. One trip to Mr. Barrett's office was enough for the day.

During class, I had a hard time concentrating. I kept trying to force Daniel from my mind, but I wasn't having much luck. I couldn't believe the way my parents were jumping up and down about my brother coming home, acting as if there wasn't anything wrong, going on as if he hadn't been accused of—I couldn't finish the thought.

He'd left us seven years ago, shattering our family. I still found it almost impossible to trust people or get close to anyone. I was always afraid of doing something wrong and driving them away. And now, just when my life was beginning to get normal, Daniel comes parading back home, disrupting everything again.

Even if he hadn't come home, it seemed as if his reputation at school was going to be a problem for me.

Mr. Barnett wasn't the only teacher who remembered Daniel. My English teacher actually seemed to turn a little pale when I admitted I was Daniel's brother. I wondered exactly how much trouble my brother had gotten into in the short time he was a student here.

It really bugged me that my parents wanted me to rearrange my schedule around Daniel, as if he hadn't rearranged my whole life by leaving. How could my parents just take him back with open arms and no questions? How could they expect me to do the same thing?

I tried to think about the cheerleader, but that just made me wonder whether I should go to forensics practice, and that led me straight back to Daniel. Part of me was dying to see him. What did he look like now? I had so many questions about how he had managed to survive for seven years on his own. I wanted to know why he left, and why he came back. Part of me couldn't wait to see him. But another part of me didn't want to see him at all.

Of course, I would have to see him. There was no way to avoid that. So under what circumstance did I want to meet him? Did I want him coming into the house with me there, waiting for him? Or did I want to come home after he was already there, showing him that he wasn't the most important person in my life anymore? Should I go straight home after school because my parents had told me to? Or should I disobey them and stay for practice, knowing that they would worry when I wasn't home on time?

All these thoughts tore through my mind like a tornado, ripping away the calm security that I had struggled to find for the last few years. When the bell rang, it felt like class had only lasted five minutes. And I had no idea what had happened. I wasn't entirely sure if the substitute had been male or female.

"So what do we do in civics?" Vernon asked at our lockers.

"I have no clue."

"What do you mean? Weren't you just there?"

"Sort of." I shook my head, shoved my books in my locker, and slammed it shut.

In the lunch line, Vernon tried to get a conversation started, but after a few monosyllabic answers from me, he fell quiet too.

We paid for our lunches, and then wandered over to the table we had been sitting at for the last two days.

As I picked up the piece of cardboard that passed for pizza in the school cafeteria, I felt bad that I had brushed Vernon off. I asked him if he had any brothers or sisters.

"Yeah," he said, "an older brother and younger sister. How about you?"

"I don't know," I said. About four years ago I had started telling people I didn't have any brothers or sisters; it was easier than explaining everything.

"You don't know?" Vernon laughed, but it was an uncomfortable laugh. "You don't know if you have brothers or sisters? You don't know what you did in the class you were just in? What are you, strung out on crack or something?"

I shook my head and put my half-finished pizza on the plate, shoving the tray away from me. "No, but I'm wondering if that might help me." I put my head down on the cafeteria table.

"Shadow, what's going on?"

Lifting my head, I stared past him through the windows. "I had a brother. When I was eight, he ran away. We never heard from him again. Until last night."

Vernon's eyes got huge. "He's still alive?"

I nodded.

"And he just showed up last night?"

"No, he called us. He's coming home today."

"When?"

"I don't know."

Vernon gave me a funny look. "Your brother's coming home today and your parents made you come to school?"

Shaking my head, I began ripping a napkin to pieces. "My brother's coming home and my parents told me *not* to come to school. They wanted me to stay there and help get a party together for him."

Vernon was quiet for a few moments, and I could tell he was trying to figure out what was going on. "Why don't you want to be there?"

"I don't know." I laughed bitterly. "My answer for the day."

"Well, I guess that explains why you're acting so weird. I fight with my brother all the time, and sometimes I say I wish he didn't exist, but...I...I can't imagine my life without him."

"That's how I used to feel—well, the part about not imagining a life without him. Now, though, I can't imagine a life with him back."

"What happened when he ran away?" Vernon asked.

Vernon really seemed to care. He wasn't just interested in the gossip. For the first time in years, I told the story.

*It was just a few days after my eighth birthday, and the most important thing in my world was my big brother. I wore his hand-me-down clothes, played with his old toys, and followed him around so much that I wanted everyone to call me Shadow, just like he did.*

*But it seemed like Daniel had been changing, since about the time I turned seven. He and my parents fought all the time, although I didn't always understand what they were fighting about. Sometimes it was about his new friends, sometimes it was about his curfew or his grades, and sometimes about the clothes he wore. And my parents fought with each other about what to do with him.*

*That summer, he wouldn't let me be his shadow anymore, and got mad at me when I tried to follow after him anyway. He started sneaking around. And I'd sneak around too, trying to be like him. Since I couldn't go where he went, I'd wait for him at the end of our street. Then I'd walk home with him, pretending we had been together the whole time.*

*One night, Mom and Dad were both in the living room, just sitting there. They were waiting for us. I got a funny feeling in my stomach.*

*Mom came over to me. "Shadow, what time were you supposed to be home?"*

*"Five-thirty," I said softly.*

*"What time is it now?"*

*I looked at my new watch, a silver one just like Dad's that I had been given for my birthday. "Almost seven."*

*"Shadow, you're old enough to tell time, and you're more than old enough to follow the rules. I want you*

*to go to your room and think about this. You're restricted to your room for the rest of the night."*

Slowly I turned and shuffled toward my bedroom. From the hallway, I was able to hear almost everything my parents and Daniel said.

"What's the problem?" Daniel asked.

"What's the problem?" my dad repeated in disbelief. "You have so many problems, I hardly know where to begin!"

"Mark—" Mom started.

"But the first problem is your attitude," Dad continued.

"Too bad," Daniel said, and I could picture his shrug.

"For you!" my dad countered. "Your attitude has got to change, and so does your total disregard for our rules."

"How about your attitude? How about your need to be in control of everyone? It drives you crazy that I'm an adult now and you can't tell me what to do anymore."

"One, you're not an adult yet—"

"Bullsh—"

"Two," Dad raised his voice to cut Daniel off, "I can tell you what to do. I'm your father and you're living under my roof. And three—"

"You're such an asshole! I can't even—"

"Watch your language!" Dad yelled.

"Please," Mom said, "Please let's just sit down and—"

"I'm outta here," Daniel said.

"That's it!" Dad shouted. I heard him jump up from the couch. It sounded like he threw the table *across the room. "I will NOT tolerate your defiance any longer! You—"*

*It was at this point that I decided I would be better off in my room, so neither Daniel nor my parents would catch me eavesdropping.*

*I'm not sure how long I lay on my bed, curled up with the stuffed tiger Daniel had given me for my fourth birthday. Eventually the shouting stopped and the house got quiet. At one point, Mom knocked softly on my door and brought in two peanut butter and jelly sandwiches and a large glass of milk. She told me good night and ruffled my hair before giving me a kiss on the cheek.*

*A few moments later, I heard her knocking on Daniel's door.*

*"Go away!" he shouted. "I have nothing to say to you!"*

*"I thought you'd like—"*

*"I don't want anything from you!" he yelled. For a while I could hear him throwing things around.*

*After that, it was quiet, almost too quiet. There wasn't a sound coming from Daniel's room, not even his stereo or TV. I sat on the floor by my door, holding my tiger, and hoping Daniel would come talk to me the way he used to. Finally, barely able to keep my eyes open, I got up, stripped down to my underwear, and crawled into my bed.*

*In the middle of the night, I woke up. I thought Daniel was in my room, but when I sat up, no one was there. I decided I must have been dreaming.*

*When I went into the kitchen the next morning, Mom asked me to go tell Daniel we were having pancakes for breakfast.*

*I knocked timidly on his door, and then a little louder. "Daniel? It's me," I said, knocking again. When there was no answer, I carefully and quietly turned the knob and opened the door.*

*The window was open and the drapes were fluttering a little, letting in bits of light. Daniel's room was always a mess, but now it looked like it had been destroyed. Torn papers and posters were everywhere, books and CDs were scattered all over, and the desk chair was lying on its side in the middle of the room.*

*But Daniel's bed was neatly made, with a piece of paper lying in the center of it.*

*I took a couple of steps into the room, toward the bed, looking around. "Daniel?" I whispered again, frightened. Only the curtains flapped in answer.*

*I looked at the paper. There were just three words, in large block letters:*

*I HATE YOU*

*I turned and ran out of the room, hollering, "Daniel! Daniel is gone!"*

*When Daniel didn't come home the next day, the police were called, the school was notified, all of Daniel's friends were questioned. No one knew where he was.*

*Every time the phone or doorbell rang, we all jumped. Mom and Dad practically raced to answer it, hoping for news. As the days passed, however, we became less hopeful, and more fearful of what the news might be. Weeks went by, and we still asked each other if anyone had seen Daniel.*

"I still remember all of us sitting quietly around the dinner table three months later, on Daniel's sixteenth birthday, wondering where he was and if we would ever see him again. And it turns out that we will get to see him again," I finished. "We just had to wait seven years."

"So that's where you got your nickname," Vernon muttered.

"What?"

Vernon kind of shook his head. "I didn't want to ask so I just kind of assumed that you took the name Shadow 'cause, you know, it's better than Ernest."

I got up and threw my lunch away. When I returned, Vernon was kind of toying with his empty milk carton. "You going to practice today?" he asked, pushing his glasses up on his nose.

"I haven't decided yet."

"I know it's none of my business, and you haven't asked, but I think you should skip practice. I'll tell you everything that happens. Go home and see your brother."

# Chapter Four

**C**autiously I opened the front door, actually afraid of what I might see. I couldn't begin to imagine what Daniel looked like now. Would he look like Mom? Or Dad? And the fact that he had been in prison was setting my imagination on fire. Would he have long, scraggly hair, or would he have shaved it all off to look tough? How many scars would he have on his face? After all, I was pretty sure that all accused murderers must have at least one scar.

I peeked around the door, not stepping immediately into the house. All was quiet. The living room drapes were drawn and there were no lights on. The house had an empty feeling to it. Sighing, I went inside and headed for the kitchen. I wanted to grab some food and then get to my room as quickly as I could.

"What was that sigh for?"

I probably jumped a foot straight into the air. As I landed, I kind of crouched, ready to ward off blows.

"Jeez, Shadow, you're jumpier than a cat!"

I took my sunglasses off, but in the dim light I could barely make out the person sitting in the armchair by the fireplace. I straightened up.

"I didn't think anyone was home."

"I noticed," he replied. "Mom and Dad went to pick you up. Apparently they missed you."

Neither of us said anything for several moments that felt more like years. I didn't move. I didn't want to go into the living room, because then I didn't know how I'd escape later. Questions kept flying through my mind, but I rejected them quickly. They all sounded accusing, even to me.

"I don't think I would have recognized you on the street," he finally said. "Looks like you got Dad's height."

"Almost," I said.

"Give it another year. I bet you catch him."

I had nothing to say to that. Daniel was sitting down and I had no idea how tall he was. As my eyes adjusted, though, I could tell that Daniel was stockier than Dad and I were, and his hair was short, but not shaved. His haircut looked almost trendy. He had dark hair like me and Mom, but he had Dad's strong chin. In fact, the way he was relaxing there in khaki pants and a rugby shirt, I would have never guessed he had just come from jail.

"I guess school just started. You a freshman now?"

"Sophomore."

"Watch out for the dean. I can't remember his name, but he is one big jackass."

"You mean Barnett?" I asked.

"Yeah, that's the dude," Daniel agreed.

"He's only a jackass to troublemakers and delinquents." *You know,* I added in my mind, *the kind that get arrested later in life.*

Before Daniel had a chance to respond, the door to the garage slammed, and Mom and Dad came rushing into the house. "Oh, good, Shadow, you're home," Mom said. She barely looked at me as she hurried over to Daniel.

Dad, however, did look at me. Sternly. "We don't appreciate what you did this morning. We'll talk about it later."

"...made reservations, just in case," Mom was saying to Daniel. She reached out and patted an imaginary stray hair back in place. "It's entirely up to you. We can go out to dinner, or we can stay here and have steaks."

Daniel shifted uncomfortably in his chair, leaning away from Mom a little bit. "Either way is fine. I don't care."

I started to walk down the hall toward my room.

"Shadow, what do you want to do?" Daniel asked.

"They didn't ask me." I stepped into my room and shut the door behind me.

It didn't stay shut long. I had just put my backpack on my desk chair when the door swung open again.

"Young man, I don't know what your problem is, but you had better get over it right now!" Dad hissed.

"What?" I exclaimed. "I just came in here to drop off my books and take off my shoes."

Disbelief was plain on Dad's face, but all he said was, "Come back into the living room, and bring an adjusted attitude."

*Which attitude?* I wondered. *The one where I fawn over Daniel for killing someone? Or the one where I thank my brother for ruining our lives without a second thought?*

"I'd rather stay here," I said.

"Then you'd better be ready to stay here for a long time," he said, glowering at me.

"Fine! Just tell Daniel I'm sick again. I'm sure he'll believe it now."

"Shadow," Mom said gently. Dad and I both jumped. Neither of us had seen her in the hall behind him. "Please. Your father and I just want to have our whole family back, okay? We want our family." Her voice quavered just a little. "Could you please try? I don't know why it's so hard for you, but could you just try for us?"

I couldn't remember my mother ever begging me for anything. "Okay," I said, shrugging uncomfortably. "I'll try."

Her eyes shone across the room. "Thank you, honey." She turned and disappeared down the hall.

I went back to my bag and began pulling my books out, stacking them on my desk.

As Dad started out of my room, he said, "You know, this isn't easy for any of us."

I raised my head slightly, but didn't say anything. It didn't seem to be all that hard for Daniel, and I didn't see Mom or Dad being really bothered either.

"Don't take too long," Dad added.

I didn't rush, but I didn't take as long as I could have, either. After I unpacked my books, hung my coat on the back of my door, and ran a comb through my hair, I took a deep breath and went back to the unknown.

In the living room, I walked into silence. Mom seemed eager to break it. "Daniel would like to stay home for dinner tonight, where we'll all be more comfortable."

"Good," I said, thinking that if this was supposed to be comfortable, I would rather die than go out where it would be *un*comfortable.

"Mom, I've told you I go by Dan now," my brother said, a little sharply.

"Oh, yes, yes," Mom said. "I'm sorry, honey. I'll really try to remember."

"You'll have to give us a little time," Dad said, "to get used to all the changes, Dan."

I decided not to sit down. "I think I'll get a soda," I said. "Does anyone else want something to drink?"

"I'd like an iced tea, please," Mom said, smiling at me.

"Got any beer?"

My parents both stared at Daniel for a minute, not answering right away. Daniel had only been fifteen when he left, but now he was twenty-two. Mom spoke up slowly. "I...I think there are a couple of light beers stuck in the back of the fridge," she said to Dad. "From the last office party we had."

Daniel wrinkled his nose slightly, but nodded. "I'll take one."

"Let me help you, Shadow," Dad said, getting up quickly.

He followed me into the kitchen with a tight face. I took four glasses out of the cabinet, then put one back and got a beer mug instead. Dad just stood there in front of the fridge.

After a couple of seconds, I said, "Dad? If you don't want to help, could you at least get out of the way?"

He flinched a little, and then opened the refrigerator. He handed me the pitcher of iced tea and a can of soda. He bent down, muttering to himself.

"What do you want?" I asked. He didn't answer right away, but then he stood up with two beer cans in his hand.

I raised my eyebrows but didn't say anything as I put one of the glasses back and got another mug. My parents occasionally had a glass of wine with dinner, but that was about it. We used the beer mugs mostly for root beer floats.

Back out in the living room, Dad handed Daniel his beer, and then lifted his mug for a toast. "To our family. May it stay whole for a long time to come."

Mom clinked her glass against mine. She turned to Daniel, but he was already drinking. She clinked Dad's glass and looked over at Daniel again. "Well, if we want to eat tonight," she said, "I'd better start getting dinner ready."

I stood up quickly. "I'll help."

"Oh, no, really, that's okay," Mom said, gesturing toward my chair. "Keep Daniel—Dan—company."

That was the last thing I wanted to do. But I had promised to try, so I sat back down.

It was quiet for a while. Even Dad seemed a little unsure about what to talk about. Daniel was staring into his mug, so I took the opportunity to study his face.

The haircut made him look preppy, but something about his eyes made him look…hard. He was frowning, and the lines on his forehead reminded me of Dad. I peeked at Dad; the lines on his face only made him look tired. When I looked back at my brother I noticed that he *did* have a scar—one on his left cheek, just under the eye.

"What'd you do to your face?" I asked, trying to sound casual. I was trying to think of what could have caused the scar. It was too small for a knife wound. Maybe he had gotten into a fight with someone wearing a ring or something.

"What?" Daniel sounded defensive.

"The scar." I pointed to my own cheek. "What'd you do?"

"I tried to pull a little brother out of a cactus bed when I was eleven. I've got a couple more on my neck and arms, if you want to see them."

"Oh," I said. "No, that's okay."

"You look good, Dan," Dad said. "Staying pretty fit."

Dan shrugged. "Small meals and needing to move fast was good for me, I guess."

"Moving fast?" Dad repeated blankly.

Dan made a dismissive gesture. "Nothin'."

"So did you have roommates?" Dad tried again.

"Yeah."

Dad waited for more, but Daniel apparently thought that was answer enough. "So..." Dad cleared his throat. "Um, Dan, what kind of job do you think you're going to get?"

Daniel looked up from his beer. "You mean if I don't go to the joint?"

Dad winced, but pushed on. "I just wondered what kind of work you were interested in."

"Don't know," Daniel said, shifting in his chair. "Hard to get a job without a diploma." He nodded toward me. "Remember that. Stay in school till you get one."

I felt like I was in a bad ad for public education.

"Surely you've had jobs," Dad pressed. "You must have some idea of what you want to do."

"I've done all kinds of jobs at one time or another. Didn't ever like any of 'em enough to stick with it."

"Like what?"

"Sales, services, errand boy, bookkeeper, entertainer, all sorts. Never stayed with any of 'em very long."

Dad was quiet for a moment, then chose what would seem to be the safest job to discuss. "What kind of sales? Furniture? Clothing? Did you work in a mall or a department store?"

Daniel snorted. "Not quite."

"So what did you sell?" I asked.

He looked at me out of the corner of his eye. "Nothing you'd be interested in."

"Where have you been?" I continued. "Where were you staying all that time?"

"I'd rather not talk about it right now." His voice had a sharp edge to it.

"Okay," I said slowly. He didn't want to talk about his future; he didn't want to talk about his past. I didn't know what to make of this stranger who was supposed to be my brother. "Did you really kill someone?" I blurted out.

"Shadow!" Dad exploded, sitting straight up in his chair. "That's enough!"

"It's okay," Daniel said, shaking his head. He turned cold eyes toward me.

I tried to meet that icy stare, but I couldn't. It was my turn to study my drink. Fortunately, Mom came bustling back in. "Okay, the steaks are seasoned, and the scalloped potatoes are in the oven. Whenever you're ready, you can start the grill," she said to Dad.

"I'll do that right now," he said, jumping up from his chair.

Envious, I watched him leave the room. Mom pulled a chair over closer to Daniel. "What did I miss?"

Daniel and I glanced at each other before looking

away and simultaneously saying, "Nothing." For a moment, it was almost like old times—in the interest of self-defense, we both wanted to keep our problem to ourselves.

"Well, Dan, so much has changed," Mom said. "I don't even know what kind of food you like or anything. You'll have to give me a list of things you like, so we can get them for you."

"Don't worry about it. I probably won't be staying long."

I could have killed him for saying that. Mom looked like he had just knocked the wind out of her.

"Why not?" I demanded.

He smiled bitterly at me. "My trial will be coming up soon."

The hairs on the back of my neck rose. If he didn't think he'd be back after the trial...he must have done it.

Mom floundered, at a loss for words, but finally she patted his arm and said, "Honey, we're going to meet with a good lawyer tomorrow. Don't give up."

"The public defender told me the best I could hope for is ten to fifteen years for voluntary manslaughter."

"He didn't care about your case. He's swamped and looking for an easy way out. We're going to get you the best lawyer and—"

Dan shifted away from her. "Don't waste your money," he said.

I felt sick. It was hard enough to have him home again; I couldn't think of him going to jail. I stood up, trying not to wobble. "I'll go set the table," I said. I passed Dad as he came back into the living room.

I put out four plates, remembering back to the first year that Daniel had been gone. Mom had made me set four places at the table month after month, just in case my brother came home in time for dinner. The day Dad quietly told me that I only had to set it for three, Mom had spent an hour locked in her bedroom. When she came out, her face was puffy and her eyes were blood-shot. That was the last time I had seen her cry.

The timer went off. "Got it!" I called. I turned the buzzer and the oven off, but left the potatoes in to keep warm. Dad went out to the grill to flip the steaks. On his way back through the kitchen he managed a strained smile.

I glanced into the living room. Daniel had picked up a small statue off the fireplace. I wondered if he was pricing it. Suddenly I flashed back to the night Daniel had left and I had "dreamed" he was in my room. Two weeks later, when I was unable to find my piggy bank anywhere in my room, I realized that I hadn't been dreaming. I lost not only my hero that night, I had lost my Playstation savings as well.

Clearly I needed to settle down before I went back in there. I put the salad on the table and got out three types of dressing. Mom had set out a loaf of French bread on the counter. I sliced it slowly and put it in a basket. Desperately, I looked around the kitchen again, but couldn't find anything else to do. I went back to the living room.

Daniel was still standing by the fireplace. "The house looks good," he was saying. "Not much has changed. I thought maybe you'd be in a bigger house by now."

"No," Mom said quickly. "We're very happy with this house, and we love our neighbors. Besides, it's the perfect size for us."

I looked at Dad, but he was staring off through the window. My parents didn't disagree often, but they had fought several times over the last few years about moving. Dad did want a bigger house, at least one with a three-car garage, but Mom refused to even consider it. If we moved, she had always asked, how would Daniel be able to find us?

"How much longer for the steaks, Dad?"

"Hmm?" He blinked, then looked at his watch. "Oh, they should be ready any minute. We could probably move to the dining room."

"Any more beer, Shadow?" Daniel asked.

"I'm afraid those were the last two, son," Dad said.

So that was the reason Dad had taken a beer.

"We'll get some, the kind you like," Mom said. "We just don't drink much around here."

"There's Coke, Diet Pepsi, and 7 UP," I told him.

"I'll take a Coke," he said.

I almost offered to show him where he could find them himself, for future reference, but I firmly reminded myself I had promised Mom to try. Instead, I took the empty beer mug from him and went to the kitchen to get his Coke. I needed another one anyway.

By the time I had poured the two glasses, Dad was back in with the steaks, and Mom and Daniel were sitting at the table.

At least while we were eating we didn't have to talk. There was the minimal pass-the-salt and the-potatoes-are-really-good conversation, and that was about it. The quiet was almost a relief.

But then Daniel asked about our cousin Bruce, and that led to questions about other family members. In a few minutes they were having a great time, reminiscing.

Old events, so old that I couldn't remember them, were brought back to life. Mom, Dad, and Daniel were talking over each other and laughing. It was just like the time Dad had an old college buddy over to dinner. I felt like an extra in a movie scene. I listened and put one forkful of food into my mouth after another.

When I finished my dinner, I stood up to clear my place.

"We've got apple pie for dessert," Mom said.

"I used to dream about your homemade apple pie," Daniel said.

"I'm full," I said, even though I had only had one helping of everything. "And I've got a lot of homework tonight."

"You get good grades, Shad?" Daniel asked.

I shrugged.

Mom smiled. "You can do better than that, Shadow." She turned to Daniel. "He's been on the honor roll for the last three years."

"Very good," Daniel said, doing a golf-clap. I couldn't tell if he was mocking me or not. "What sports do you play, other than basketball?"

As I opened my mouth, Dad answered for me. "He doesn't."

"Just sticking with basketball, huh?"

"No, he doesn't do any sports, not even basketball."

"Really?" Daniel seemed surprised. "So what do you do?"

"Hang out mostly," I said before Mom and Dad got a chance to say anything. "Read a lot, surf the Internet, just do stuff."

"He's thinking about the Speech and Debate team this year," Mom added.

Daniel's eyebrows rose. "That's...uh...different."

"That's exactly what I said!" Dad exclaimed, gathering dishes from the table.

I glared at them both and then took my plate into the kitchen. Dad was right behind me.

As I left the kitchen, he said, "Shadow, try to hurry with your homework tonight, okay? Don't just stay in there reading. Come back out and join us."

I couldn't decide if he was ordering me to do it, or if he was asking because he wanted a little help with conversation.

My trig assignment took the most time, because I hadn't been in class to start it. I also had short assignments in chemistry and American lit. After I was done, I sat at my desk, staring at my library book. I had no idea what to make of Daniel. I wondered if he was just using my parents for the bond money. Would he skip town again and leave them with a huge debt to go with the shattered hopes?

I really didn't want to go back out to the living room. Daniel was the shining star tonight. I wondered how long his "guest" status would last. Would my parents ever treat him as their son again, as someone they could be honest with and voice their disapproval to? I had a sinking feeling that the time for that was long since past. Daniel had been gone too long to ever really be a family member; he would always be treated as a guest in our house.

With a sigh, I forced myself to get up from my desk and walk down the hall. It wasn't as quiet in the living room this time, because the TV was on. Everyone was looking at it, but I had the strange feeling no one was really paying any attention to the sitcom on the screen.

"Everything done?" Dad asked as I walked into the room.

"Yep."

"There's a piece of apple pie waiting in the oven for you, Shadow," Mom said.

"Thanks. I'll get it later."

Daniel glanced at me. "So, you still go by Shadow. When I started calling you that, I never thought it'd stick."

I did my best to keep my voice even. "Just because you left didn't mean everything about my life had to change. I liked the name Shadow. I still do."

"You look like one now, all in black like that."

"Thanks," I said, flashing a huge fake smile at him. I wasn't going to let him know he upset me. I wasn't going to let him control my feelings anymore.

I stood up without realizing I was going to move. Once I did, I had to go somewhere, so I headed for the kitchen.

"Hey, Shadow, catch me another Coke, would ya?"

"Right," I muttered. "Anybody else?"

Mom and Dad said no.

From the kitchen I heard Daniel ask Dad, "Ya got any rum? It might make the Coke go down easier."

It was Mom who answered. "Yes, I think we have some rum. Don't we, honey?"

"I can fix a drink for you," Dad said in a tense voice. I could hear him rummaging around in the dining room cabinets.

I was pulling the pie out of the oven when Dad came in and got the Coke from the refrigerator. "Want another one, Shadow?"

"Does mine come with rum?" I asked, trying to joke.

Bad timing. Dad gave me an unreadable look.

"I'll take milk," I said quickly. "It goes better with pie."

Dad poured the rum into the Coke, shaking his head the whole time.

"What's wrong?" I asked.

"Nothing," he replied curtly. A lie if I ever heard one.

Daniel had the remote and was flipping through channels when we got back. Dad handed him his drink and he took it without saying anything. Dad's mouth tightened in a thin line, but he was quiet as he returned to the couch.

"This is a good show," I said, when Daniel paused for a moment on channel four.

He waited a few seconds, then grunted, "Nah," and kept moving through the channels.

I turned my attention to my pie, resolving to finish it and then go to bed.

The phone rang, and I hoped fervently that it would be Vernon, calling to tell me about the afternoon's meeting. Mom picked up the phone, and in a few short words she told the telemarketer that he was interrupting a very important evening. She slammed down the receiver. I had never seen my mother come that close to being rude before.

A few more bites finished the pie. After I put the plate in the dishwasher, I stopped between the living room and hallway.

"Well, good night," I said.

"You're going to bed already?" Daniel asked.

"Yeah," I said, yawning as big as I could. "I had a long day. Besides," I added with a sidelong look at my parents, "I'm still fighting that cold."

"Just a minute, Shadow," Mom said, turning to Dad. "We need to decide what's happening tomorrow."

"What do you mean?" he asked.

"I can't take tomorrow off," she said. "Someone should stay home with Daniel."

"Not me!" I said instantly. "I'm not old enough to baby-sit him."

"I don't need anyone to stay home with me," Daniel said. "As long as there's a car I can use."

"No," Dad said before Mom could open her mouth. "I'm afraid that won't be possible." He gave Mom a meaningful look, which she chose to ignore.

"I could probably get a ride with Sonia," she said, "and you could use my car."

"Caroline," Dad said in a hard voice. "I said he can't use our cars."

Mom and Dad locked in a stare-down. Mom was clearly upset. I knew Dad was angry, but he looked calm.

"Hey, no big deal," Daniel said, shrugging it off. "I'll find a way to get wherever I need to go."

"I think it would be best if you stayed in the house," Dad said, not taking his eyes off Mom.

"You're not trying to ground me again, are you?" Daniel's tone was almost light.

Dad smiled, but there wasn't any humor in it. "Merely making a suggestion. You don't have money to buy gas anyway."

Mom turned back to me. "Are you sure you can't stay home tomorrow?"

Stubbornly, I shook my head.

Daniel laughed. "I think he's afraid of me."

"No," I shot back. "I just have better things to do."

"Boys," Dad said, refereeing just like he had when we were younger.

Mom ignored the whole side play. "Then I want you to come straight home after school," she said.

"I'll try."

"You'll try?"

"Yeah." I got defensive. "I missed practice today. I've got to find out what's going on. I might need to stay after a little bit."

"I'm sure it can wait till next week," Mom said firmly. "Come straight home."

I rolled my eyes. "Good night," I said again, escaping the room before I could be given another command.

I went to bed, but I stayed up reading. Dimly I was aware of Daniel and my parents coming down the hall and saying good night to each other. The house was quiet, and it was my favorite time to read. The book drew me in, and before I realized it, I had read the last hundred pages.

With a sigh and a stretch, I put the book down and blinked at the clock. Just after one. I yawned and decided to go to the bathroom.

When I opened my door, I was surprised to see a light coming from under my parents' door. They were never up this late.

Quietly, I walked to the door. I could hear murmuring, but couldn't make out any of the words. Just as I was about to knock and ask if something was wrong, the voices got a little louder.

"Caroline, I meant what I said!"

"We can't just leave him with a public defender!"

"I didn't say that! I said we can't afford Maclean! The bail alone set our investments back almost ten years! And Maclean's the most expensive lawyer in town!"

"Because he's good! Doesn't Daniel deserve the best?"

"Yes, but Bryce is a very busy—"

"You don't think he could work the son of his tennis partner into his schedule?"

"Of course, but—" Dad was almost shouting.

"Shhh! Do you want the boys to hear?" she asked.

Their voices became an indistinct murmur again. I returned to my room. I wondered how long Daniel—and their fights—would remain under our roof.

# Chapter Five

The next morning when I went into the kitchen, I was surprised to find Mom there, already dressed for work and talking on the phone. She usually didn't get ready until after Dad and I left. "Thanks, Sonia, I really appreciate it.... Okay, see you in twenty minutes."

She hung up the phone. "Good morning, Shadow." She smiled, but she looked pretty frazzled.

"Morning. What was that all about?"

"Oh, Sonia's going to come pick me up today."

"Something wrong with the car?"

"No. But your father and I discussed it some more last night, and we decided to let Danny—Dan! I've got to get that right!—to let Dan borrow the car today."

"You and Dad both decided that?"

She was writing a note, so it took her a moment to answer. "Well, it makes more sense. If we can get an appointment today, I would have to leave work, drive home to pick him up, and then take him back downtown. This way Dan won't have to wait on me. He can just drive the car to the lawyer's office himself."

I nodded, even though it sounded weak to me. "Where's Dad?"

"He had to go in early to see about getting an appointment with Mr. Maclean." Mom put the note in the center of the countertop. "Now, I've got to go finish getting ready. Don't forget to come straight home this afternoon."

"I'll try," I said.

"Do better than try, Shadow. Be here." As an after-thought, she added, "Have a good day."

"You too," I muttered.

I glanced at the note. It was for Daniel, of course. It said that Dad would call later with the appointment time and that we would be having dinner at 6:30.

I grabbed my breakfast bars and headed out for school. Vernon was waiting for me at the corner.

"Two more minutes and I would have left without you," he said in greeting. "I wasn't sure I wanted to wait as long as I did yesterday."

"Fair enough," I said.

"So?" he said as we turned down the street. "How'd it go last night?"

"It was..." *How was last night?* I shook my head. "I don't know."

Vernon laughed. "Sounds like you're in the same condition you were in yesterday."

"Yeah," I said, "and it really sucks." I relayed bits and pieces of last night's conversations, skipping over anything that had to do with Daniel's arrest and upcoming trial.

"Sounds uncomfortable," he said when I finished.

"Yeah, that's a pretty good word for it." We were both quiet for a minute. "So what's up with the speech club?"

"You mean our opportunity to join the NFL?"

"Huh?"

Vernon grinned and pushed his glasses up on his nose. "The National Forensics League, of course. The NFL."

I laughed. "Right. Maybe that'll get my dad off my back about sports. I can just tell him I'm in the NFL."

"Well, you've got to start coming to practices first," Vernon said. "We have to earn points to become members, and we earn points at the meets. I have a booklet to give you. Yesterday the upperclassmen did demonstrations of the two types of debate and a couple of the interpretive readings."

"How was that?"

"Pretty cool. You can debate with a partner, or you can do it alone. I can't remember the names of them right now, though. They gave us this year's topics for the debates and guidelines for the interpretive stuff, and we're supposed to practice them. Next week they'll go over some of the other speeches, and we can start deciding which ones we'd like to prepare for."

I was having a hard time keeping my mind on debate.

"Hey, are you listening?" Vernon asked.

"Yeah, I'm sorry. Did you say how long we have to prepare?"

"Since the topics are assigned for the whole year, we've got plenty of time to polish our speeches and get as many sources as possible."

"We work on the same speech for a year before we give it?"

"No, no. Mr. Souza said we have several meets during the year. We're supposed to keep trying to perfect our speeches, so we'll kick ass at State. Our first meet is in three weeks," he said. "And it's on a Friday, which means we get out of school."

"I can handle that," I said, trying to be enthusiastic for Vernon. "So what are the topics for the year?"

"For the ones with partners, it's the minor's right to privacy. For the solo debates, it's the death penalty."

"Who all was there yesterday?"

"Let's see. Our sponsor, Mr. Souza, was there, obviously. But he said he leaves the sophomore training to our captains. Remember that guy from registration?"

"Arrogant wrestler dude?"

"Yeah. The guy named Pat. He's a captain. And remember that cheerleader who was with him, Tess? She's the other one."

"What about the kids from the first meeting?"

Vernon wrinkled his forehead, trying to remember. "There were a lot more people at the practice yesterday, so I don't know."

"Really? How many?"

"I'm not sure. There were probably eight upperclassmen, but they don't have to come to the after-school practices, except for the captains. And I'd say there were about fifteen others."

"Wow. Sounds like a big group. Does everyone get to be in the meets?"

Vernon shrugged. "They didn't say. But they did say we have to be at the practice the week of a meet in order to be able to compete. And if we sign up to be in a meet and then don't show up, we have to pay the entrance fee. I've got this whole packet to give you," he repeated. "It's in my locker."

We were almost at school.

"So was that other girl there? You know, the one who sat way back in the corner?"

Vernon thought for a moment then shook his head. "I really can't remember. Tess asked about you, though."

"She what?"

"She asked me where you were."

"You're lying!"

"I'm serious," he insisted.

I cuffed him on the shoulder. "Why didn't you tell me that before?"

He grinned. "I wanted to see if you would ask about her."

The first bell rang as soon as we got to our lockers, so we split up to go to our classes.

At lunch, Vernon led me to a different table, where a few guys were already sitting. He introduced me to Ryan, Don, and Russ. I recognized Ryan from two of my classes. Vernon said that all three of them were joining the forensics team. Don tried to talk everyone into joining the chess club too.

At first I was a little uncomfortable, but the others talked so much, they didn't even notice I was being quiet. Don and Russ didn't stick around long. They wolfed down their food and then went off to use the computer lab.

"Hey," Ryan said. "A few of us are going to stay after school today and tomorrow to do some practice rounds. Want to come?"

Vernon bobbed his head enthusiastically.

"I can't today," I said. "I'll come tomorrow though. Where?"

"We'll meet in the same room we practice in, room

115. Mr. Souza doesn't care if we come practice in there as long as we leave when he does."

Just then, I happened to glance across the room. Without really thinking, I jumped up. "Be back in a minute," I said.

"Where's he going?" I heard Ryan ask.

I cut between the cafeteria tables. She was standing by the cash registers, holding her tray and looking around uncertainly.

"I didn't know you had lunch this hour," I said. Robin jumped a little, flinching away from me nervously. "Oh. It's you," she said. She continued to peer around the room. "I don't—I mean, I didn't. I had to get my schedule changed, and it took till today to get it all straightened out. Now I've got this lunch."

"Cool," I said.

"Not really. I don't know anybody who has this lunch."

"You know *me*," I began.

She rolled her eyes.

"No, really, I promise to be nice. You can come sit with us." She hesitated, and I added, "At least for today. Until you find someone else you want to sit with."

"Okay," she said finally. "Thanks."

She followed me across the cafeteria to where Vernon and Ryan were waiting. I pulled out a chair for her. She looked at me funny before she sat down, muttering something under her breath that I couldn't hear.

"In case you don't know them, these are other members of the forensics team," I said, introducing her.

She smiled and said hello, and then tried to turn her attention to her lunch. She barely got her fork to her mouth before Vernon and Ryan started firing questions at her.

"So what junior high did you go to?" Ryan asked.

"Who do you have for American lit?" Vernon wanted to know. "What hour? We must be in the same class."

"Do you have CP chemistry?"

"What are your electives?"

"What kind of books do you read?"

"Do you play any sports?"

Thank goodness for Vernon and Ryan. With their blunt questions, I learned more about Robin in five minutes than I knew about my own brother. I almost felt sorry for her, but she quickly turned the fire back on them and bombarded them with questions. And then she turned on me.

"So where were you yesterday?"

"Yesterday?"

"The forensics meeting? You said you were going to join, but you weren't there," she said to her apple before she took a bite.

"I couldn't make it," I said. "Family obligations." I smiled. "But I'll make sure I'm there next time."

"Some of us are going to practice today and tomorrow after school," Ryan cut in. "You can come if you like."

She thought about it for a minute. "I'll see what I can do."

The bell rang. Robin still hadn't finished her lunch. Ryan and Vernon got up, but I stayed where I was.

"Catch you later," I said to them.

"See ya," they said as they joined the mass exodus out of the cafeteria.

"You don't have to wait."

"Sure I do. It's the polite thing to do."

"The polite thing? After your friends ask me so many questions I can't get three bites of food in, you're now going to sit there and stare at me while I try to eat? You consider that polite?"

I grinned and turned in my chair. "I won't stare," I said, looking in the other direction.

She shook her head and again muttered something that I couldn't catch. After a minute, she said, "So what was your family obligation?"

"Oh, nothing exciting," I said. Then, so I wouldn't sound like I was brushing her off, I asked, "What type of debate do you want to do? The one with a partner or the solo one?"

She sighed. "I'll do whatever they'll let me do in meets. I'd probably do better on my own, but I guess it'd be good for me to work with partners too. What about you?"

"I don't know. I haven't made up my mind."

"But you said you were coming next week."

"I'll probably give it a try," I said. "I'm not sure yet if this is for me."

"You don't want to compete?"

I shook my head. I wasn't sure I'd even be able to do a practice speech in front of my friends, but I didn't want to say that. Then she'd probably want to know why I was joining the team at all.

She pushed her chair back. "We better get going," she said, "or we'll be late."

I picked up her tray and emptied it into the trash can before stacking it. She was looking at me funny again. "What?" I asked.

"You pull out my chair, you clean up my tray... Are you a psycho, or are you the last gentleman left on the planet?"

I gave her a full smile. "I guess you'll have to get to know me better to find out."

"I was afraid you'd say that," she said as we got to the hall. "My locker's down this way, so I guess I'll see you later."

"How do you know my locker's not that way?"

She blushed as she said defiantly, "Well, is it?"

"No—but I think you already knew that." The hall suddenly seemed warmer.

Her blush deepened. "I've got to get going," she said quickly and turned to go.

"Yeah." My voice cracked, but I cleared my throat and kept talking. "Join us for lunch tomorrow if you want to."

She smiled and waved. I ran to my locker and then down the hall, slipping through the classroom door just as the late bell rang.


"Hello!" I called as I opened our front door. I didn't want a repeat of yesterday. "Hello?" I yelled again when there was no answer.

I dropped my backpack on the floor and went out to check the garage. It was empty.

"Terrific. I come straight home to be here for Daniel, and he's not even here," I muttered to myself, grabbing a Coke and a bag of chips from the kitchen.

It took me less than an hour to finish my homework, and since I had finished my library book the night before, I had nothing else to do. I was watching TV when Dad got home a little after five. "How was your day?" he asked on his way from the garage to his room.

I waited the five minutes it took for him to change into jeans and a T-shirt and come back to the living room. "It was fine. How was yours?"

"It was all right. You get all caught up from yesterday?"

"Yeah."

"Was your friend able to fill you in on that speech stuff?"

"Yeah. A few of us are going to practice after school tomorrow."

"Good," he mumbled absently as he flipped through the mail.

"I thought you might come home early today."

"Oh? Why's that?"

"Since you left so early this morning," I said.

"Nope," he said, taking the bills to the office. "Just had a lot to do today." He came back and glanced at the clock. "Dan's not back yet?"

I shook my head. "I'm the only one here."

Dad frowned. "I didn't think his appointment with the lawyer would take so long. I wish he had let one of us go with him."

He got a Coke from the kitchen and joined me on the couch, watching the news. Mom got home fifteen minutes later.

"Hello!" she called from the front door. "Sorry I'm late!" She came into the living room with a puzzled look on her face. "Where's Daniel?"

"Maclean's secretary said he could work him in around three," Dad said.

"The appointment wouldn't take this long, would

it?" She didn't give him a chance to answer before she turned to me. "Has he called?"

"No," I said.

"That's strange. Well," she said, "I'm sure he'll be home in time for dinner. I told him six-thirty. Shadow, will you get out the chicken and some frozen vegetables while I change?" She started down the hall without stopping to kiss Dad hello the way she usually did.

"Sure." I got up and went to the kitchen.

Mom joined me a few minutes later. She had me set the table and then shooed me out, claiming I was in her way.

The six o'clock news ended. Dad and I stayed in the living room, watching a game show. The smells coming from the kitchen made my stomach rumble loudly.

At quarter till seven, Mom came in and sat down. No one said anything. She and Dad didn't even look at each other. They just stared fixedly at the TV. The tension in the house seemed to increase every minute.

Half an hour later, my stomach growled again, even louder this time.

"Is dinner ready?" Dad asked.

Mom gave a quick nod.

"Maybe we should go ahead and eat."

"He'll be here. We can wait."

"How long do you plan on waiting, Caroline?"

"He'll be here!" she snapped.

During the next commercial I hesitantly asked, "What happens if he doesn't come back?"

Mom made a small noise in the back of her throat. She stood up quickly. "I can't believe...you don't..." Finally she blurted out, "Fine, go ahead and eat!"

She started out of the living room. Dad stood up and

tried to stop her, but she pushed him away and ran down the hall.

He bowed his head down for a moment and then turned to me. "I guess it's just the two of us for dinner."

We fixed our plates in silence. Dad started toward the table, then stopped, looking at the four empty chairs surrounding the table. "What do you say we just eat on the couch tonight?"

"Sounds good."

While we ate, a reality show rerun came on; neither of us bothered to change the channel.

"I didn't mean to upset Mom," I said.

Dad sighed. "It's okay, Shadow. It's like I told you, this isn't easy for any of us." He was quiet for a few minutes. "The night Daniel left, it was my decision to come down hard on him. Your mother thought I was being too strict. We had discussed punishment several times before, but she was always against it. She thought that he was just going through a phase, that he'd snap out of it. I went along with her decision, until that night, when I had had enough." Staring at his empty plate, he shook his head. "For a long time, I blamed myself for Daniel leaving. It was easy to feel guilty, because every time I looked at your mother, I knew she was blaming me too."

"Dad..." I began, but I had no idea what to say. He had never talked to me about that night.

"So now," he continued, "Daniel's come home. And your mother doesn't want anyone to refuse him any-thing, because she doesn't want to lose him again."

"But we have to have him back before we can lose him," I muttered.

Dad flashed me a sad grin. "You've always been an

insightful kid." He paused, then quietly added, "Your mother thinks he's back."

"He's here, but he doesn't act like he plans to stay."

"I'm afraid he doesn't. When he called, he said he just wanted to let us know he was alive and okay. He didn't ask us to bail him out, and he didn't ask if he could come home. Your mother just took over."

"How much was the bail?" I had been curious, but there hadn't been a good time to ask until now.

"More than we can afford to lose."

"We might lose it?"

"If Daniel skips town."

"Do you think he will?"

Dad shrugged. "As you pointed out the night he called, we don't really know him anymore. But the judge was willing to set bail for two reasons. One, he's never been arrested before. And two, we agreed to be responsible for him."

"Is that why you didn't want him to use a car?"

"That's part of it. The other part is that I don't know how well he drives. I don't even know if he has a license."

"So why did Mom give him her car?"

"He's her baby, Shadow, the same way you are. And she doesn't want anything to hurt either of you. For the last seven years, she hasn't been able to do anything for Daniel, so she wants to make up for it now. She wants to give him everything. I'm already looking like the bad guy, already saying no to him." Dad sighed and ran his hand through his hair. "I'd like to know what he's been doing these last years, because that might explain a lot, but he won't talk about it and your mother won't press the issue. She doesn't want to upset him."

"She doesn't want to upset him?" I asked. "Or she doesn't want to be upset by what she hears?"

Dad looked at me but didn't say anything.

I started gathering the dishes. As I headed to the kitchen, Dad stood up. "I'll go check on your mother. These next few weeks are going to be hard, Shadow, for everyone."

I had never seen my father look so old, so tired.

It took Dad a while, but he finally talked Mom into coming back into the living room. She jumped every time the clock chimed, and when the phone rang a little before nine, she raced for it. It was a wrong number. A few minutes later, it was Vernon.

As she handed me the phone, she covered the mouthpiece and said, "No more than five minutes. We have to keep the line clear."

Vernon wanted to know if I had written down the page numbers for our chemistry assignment. It took me a few seconds to find the right page in my notebook. After I read the numbers out to him, I lowered my voice a little. "So Robin's in your American lit class, huh?"

"Yeah. I didn't realize it before, because she sits a few rows over and behind me. Besides, she's good at making herself invisible."

"You mean she's quiet in class?"

"Well, yeah. Seems to me she's pretty quiet everywhere. She hardly talked at all during lunch."

Mom cleared her throat loudly. I glanced at her and she gave me an impatient look.

I turned around and walked a couple of feet down

the hall. "What do you mean? Robin talked a lot today. You guys didn't give her a chance to be quiet. You asked her so many questions she couldn't even eat her lunch!"

Vernon laughed. "I guess that's true. Is she in any of your classes?"

Before I could respond, Mom snapped, "Shadow, your five minutes are up!"

I went back to the living room and sat down, phone to my ear. She stood up, hands on her hips, glaring at me. I glared right back.

"Just a second!" I said.

"You've had your second! Hang up the phone!"

"Hey, man, I've got to get going anyway," Vernon said.

"You sure?"

"Yeah. See you tomorrow morning."

"See ya."

I hung up.

"Thank you!" Mom said. I handed her the phone and sank further into my chair. She returned to the sofa, clutching the phone.

The garage door finally opened a little after nine. Mom ran out to meet Daniel. Dad and I exchanged glances, but neither of us moved.

A few minutes later, the two of them came in together. Daniel carried in two six-packs of beer and put them in the fridge on his way to the living room. Mom was hovering behind him.

"Hey," Daniel said easily. "Sorry I'm late. Lost track of time."

Even from across the room, I could smell the cigarette smoke.

"Where were you?" Dad asked. His face was blank, his tone bland.

"I stopped at JR Rocker's on the way back from the lawyer."

Mom jumped in eagerly. "How did the meeting go?"

Daniel shrugged. "Fine. I still don't think we need this guy, though. The case is going to be the same if you pay for a fancy lawyer or if the state just pays for a public defender."

"Oh, no," Mom said. "Mr. Maclean is the best lawyer in town. I'm sure—"

"Something smells good," Daniel cut in. "Is there any left?"

"Of course," Mom said, bustling off to the kitchen. "Sit down and I'll get you a plate."

"Anything good on the tube?" Daniel asked, flopping down in a chair.

I picked up the remote. "We're watching a movie," I said, turning the volume up a notch. I kept the remote in my hand.

"So, what else did you do today?" Dad asked.

"Nothing, really. Just went to that meeting and then to the bar."

"How long did the meeting take?"

"About forty-five minutes."

That meant he had been at Rocker's from around four o'clock till almost nine. I could tell Dad was thinking the same thing I was.

Mom brought the plate of food out for him, along with one of the beers. "Here you go, honey."

"Thanks." He smiled up at her. "Looks great."

"Aren't you going to eat, Mom?" I asked.

She shook her head, smiling, without taking her

eyes off Daniel. "I'm not hungry."

"Hey," Daniel stopped shoveling food in his mouth and swallowed. "Can I use your car again tomorrow?"

"No!" Dad said immediately.

"Mark—"

"Caroline, he's just driven himself home in our car after spending nearly five hours in a bar! He could've ki— " Dad broke off, but we all knew what he had been about to say. His face turned so red it was almost purple.

"Hey, Dad, I'm not entirely stupid," Daniel said with a weak grin. "I wasn't drinking."

Dad raised an eyebrow.

"I wasn't drinking before I drove," Daniel amended. "I had two beers the whole time I was there. Swear to God."

Dad was watching Mom. She glanced at him and he shook his head. She looked back at Daniel and sighed. "Yes, you can use the car tomorrow, but that will be the last time for a while. I've got a busy schedule coming up at work."

Dad closed his eyes.

"Thanks, Mom."

"You've got to be home by five though. And no drinking!"

I excused myself and went to hide in my room. I thought about calling Vernon back, but I was afraid it might be too late. I dug through my old books and found a favorite I hadn't read in a while and climbed into bed with it.

A few minutes later, there was a knock at my door. "Yeah," I said, thinking it would be Dad. It was Daniel.

"Hey, man. What's up?"

"What do you want?" I asked suspiciously.

"Just want to talk," he said, wandering over to the shelves by the window. He picked up an old model Mustang, turned it over in his hands, and put it back.

"I never got another piggy bank," I said, "if that's what you're looking for."

"Is that why you've been so pissy to me? Just 'cause I took some of your change seven years ago?"

I thought he wouldn't remember what I was talking about. For him to admit to the theft so callously only made me mad all over again. "No, Daniel, you didn't just take some of my change. You took all the money I had saved. So why don't you just leave?"

He sighed. "I came in here to make up, Shadow." He reached in his back pocket and pulled out a wad of bills. "Here. This should take care of my debt."

My anger shifted to fear. "How'd you get that? Dad said you didn't have any money."

He shrugged easily. "I know how to make money. It's one of the things you have to learn when you're living on the street." He paused. "I'll tell you where I got it if you really want to know."

I did. I really did want to know all about him, but a cowardly part of me was afraid to find out. I guess Mom wasn't the only one who was afraid of being upset by hearing what he had to say.

"Look," I said uncomfortably, "it's late. I've got to get up early tomorrow."

"Sure," Daniel said. "Where do you want this?" He waved the bills around.

"Keep it," I said. "You didn't take that much."

"Oh, consider this interest," he said, flashing a big grin. I had forgotten that he had two dimples.

"I don't want it," I said. And it was true. I had never really cared that he had taken the money from me. I would have given it to him if he had asked. It was that he had taken himself and my trust away too.

He walked over to my desk, picked up my backpack, and slipped the folded bills inside a side pocket. "In case of an emergency," he told me, winking. He walked out of my room and shut the door behind him.

As tired as I was, I lay awake for a long time.

# Chapter Six

The next afternoon, I went to the voluntary forensics practice. Of the eight people there, Vernon, Ryan, and Russ were the only ones I knew. Vernon introduced me to two girls, Erica and Lia. I was disappointed that Robin didn't show up. A couple of guys came in late to work on their own interpretive speeches and didn't talk to us much.

The rest of us practiced debates. We decided to do a Cross-Examination debate first, and then try Lincoln-Douglas debates if we had time. The CX debates involve partners, and the L-D debates are done solo. Since Erica and I had missed the official practice on Wednesday, we were the judges. Mr. Souza gave us a box of debate topics and a CX debate ballot so we could mark the scores. Vernon paired up with Lia for the affirmative side, and that left Russ and Ryan on the negative team.

I drew a debate topic from the box and Erica read it to the team. "Resolved: The U.S. needs to change its foreign policy with China."

"How much time do we get to prepare?" Russ asked.

I looked at the guidelines. "It says here you get ten minutes to prepare opening speeches, and then five minutes per team before your speeches during the debate."

The two teams went to the file cabinets, looking for articles relating to the debate topic. Apparently the forensics team kept files on everything from toxic waste to cloning to affirmative action laws. Vernon said we were all expected to help keep the files current by bringing in new articles on different issues. They also maintained a list of active websites and message boards.

The CX ballot broke down pretty clearly what was expected from the debaters and gave us the scale for judging them. I had read the information Vernon had given me, but Erica said she hadn't looked at her stuff yet. We went through the ballot together, and I explained what I could to her.

"Wow," she said, looking at the times.

"What?"

"They get an hour for speaking," she said, pointing to the alternating speaking schedule. "And that doesn't include the time they can stop to prepare. I don't think we're going to have time to practice much else today."

We settled in for the debate. It was hard work for all of us. Vernon seemed nervous, even though he knew everyone in the room. Russ spoke too fast, and Ryan wouldn't look up from his notes at all. Lia really seemed to enjoy being the center of attention, but she went over her allotted time each time she spoke. Erica and I had a hard time keeping track of the time, and we messed up twice. The whole debate took us an hour and twenty minutes. Through it all, Mr. Souza sat at his desk, grading papers. At least, that's what I thought he was doing.

"That was impressive," he said as we began gathering our things, "but next time you might want to do just the first half of the debate and really tighten up your speeches. At practice, it's okay to stop speakers, give them some pointers, and then have them start over. It's a lot easier than trying to remember everything that's been said in the last hour." He smiled at Erica and me.

"I usually don't stay more than an hour after school, but it was worth it to stay a little later today. I don't often have a group of sophomores come in on their own to practice a CX debate the first week of school. It can be a little overwhelming for beginners unless there's an upperclassman involved. I hope you all can maintain this level of energy and dedication for the year." He flipped through the stack of papers. "Let's see. Vernon. Lia. Ryan. Russ." He handed each one of them a sheet. "These are just some of my notes and observations. I thought they might help."

They looked at each other in surprise and murmured their thanks.

"Will you help us with the Lincoln-Douglas debate on Monday?" Vernon asked.

Mr. Souza grinned. "Why don't you all take Monday off? I'll make sure at least one of the upperclassmen comes in to help on Tuesday."

We nodded in agreement and began filing out the door.

"Have a good weekend, Mr. Souza," Russ said.

"You too."

The girls stayed behind so Lia could talk with Mr.

Souza about her evaluation sheet. Vernon, Ryan, Russ, and I headed down the deserted halls.

Russ was pumped up about the comments Mr. Souza had given him. Ryan was a little bummed about his. After they had finished comparing notes, Vernon suggested we all go out and do something over the weekend.

"Yeah!" Russ bobbed his head. "Let me get your number." He pulled a scrap of paper out of his pocket. "Anyone have a pen?"

"I do," I said, swinging my backpack around and fumbling with the front pocket. Out of the corner of my eye, I sensed movement, and glanced up to see Mr. Barnett stepping out of his office. My hand found a pen, and as I pulled it out, the wad of bills fell to the ground. Right at Mr. Barnett's feet.

He bent down, scooped up the money, and looked at us in surprise. "Mr. Shadow. Gentlemen. You're here late today."

"Forensics practice," Ryan said.

"I thought that was on Wednesdays."

"It is," Russ said, "but those of us just starting need some extra help."

"I see. And how are things going for you, Mr. Shadow?" He turned his sharp eyes to me. "Any more problems with the alarm clock?"

"Nope," I said, shaking my head.

"And this is yours?" he asked, waving the roll of money as he pulled his walkie-talkie off his belt with his other hand. "Mr. Morse," he said into it, "could you please meet me at the office?"

"Right there," the radio crackled back.

Vernon and I exchanged glances.

"Shadow?" Vernon whispered. "Is that yours?"

I nodded.

We all just stood there silently in a loose circle for almost a minute before Mr. Morse, one of the campus security guards, came around the corner.

"What's going on?" he said, smiling but obviously sizing us all up.

Wordlessly, Mr. Barnett handed him the money.

Mr. Morse flipped the folded bills open and sniffed them. He looked at Mr. Barnett, then turned to us. "Whose is this?" he asked.

"Mine," I said.

"Do you mind if I take a look at your backpack?" Mr. Morse said easily.

"Why?"

"Just want to make sure you're not carrying anything on school grounds that you shouldn't be."

I just stood there.

"You don't have to give it to me," Mr. Morse said. "We could step in the office and wait until your parents and the sheriff show up instead."

"For what?" Russ said indignantly. "We're just going home."

"Late, very late. And with a large amount of money. This is probable cause in the world of narcotics."

I handed my backpack over to him, and he rummaged through it. "Got anything in your pockets, big guy?"

Instead of answering, I pulled my pockets inside out. He finished inspecting the bag and then handed it back to me.

"You sell very often?"

"Sell what?" I asked, confused.

Mr. Morse looked at me for a long second, and I could feel him weighing my answer in his mind. He smelled the bills one more time, and then shook his head at Mr. Barnett.

"Can he have his money now?" Russ demanded.

"Sure," Mr. Morse said, refolding the bills. As he held them out, he said, "You probably shouldn't bring that much to school. You know we're not responsible for anything that's stolen from lockers or backpacks."

"I'll be sure to remember that," I said, relieved that my hand didn't shake as I took the money.

"What are you doing carrying so much cash at school?"

I shrugged. "It's not that much," I said, although I had no idea how much was really there.

Mr. Morse raised his eyebrows. "Not that much? Maybe you could just give it to me, then."

Russ and Vernon chuckled nervously.

He studied my face for a moment. "Are you related to Daniel Thompson?" he asked.

Through stiff lips, I managed to say, "He's my brother."

"Has your family heard from him?" Mr. Barnett put a caring and concerned expression on his face.

"Yeah." That was all I said. I wasn't going to let him rattle me anymore.

"I saw a Daniel Thompson mentioned in the Denver paper, about a month ago, wasn't it?" Mr. Barnett glanced at Mr. Morse, then back at me. "Was that him?"

So much for not letting him rattle me. My stomach seemed to have frozen inside me. I couldn't think of a thing to say.

"Nah," Vernon said after a few seconds of my

silence. "If Shadow had a famous brother, he would have told everyone."

"Good," he said, turning to Vernon. "And you're Glenn Thomas's brother, aren't you?"

"Yeah," Vernon mumbled, not looking at Mr. Barnett.

"How's he doing? What's he up to?"

"He's taking some courses at the community college," Vernon said, "and working a part-time job."

Mr. Barnett nodded as if that's what he expected to hear. "Tell him I said hello."

"Uh-huh," Vernon said.

"Okay, gentlemen. Enjoy your weekend. And stay out of trouble." He and Mr. Morse turned and headed down the hallway, talking quietly.

None of us said anything until we were outside.

"'Tell him I said hello,'" Vernon mimicked. "Yeah, I will, when I want to wreck his day! My brother hated Mr. Barnett!"

"Watch yourself now," Russ warned. "If he didn't get along with your brother, he might take it out on you."

"I'll just stay out of his way."

I pulled the bills out of my back pocket and sniffed them. Ryan watched with interest.

"What's it smell like?" he asked.

"Nothing." I smelled again. "Cigarettes, maybe..." I sniffed one more time. "No. Never mind. Just nothing."

"Why'd he smell it?" Ryan wondered out loud.

Russ laughed and shook his head at him. "To see if it smelled like dope, you dope!"

Vernon was laughing too, but he stopped suddenly. "Really?" he asked.

I was quiet. Daniel had only gone to school here for a year, but Mr. Morse had remembered him—remembered him enough to put us together.

"From what I hear, everyone hates Mr. Barnett," Ryan said. Then he turned to me. "What did he mean about your brother?"

"My brother ran away from home a week before his junior year began," I said simply.

"How long was he gone?" Russ asked.

I hesitated.

"He was gone for a while, but then he came back," Vernon said, saving me once again. "It's no big deal."

When we came to the corner, we split up, because Ryan and Russ lived in a different neighborhood.

"See ya Monday," Russ said.

"See ya," Ryan echoed.

"Later." Vernon waved at them. I stayed quiet.

After a few minutes, I cleared my throat. "Thanks, man."

He waved it off. "Like I said, it's no big deal."

"Actually, it kind of is. You may have just lied to Barnett for me."

"What do you mean?"

I took a deep breath. "My brother has to go to court in a few weeks."

"What for?"

"He's been charged with homicide."

Vernon stopped short. "I'm sorry...did you just say—"

"Yep." I kept walking.

Vernon trotted to catch up with me. "Homicide? As in a dead body?"

"Yep."

After a moment, Vernon whistled low. "Wow. I guess that's why you weren't too crazy to see him when he got back, huh?"

"Pretty much."

Vernon hesitated. "Did he do it?" he asked.

"I don't know."

A few more minutes of silence, and then Vernon asked, "Do you think he did?"

"I don't know."

Daniel wasn't home when I got there. I headed straight down the hall toward the bedrooms. I knew I only had a few minutes before Dad would be coming in from work.

The door to Daniel's room was shut. It had been left open for so long, reminding us all of its emptiness, that I was almost afraid to turn the knob. As it swung open, it revealed a room different from the one I remembered. All the posters were off the walls. There were several paper bags stacked by the wall, and I saw the rolled posters sticking out of one of them.

Walking over, I discovered that the other bags were full of his CDs and neatly folded old clothing. He was cleaning everything out. Now it didn't look like Daniel had ever lived there. It looked like a guestroom.

I scanned the room again. There had to be a place where I could leave the money, a place where he would find it.

Then, sticking out of a pocket of the khaki pants he had worn the night before, something green caught my eye. It was another wad of bills. Most of them were ones and fives, but there were at least a couple of twenties too. Quickly I shoved the money he had given me in the other pants pocket. He would find it there, but hopefully he wouldn't realize I had returned his payment, including the interest.

I left the room as fast as I could. I was afraid of what else I might find in there.

Mom and Dad came home from work together. Apparently he had picked her up, instead of having her wait for her friend. She also had a bouquet of flowers in her hand, but they were arguing.

"Caroline, we have to present him with a united front. We can't let him play us off each other."

"We tried the united front before, and it drove him away."

"So you're willing to let him destroy our family?"

"Mark!" Mom exclaimed, looking pointedly at me. "We'll talk about this later."

"It's okay," I said, even though it really wasn't. "I know you guys fight."

"We don't fight, Shadow," Mom said soothingly. "We just disagree sometimes."

"Mom, I'm not a baby. It's fighting."

"No, it's not. It's—"

"This one is going to be a fight if we don't get some things settled," Dad muttered.

Mom glared at him and headed for their bedroom. Dad sighed and shook his head as he flipped through the mail.

"Dad, how much money did you say Daniel had?"

He glanced up at me. "He didn't have any, but I think your mother gave him money for some new clothes before she left for work yesterday."

"Oh," I said. I looked in the fridge for something to munch on.

"Why?"

For a moment I thought about telling him. I knew he already felt left out of what was going on in the house. But at the same time, I didn't want to cause more tension by putting him in another awkward position. "Just wondering."

"Is he home yet?"

"Nope."

Dad sighed again and then headed to their bedroom.

I took my soda to the living room, and Mom joined me. She must have passed Dad in the hall.

"How was your day?" I asked her.

"Fine," she replied absently. "Where's Daniel?"

I shrugged.

Dad came back, in jeans and a T-shirt. Mom *tsk*ed and shook her head. "What?" Dad asked.

"I told you I thought we should go out to dinner tonight." She was still wearing her skirt and blouse.

"I didn't realize you meant someplace dressy," Dad said. He sat down on the couch.

"You'll have to change."

Dad picked up the remote. "When Daniel gets home for dinner, I'll change. We have no idea when that will be."

He clicked the TV on, which was good, because he had just clicked the conversation off.

Daniel wasn't exactly on time for dinner, but he wasn't three and a half hours late, either. He came strolling in at seven-fifteen, carrying a bag of groceries.

"Hello!" he called cheerfully as he came in the door. "Is anybody hungry?"

"Yeah, but that's because we usually eat at six-thirty," I said.

"Shadow!" Mom hissed at me. Dad hid a grin.

"I've got dinner, but I'm going to need a little help cooking it," my brother said, coming out of the kitchen.

"Well, actually, we were going to..." Mom began, but then she just smiled. "I'd love to help you cook. What did you get?"

"Potatoes, salad, and lobster tails!"

For a second, Mom and Dad just looked at him. They both spoke at the same time. "That sounds wonderful," Mom said, while Dad was demanding, "Where did you get the money for all that?"

Daniel looked hurt. "Mom slipped me a little just-in-case cash yesterday. I didn't use any of it, so I thought I'd get us dinner."

Dad clearly didn't believe him. He opened his mouth, but Mom shot him a look and he closed it again. I chewed on my lip. My brother certainly had plenty of cash lying around in his room, and I was pretty sure he had more in his pockets right now. But I didn't say anything.

"Just give me a minute to get changed, and I'll start dinner," Mom said, kissing Daniel on the cheek as she left the room.

Dad cleared his throat. "You did hear your mom ask you to be home at five, didn't you?"

"Sorry," Daniel said. "I'll try not to be late again."

I returned to the couch, and Daniel took what had already become his chair.

"Man, who died?" he asked me.

"What?"

"Who died?" he repeated. "What's with all the

black? It's all you've been wearing this week."

Mom came back through the living room just in time to hear. "That's been his thing for the last couple of years," she said, shaking her head. "I've tried talking him out of it, but he insists. Maybe you'll have better luck."

Daniel raised his eyebrows at me. "It makes you look sick."

"Thanks, Daniel," I said dryly.

"It's Dan."

"Well, Dan, thanks for sharing your opinion. I'm overcome with the need to go put on a bright blue shirt and green pants right now."

"No, seriously, it makes you look sick and pale."

I shook my head and kept my eyes on the TV.

"You could use a haircut too."

I stared at him in disbelief. "What?"

"You look like some kind of troublemaker, with your hair all long and wearing all black like that. You should clean yourself up, try to look good."

I was pissed. "Why do I need to look good?" I demanded. "I'm the one who stayed in school. I'm the one on the honor roll. You might look all 'clean' and 'good,' but you're the criminal! Why would I want to look like you?"

Dad put a hand on my arm. I jerked away from him. "Come on, Shadow," he said, gentle and firm at the same time. "Take it easy."

"I don't want to take it easy," I said. "What right does this convict have to—"

Mom came out of the kitchen. "Shadow!" she yelled, hands on her hips.

"What?" I asked her. "What right does he have to

come in here and judge me when he doesn't even know who I am? What right does he have to criticize anyone when he's been arrested for murder?"

"Shadow!" Mom said sharply. "I think you've said enough."

"Just not saying something doesn't make it go away, Mom." I plowed on. "He left this family a long time ago and now he's been arrested. Those are the facts. He's got no right to blow back in here and start criticizing when we eat, what I wear, or anything else!"

"I think you should go to your room to cool off," she said.

"Fine," I said, standing up. "I'd rather be there anyway!"

"You can come back when you're ready to apologize."

"Caroline," Dad began.

"Then I won't be coming back," I told her flatly. "He owes me an apology, and he owes you and Dad an apology. But you're so concerned with keeping him happy that you don't care about anyone else's feelings now. Not even the people who have actually been here to care about you!"

When I got to my room, it was all I could do to keep from slamming the door shut. I could hear their voices through the wall. I turned my stereo up so I wouldn't have to listen to them.

I flopped down on my bed. A few minutes later, I heard a knock on my door. "Go away," I said. Someone knocked again. "What?" Another knock. "Okay, okay, come in already!"

Daniel stuck his head in. "Come on back, Shadow," he said.

"No thanks. I'm fine here."

"Look, I'm sorry about what I said. You were right. I shouldn't have dissed you."

I didn't say anything, just scowled at the ceiling.

"I'm sorry things are so weird. I just...I just don't know how to act around you guys. I don't know what to say and when I try to talk it all comes out wrong. That's why I got the lobster. I wanted to apologize."

"Oh, what a nice apology. Come home late, and 'Oh, by the way, Mom, I brought stuff for you to cook for me.'"

"Shadow, I'm sorry! I'm just not used to how things work around here."

"And whose fault it that?"

"Mine," he said simply. "And if you don't think I've been paying for it for a long time, you're a fool...even if you are on the honor roll." He sighed. "Look, I'm trying, okay? Could you at least try too?"

That was almost exactly what Mom had said. Why didn't anyone think I was trying?

"Come back out to the living room, Shadow. I promise to lay off."

I still didn't say anything. He backed out and shut the door. I waited a few minutes, trying to gauge how long I could stay in my room before one of my parents came to chase me out.

Finally, I got up. I met Dad in the hall as I stepped out of my room.

"Coming to join us?" he asked.

"Coming to get me?"

"No," he said. "Just going to the bathroom."

I didn't believe him, but how do you accuse someone of lying about that? "See you in a few minutes then."

Daniel didn't look over when I came in and sat down on the couch. A few minutes later, Mom stuck her head in to tell us to move to the dining room for dinner. I knew she was disappointed and frustrated with me, but at least she didn't say anything.

After dinner, while Dad and I did dishes, Mom and Daniel ran out to rent a movie. The movie was Daniel's suggestion. It irked me that even though this extravagant dinner had supposedly been his way to say thank you, he hadn't done any of the work. He was still acting like a guest.

"Shadow, for what it's worth, I agreed with you earlier," Dad said. "I don't think Daniel's in a position to criticize much of anything right now."

I glanced at him out of the corner of my eye. "Even though you agreed with what he was saying?"

Dad grimaced. "You know your mother and I aren't crazy about the way you dress, and I've never approved of your long hair. However, that's not the point. I didn't agree with the way he was saying it, or the reasons."

"Mom didn't seem to think it made a difference."

He sighed. "I tried to explain to you the other night, Shadow, how hard this is on all of us. But it's even more difficult for your mother. She's terrified of losing him again."

"Are you?"

"Yeah."

"But you're not all wigged out about it."

He smiled. "I guess I hide it well. But believe me, inside, I'm very wigged out."

"I just don't get it. He screwed up big time, and he keeps screwing up while he's here, but she yells at me instead."

"There are times when she'd like to yell at him, but she doesn't want to drive him away. So she's yelling at you—and at me too. It's not very fair, but there it is."

"Yeah, well maybe I should run away too."

"Shadow, don't even joke about that! Your mother still loves you very much, and if she ever thought she might lose you... I don't even want to think about what would happen."

We finished the dishes in silence, and then waited for Mom and Daniel in the living room.

"Hey, Dad. Did Daniel get in a lot of trouble with Mr. Morse at school?"

Dad blinked. "Daniel got in quite a bit of trouble with just about everyone at the end of his sophomore year. Why?"

I shrugged. "Mr. Morse asked me about him today."

"That last semester, Daniel skipped a lot of classes. One of the administrators gave him detention for it several times, and finally in-school suspension, but it didn't stop Daniel. A couple of times they asked us to come in for a conference, but..."

"But what?"

"Your mother—she and I—we didn't realize how bad it was. We thought we could handle the problems with Daniel at home."

"Was he in the paper?"

"What?

"Was there an article about Daniel and the murder in the paper?"

"I haven't seen one. Why?"

"Just wondering if his case was getting much media attention."

"Not that I know of. Not here. Not yet."

I didn't get to ask him anything else, because right

then Mom and Daniel came in together, laughing. On the way home from the movie rental store, they had stopped and picked up ice cream sundaes for all of us.

We ate our ice cream in the living room, sampling from each other's flavors, and started the movie. Although we didn't talk much while we watched the video, it was the most comfortable evening we had spent since that phone call.

We were almost like a normal family.

# Chapter Seven

On Saturday, I slept in until almost ten. Usually my parents wake me up by nine, because they don't like to see me waste the whole morning in bed.

After I showered, I went out to the kitchen. Mom was sitting at the dining room table, going through some papers.

"Morning," I said.

She looked up. "Good morning, honey."

I started to get some cereal.

"I'll be making pancakes, if you want to wait until your brother gets up."

I hesitated. She hadn't made pancakes for breakfast in months. "No, thanks. I'm really hungry right now."

I poured the milk over my cereal, got a spoon, and started to head to the living room.

"Why don't you eat in here?" Mom suggested.

I couldn't think of a reasonable objection. "Okay."

I sat down at the table across from her and began to eat. "What are you doing?" I asked, glancing at the various bank statements she had in front of her.

"Just catching up on bills and finances," she said distractedly.

I stirred my cereal. I wasn't really hungry anymore, but if I didn't eat it, Mom would think something was wrong.

"How did the meeting with the lawyer go?"

"I don't know," she said. "Dan didn't want to talk about it."

"Couldn't you call the lawyer?"

"I can't do that. Lawyer-client confidentiality."

"Even though you're paying for it?"

"Um-hmm." She was still flipping through papers, looking for something.

"But you and Dad got this expensive lawyer for him. He could at least tell you what's going on."

"He's an adult, Shadow." She sighed. "But he's our son—your brother. We have to help him however we can."

*She's still afraid to know what happened,* I thought. "Where's Dad?" I asked.

"He went in to the office for a little bit."

"He what?" I stared at her. I couldn't remember Dad ever going in to work on a Saturday.

"He's got a lot of work this week."

"I guess," I said, not making any effort to keep the sarcasm out of my voice. "He went in early twice this week and now today. He *must* be busy. It's not like we've got any problems at home that he'd be avoiding."

She slammed her hand down on the table, and it was so unexpected that I probably jumped a good six inches into the air. "I don't know what you're trying to imply, but I do not like the tone of your voice, young man!"

I thought about asking if she wanted me to draw her

a picture, but then I took another look at her anger-flushed cheeks and decided against it. Instead, I pushed back from the table and picked up the bowl.

"Where are you going?" she asked as she picked up the phone.

"To my room to finish my homework."

"Keep your stereo down, please. Dan's still sleeping."

I clenched my teeth and put my dishes in the dishwasher.

As I walked down the hall, I heard Mom saying, "Yes, I was calling to find out the penalty for early withdrawal on a CD, and what your interest rates on loans are right now."

I turned on my stereo as soon as I was in my room, controlling the urge to turn the volume way up. It only took me twenty minutes to finish my homework, but I didn't feel like going back out to the kitchen or living room. I decided to clean my room. I tore it apart first, digging through drawers and shelves, pulling everything out and checking each item. I made one stack of things to keep and another one of things to throw out. Before I knew it, almost three hours had passed. I was starving.

Stepping out in the hall, I glanced down to Daniel's room. The door was still shut.

Mom was sitting on the couch, reading. She looked up as I came in, and gave me a weak smile. "You must have had a lot of homework."

"Actually, I barely had any."

"So what have you been doing in there?"

"Cleaning out my desk and book shelves."

"That's a big job. How far did you get?"

"I'm finished."

She raised her eyebrows. "You cleaned everything out?"

"Uh-huh."

In the kitchen, I began pulling out stuff to make sandwiches.

Mom called in, "We'll be going out to lunch in a little bit, if you can wait. Otherwise, just have a snack."

I stuck my head back in the living room. "How soon is a little bit?"

"As soon as Daniel gets up."

"He's still asleep?"

She nodded.

"Good thing I didn't wait for pancakes," I muttered, going back into the kitchen.

I made myself two sandwiches and grabbed an apple. When I turned to go into the dining room, there was Mom in the doorway, watching me with a frown.

"That looks like more than a snack," she said.

"I'm hungry," I said. "And who knows how long Daniel will sleep."

"I'm sure he'll be up soon."

"You said that a few hours ago," I pointed out as I set my lunch on the table.

She gave me one of those looks that let me know she was upset with me, but she didn't say anything.

I went back to the fridge to get a soda, and she was still staring at me. "What?"

"We'll be going out soon," she repeated.

"Where are you going?"

"We're going shopping. And I want you to come with us."

"Why?"

"So we can all be together."

"I don't need anything."

"I'd like you to come with us," she repeated, raising her voice just a little.

"Mom, I hate the mall, I don't need anything, and I've got other things to do. I'm not going."

"Don't use that tone of voice with me! I'm not asking if you want to come, I'm telling you that you're coming with us."

"Why?"

"Because it will be good for you to spend time with Daniel."

"I spent enough time with him for the last two nights. I need to go to the library today."

"You can go to the library later this week."

"No!" I suddenly shouted. "You keep pushing back everything that I want to do!"

"Shadow, you said you would try—" she began.

"And I have tried. But I'm not going to spend every minute with him!"

"He's only been here a few days—"

"I know. And I've rearranged my entire life for him because you asked me to, but today I've got stuff I need to do. Maybe if he decides to stick around, I'll spend more time with him."

"I know you've been an only child for a while, Shadow, but there's no reason to be this selfish. You're acting like a spoiled brat."

I wanted to scream. She really just didn't see what she was doing. Shaking my head, I grabbed my two sandwiches and my soda and headed out the back door.

"Where do you think you're going?"

"I'm going to the library. I'll be back later."

"Young man, you get back here!"

I stepped off the back porch and went to the gate. I looked up at the gray sky, and hoped it wouldn't decide to rain on me. I had left my jacket in my room, but I wasn't about to go back and get it. The way she had shouted at me, I half expected her to come chasing after me. She didn't.

The library was calm and quiet, which was exactly what I needed. The cool air felt good on my hot cheeks. I had allowed myself to rant and cuss all the way over, sometimes under my breath and sometimes not. How could my mother accuse me of not trying? Why was she trying to force us into the perfect family model right away? Why couldn't she see that Daniel was just using us?

Entering the library, I told myself I wasn't going to think about Daniel anymore. He had taken up enough of my morning. I checked the new arrivals shelf and picked up a book that looked interesting. I found a couple more in the fiction section, then went to find a table.

On a whim, I went to the back table where I had sat with Robin. She was there again, sitting with Lia.

"Hi," I said, "mind if I join you?"

They looked up from their books and then glanced at each other. "Sure," Lia said, shrugging. "Why not?"

"If I'm not wanted, just say so," I said, stung that Robin hadn't immediately said yes. After all, I had included her in our group at lunch.

"We're working on a debate, Shadow," Robin said, "so that means no gossip."

"Me?" I put my hand dramatically to my chest. "I don't gossip. I never gossip."

"Whatever," she said.

Lia was a little friendlier. "We've just got a lot of work to do," she explained.

"So this is for an L-D debate?" I asked, pulling up my chair and moving some of their papers over.

"Shadow," Robin warned.

"What?"

"We're working."

"Maybe I can help. What's the resolution?"

"Shhh," said Robin. "You'll get us kicked out of the library."

Picking up a piece of paper, Lia quietly read, "Resolved: Capital punishment should be abolished." Robin went back to a book and started taking notes.

"Are you on the affirmative or negative?" I asked, keeping my voice down.

"Robin's affirmative," Lia said. "I'm negative."

"For the debate," Robin muttered.

Glancing at Robin, I asked, "Really? What about personally?"

"What do you mean?" Lia asked.

Robin groaned. "Shadow, we've got work to do!"

I ignored Robin and asked Lia, "Do you really believe that capital punishment should be abolished?"

"Absolutely," Lia said.

Robin put her book down. "You're kidding."

Lia looked surprised. "No. You don't agree?"

"I think capital punishment is a good idea," Robin said. "Especially for violent criminals who are repeat offenders."

"But killing is wrong."

"Not when someone deserves it."

"Hey, you guys," I said, glancing around. "Better keep it down."

"Who are you to judge who deserves it?" Lia demanded, ignoring me.

"I'm not," Robin said. "That's what the judge and jury are for."

"Who are they to decide? The only one who should have that right to decide is God."

"Then why did the murderer get to decide someone else should die?" Robin countered.

"I'm not saying the murderer shouldn't get punished, but they don't have to die. They deserve a second chance."

"Tell that to the person who was murdered!" Robin retorted.

Lia turned to me. "What do you think, Shadow?"

"Whoa, slow down here," I said, holding my hands up. "I was just asking a question. Besides, you'll have to argue both sides anyway."

"Yeah," said Lia. "Mr. Souza says that the best debaters know both sides of their argument, and that's why they're always ready with the rebuttals."

Robin looked at Lia. "He's right. Maybe that's how we can prepare. We'll debate each other first, so we'll know both sides of the issue."

"Let's get some more notes taken first. Then we can argue and see what angles we missed."

"*Debate*," Robin said. "We'll debate. We're not supposed to argue."

"What's the difference, anyway?" Lia asked.

"You get emotional in an argument," Robin began.

"And when you argue there aren't any rules," I added. "In a debate, you're limited on time and topics."

They went back to their notes and I skimmed

through the books I had picked up, trying to decide which ones to check out.

After a few minutes, Lia turned to me. "You never did answer the question."

"What question?"

"Do you believe in capital punishment?"

"I don't know," I said.

"That's not an answer," Robin said.

I shrugged.

"We told you what we think."

"I really don't have an opinion," I said.

Robin and Lia both shook their heads and then went back to their books.

They didn't believe me, but it was true. I used to just assume that the death penalty was necessary. If you decided to kill someone else, you should give up your right to live too. But now, I wasn't so sure.

After about an hour, Robin and Lia left to go practice their debate at Lia's house. As I checked out the two books I had chosen, I looked over toward the computer banks in the back of the reference room.

On impulse, I did a search for the Denver paper. It took several minutes and a lot of backtracking to finally find the archived article.

It was just a tiny article buried in the back of the regional news section.

### Local Man Charged with Murder

Daniel Thompson, 22, was arrested in connection with last month's murder of Reggie DiGallo. DiGallo was found dead

in the Landon Arms Apartments on the
24th. Authorities had no comment on
details of the case. A $250,000 bail has
been set.

Two hundred fifty thousand dollars! And that didn't
even count the lawyers' fees. No wonder Mom was
worried about the finances. There was no way my parents had that much money.

Although finding the article didn't make me feel
any better, at least I knew a little more. Wondering how
the bail system worked, I did another search. I finally
found a site that had the information I was looking for.
It said that usually only 10 percent of the bail was
needed to bond someone out of jail. But still, twenty-
five thousand was a lot for my family. And if Daniel
skipped out, we'd have to pay the entire amount.

I left the library, deep in thought. It was hard for me
to believe that my brother could have killed someone.
But if he wasn't guilty, why did he refuse to talk about
what happened?

The skies looked heavy and I knew it would probably start raining soon. I didn't want to go home yet, so
I stopped at the corner store and wandered up and
down the aisles. The man at the counter started eyeing
me like I was a shoplifter or something, so I bought a
twenty-ounce Coke and a candy bar and left.

Just as I turned onto our street, I saw my mother's
car back out of the driveway and head toward the mall.
Relieved, I walked home quickly, hoping to beat the
rain. There was a note waiting on the counter, for both
Dad and me. It simply said Mom and Daniel would be
back from shopping in time for dinner at 5:30, and
since we would be home first, dinner was our job.

*Great,* I thought, and propped the note back up so Dad would see it when he came in.

As I walked down the hall, I felt a strong breeze. Daniel's bedroom door was open. Thunder cracked outside. I put the Coke and candy bar on my desk, tossed the books onto my bed, and then went into Daniel's room. The window was wide open, and the first raindrops were splattering on the windowsill.

I slid the window shut, and then hesitated as I turned to leave. For the last seven years, this room had felt strange, like it was waiting for someone. Now it seemed strange because there was someone staying in it. I looked around, feeling like I was trespassing.

The bed was neatly made and the clutter on the stereo was gone. The closet door was open, showing off its empty hangers and bare floor. It looked like a hotel room.

As I walked by the dresser, I glanced down. A CD case was on top of his otherwise immaculate dresser. I picked it up, wondering which musician Daniel found worth keeping. There wasn't a cover or CD in the case. Instead, there were photographs. *What a weird place to keep pictures,* I thought. I opened the case and took them out. The one on top was of Daniel with a girl. The other two were pictures of the same girl. She was pretty, although her smile seemed shy.

"Hello? Anyone home?" The garage door slammed shut.

I shoved the photos back in the jewel case and hurried out of Daniel's room. I managed to make it look like I was coming out of my room when Dad turned the corner in the hallway. He started a little bit.

"You could have at least answered," he said.

"Sorry."

"Where's everybody else?"

"Mom took Daniel shopping."

"Why didn't you go with them?"

"I needed to go to the library. Some of us were doing research for forensics."

He frowned. "I'm glad you're so excited about forensics," he said, "but I hope it won't interfere with your class work."

"It won't," I said. "I finished my homework this morning."

"Good," he said, nodding. Then he asked, "Did your mom say when they'd be back?"

"There's a note for us on the counter. It says we're in charge of dinner tonight."

He looked at me for a second, and then together we said, "Pizza."

He laughed. "We can order it later. I've got to check my e-mail."

In my room, I had to turn the light on because it had gotten so dark outside. The wind had really picked up too. After twenty minutes, the power went off. Dad and I went out on the porch and watched the storm together for a while. When we went back into the house, it was really dark. Dad found some candles and lit them. We tried ordering the pizza but the phone lines were down too. At about five minutes to six, Mom and Daniel came in.

"Sorry we're late," Mom said, kissing Dad on the cheek.

Daniel was right behind her, carrying two pizzas. "When we heard on the radio the power was out on this side of town, we decided we should stop."

So we had a candlelit pizza dinner. It was the most relaxed meal we ate all week. Mom and Daniel described the hard time they had getting out of the parking lot at the mall. The traffic lights were out and cars were backed up for blocks. That launched Dad into his story about canoeing down the main street during a flood when he was a kid, a story I'd heard every time it rained for more than an hour.

I kept waiting for Mom to say something about me walking out that morning, but she never did.

The power finally came back on a little after nine. We turned on the news and watched the footage of the storm damage. Several big trees had blown over not far from our neighborhood.

After the news, I said good night. I had just settled in with a book when there was a knock at the door.

"Yeah," I called.

"Mind if I come in for a minute?" Daniel asked, sticking his head in the door.

I shook my head and set my book aside. He sat down at my desk and peered into my backpack. He pulled out my chemistry book.

"How do you like chemistry?"

"It's a class," I said, not sure where this conversation might go. "It's not as boring as some."

"Is it your favorite?"

Shrugging, I said, "Yeah, I guess it is right now."

He was thinking. "I didn't have chemistry. I had some other science class."

"Earth science?"

"Yeah, that was it."

We were quiet for a few seconds.

"I don't see the money in here," he said, opening the front pocket of my backpack. "I wonder where it went."

I didn't take the bait. He had given me the money—

forced it on me, really—so what I did with it was none of his business. But if he knew I gave it back, why didn't he just say so?

He pulled a roll of bills out of his pocket. "If I were as loaded or stoned as some of my old buddies, I probably never would have noticed."

I picked up my book again.

"You don't like money?"

"I like money just fine. I don't like not knowing where it came from."

"It came from me."

"But I don't know where you got it. I don't want any of your money and I don't want to know what you did to get it."

Daniel leaned forward. "I think you do want to know how I got it. You're dying to know. You're just afraid of the answer."

"Yeah," I said, meeting his stare. "You're right."

I could tell I had surprised him, admitting it like that. But then he sat up with a grin. "You're okay, Shadow. You still call it like you see it, just like you always did. Let me tell you where I got this money, so you can take it with a clean conscience. It's not drug money."

I was proud that I didn't blink. I kept my face straight, even though I had been sure that the only way he could make that much money that fast was with drugs. "I sold drugs for a while. I got out of it almost two years ago. You make quick bucks, but the risks are too high. I switched to hustling pool."

"You can make that much money playing pool?" I asked. I had no idea.

"No, man," Daniel closed his eyes and shook his

head a little. "You make money on the books. I get a little pile of money going from the hustling, and then I
play the books."

"What do you mean?"

"Betting? Bookies? The track, football, basketball,
you name it, you can bet on it."

"I thought you'd been at the bar, not at the track."

"It's called off-track betting."

"Oh."

We were quiet again.

"Do you use drugs?" I asked.

"Not any more."

"Honestly?"

He snorted. "Why should I lie about using drugs?
That's nothing compared to—" He broke off suddenly.
"So, can I put it back here?" he asked, opening my
backpack pocket.

"No. I don't want it." I almost told him about my
encounter with Mr. Morse, but something stopped me.
I wanted to believe he was being truthful, but I didn't
quite trust him.

"It really is yours. I owe you."

"I don't want your money."

"You're the first," he mumbled.

"What?"

"Shad, everyone on the streets wants something
from you, and it almost always comes down to cash.
And if you don't pay your debts with cash, you pay
with something else."

*Like what?* I wanted to ask. When Daniel picked up
a couple of my CDs, I blurted out, "So who's the girl?"

He glanced behind him. "What girl?"

"The one in the pictures on your dresser."

"What were you doing snooping around my stuff?" His tone sounded just like it did when I was little and I had gone into his room without permission.

"You left the window open during the storm. I went in to shut it. Next time I'll just let your room flood."

He seemed to relax. A little.

"So, who is she?"

He started to walk away. "Her name's Robin."

"You're joking!"

He whipped around and stared at me. "Do I look like I'm joking?"

"I just—" The look in his eyes scared me. "Never mind. So, is she your girlfriend?"

He opened the door. "It's late. I'm sure you want to get back to your book. Good night." He shut the door behind him.

# Chapter Eight

On Sunday, Mom decided we would take a family trip to the museum. I looked at Dad, waiting for him to object or come up with an excuse, but he merely continued eating his cereal. I still wasn't worried though; I was sure Daniel would be as thrilled about going to a museum as I was. Besides, there was also the chance he wouldn't even wake up before it closed.

It was shocking, then, to find myself in the backseat of the car before ten. Not only had Daniel not objected to the plan, he'd expanded on it: "That sounds great! Why don't we go to the zoo first? Before it gets too hot."

I tried not to stare at Daniel too much. I was having a hard time matching what he had told me last night with his behavior today; it simply wasn't lining up. At first I was really on edge, waiting until Daniel said something to spoil the mood, but as the day went on, I began to relax. We spent the day doing things I never thought we'd do again—wandering the zoo together for two hours in the morning, eating a leisurely hour and a half lunch, and touring the museum all afternoon. I didn't think anyone was acting; we all seemed to be enjoying each other's company. On the ride home, I could especially tell how happy Mom was. I silently apologized to her for my earlier doubts. I had had a good time.

I went in to do some reading when we got home. When I came out of my room, I was surprised to find Daniel in the kitchen, helping Mom fix dinner.

"Anything I can do to help?" I asked.

"You could set the table," Mom suggested.

As I put out the plates and silverware, I could hear them talking and laughing together. After I finished with the table, I asked if there was anything else I could do. They didn't hear me. They were too busy discussing the recipe. Ignoring the hollowness in my stomach, I left the kitchen.

Dad was in the living room reading the newspaper. He smiled up at me as I came in and sat down, but didn't say anything. I wondered if he was feeling left out too.

Everything went fine at dinner. Just as we were finishing the dishes, Dad spoke up. "So, Dan, what are your plans for tomorrow?" he asked.

My brother shrugged. "I hadn't given it much thought," he said, turning to Mom. "Can I borrow your car tomorrow?"

Dad didn't move, but I could almost feel him tense up.

Mom hesitated, and then shook her head. "I really need the car tomorrow and Tuesday. Maybe on Wednesday, but we'll have to see."

It seemed to me that the tension drained out of Dad

and went directly to Daniel.

"Well," Dad said, sounding casual, "if you don't have anything planned for tomorrow, you could mow the lawn."

That was my job, but if Dad wanted Daniel to do it, why should I care?

"Sure," Daniel said. "If I have time." He reached in the refrigerator and got a beer.

"Never mind," Dad said. "I'll do it when I get home from work." The nice feeling from this morning and afternoon had disappeared.

I escaped out the back door and sat on the steps. I had only been there a few minutes when Daniel came out and sat down beside me.

"Hey," he said.

"Hey."

"I get the feeling Dad's not real happy."

"Glad you could pick up on that," I said.

Daniel shot me a look. I didn't care. We had had a good weekend, and it was his fault that everything was falling apart again.

"Well, there's nothing I can do about it now," he said.

"You could mow the lawn before he gets home tomorrow," I pointed out. "And if that's too much, why don't you try getting home on time?"

"Thanks for the tip." He folded his arms across his knees and put his head down.

"What's wrong?" I asked.

"You mean other than being accused of murder? I don't know. Haven't really had time to think about much else."

"You act like it's the end of the world."

"Isn't it?" he asked. Before I could respond, he continued, "No. You're right. It's not the end of the world. It's just the end of my freedom."

"I thought—"

"Unless I get the chair," Daniel continued. "Then it's the end of my life."

"But Mom said that lawyer is—"

"Shadow, it looks bad, okay? Even if I plead not guilty, no one's gonna believe an ex–drug-dealing, pool-hustling punk like me." He stood up. "Guess I'll see you tomorrow afternoon," he said.

"Daniel?"

"It's Dan," he said, turning around.

"Why did you leave?" I managed to keep my voice steady.

Running a hand through his hair, he sighed. "You know, it's stupid, 'cause I don't even remember. I never intended to stay away so long, though. I remember thinking I'd stay away for a week, just to show them. Then the week became a month, and six months went by. After a while it was just too late to come home."

"It was never too late, Daniel."

He gave me a weak grin. "I didn't know that."

"Where did you stay?" I pressed. "What did you do?"

"You don't want to know."

"I wouldn't ask if I didn't want to know."

Daniel looked at me for a long moment before he shook his head. "Maybe if I don't tell you, I can feel like I've done something to protect my little brother. Good night, Shad." He opened the back door.

"Dan, Mom and Dad have done a lot for you in the last week," I said quietly. "They would have done it every day of your life if you hadn't run away. Think about it."

In spite of Sunday night, the week seemed to start pretty well. I don't know what Dan was doing to pass the time, but he was home every day by the time I got there. When Mom apologetically told him that she still needed the car on Wednesday and Thursday, he didn't get an attitude about it.

School was fine. I only saw Mr. Barnett in the hall once, and he was so busy chewing out someone else that he didn't even notice me. I went to Vernon's after school on Monday, and on Tuesday we stayed at school to practice a Lincoln-Douglas debate. I was disappointed that Robin didn't join us after school, but she promised to be there for regular practice the next day.

Vernon and I were in room 28 by 3:02 on Wednesday. Lia and Erica were already there. Ryan showed up next, and told us that Russ had gone home sick and wouldn't be coming. Several people I didn't know came in and started going through file cabinets. Pat walked in with another upperclassman, and around ten after, Tess made her entrance. She gave Pat a quick kiss.

Vernon nudged me with his elbow. "Looks like you waited too long," he whispered.

"I told you she had a boyfriend," I whispered back.

Together, Pat and Tess began to explain the interpretive speeches. There were several different kinds, but they all basically fell into two categories: speeches you memorized and prepared ahead of time, and speeches on topics that were given to you five minutes before you presented them.

Pat was in the middle of explaining "The Interpretation of Humorous Literature" when Robin walked in. He stopped talking and gave her a dirty look as she looked for a place to sit.

"Hey, Robin," I called out. "Over here! We saved a seat for you." For my trouble, all I got was a dirty look from both Pat *and* Robin. She sat down four desks away.

Tess and Pat took another fifteen minutes explaining the different events. Then Tess told us to break up into two groups. "Those of you who think you'd like to try the interpretive readings go to the right side of the room," she instructed, "and those of you who want to do the impromptu events go to the left. You'll get the chance to try the other events later if you want to. This is just to get started."

Vernon turned to me. "What are you going to do?"

"I don't know," I said, glancing at Robin. She moved over two desks, to the left side of the room.

"I think the impromptu stuff sounds fun," I said. Getting a topic and only having five or ten minutes to prepare it did sound more challenging than just reading something.

Vernon made a face. "I really think I'd do better at the readings," he said slowly.

"Okay, see you later," I said. I could tell he thought I was trying to get rid of him. "We can compare notes on the way home," I added.

Vernon picked up his bag and went to the right side of the room. Ryan went with him. Erica and Lia were discussing where to go. I got my stuff and moved over next to Robin.

"Sorry," I said.

She didn't look at me.

"I was trying to help."

"You thought embarrassing me would help?"

I winced. "I wasn't trying to embarrass you. I was trying to get Pat's attention away from you."

"By calling my name in the middle of what he was saying?"

"I said I was sorry."

"You should be."

"Do you accept my apology?"

She looked at me out of the corner of her eye. "I'll think about it."

By now Erica and Lia and one other sophomore, a guy named Paul, had seated themselves by us, and everyone else was on the other side of the room. Pat and Tess picked up some papers, and I tried not to groan when Pat came over to our group.

"We'll try to get two kinds of speeches done today," he said. "The first one is Creative Storytelling. I'm going to give each of you a piece of paper with characters, setting, and a situation written on it. You'll have fifteen minutes to prepare. You can write ideas down, but you can't use any notes during the presentation." He started passing out half-sheets of paper. "Um, this is going to be a little different from a meet, because in a meet situation you're given three story outlines to choose from, and you have to stay within the time limit. Today, since we're all going to listen to each other's stories, you'll only be given one story option, not three. And those of you who go last will actually have a little longer than fifteen minutes. Any questions?"

"How long should our story be?" I asked.

He gave me a killer glare, and I could tell he thought

I was trying to piss him off. I really wasn't. He hadn't said anything about the length of the stories.

"Between three and five minutes. Any other questions?" His stare dared me to ask one, but I was ready to get this over with.

"Good," he said. "Your fifteen minutes start now."

My paper said:

Characters: Princess, Prince
Setting: Castle in Ireland
Situation: The Princess's mom is coming to visit

*Are the topics all this stupid?* I wondered. *Or did Pat give me this one on purpose?* Maybe he was trying to make a point with me. I tried to glance at Paul's and Robin's papers, but they were both bent over their desks, already writing away. I pulled out a blank piece of paper and started scribbling. After a minute, I felt someone staring at me. I glanced up, right into Robin's brown eyes. She immediately looked down at her paper, blushing.

"What?"

"Nothing."

"What?" I demanded.

"Nothing!" She glared at me.

"Fine." I shrugged and went back to work. Every once in a while, I thought I could feel her eyes on me, but I never caught her looking at me again.

"Time's up," Pat said.

I wasn't the only one who groaned as I put my pen down. I had barely gotten my story completed. I hadn't even had time to run through it once.

"I'll need your papers before you speak, so I can

check that you did the right story and write my comments."

I picked up my pen to change part of what I had written. Pat cleared his throat loudly. I sat back in my chair, but I didn't put my pen down.

"So who wants to go first?"

We all shifted uncomfortably in our chairs.

Pat paused for a few seconds and then smiled. "How about you, Shadowman? Why don't you start us off?"

I swallowed hard and stood up. There was no point in arguing. It was only a practice run, but I still felt almost physically ill. I had been telling myself that this really wasn't a speech, that I could handle talking in front of our team. But I was wrong. As soon as I turned to face the others, the last drop of saliva in my mouth evaporated. I have never wanted so badly to run away.

I cleared my throat twice. I glanced nervously at the other side of the room, but they were all discussing their readings and not paying any attention to us.

"Sometime today," Pat said.

Not even being pissed at him could get me over my fear. I cleared my throat again, praying that my voice wouldn't crack on me. Then I began.

"Once upon a time, a long time in the future, a princess and prince were living in their castle in Ireland." There, I had stated almost all of my required subjects. Quickly I added, "Princess Lori was getting excited about her mother's visit. She was coming all the way from the planet Zitzoid."

I saw Paul whisper something to Lia.

"Prince Jim, however, wasn't too crazy about having his mother-in-law to visit. He wanted to go star-surfing instead. He begged and pleaded with the princess, but she said if he didn't stay for the visit, she would cancel his membership with the Cha-Tet." I could see the confusion on the faces in my audience.

"Um...the Cha-Tet was the elite star-surfing club. Only the best star-surfers could join." I still had my pen in my hand and I began twirling it between my fingers.

"'When will she be here?' Prince Jim asked.

"'She can beam over here tonight,' the princess replied. 'Maybe we could all go surfing together.'

"'Why would we want to do that?'

"'Because she'll pay for everything.'

My voice squeaked on the last word. I took a deep breath and tried to slow down. I was going too fast and knew there was no way my story would last for three minutes.

"'Your mother couldn't surf a star if she held it with all of her hands,' the prince said. 'How long will she be staying anyway? She'd better be gone before the championships.'

"'My mother can stay as long as she wants to. After all, she gave us the Xanium to fill the moat. You always say the Xanium makes you the best star-surfer.'"

I paused in hopes of a laugh or a giggle or some kind of response. Nothing. I was dying.

Desperately, I tried to move my story along.

"The mother-in-law was more like a mother to the prince than his own mother, but he still didn't want to spend any time with her." I switched the pen to my left hand and kept twirling it. "Princess Lori knew why her mother was coming to visit, but she didn't want to tell the prince yet." My voice cracked again. Pat snorted. "It was supposed to be a big surprise."

I was so rattled, I couldn't even remember my character's names. "That night, the mother-in-law beamed over in her convertible space rocket.

"The prince was just about to slip out the back door of the castle when the princess stopped him. 'Wait,' she said. 'Mother has something for you. An early birthday present.'"

Suddenly, the pen flipped out of my hand and bounced off the desk, clattering to the floor. At least Erica and Lia were smiling now. I didn't dare glance at Robin.

I couldn't stand much more of this. I had to finish quickly. I didn't care how short the story was.

"The prince couldn't believe his eyes. His mother-in-law was holding in her hands a brand-new, state-of-the-art Asteroidian Star-Surfboard!

"'This is great!' said the prince. 'Simply stellar! I'll be sure to win the star-surfing championship now!'"

I practically dove into my seat, leaving my pen on the floor.

"You're not allowed to use props, especially flying pens," Pat said as he made a couple of notes.

Everyone giggled.

"You didn't say anything about props when you gave us directions," Lia said.

Pat glared at her. "Okay. Does anybody have any comments?"

"I thought it was good for a first try," Lia said.

No one else said anything. They were all staring down at their papers. I suddenly realized that most of them had probably been paying more attention to their own notes than to what I had been saying.

"Let's see," Pat said, scanning his critique sheet.

"That was kind of short. And it didn't make a whole lot of sense. You should have explained what star-surfing and Xanium were. But you did use all of your elements. Another thing—you need to slow down. You were really rushing at the end."

"I just wanted to sit down," I mumbled.

He ignored me and continued, "You need to look at your audience. Eye contact counts." Pat checked his notes again. "Your ending was really weak."

"That's because I changed it as I went."

Pat shook his head. "That's never a good idea. How many times did you run through it before you got up there?"

"I didn't."

He nodded smugly. "You need to be able to create the story and practice it at least three times in the fifteen-minute prep time," he said. "That's the big thing, making it within the time limits. If you go over or under, they automatically rank you fourth or last." He put down the sheet and looked around the group. "Who wants to go next?"

I was the only one not trying to melt into my chair, because I had already gone. Pat waited a little longer this time for a volunteer before choosing Robin.

She handed him her outline and gave me an unreadable look before starting her story. I guess she figured Pat wouldn't have known her name if I hadn't called it out when she came in.

Her voice started off a little too soft and quiet, but as she went along, it got stronger. Her story was a cute one about a dragon stuck in a damp cave who couldn't remember how to breathe fire.

She sat down.

"Good job," Erica said.

"That was really good," Paul said. "I could almost picture that dragon."

"Nicely done," Pat agreed, finishing his notes. "It was three minutes, forty-five seconds. You used all of your elements, and you didn't rush too badly. Your eye contact wasn't bad, either. You do need to work a little on your volume, though, because you were hard to hear at the beginning. Okay, who wants to go next?"

Erica, Lia, and then Paul all did their stories. Robin's was the best one by far.

Pat stood up. "Well, it's almost four-thirty, so there's not enough time to try another type of speech. We'd better stop now. Don't forget, the story outlines are found in the filing cabinet, if you want to practice them from time to time. There's also a file with impromptu topics, so you can practice those. Of course, for the impromptu speeches, you only get five minutes to prepare, but you can use note cards while you give the speech." He gave us the critique sheets he had filled out for each of our stories.

Vernon's group was still working. Robin picked up her bag and walked out the door. I looked over at Vernon, hesitated for a moment, and then went after Robin. I had to run to catch her.

"Hey, Robin!" I called.

She glanced over her shoulder and slowed down a little, but she didn't stop. She was heading toward the door on the opposite side of the building from the one I normally used.

I caught up with her just as she stepped out of the building. "I guess this means I'm not forgiven," I panted.

"I still haven't decided."

"Your story was great."

"Kissing up is not going to get you forgiven."

"No, I mean it! Your story was the best. Mine stunk."

"I wouldn't say it stunk…" she began.

"But you certainly can't say it was good." I finished her sentence for her.

"You looked really nervous."

"I was," I said. "And if I was that nervous just for our teammates, how am I going to be in front of strangers? Maybe I should try the impromptu stuff, so I can have a note card to stare at instead." We came to the first corner and turned left.

"The eye contact is what kills me," I continued. "I can't handle looking at people when they aren't responding to what I'm saying."

"So don't look at them."

"Then I don't get the good marks," I said, holding up the critique sheet Pat had filled out.

"I don't look at people," she said.

"You did today."

"No, I looked *through* them. It's a trick I learned from my dad. He has to do a lot of public speaking. I let my eyes move around the room, but I'm not really focusing on anyone. It's hard to explain," she said, noticing my confused look. "You kind of let your eyes fuzz over, so it looks like you're making eye contact, but you don't really see anyone."

"I think I understand," I said slowly. "I'll have to try it next time. Thanks."

She nodded her head a little. We walked on quietly for a few minutes, turning another corner.

"I didn't know you lived over here," she said finally.

"I don't."

Robin stopped and stared at me. "Then why are you walking this way?" she demanded.

"I wanted to talk to you. You wouldn't stop walking, so I just walked with you."

"So where do you live?"

I pointed back in the direction we had come from.

"You walked all this way just to talk to me? Why?"

I started to answer and then stopped. Ahead, just past the next street corner, I could see a big sign.

"Want to go get a burger?" I asked.

She looked at her watch. "Okay. Sure."

We walked over to the fast food place, and I bought us each a burger, large fries, and a Coke. We sat down in a booth in the back. At first Robin did most of the talking, but then she started asking me questions. Before I knew it, I was telling her about some of my failed sports attempts, making her laugh. We were both having fun. Suddenly, we realized that the sun was almost down.

"I'd better get going," Robin said.

"Yeah," I said. "I didn't realize it was this late."

We left the restaurant and walked back the way we came. She tried to tell me to go home when we got back to the corner.

"I'll walk you home first."

"You don't have to do that," she said.

"Sure I do."

"What if I don't want you to know where I live?"

"Look, I'm not going to let you walk home alone. Either we walk together or I walk fifteen feet behind you, but either way I'm going to make sure you get home okay."

She laughed. "You're really sweet, you know that?"

"Don't tell anyone," I said, flipping up the collar of my leather jacket and hunching down a little. "I don't want to wreck the terrifying reputation that I worked so hard to get."

She laughed again. "You? Terrifying? I don't think so."

I walked her the rest of the way home. When we got there, I resisted the urge to ask to use her phone. I could be home in fifteen minutes if I walked fast.

"Thanks for the burger," she said.

"No problem," I said, shifting from one foot to the other. She looked over her shoulder at the door. I thought I saw someone move behind the glass. "I guess I'll see you tomorrow."

"Yeah," she said. "At lunch."

I turned and walked down the driveway.

"Oh, Shadow?"

"Yeah?" I swung back around.

She was standing in the door. "You're forgiven."

I grinned. "Thanks."


I tried to jog home, but I wasn't used to running and my backpack bounced awkwardly against my shoulder. It was nearly six-thirty when I walked in the front door.

"Where have you been?" Mom demanded before I even had the door shut. She jumped out of her seat and hurried toward me. Dad and Daniel were in their regular places in the living room.

"I had forensics practice today. I told you that."

She got up in my face. "Don't lie to me!" she nearly shouted.

"I'm not lying!"

"Where were you?" She was shaking.

I began again. "Forensics practice—"

"Vernon called here almost two hours ago, looking for you," she cut in. "Forensics practice ended at four!"

"Four-thirty," I corrected.

Mom slapped me, hard across the face.

Absolute silence descended. I slowly raised my hand. Mom was pale and there were tears glistening in her eyes as she took a half step back.

"Shadow." Dad's quiet voice had steel behind it.

Until Dad spoke, I wasn't really aware of what my hand was doing. It was kind of a shock to realize I had been ready to slap Mom back. Instead, I touched my cheek, then simply walked out of the living room, down the hall and into my room, slamming the door behind me.

My parents rarely ever raised their voices to me, and neither of them had ever hit me before.

I threw my backpack over by my desk. I was too angry to sit down. I paced back and forth in my cramped room, my long strides making it almost seem like I was just spinning around. Finally I drew a deep breath, and then another. I sank down into the chair and picked up the phone.

There was a knock at the door.

"I'm on the phone!"

The door opened anyway.

"I said I'm on the phone!"

Dad came in, followed by Mom. "We need to talk, Shadow," he said.

"I have nothing to say."

"Put the phone down."

I glared at him, and he calmly met my eyes. Mom

wasn't looking at me. I slammed the phone down and stood up.

"Thank you. I'm sorry to be interrupting your call, but we need to talk before this gets out of hand."

"Mom seems to have everything in her hand," I said bitterly.

She looked up at me. Tears were streaming down her face. "Shadow." Her voice broke. "Shadow, I'm sorry. I'm so sorry." She dissolved into quiet sobs.

Dad waited for me to say something, but when I didn't, he put his arm around her. "Your mother was extremely upset."

"So that makes it okay?"

"I'm trying to explain this to you," Dad said, a bit sharply. He took a deep breath. "You know you're supposed to call if you're going to be late. We had no idea where you were or if you were okay."

"I just lost track of time."

"You know how important it is for us to know where you are," he said.

"If I were going to run away, you should know I'd be nice like Daniel and leave you a note," I said.

Mom's sobs got louder. She covered her face with both hands and stumbled out of the room. I felt less than an inch tall, but I was still pissed. I was late for the second time in seven years and I got slapped for it, before I even got a chance to explain where I was. It wasn't fair.

Dad turned and looked at me, anger evident in his face. "You will apologize to her for that last remark."

I simply nodded as I sank back down into my chair.

"What happened this afternoon?"

Stubbornly, I didn't answer.

"Shadow, I don't like this change in attitude." I had to admire Dad. His face was all tense and red, but his voice was as calm as ever. "You've always been such a good kid—"

"Yeah, and instead of being trusted because of it, I get punished the instant I make one tiny mistake!"

Sighing, he sat down on my bed. "I know this isn't going to help much, but you just picked the wrong day to lose track of time."

"What do you mean?"

"Your brother came in, oh, maybe fifteen minutes ago."

"So we were both late. Did she slap him too?"

He glared at me.

"Sorry," I muttered, stubbing the toe of my shoe into the carpet.

"His shirt was torn and dirty, and he's got a black eye."

"What happened?"

"He won't tell us. Mom was worried about both of you, but when he walked in hurt like that... Well, her nerves have been stretched pretty tight anyway. So you walked in, she saw you were okay, and it was like everything snapped."

"Across my face."

"If you don't quit making those comments, you're going to get slapped again!"

I stared at the desk. Dad took another deep breath.

"It was your smart-aleck tone that earned you the slap."

"I wasn't being a smart aleck," I protested.

"It's your tone of voice, Shadow," he cut in. "And you're doing it again."

"Sorry," I said, thinking that I needed to tape record my voice so I could start figuring out which tone was the smart-aleck one. Lately it seemed to come out a lot more than I intended.

"So where were you this afternoon?"

I shrugged. "I walked a girl home after practice, and we stopped for a burger, okay? We were talking so much, we didn't realize how late it was."

He just looked at me, but I could tell he was trying to decide my level of honesty. I'm glad he didn't question it out loud though; I wasn't sure what my response would have been.

"Can I make my call now?" I asked.

"Dinner will be ready in a few minutes," he said, standing up. "So make your phone call quick."

"Right."

He tried to grin. "So is she cute?"

I rolled my eyes at him. "Dad," I moaned.

He looked at me like he wanted to say something else, or maybe he was expecting me to say something, but then he just stood up and left. Part of me wanted to crawl into bed and wait until everything sorted itself out. The other part of me wanted to grab everyone in a huge hug and hold them there until we could all talk like rational human beings.

Instead, I picked up the phone again and called Vernon.

"Hello?"

"Hey, Vern," I said.

"Thanks for ditching me, man."

"Sorry," I said. "Your group was still talking."

"You could have waited for me."

"I know, I know."

"So where'd you go?" he asked.

"I walked Robin home."

He started laughing. "Boy, you don't waste any time. Find out one girl's taken and you just move on to the next."

I didn't say anything. It would be pointless to remind him I'd never said I was interested in Tess.

"So are you two going out now?"

"I don't know. Ask her. Look, I've got to go eat. Have you done the trig yet?"

"Half of it. It's actually kind of tough tonight."

"Great," I said. "Maybe I'll call you later for some answers."

"Sure," he said, "I only charge a hundred dollars per answer, or for five hundred, you can get the correct one."

"You're weird, Vern," I said, hanging up. Hesitantly, I walked down the hall to the living room. Dad and Daniel were in their seats. If I hadn't known better, I would have said neither of them had moved since I came in. I could hear Mom clattering around in the kitchen.

I took a deep breath and stepped into the kitchen. "Smells good," I said. "Need any help?"

"No thanks," she said, clearing her throat. "I think everything's under control."

"Can I set the table?"

"Daniel already did."

"Oh." She wouldn't look at me, and it felt awkward. Finally I just blurted out, "I'm sorry, Mom."

She made a sad smile. "Me too, honey."

I felt like we should hug or something, but she stayed where she was, stirring something in the pan.

Feeling a little empty, I went back out into the living room.

Needless to say, dinner that night was extremely uncomfortable. It was at least as bad as the first night Daniel had come home, if not worse. Mom had been carrying almost all of our meal conversations, and she hardly said a word. It was too bad we hadn't gone out for dinner, just to get a change of pace.

We finished dinner, and I practically leapt up. "I'll do the dishes," I said, grabbing the salad bowl.

"I'll help," Daniel said.

Together we cleared the table and put the dishes in the dishwasher. Mom and Dad went out to the living room. Daniel didn't say a word until we were putting the last glasses in the washer.

"Boy, Mom really freaked about you being late."

"She was freaked about both of us," I said. "What happened to you?"

He shrugged. "Just a fight. But I don't think she really even noticed that. She just..."

"Flipped out because you weren't home yet?"

"Exactly! What's the big deal about being a little late?"

"It's a big deal if you're afraid someone might never come home again."

"Oh. Guess I kind of screwed things up for you, huh?"

"Not just for me," I said. "For all of us."

"Maybe I should go stay somewhere else," he said.

I snorted. "You really hate us that much?"

"It would be easier—" he began, but the phone interrupted.

I picked it up as I followed Dan to the living room. "Hello?"

"Hi, this is Jan Moore from the *Denver Post*."

"Oh, we already get the—"

"No, no," she said quickly. "I'm not calling for sales. I'm a reporter. I'd like to arrange an interview with Daniel Thompson, or with someone else in the family. "

My mouth went dry.

"Are you his brother? Could I ask—"

I hung up.

"Who was that?" Dad asked.

I was staring at the phone. It rang again in my hand. "Hello."

"Hi, this is Jan Moore again. We must have been—"

I hung up the phone again, then set it on the table.

"Shadow?" Mom asked.

"What's going on?" Dad demanded.

"A reporter from the *Post*," I said.

"Damn it! Why won't they leave us alone?" Dad practically shouted. "If this keeps up, we're going to have to get an unlisted number." He picked up the handset and began fiddling with it.

"Mark," Mom pleaded.

"They've called before?" I asked, startled. "Why didn't you tell me?"

"We didn't want to upset you, honey," Mom said soothingly.

"Mom, you have to stop protecting me!" I looked at Daniel. "Did you know about this?"

"Yeah. They called a couple of times during the day. Maclean said not to talk to the media, but I gave the reporter a few quotes before I hung up. Stuff they can't put in the paper."

"There," Dad said. "I've turned the ringer off for now. If they want to keep calling, they can just listen to our voice mail message."

I escaped to my room and worked on homework for almost an hour. I tried calling Vernon a couple of times, but his line was busy. I had just picked up my library book when I heard someone coming down the hall.

"Hey, Shadow. You still awake?"

It was Daniel.

"Yeah. Come in," I said.

"Hey," he said, opening the door.

"Hey. What's up?"

He shook his head. "It's not much fun out there."

"I'm glad it's not just me."

"So why were *you* late?"

"Lost track of time," I said.

He dropped down on the floor in the middle of my room. "I used to use that excuse. What were you doing to make you lose track of time?"

"Walking around with a friend," I said.

"Who? Someone from that speech team?"

"Yeah."

"Was it a girl?" His grin got a little devilish. He almost looked like the old Daniel I remembered.

"Yeah." I shifted uncomfortably.

"So what's she look like?"

"Brown hair, brown eyes."

"Cute?"

"Sort of."

"What's her name?"

"Robin."

He stiffened up. "That's not funny."

"I'm not joking."

Daniel stared at me. "You're serious?"

"Yeah."

"That's weird, man."

"I know."

We were both quiet for a minute.

"Where's your Robin now?" I asked. "You still talk to her?"

He shook his head but didn't answer. He didn't leave, though, and I took that for a good sign.

"So how'd you get the black eye?" I asked.

"At Rocker's," he said, cocking an eyebrow at me. "Where else?"

"So why didn't you just tell Mom and Dad about that?"

Shrugging, he said, "I don't think they'd want to hear all the dirty details."

"Maybe not all of them," I agreed. "But surely they'd like to know why you came in looking like that. Was the fight over a bet or your pool game?"

"My pool game." He pulled at a strand of carpet. "I don't want to tell Mom and Dad what's going on. I don't think I can stand to disappoint them any more than I already have."

"So don't. Quit going to the bar and—"

"Shadow, I know you're trying to help," he broke in, "but lay off, okay? I'm going to disappoint them again. There's no way to avoid it." He muttered to himself, "I never should have called that night."

I was searching for a response to that as he stood up. He turned around when he reached the door. "You asked about my Robin. I don't see her anymore. I can't. She's dead."

145

# Chapter Nine

Having spent the last few days avoiding Daniel, I now found it frustrating that I couldn't find any time alone with him. I desperately wanted to ask him about his Robin, but was sure he wouldn't talk about it in front of Mom and Dad. He had to know I wanted to talk to him, but now it seemed that he was avoiding me.

Over the next week, I checked the on-line edition of the Denver paper every day, but I didn't see anything else about Daniel's case. Not a word was said in our house about lawyers or trials or my brother's dead girl-friend.

Daniel occasionally did small chores around the house during the day; usually he was asleep in his room when I got home from school. Sometimes he was up by the time Mom came in from work, but not often. He wasn't eating much, either, no matter what favorite dish Mom cooked for him. The new clothes she had bought him hung on him like he was no more than a wire hanger. Mom was disappointed when Daniel repeatedly refused her offers to fix up his room.

Although the tension between Mom and Dad

seemed to have eased off, the tension between Mom and me had gotten worse. I had apologized for being late, and she had apologized for slapping me. There was still something between us, though, and I didn't know how to fix it. I wondered if that was how Daniel had felt all those years ago when he was fifteen. My conflict with Mom was nothing compared to some of the fights Daniel had had with Dad.

I remembered one time in particular. Daniel had plastered posters on his wall and replaced all of the lightbulbs in his room with black lights. Only six, I had been in awe of the way my shirt had looked in the eerie light. Dad hadn't paid much attention to our clothing, however, because he had been livid about the posters. I never really had much of a chance to look at them, because Dad had ripped them off the wall so fast. He ordered me out of the room, but the yelling started before I got through the door.

Looking back, I realized that other things must have been going on that I simply wasn't aware of.


On Saturday, I met Robin at the library. After we studied for a while, I walked her to her house. On the way, we passed through a park. Somehow, we ended up racing for the jungle gym.

"Can I ask you a personal question?"

I looked at her as she climbed past me. "You can ask, but I might not answer."

"Why do you always wear black?" She stopped just a little short of the top.

"Because," I whispered, trying to sound mysterious. "I'm really a vampire."

"Shadow—"

"To maintain my terrifying image," I said in my best Dracula accent.

"Never mind," she said in an exasperated tone just like my mother's. "Sorry I asked."

"I don't really have a reason." I managed a grin, but I felt embarrassed and self-conscious. I climbed to the triangle just below her. "I started a couple years ago, to be different, I guess. Now, it's more of a habit."

She had a gleam in her eye. "What would it take to get you to wear something besides black?"

"I don't know," I said. I had actually considered wearing another color several times, but the thought of the grief I would get the day I did had stopped me. I had trapped myself very neatly.

"Are you going to wear black to the meets?"

"Sure. I've got a real nice black silk button-down shirt."

She moved gracefully to the top, and looked down at me thoughtfully. "So you wear black everywhere you go? What if you were playing tennis?"

"I don't play tennis...or golf," I added, trying to stop her line of conversation.

"What about Homecoming?"

The Homecoming dance had been announced earlier this week. It was still almost a month away. "I've never gone to dances," I said slowly. "But if I did go..." I stopped to think for a moment, but then shook my head. "...I'd probably wear all black there too."

She slipped between the bars and swung, hand over hand, till she was back at my level.

"You part monkey?"

Robin laughed as she pulled herself up through the bars. "I loved hanging around the jungle gym when I was in elementary school."

"Obviously," I said, and she gave me a light swat on the shoulder. "Okay, my turn for a question."

She gave me a measuring look. "You can ask, but I might not answer."

"You told me you were doing debate for your career, but you never would tell me what you want to do. Will you tell me now?"

She shrugged. "It's really no big deal," she said.

"That's avoiding the question," I said.

"I didn't promise to answer it," she responded.

"Tell me this: Was one of my guesses right?"

Flushing, she nodded.

"Well, then I'm sorry for whatever insult I added to your chosen career."

She smiled at me and then jumped lightly off her perch. I followed with a little less grace.

"When are you and Lia debating the death penalty?"

"Wednesday."

"Are you ready?"

"I think so. We've got our arguments outlined, and we've done a practice run at home. It's been hard, though, because Lia is really against the death penalty, and she can get a little emotional about it."

"And you still believe in it?"

"Yeah. It's kind of personal for me. Four years ago, my dad's cousin and his wife were murdered."

"Wow. I'm sorry."

"They lived in Los Angeles, and we didn't see them a whole lot. The police caught the guy who did it. But even though he was convicted and sentenced to life in prison, he could be out on parole in only eight more years."

I frowned.

"It just makes me mad, you know?" Robin continued. "I mean, this jerk not only took two lives, but he devastated my grandparents and aunts and uncles, and all he has to do is sit in a cell and get fed three meals a day. He's even got cable and access to a gym! And do you know why he did it?"

I wasn't sure I wanted to know, but it was a rhetorical question.

"He needed money for drugs. He broke into their house, started stealing stuff to sell, and when they walked in on him, he just killed them. Because they were in the way," she said bitterly. "They had the nerve to walk into their own home and he killed them."

There was nothing I could say.

After a few moments, she said, "You never did tell us which side you were on. Are you for it or against it? How would you feel if someone in your family had been murdered?"

"Wait. I bet I know," I said, determined to change the conversation. "You joined debate to practice being a lawyer."

"Now who's avoiding the question?" she teased.

"Let me guess. You want to be a prosecutor."

She nodded, looking a little self-conscious.

"You're going to put the scum of the earth away for life."

"Okay, okay. You've made your point," she said, laughing. Then she looked at me carefully. "Now back to my question. Are you for the death penalty?"

"I used to be for it," I said, after hesitating for a second. "But now I'm not so sure."

"What do you mean?"

"It's personal for me too."

"How so?"

Briefly, I told her about Daniel.

When I finished, Robin was shaking her head. "I can't believe you let me go on about the death penalty like that. Why didn't you just tell me to shut up? I don't know what I'd be feeling if I were you."

"I've spent the last couple of weeks trying to figure out how I feel."

"Have you been able to talk with your brother?"

"Not really. It's hard, because I really don't know him. He's not like he used to be. At least not like I remembered him." I tried not to think of Daniel's comment about his Robin, the flat tone of his voice when he told me that she was dead.

"Do you think he killed someone?"

"I don't know."

She looked at me carefully. "Yes, you do. You have an opinion."

She was right. I did know what I thought. I just couldn't bring myself to say it out loud. "I don't know," I repeated stubbornly.

"You know, what you said before about me putting all the scum of the earth away for life? That doesn't necessarily mean your brother."

"I know," I said, but I wasn't convinced.

"Has he told you anything about what happened?"

"No." The brief newspaper article flashed through my mind. "That's what makes it so hard. He never wants to talk about it."

"Maybe he did it, but it was self-defense. Or maybe it was an accident."

"Maybe," I said.

Conversation kind of dragged after that. I walked

her home again, even though she kept protesting that it was too far out of my way.

Right before she disappeared into the house, she suddenly said, "Red."

"Red what?" I asked, confused.

"You should wear red. It would look really good on you." And she ducked inside the door, not giving me a chance to respond.

When I got home, Daniel was out mowing the lawn. I dropped my books off in my room, and then went out to start the edging. He grinned at me over the mower and waved. We finished about the same time.

As we put the mower and edger away, he wiped the sweat off his forehead. "Thanks for the help, man."

"No problem. Where are Mom and Dad?"

"They went out to get stuff for dinner."

We went in through the garage. I stripped off my shirt.

"I could really go for something cold," Daniel said, heading to the kitchen.

"Me too," I said. I went out onto the back porch, where the shade from the big oak kept it nice and cool.

"Here." He pressed a can into my hand.

I lifted it halfway to my mouth before I realized what it was. "You gave me yours," I said, turning to give him the beer.

He had another one in his hand. He sat down, lifted the can, and grinned at me. "Cheers."

"Dan, I don't want this," I said.

"Mom and Dad aren't around."

"I don't drink," I said, setting the can down on the table in front of him. I went and got myself a soda.

"Sorry, Shadow," he said. "I started drinking when I was fifteen. I figured you did too."

"You know that it bugs Mom and Dad that you drink so much, don't you?" I asked.

"Yeah, I know."

"So why don't you stop, or at least slow down?"

He sighed. "I know I'm not the son they wanted, but it's too late to change. I'm not going to pretend to be somebody I'm not."

"It's never too late to change," I said.

"Wait till you've got a few more years behind you," Dan said. "When you decide to quit wearing black, we can talk about when it's too late to change."

It spooked me that he could see into my head like that.

We were quiet for a few seconds. I was trying to gather the courage to ask him about his Robin.

"So what do you want to do tomorrow?" Dan asked, before I could get my question out.

"What do you mean?"

"I have this feeling Mom will want to do something as a family. Maybe it'd be a good idea to come up with something we'd like to do ahead of time."

"Yeah," I said. "I guess."

We kicked around a few ideas, and finally decided on going to a movie.

"What did you do today?" he asked.

I told him about going to the library and playground with Robin.

"So what's this chick like?"

"She's kind of cute, but really quiet most of the time."

"How long have you known her?"

"Just met her a couple weeks ago. She joined the debate team."

"You going to ask her out again?"

"Probably. Don't say anything about it to Mom and Dad though. They'd want to meet her, and I don't think she's ready for that yet. I know I'm not."

He nodded and kind of grinned.

I hesitated, and then asked, "How long did you date your Robin?"

"Couple of years."

"Wow. That's pretty serious."

"You could say that."

"What was she like?"

He shrugged. "Smart. Cute—you've seen the pictures. She had a great body and a great laugh. She'd always laugh at the stupidest things." He smiled, shaking his head over a private memory. "And she was tough. Because she had to be."

"Why?"

"You don't make it on the streets if you're not tough," he said flatly.

"Oh," I said. "How old was she?"

"A year younger than me."

"Where did she...who...were you living together?"

"Yeah."

"What happened...I mean, how did she die?"

He looked at me for a minute, and I was afraid he was going to walk away again. Instead, he said, "She was stabbed."

"Oh man, that's terrible," I said, wishing I hadn't asked. "I'm so sorry," I added lamely.

He shrugged again, toying with the beer can in his hands. "You really loved her, huh?" I asked.

He took a deep breath, staring at the can. "We were going to have a family together. And it was my fault she died. I should have never..."

"Hey, guys! How about a hand in here!" Mom called from the kitchen.

My mouth was so dry, I couldn't even swallow, let alone say anything to Daniel.

There was a thump as Dad set a few bags on the countertop. "The lawn looks great, Dan," he said.

Dan stood up and headed into the kitchen. "Thanks, Dad," he said. "Shadow helped out."

I didn't get many chances to talk with Daniel for the next two weeks. He had several meetings with the lawyers, and when he was home he always seemed to be sleeping or just zoned out. I stayed late nearly every day after school, practicing different kinds of speeches. I felt more comfortable with the interpretive events than I did with debating. That was Vernon's thing. He teamed up with Lia, Russ, and Ryan to do a Cross-Examination debate late in the week, so Erica, Robin, and I spent our time practicing our events in a separate room.

Erica was pretty good at the interpretive humor readings, and even better at the poetry. But she had a hard time keeping her voice strong, and sometimes when she got flustered, she'd just give up. I could sympathize because it's hard to recover when you let your concentration slip during a speech.

I thought I was about the same level as Erica. I was able to stay calm when presenting, mostly because of Robin's trick of letting my eyes unfocus, but that didn't make it easy. I still hadn't given a speech that met the minimum time standard. My storytelling, although still a little rushed, had gotten better. My impromptu speeches seemed to be missing some "oomph," as Mr. Souza put it. My points were clear enough but I wasn't able to get much passion into my voice.

Neither of us had Robin's gift. She could do a Solo Acting reading, and without a single prop she could make you see the whole town as she walked through it. It was the Creative Storytelling, though, where her talent really shone. Within minutes, she could create a person, conjure up a crisis, and then resolve the problem in the most imaginative way possible.

Mr. Souza watched us more than he let on, and during those last few days before our first meet, he observed at least one speech and one debate by each team member. Our first meet was coming up on Friday, so that meant Wednesday's practice was mandatory if we wanted to go to the meet.

On the way to practice that day, Vernon and I stopped at the school store for a soda. When we reached room 28, Pat was outside the doorway, hanging out with three or four other guys I'd never seen before. He stepped in front of the door as I tried to go through.

"Hey, Shadowman," Pat said. "Your last name's Thompson, right?"

"Yeah," I said, glaring at him.

"You got a brother named Daniel?"

"Yeah," I said. I forced myself to keep eye contact.

"The one who was arrested for murder?"

I broke out in a cold sweat. I wondered if I had missed another article about Daniel in the newspaper.

"What?" one of Pat's buddies exclaimed.

"What are you talking about?" another one asked.

Vernon was looking at me anxiously.

"It seems this kid's brother is a killer—"

"He is not." I wanted to shout it, but the words barely even came out. After all, I wasn't sure. Maybe he *was* a killer. He must have done *something* to get arrested.

"Come on, Shadow," Vernon said. "Let's go in."

Pat smirked. He knew he had gotten to me.

Just then Mr. Souza stuck his head out the door. "Will you be joining us, gentlemen? I'd like to finish this practice as soon as possible."

Vernon and I quickly found seats. Pat and his buddies sat a few feet away, whispering to each other. I was sure I knew the topic of their conversation.

It was the biggest practice we'd had all year, because it was mandatory for everyone going to the meet. Almost twenty people were there.

Tess went first. As always, her original oratory dazzled everyone in the room. Everyone except me, that is. I couldn't keep my mind on the speeches. *How did Pat know about Daniel?* I wondered. *Who else already knew?* I tried to concentrate when Lia and Russ performed a Duet Acting, but my mind was racing. *What would people think about my brother?* I managed to listen a little more closely while Robin told an original story—something about fairies living under a mushroom.

Next, Pat was called to the front of the room. That got my attention. He and Vernon did a mock Lincoln-Douglas debate over teen curfews. When the class and Mr. Souza voted Vernon the winner, Pat stormed out of the room.

By the time I drew my choices for an impromptu speech, my mind was churning. I quickly read the sentence: The American Dream has been killed with frivolous lawsuits.

At first I thought it said ferocious, and my heart seemed to stop. Then I read the sentence again. *Frivolous* lawsuits.

I flubbed my way through my speech. Not only was it almost a minute short, it was so unfocused that it was almost pointless. I just couldn't concentrate.

At the end of practice, I was disappointed, but not surprised, to discover I was not among those who would be competing in our first meet. I congratulated Vernon, Robin, and Lia, the only sophomores who would be going with the team. Mr. Souza reminded us all that there would be many more meets to go to. Before he dismissed us, he emphasized that if any participants could not attend the meet, it was up to them to find a replacement for their event. If they couldn't get someone to go in their place, they'd have to reimburse the school for the entry fee.

"I'm sorry you're not going," Robin said as I walked her home.

I shrugged. "No big deal. I'm not sure I really want to compete in front of a judge anyway," I said. I kicked a stone and it ricocheted off a fence post. "I can't believe Mr. Souza is still taking Pat after he stormed out like that."

"He *is* one of our captains. And he's really good, usually."

I didn't like to hear her stick up for him. "Yeah, but that doesn't give him the right to act like a spoiled brat. Why does he always thinks his speeches are automatically the best?"

"It probably runs in the family. Remember when I said forensics would be good for my career? Pat's here for the same reason. My mother knows Mrs. Riley.

Pat's brother's at Harvard Law School, his sister's a big shot D.A. in Denver, and his father's a judge. I'm pretty sure they expect Pat to be a lawyer one day."

"Instead of being a lawyer, he's going to *need* one if he doesn't get a grip on his temper," I said.

We walked in silence for a few moments. I didn't really want to talk about forensics. At least now I knew how Pat knew so much about Daniel. I wondered if Pat's sister was actually involved with the trial.

"How's your brother doing?" Robin asked.

"He's all right, I guess," I said, startled by the question. How did she know what I was thinking?

"Why?"

"Just wondering how everything is going. Is his trial soon?"

"Trial starts Friday."

"So you couldn't go to the meet anyway," she said.

"Probably not."

"Probably not?"

"The trial is going to last several days," I said.

"Yeah, but shouldn't you be there for the first day?"

"I'm sure my mom will think so."

"You don't?"

"I don't know. I mean, it's not like he's been around to support *me*. Other than slip me cash from God-knows-where and offer me a beer that I didn't want, he hasn't done jack."

"But he's still your brother. And what about your parents?"

"I'm sick of hearing about my brother. And I don't care what my parents think."

"I thought you said he's been better at home."

"Yeah, he has been. But it's a little too little a little too late, you know?"

She looked at me like she was disappointed or something. But then she said, "I haven't seen anything about it in the papers."

"You've been looking?"

She seemed a little uncomfortable. "I was just curious."

"It's not really a big case, especially here. The Denver paper's keeping up, sort of," I said. "The guy who died was a drug dealer or some other kind of lowlife scum."

"According to your brother?"

"No. He still hasn't told us anything about it. I'm guessing from a comment in a newspaper article I read a few days ago. But as you pointed out, there hasn't been a lot of media coverage up till now." I was grateful for that. There was bound to be more coverage once the trial started. I wondered how it would affect my parents. I wondered how it would affect me.

"Do you still think he did it?"

"I never said I thought that."

She just looked at me.

"I don't know," I said, sticking with the safest phrase. "I don't know any of the details of the case, and I still don't know Daniel."

"You know him better than you did."

"Yeah."

"So has your opinion of him changed?"

"I never had an opinion!" I exclaimed. "I don't know him! I thought I knew him when he was fifteen, but I was wrong. I certainly don't know him now."

"I'm sorry," she said quickly. "It's none of my business."

"It's all right," I said, shrugging it off and watching the ground as we walked on.

"So," she said hesitantly, "what are you doing Saturday night?"

"I don't know."

"Want to do something?"

"Sure," I said, my mind still on Daniel.

"Shadow?" She stopped walking.

I looked back at her and was surprised to see her blushing. I stopped too.

"Are we just friends?"

"What do you mean?"

"I mean, are we just friends, or are we..." She blushed even more.

"Dating?"

She nodded, not looking at me.

I felt my face get hot and wondered if our blushes were matching shades. "What do you want?"

"I asked you first!"

"No, you asked me what we *are*. I'm asking you what you *want* us to be."

She threw her hands up in the air. "Never mind!" She started walking.

I tried not to laugh as I grabbed her hand and stopped her. "I think we've just been friends," I said, "but maybe Saturday night could be a date."

She smiled at me. I heaved a sigh of relief for picking the right answer. We began walking again, still holding hands.

"So what do you want to do?" she asked.

"What?"

"On Saturday. What do you want to do?"

"Oh. I don't know," I said. "Go see a movie maybe?"

"Sounds good."

That evening, Daniel was in a terrible mood. He snapped at Mom three times during dinner and once at Dad. He virtually ignored me. Instead of helping clean up after dinner, he just sat in the living room and steadily drank his way through two six-packs.

The tension level had been increasing in our house all week, and by eight o'clock it was almost as high it had been when Daniel first came home.

I was grateful to have a load of homework to do. As I was excusing myself to go work, Dad stopped me.

"How's forensics going?"

"Pretty good," I said. I didn't really think he was interested in forensics. I figured he was trying to make up for the awkward lack of conversation at dinner.

"Is it getting easier to speak in front of people?"

"A little bit," I said. "But so far I'm just speaking in front of Mr. Souza and the other team members. I don't know what it will be like in front of strangers and judges."

"When's the first meet?" Mom asked. "Do they need any parent volunteers?"

"They're always looking for volunteers. Our first meet is on Friday—"

"You can't go on Friday!" Mom interrupted. "Absolutely not!"

"But I'm not—"

"No, Shadow. You cannot go. This is not open for discussion."

I was furious she cut me off like that. Never mind the fact that I wasn't on the team chosen to go. She hadn't even given me a chance to explain. My anger boiled up to the surface. "I've spent the last month getting ready!" I shouted. "It means a lot more to me than the first day of some stupid trial!"

"Shadow!" Mom gasped.

I felt rotten for saying that in front of Daniel, but it was true. "He won't even talk to us about what happened! Why should he care if we're there or not? Why should I want to be there?"

Mom and Dad just stared at me for a minute.

"Let him go," Daniel said from his corner. "He's got his own life."

"He's got a family," Mom said firmly. "And family is the most important thing."

"I haven't been a part of this family for a long time," Daniel said. "And I'll be out of it again soon."

"Why?" Mom asked, turning toward him with tears in her eyes. "Why do you keep saying that? Why have you given up?"

Daniel looked at her. "Because I know what I'm charged with, and I know what I did. And I'd do it again if I got the chance."

Mom got very pale. Dad was watching Daniel with a blank look on his face.

*You really did it.* I wanted to say the words, but nothing would come out. This was what I had been afraid of all along.

He was my brother. He was sitting less than fifteen feet away from me. And he had killed a man.

# Chapter Ten

At school the next day, I couldn't focus on anything. I vaguely remembered going into my room and doing my trig homework after Daniel's bombshell the night before, but when it came time to turn in our assignment, I couldn't find anything in my folder. In chemistry and American lit the teachers called on me, confident I would have the answer as always. I didn't even understand the questions they were asking. The day was over before I could formulate a coherent thought.

The Denver paper had run a longer article about the upcoming trial that morning. This one mentioned that Reggie DiGallo was a known gang member, and that the altercation with Daniel may have been either gang or drug related. DiGallo had been stabbed twice, once in the leg and once in the chest. The last paragraph said that our family had no comment.

I was in a daze. All I could hear, over and over again, was Daniel's voice. *I know what I'm charged with, and I know what I did. And I'd do it again if I got the chance.* His words had sounded so cold, so uncaring. The tone he had used the first couple of days was back, and so was the distance. He hadn't come to my room to talk for four nights in a row. It was as if any progress we had made had been erased.

*I know what I'm charged with, and I know what I did. And I'd do it again if I got the chance.*

As I looked back, I realized that I had started to open up to Daniel, and I thought he had been opening up to me. He had told me about his Robin; he had even teased me a little about my Robin. I had to admit that I had started to care about him again.

But how could I care about someone who had torn our family apart?

How could I care about a killer?

*I know what I'm charged with, and I know what I did. And I'd do it again if I got the chance.*

What would make a person want to kill someone? What kind of person kills without regret? I couldn't imagine stabbing someone, being face to face with them as they died. The overwhelming feeling that I didn't know Daniel at all washed over me again.

After school I decided to skip forensics practice. It would be too depressing, watching everyone else practice for tomorrow's meet. And besides, I still couldn't focus on anything. Walking along the street, I let my mind drift again. Daniel had admitted to selling drugs, hustling pool, and gambling. None of those were activities I could respect. But, I had to admire him a little. I could only imagine how tough living on the street must have been. He had never asked for help from anyone; he had survived on his own.

And as we had talked about our Robins, I had begun

to look at him in a different way. It was clear that he had really loved her, and that they had both been trying to change their lives for the better.

I nearly jumped out of my skin when a hand came down on my shoulder from behind.

"God, Shadow, why are you so jumpy? Didn't you hear me calling?"

I shook my head. "What are you doing here?"

"Looking for you," Daniel said, falling into step with me.

"Why?"

"I wanted to make sure that you're going to go to your meet tomorrow."

"Why?" I asked again.

"'Cause of what you said last night. You've worked hard for this. It means a lot to you." He shrugged. "It's more important for you to be at the meet than it is for you to be at the trial," he said.

"You mean you don't want me there."

He stopped and gave me a sad little grin. "You cut right through the crap and call it straight, don't you? Okay," he said, looking me in the eye. "You're right. I don't want you there. I don't want Mom and Dad there either."

I didn't understand why he wouldn't want us there, why he wouldn't want the moral support. "Why not?"

"Because of the things that will be said. You guys don't need to hear any of it."

"Maybe we do," I replied evenly. "And it looks like we're never going to hear anything from you. The only way we'll ever hear it is at the trial."

"Look, Shadow, it's not a lot of cool stuff."

"I know," I said. "But it's part of where you've been,

part of what's taken you away from us for the last seven years. It might make things easier if you'd just talk to us."

"I never should have called," he muttered.

"Then why did you?" I asked bluntly. We were standing in the middle of the sidewalk, in the middle of the block. This was hardly the time or place to have this discussion, but I wasn't going to let him get away again without telling me something.

He spread his hands helplessly. "I...I wanted to say I'm sorry. I didn't want Mom and Dad to find out through the papers. I owed them at least that much. I wanted to...maybe...I just wanted to say I'm sorry."

"You can't just call up to say you're sorry and expect to be forgiven right away, especially when it's something this big."

"I didn't know what else to do. And anyway, I'm not looking for forgiveness."

"Then why apologize?"

He shrugged again. "I don't know," he said in a tone eerily like mine.

"Well, I'll be there tomorrow anyway," I said. "I'm not going to the meet."

"I wish you would. It's not just that I don't want you at the trial," he added quickly. "It's time for you and Mom and Dad to look to the future, not the past. That's all this trial is. Crap from the past."

"But the past is all part of who we are. If we understand our past, maybe we can have a better future."

He looked at me long and hard. "That's a nice thought, Shadow, but it doesn't look as if I have much of a future now." He turned away from me. "They'll never believe me." He spoke so quietly the noise of the passing traffic almost swept his words away. "Besides, I did it. I killed him."

I wanted to shut my ears. I wanted to run away and never come back.

"My only regret is I didn't do it sooner. I was too late."

I hesitated, almost afraid to ask. "Too late for what?"

He looked around at me. I had never seen him look so desperate. "To save Robin. To save our family."

"You mean the guy you killed?..."

"I came home from the pool hall one afternoon. I was way behind on payments to DiGallo, and he was pounding on my apartment door. I had told him I didn't want him around my girl, and I shouted at him to get away from our apartment. He started yelling back about the cash I owed him. Robin opened the door, telling us to shut up before someone called the cops. Reggie pushed his way inside.

"He started waving this big knife around, saying that he'd get the money out of me one way or another. I told Robin to go into our bedroom, but she wouldn't listen to me. By that time Reggie was in a full-blown fit. He was a wild man. I was trying to calm him down, to edge him toward the door, when he started lunging at me with the knife. Robin ran over, screaming at us to stop—she never could stand fights—and the next thing I knew, she was on the floor, bleeding." Daniel stared at the sidewalk. "I'm not sure about what happened next. I think I tackled Reggie. I must have knocked the knife out of his hand, because I remember picking it up. All I could think of was that he had hurt Robin. I guess I stabbed him. When he fell, I went over to help Robin."

I had to strain to hear his next words.

"I was too late. She never regained consciousness."

He took a deep breath and let the air out in a long sigh. "We were gonna move, get out of town and start over, go someplace safe. But we were too late. I lost my family."

"Your family?" I asked, bewildered. "You mean…"

"What do you think I mean?"

I turned in a slow circle. I wanted to sit down, to absorb everything. Daniel was going to be a father? I would have been an uncle?

"Oh, Dan," I finally said. "I'm so sorry."

"Me too," he said with a weak grin and hard eyes. "Me too. And the worst part is, it was all my fault. If it hadn't been for me, Robin would still be alive."

"But you tried to help her—"

"No. I mean I was the one who got us into trouble in the first place."

"I think you should tell Mom and Dad," I said.

"No," he said. "I couldn't stand it if they—" He broke off and started again. "It doesn't matter what happens to me now. I wish I'd never called them."

Hearing him say that was like a blow to the gut. I thought we were doing better. I thought we were all finally trying. And now he was going to quit. "Daniel, Mom and—"

"Just do me a favor and keep bein' a good kid. They don't need any more grief."

He turned away and started down the sidewalk.

"Daniel," I called to him. "Wait."

He just kept walking.

The house was empty and quiet. I dropped my books on my desk and then went straight to Daniel's room. The door was slightly ajar. The CD case was still on the dresser, but the only photo in it was of Daniel and Robin. I studied their faces carefully. They sure looked happy together. I looked around the room. Daniel had lost Robin and their future family, so he called his past family. But I guess we weren't enough to ease the ache he had inside.

I had resented Daniel for coming back and upsetting our lives. I had been angry at him for using Mom and Dad's money, especially when he kept them at such a distance and gave so little in return. But now I could see that when Daniel had called, he'd never expected anyone to believe in him enough to care.

He never expected our help.

He never believed we still loved him.

Suddenly I couldn't handle being alone in the house. I wrote a quick note for Mom and Dad, telling them I was at the library and would be home in time for dinner.

"Shadow!"

In spite of myself, I jumped again. "Dan? Man, you've got to—" I broke off. It was Dad. He had pulled up in his car and was waiting across the street. I checked my watch. I wasn't late.

I jogged over. "Hey," I said, climbing in the passenger side. "What are you doing here?"

"I saw your note. Thought you might want a ride home. Looks like it might rain."

"Thanks," I said, looking doubtfully at the clear sky.

"Music?" Dad asked, turning on the radio. He flipped through the preset stations, which were all talk radio, and then hit scan until some tunes came on. He turned up the volume.

The look on his face stopped me from asking what was wrong, even when we passed the entrance to our development. I knew this had to have something to do with Daniel. A few minutes later, we were pulling into the parking lot of JR Rockers'.

The lot was nearly empty, so we were able to pull into a spot right in front of the building. Dad turned the engine off, but then he just sat there. I didn't know what to say.

"I uh—" Dad cleared his throat. "Dan wasn't home yet, and I knew your mother would panic if he was late again tonight, so—I'm just going to run in and see if he's here."

"Okay," I said, and for some reason my voice sounded small.

Dad stared at the entrance to the bar. After a few seconds, he kind of shook himself all over and got out of the car.

I turned around and studied the marquee of the cheap movie theater across the street. Maybe I could take Robin to see a movie next week.

Dad wasn't inside very long. By the time I looked back toward the bar, the door was open and Dad was backing out of it, pulling Daniel with him. My brother didn't seem to be arguing with Dad so much as still trying to talk to someone in the bar.

As the door swung shut behind them, Daniel turned around and started walking, so Dad let go of his arm. Almost immediately, Dan stumbled and fell.

I started to unbuckle my seatbelt, but then Dad waved me off and shook his head. He was bending over to help Daniel up when the door to the bar flew open.

Two big guys, looking like they had just stepped out of an old Hell's Angels flick, started yelling at Daniel.

They looked almost identical, both wearing black leather and bushy mustaches. The only difference I could see at a glance was one wore a red bandana and the other heavier man wore an orange one. Dad was so startled, he let Daniel fall back down. The guy in the red bandana actually lifted Daniel up off the ground.

I was having a hard time locating the seat belt buckle release, so I had to look down and see what I was doing. When I looked up again, Daniel was back on the ground, writhing now, and Dad was trying to get between him and the two men.

The door handle seemed to have moved, because I had to look down to find it, too. Finally I got the car door open.

"—asshole owes me—" one of the guys was saying.

"Do not!" Daniel moaned from the ground.

The bigger man with the orange bandana tried to lunge past Dad, who somehow managed to stop him. Considering he had at least a hundred pounds on Dad, I was impressed.

"Wait, wait, can we please talk about it?" Dad said.

The other guy put a hand on the stocky one's arm, and I think he would have stopped him, except Daniel suddenly came flying at both of them.

He had the advantage of surprise, and he knocked the orange bandana guy flat on his back. The other one gave my father a shocked look before he pulled his arm back and decked him.

"Dad!" I yelled and ran toward them. The man standing over my dad stopped and stared at me.

"What the hell do you think you're doing, bringin' your kid to a bar?" he asked my dad.

"Trying to bring my other kid home," Dad grunted, holding a hand over his cheek.

The man looked over his shoulder to where his buddy and Dan were rolling on the ground, trying to beat the crap out of each other. "He hustled us," he said by way of explanation to my dad. "If we ever see him here again..."

I helped Dad up, but then just clung to his arm. I couldn't move.

"I'll be sure to explain it to him," Dad said. "Could you just call off your friend before he kills him?"

"Yo, Percy! Let's go!"

Orange bandana gave Daniel one more blow to the head, and then stood up. He pulled his leather vest down, hawked a loogie that just missed landing on Daniel, and walked into the bar without a backward glance. Red bandana followed.

"You okay, Shadow?" Dad asked.

"Huh?" I was looking to make sure the two guys weren't coming back. "Oh. Yeah, I'm okay. I didn't get hit."

"Then maybe you could let go of me," he said, gently prying my hand off his arm.

My brother groaned and rolled on to his side. We helped him up and somehow got him into the car. I climbed into the back seat, numb.

The ride home was absolutely silent. I wasn't sure if Daniel was still conscious, the way his head lolled around. He was trashed in more ways than one. I could smell the alcohol, even under the cigarette smoke. Through the rearview mirror, I could see that he was a mess. There were several cuts and bruises on his face, and his shirt was filthy. My heart sank. He really was beyond our help.

In the garage, it was impossible to tell if Daniel was staggering because he was hurt or because he was drunk. Dad and I followed him into the house. Mom called hello from the living room. My brother made it as far as the front entryway, where he sat down, hard.

"Ow," he said, looking up at us with bleary eyes.

"Oh, Daniel," Mom moaned. She hurried off to the kitchen, and came back quickly with a damp cloth. She tried to clean his face, but he kept jerking away.

"Stop it, Mom," he complained.

"But, Daniel," she whispered, reaching for his face again. He slapped her hand away.

"Caroline," Dad said, lifting her up off her knees.

"Call me Dan." My brother's voice was slurred, but it had an angry edge. "I'm not your little boy anymore."

"No, you're not," Dad said. "Why don't you go get yourself cleaned up?"

He struggled for a minute, trying to get up off the floor. Mom tried to step forward, but Dad held her back. Daniel finally got to his feet. He took a few wobbly steps, then turned to look at me. "You going to your...your speech thing?"

I just stared at him. He was too disgusting for words.

"Shadow will be at the trial," Mom said to his back. "We'll *all* be there."

"I don't want you there!" Daniel exploded. "It's my life, my problem. Just let me deal with it!"

"You need us—" Mom began in a trembling voice.

"No," Daniel cut in harshly. "I don't need you. I haven't needed you since I was fifteen. That hasn't changed." He turned a little too sharply, pushed himself off the wall, and then continued to stagger down the hall.

The phone rang at the same time his door slammed shut. Dad grabbed it before the answering machine could pick up. "Hello? Yes.... Who?"

"Shadow," he said curtly, returning his attention to Mom.

I took the phone, still trying to digest what had just happened. "Hello?"

"Shadow?" The voice was a hoarse whisper.

"Yeah?"

"It's Tess."

"Hi," I said in surprise. I wrenched my attention from my parents' whispered conversation and tried to focus on Tess's raspy voice.

"Look, I hate to do this to you, but you're my last chance." She tried to clear her throat. "I've lost my voice and I can't go to the meet tomorrow. Could you take my place?"

"I don't know. I haven't practiced much."

"Please. I've called everyone, and no one else can go."

"What are your events?"

"I'm doing Impromptu and a Cross-Examination debate with Pat."

"Um..."

"Please, Shadow!" she said hoarsely. "Please?"

I looked around. Mom and Dad were still whispering together. Daniel had told me to go to the meet. He had said he didn't want me at the trial. There was nothing I could do to stop his self-destruction. I spoke before I could change my mind again. "Sure," I blurted out. "I'll take your spot."

"Thank you! You know when the bus leaves and everything?"

"Yeah."

"Okay. Well, good luck. And would you tell Mr. Souza I'm sorry? I'll talk to him about it on Monday," she rasped.

"Okay. Hope you feel better."

"Thanks. Good-bye."

"Bye."

I hung up the phone.

Mom was staring down the hallway. Dad was watching her with a concerned expression.

"Um…hey," I said, uncertain how to begin.

Dad glanced at me.

"One of the girls on the forensics team got sick. She needed someone to take her spot at the meet tomorrow."

Mom tore her eyes away from the empty hallway. "Surely you didn't say you'd go!"

"Yeah," I said defensively, "I did."

"Well, call that girl back right now," she snapped. "You can't go tomorrow."

"I *have* to go now!" I exclaimed.

At the same instant Dad said, "Caroline, I think that—"

"We're all going to be there for Daniel," she said, ignoring us both.

"He doesn't want us there!" I was almost shouting. "Weren't you listening?"

"He didn't mean it." Her voice was now calm, almost serene.

"Yes, he did!"

"Caroline," Dad tried again, but Mom wouldn't let him finish.

"No," she insisted. "He's been drinking. He doesn't know what he's saying."

"He said the same thing this afternoon when I saw him after school. He was sober then!" I retorted.

"Shadow, I'm not going to argue with you!"

"Good! I'm not going to argue with you, either! I'm going to the meet!"

"How can you abandon your brother that way?" Mom yelled.

"What about him? He abandoned us for seven years!"

"Shadow," Dad began, his tone a warning.

"How can you support him?" I demanded. "How can he be so important? How can you love him so much, after all he's done to us? Look at him! He's nothing but a strung-out, drunken—"

"That's enough!" Dad finally shouted. Mom and I both looked at him. "Maclean called me the other day and suggested family counseling. I'm beginning to think he was right. We can't handle this by ourselves. But we need to be able to sit down and talk *now*," he said, trying to use his normal tone.

Mom started toward the couch, but I shook my head. "I'm out of here," I said.

"What?" Dad asked sharply.

"Maybe if I leave, what *I* want will become important too." I darted through the front door and slammed it behind me.

I took off running. I cut through a couple of yards, in case they tried to follow me. It only took me a few minutes to get to Vernon's house. I rang the doorbell and his younger sister answered.

"Is Vernon here?"

"Yeah," she said, sounding uncertain.

"Could I talk to him for a minute?"

She gave me a strange look before she disappeared into the house.

"Hey, man," Vernon said, appearing from around a corner. "What's up?"

"Could I come in?"

"Sure."

"Thanks."

I followed him back to his room.

"What's up?" he asked again. "You forget your trig book or something?"

"Any chance I can crash here tonight?" I blurted out.

"Here?" He looked surprised. "Um...I guess. What's going on? You look...really wild."

I could imagine how my face must look right now. "Big fight with my parents," I said, sitting down on his bed. "I just need a place to stay for the night."

"I've got to leave early tomorrow," he said hesitantly. "You know, for the meet." I could tell he felt bad about going to the meet when I wasn't.

I nodded. "I'm going too. Tess can't make it, and she asked me to take her spot."

A big grin lit up Vernon's face. "Really? Cool!"

"Yeah. Of course, I was her last choice, but—"

"Who cares? At least you're going now!"

"So will it be a problem if I stay?"

"Nah," he said, shaking his head. "This is perfect. I'll just tell my parents that it'll make it easier since we both have to leave so early. Let me go tell them you're here. Want anything to eat?"

I shrugged. I hadn't eaten dinner yet, but I didn't want to be a mooch. I wasn't sure my stomach could handle any food right now anyway.

"I was just going to grab a snack," he said. "I'll be

right back." He left me alone in his room for about fifteen minutes. When he came back, he had six sandwiches, a bag of chips, a stack of cookies, and two Cokes. My mouth started watering as soon as I saw the tray. "This should keep us for a while," he said.

"This is a snack? If you eat like this, I'm surprised you're not a lot bigger than I am," I said. "Or at least a lot wider." I picked up a sandwich.

"So," Vernon said, "what happened?"

Briefly I explained the argument that had followed the fight at the bar. I thought about calling home, but I changed my mind.

"He got drunk again? I thought he was cleaning up his act."

"That's what I thought too," I said. "And I believe he was for a while. But I guess he just doesn't care."

"It sounds like he's trying to push you away."

"Sounds like it? He came right out and said he was."

"Yeah, but I mean, it sounds like he thinks it will be better for you and your parents not to be close to him. You know, like that guy on *ER*—or was it on *The Practice?* Well, anyway, this guy found out he was dying, and he tried to push everyone away, so when he died it wouldn't hurt the others as much."

"Maybe. But I don't think that's it. I think he just doesn't want us in his way."

We finished our sandwiches quickly and quietly. Then we did some prep work for the meet.

Vernon had copied a bunch of stuff from the files, and had it spread out on his desk. He offered to share and also told me I could use his computer to surf the net for more info if I wanted to. I hadn't done much with the debates other than watch and judge them. I hoped I could get by with one night of cramming. As we finished the chips, a new dilemma occurred to me. I hadn't had a chance to get clean clothes or anything. "Hey, I don't suppose you have an extra shirt that might fit me? For tomorrow?"

Vernon made a face at me. "Sure, you think the shrimp is going to have some shirts big enough for the bean pole?" He shook his head. Then he said, "My brother's almost as tall as you. Let me go see if I can snag one from him."

He came back a few minutes later, carrying three shirts. "You can try these. I couldn't find anything black."

There was a white button-down, a green sweatshirt, and a red polo. I pulled on the polo shirt. It fit just fine. The next morning, we left early for the meet. So early, in fact, it was still dark out. Neither of us wanted to take the time to eat, so we just grabbed a couple of bagels and headed out. We walked toward the school in silence. After a few minutes, Vernon spoke up. "You okay, Shadow? You don't look so good. "

"I didn't sleep very well."

"I said you could take the bed—"

"It wasn't because I was on the floor. The sleeping bag was fine. I was just too worked up last night to sleep. I kept expecting my parents to call or barge in your front door."

He stared at the ground. "Well, actually, when I went to get the sandwiches, I called them."

"You what?"

"I just thought, given what your family has already been through, it would be better if they at least knew where you were."

"Thanks," I muttered. Half of me was upset by what he had done, but the other half appreciated it.

When we got to the school, Mr. Souza was standing in front of the bus, signing people in. I explained to him that I would be taking Tess's events for the day. I could sense his disappointment even though he tried to hide it.

"I'll do the best I can," I said.

"I'm sure you will, Shadow."

Vernon and I climbed onto the bus. I expected exaggerated gasps when people saw the red shirt, but no one said anything. We took the seat in front of Robin and Lia.

"What are you doing here?" asked Lia.

I went through the explanation again about Tess asking me to take her place.

Robin looked at me carefully. "I thought you had something else to do today."

"Nope," I said, not meeting her eyes.

Vernon asked Robin and Lia a question about one of the events, and soon the three of them were talking excitedly about the meet. I leaned my head against the window and watched the sun come up.

I knew I should try to prepare for Tess's—*my* events, but I couldn't stop thinking about Daniel. Had he gotten drunk last night just so he'd be able to sleep it off instead of spending the entire night thinking about the trial? No matter the outcome of the trial, Daniel had a hard road ahead of him, and he would have to travel it alone. Either he would be found guilty and would have to spend years in jail, or he would be found not guilty, and he would have to come to terms with his alcoholism, loss, and screwed-up life. This could be one of his last days with any kind of freedom. *The next time I see him,* I thought, *we might be looking through a thick plastic window, talking to each other on a phone.*

Maybe Vernon was right. Maybe Daniel really was trying to make it easier for us by pushing us away. He had been gone for so long and had become so used to relying on himself that he didn't realize how much it hurt Mom and Dad when he wouldn't let them get close to him.

"Shadow?"

I looked back over the bus seat.

Robin was leaning forward. "Are you all right?" she asked in a low voice.

I nodded.

"You sure? You look kind of upset."

I tried to grin for her. "I'll be all right. I just don't feel like talking right now."

She flashed a small smile at me. "Okay. I'm here if you need me."

"Thanks."

When we got to the meet, we followed the upperclassmen to the registration tables. We were given times and room assignments for each event. Robin, Lia, Vernon, and I got back together to compare assignments. I was the only one with an eight o'clock event, so they decided they'd come be my moral support. Vernon and Lia had ten o'clock events. Robin's event was after the lunch break. If my debate finished in time, I just might get to see her do the storytelling.

Together we headed toward the room for Impromptu Speaking. It was my favorite event during practice, but I was really nervous. I wished I could watch some other events before I had to speak.

We found the presentation room. A woman with a clipboard was directing the participants into a separate side room where we were to pick up our cards and prepare our speeches.

As Vernon and Lia went through the door to the presentation room, Robin kind of hung back. "Remember," she told me, "look toward the audience, but don't look at them."

"I'll let my eyes unfocus," I said.

She shifted from one foot to the other. "I was right, you know," she said shyly.

"About what?"

"About red. You look really good today." Robin blushed almost the same shade as the polo. She took a step toward me, reached up, and kissed me quickly on the cheek. "Good luck," she said.

# Chapter Eleven

I n the side room, there was a hushed air of tension. It felt like we were all waiting for a final exam, but none of us had been allowed to study. The woman went over the rules and gave us each different times to go and draw our topics. I had twenty minutes to wait. The event was carefully structured so each speaker had no more than five minutes to prepare. We could write notes on a 3x5 card, but we couldn't bring anything else with us for the presentation.

I set my cards aside, afraid that if I allowed myself to touch them, they'd be shredded before my name was called. With increasing nerves, I watched the other students draw their topics. They would write feverishly, then disappear into the room next door, where the judge and audience were waiting. I was beginning to regret eating the bagel.

Finally, it was my turn.

I stared at the piece of paper I had drawn. Three topics were listed—a word, a phrase, and a sentence. I had to choose one. The sentence was "California's 'three-strikes' law is unjust." That one held promise; I had brought in a few articles about it for our files at school, and I thought I could remember some specific information. The phrase was "character education." I discounted that one. As far as I knew, I had never received any structured character education.

The word was "forgiveness."

That stopped me cold. It felt like my brain skidded to a halt. Of all the words for me to draw in a competition, why would I get that one? I looked back at the sentence. I didn't have to do the word. So why was I looking at it again? I only had five minutes to prepare a three- to five-minute speech; I didn't have any time for indecisiveness.

I put my pencil tip on a 3x5 card, but I couldn't write anything. My mind was a murky fog. My thoughts were jumbled; I couldn't make sense out of any of them. I waited for my pencil to start writing anything about three strikes, but it just sat there and my 3x5 card remained blank.

"Shadow Thompson."

I jumped and looked at the judge.

"You're up."

In disbelief I stared at the clock. My five minutes had evaporated, and I had nothing on my card, nothing in my brain.

Numbly, I got up and followed the judge into the room. Mr. Souza was probably somewhere in the back of the room. So were Lia, Robin, and Vernon. I didn't look, just scanned the room. If I let myself see individual faces, I'd never make it.

I handed the topic paper to the judge.

"Which one will you be doing?" she asked.

"I'll use the sentence." I just wished I knew what I'd use it for.

She marked her ballot. I went to the podium at the

front of the room. My mouth was dry and I wasn't sure I'd be able to speak at all. The judge must have had the same thought, because she cleared her throat and nodded toward me.

"California's 'three-strikes' law is unjust." I folded the blank card in half and put it in my pocket. "In the first place," I began, forcing myself to look straight ahead, "basing a law on a baseball expression is ridiculous. After a player strikes out, he knows he'll have another chance his next time at bat. When someone is convicted under the three strikes law, he never gets another chance. 'Three strikes' is a bad idea for a law."

I felt pretty good. I wasn't sure where I was going with this, but my voice hadn't broken and my heartbeat had calmed down. I was seeing a very unfocused room in front of me—nothing but shapes and colors.

"This law implies that people can't reform...that they can't learn from their mistakes." I paused for a second to take a deep breath. "Imagine someone who has been imprisoned twice for a crime like petty theft. He serves his time, gets out, and stays clean for years. Then he makes one mistake, and he has to pay with the rest of his life. Even if all three of his offenses have been petty theft, he gets locked up. That's it. No more chances.

"I think people can reform if they are given a fair chance. They shouldn't have to spend the rest of their lives looking over their shoulders. The three strikes law is...well, it's unforgiving."

*Do all criminals deserve to be forgiven?*

"After three strikes," I went on, "a juvenile offender who has been caught shoplifting the third time could spend the next fifty years in jail." I paused. Now that I'd said it, I wasn't so sure. Maybe juvenile offenders didn't fall under the three strikes law. I felt panic begin to creep in.

"Um...even hardened career criminals deserve a second chance." I plowed on, hoping to regain my train of thought. "Or, rather, they deserve more than a second or third chance. They deserve however many chances it takes to get their lives together." I was sinking. I couldn't believe what I had just heard myself say.

"Doesn't that sound stupid?" I asked, trying to show that I was being sarcastic. "Some people really think that way. But you...but we can't keep giving criminals more chances to harm people. Yeah, the first time it was only shoplifting, but that's a...a gateway crime. The next one could be a mugging, a rape...or even a murder."

*We gave Daniel a second chance. He blew it. Why should he get a third?*

I had to fight to keep my mind on the speech.

"Well, then, is three strikes too many? Should we lock all criminals up forever?

"No. We can't do that. And we can't let them all go. So what do we do? Maybe three strikes is the best we can do."

I felt like I had been talking for days. But the logical part of my mind knew only seconds had passed.

"In a perfect world, there's no crime, no broken families, no hungry people. In a perfect world, no one gets hurt, and parents and kids love each other no matter what. No one ever has to say they're sorry. No one has to ask for forgiveness."

*Daniel left me.*

"But this world isn't perfect. People do get hurt and they get hurt by other people."

*Daniel hurt me.*

"And we look for someone to blame, for someone to pay the price. Sometimes, there's no one who can be blamed, but we try anyway. We won't accept an apology. We want someone's time, someone's tears, someone's blood. Even though the crime may have been committed out of need, out of desperation, out of...some kind of basic human survival instincts, we still demand that someone pay for it."

*Why can't I forgive Daniel? Doesn't he deserve another chance?*

"Maybe making laws is our way to balance out an imperfect world. Maybe we need to give people a chance to apologize, to make up for what they have done. And maybe sometimes people deserve more than three chances."

*Daniel's my brother. The only one I'll ever have.*

I rushed through my concluding sentence. "We're all flawed, and therefore so is our justice system. But as flawed as our laws are, we need them, even though they fall short of achieving the forgiveness and redemption that truly matter."

I drew a deep breath. I felt like I had run a hard mile. I couldn't remember much of what I said, and I was pretty convinced that I had rambled off course, that the speech didn't have a tight coherent message. But that didn't matter to me. What mattered was that I had finally realized that I could forgive Daniel. I had to find a way to tell him before it was too late.

Through the light, polite applause, I walked back to where Robin and the others were waiting. Mr. Souza stopped me.

He was smiling. "Nice job, Shadow."

"Really?" I asked.

He shrugged. "Well, you did wander a bit. You should have stated your thesis a little more clearly and stuck with it, but you maintained eye contact, and your voice carried the emotion without getting overly dramatic. I'd say it was a decent first competition speech."

"Thank you," I said. "Um, Mr. Souza, I need to go."

"Go? Go where?"

"I have an appointment I need to go to."

"What about your debate?"

"I'll pay for the registration cost," I began.

"I can cover your CX debate," Robin said quickly.

"Thanks," I said, relieved. Hopefully there would be a bus stop nearby. If I could get to the Greyhound station, I might be able to get to Denver by early afternoon.

Mr. Souza was shaking his head. "I'm sorry, Shadow, I can't let you go without parent permission."

I opened my mouth to argue, but a hand came down on my shoulder.

"He has it."

"Dad?" I turned around to stare in disbelief at my father.

He grinned at me, then held out his hand to Mr. Souza. "Mark Thompson, Shadow's father. I'm sorry to take him away from here, but we have a family emergency."

"Oh, of course," Mr. Souza said quickly, shaking Dad's hand. "Well, in that case...I hope everything is okay."

"Thank you," Dad said. "I do too." He put his arm around my shoulders and gave me a brief squeeze as we walked toward the doors.

"I'm very proud of you, Shadow. That was an impressive speech. How long had you been working on it?"

"About thirty seconds." I laughed. "It was impromptu. I'm not even sure I remember what I said."

He squeezed me again with his arm. "I sure wish your mother and brother could have heard you."

"Thanks, Dad, for letting me do at least that event."

"I would have let you stay for the rest, if you'd wanted to," he said. "Your mother and I had a long discussion last night after Vernon called. We decided that we need to be supporting you as much as we need to support Daniel."

"You don't think we'll be too late, do you, Dad?" I asked as we left the building.

"No, Shadow. I don't think so."

# Chapter Twelve

The judge slammed the gavel down. Everyone around me stood, glad for the ten-minute recess. Maclean's opening statement and various motions had taken the better part of the afternoon.

Mom and Dad leaned over the rail that split the courtroom, talking urgently with Maclean. Daniel was standing a few feet away, pointedly ignoring the guard who took steps that mirrored his.

I stood up and moved over to the rail next to Daniel.

"What are you doing here? Thought you were going to your speech thing."

"I was," I stammered. "I mean, I went, but I...I decided—"

"I wish they had let you go," he interrupted, ignoring my sputtered protests. "Man, I'll be glad when it's all over." He glanced at me. "I'm sure you're just as eager to get this over with."

"What do you mean?"

"As soon as the jury's verdict comes in, you'll finally be able to decide how you feel about me."

"Dan, that's not—"

"I'm sorry," he said quickly, interrupting me. "That wasn't fair. You've been incredibly cool, considering the circumstances," he finished with a twisted grin.

"Thanks," I said. "And I wanted to talk to you about—"

"I never should have called."

"No, Dan, don't—"

"Your life would be so much better if I had just stayed gone."

"Would you let me speak!" I suddenly burst out. The guard and the prosecutor looked over at us, but everyone else was still involved in their own conversations. Forcing myself to lower my voice, I continued, "That's what I wanted to talk to you about."

"What?"

"I'm really glad you called, Dan."

The disbelief was plain on his face. "Shad, you don't have to BS me."

"No, let me finish! I never even realized how angry at you I was when you left, at least not until you came back. We needed you back. I didn't know how much I really missed you until you came home, and now—" I stopped, choking on the tears I promised myself I wouldn't cry any more.

Suddenly he reached across the rail and pulled me into a rough hug. I almost started bawling right there. He clapped me twice, hard, on the back, and then stepped back. His eyes were glistening.

He cleared his throat twice, then said, "Thanks, Shadow, for giving me a chance. I'll do my best not to blow it this time. But whatever the verdict," Dan continued, "I won't be around for a while."

Startled, I asked, "Why not?"

"I need some help. No, I need a lot of help. If

Maclean can convince the jury to believe the truth, then I'm going straight to rehab. I need to get cleaned up so I can go to my brother's speech meets and understand what's going on."

"You're going to rehab?"

"Yeah," he said, and his face was pale. "It might kill me, not being able to drink the pain away, but at least I won't cause you and Mom and Dad any more."

"Dan—"

"It's true," he said harshly. "I've been so selfish all my life. It's time for me to do something for someone else. Time for me to do something for the people who care about me."

"Taking care of yourself is all we want you to do."

"Thanks." Maclean was motioning to him, and Daniel stepped toward him before stopping to say, "Oh, hey, could I borrow that tie Mom bought for you a couple of days ago? The one with the race cars?"

"I thought you said it was for a little kid!"

"Yeah, but sometimes bein' a little kid ain't all that bad."


"You'd look great in that tie," Mom whispered, "if you'd just stop fidgeting with it!"

I was wearing my black dress pants and black silk shirt, with a red tie. I thought I looked pretty good too. Dan had said I looked like a pimp.

Mom and Dad were alternating nights in Denver with Daniel; the judge wanted him staying in town. I had made it to Denver as many times as I could during the trial. After the first three days, the quiet in the courtroom had really gotten to me. The lawyers' speeches and questioning techniques were interesting, but in between there were long lulls. If it had been my butt on the line I would have started begging for mercy the first day. Daniel just sat quietly, separated from us by the court banister.

This was the last day of the trial, though, and I was listening carefully to every word. My nerves were shot by the time the prosecuting attorney finished his closing arguments and sat down. Mr. Maclean, Daniel's lawyer, shuffled some papers. He leaned over to whisper to Daniel and patted him on the shoulder. Maclean stood up and wandered over to the jury.

"Ladies and gentlemen, in the last few days you have heard about three lives that have been lost—Reggie DiGallo, Robin Grant, and her unborn child. And there's nothing that can be done about that tragedy. But a fourth life now hangs in the balance, and that you *can* do something about.

"My client has not led an ideal life, and he's made mistakes. He ran away from home at fifteen, and he's been paying for it ever since. Along the way, he learned how to survive. He did his share of drugs, hustling, and gambling. That's how he got involved with Reggie DiGallo, collecting money for him."

I looked over at Dad. He was kind of pale, but he almost looked flushed compared to Mom's white and drawn face. He had his arm around her. I turned my attention back to Mr. Maclean.

"And then Daniel met Robin," he continued. "They fell in love, and together they were trying to build a better future for themselves. She had started working as a waitress, and he had just been hired as a construction worker. They got an apartment, and were ready to start a family when their dreams came to an end.

Maclean went on to describe how DiGallo had come

to Daniel's apartment, trying to collect some money he was owed. The lawyer traced the events of that evening step by step, connecting the dots for the jury. It sounded almost exactly like what Daniel had told me on the sidewalk that day.

"This should be a simple case of self-defense," the lawyer continued. "Unfortunately, because there were no eyewitnesses, the prosecution has pressed for homicide. They want you to believe that Dan found Reggie and Robin together in a compromising situation. That, ladies and gentlemen of the jury, is not true.

"The facts are clear. We have the deaths of three young people. That is very sad, and we want someone to blame. But the only murderer was Reggie DiGallo, and we cannot punish him anymore. As I said, this was a case of self-defense. Mr. Thompson acted as any of you would have done if your home and your loved ones had been threatened. He is innocent of the murder charge."

After finishing his closing remarks, Maclean returned to his table. The judge gave the jury their instructions and they were escorted out of the courtroom. It was already so late, the judge ordered the jury sequestered for the night. We wouldn't hear the verdict until tomorrow.

Daniel stood up and turned around. Mom leaned over the banister and hugged him. He smiled and winked at me over her shoulder as he hugged her back.

In the past few weeks, as the details of the case had come out, Dan had relaxed more and more. His eyes no longer slid over people or looked through them. He could look people in the eye now, and I thought I knew why. Daniel had finally realized that he didn't have to go through this alone.

Mom and Dad had forgiven him a long time ago. Although it had taken me a while, I had forgiven him too. But for our family to be able to move on and try to have a future together, we had to wait until Daniel forgave himself. And he finally had.

By the time we pulled into our driveway, it was already dark. The phone was ringing when we walked into the house. "I'll get it," I said. Mom headed toward her room, already starting to unbutton the sleeves on her nice blouse. Dad was staying with Daniel in Denver.

"Hello?"

"Hi, Shadow."

"Hey, Robin, what's up?"

"Just called to see how things are going."

"Jury's still out, so we don't know anything yet."

"That's good, though, right? The longer they take to make up their minds, the more likely they've found a reasonable doubt?"

"I guess so," I said. "I hope so."

"You doing anything right now?" she asked.

"Actually, Mom decided we should go bowling tonight. Try to get out and move around after sitting all week."

"Sounds good."

"Yeah, but I really suck at bowling." I thought about asking her to join us. Instead I asked, "What are you doing tomorrow?"

"No plans right now."

"Want to go to a movie or something?"

She hesitated. "Won't you need to be with your family? When the verdict comes in, I mean?"

"Yeah, you're right. Maybe next weekend."

"Yeah, that'd be great," she said. I could tell she was smiling.

"Okay. I've got to go. I'll call you tomorrow."

"Okay. Bye."

I hung up just as Mom came back into the kitchen.

"I thought we were going to Olympic Lanes," she said.

"Yeah, just give me a second to go get changed."

"Who was that?" Mom asked.

"Robin."

Her eyebrows went up. "You want to invite her to join us?"

"No," I said. I was looking forward to some time with just my mom.

As I walked down the hall, I noticed that the door to Daniel's room was open. I went in and looked around. For the first time in years, it felt right. It didn't feel abandoned or forced. A pair of shoes was at the foot of the bed, and a sweatshirt was hung casually from the bedpost. There were a few rolled posters in the corner and the partially opened closet door revealed clothes hanging and some even on the floor. The CD case was still sitting on the dresser, with the picture of Daniel and his Robin smiling out of it.

I didn't know what the jury would decide. I didn't know how all our lives were going to play out. But I knew we were going to be okay, because we could depend on each other.

"Hey, Shadow. I'm waiting," Mom called.

"Be right there," I yelled back. Our family had done enough waiting.

*The Balancing Act* is an extraordinary and impc ... critical need of balance. Sharon Seivert has created a system that moves individuals and organizations beyond the traditional into the universal possibilities for success.

—*Shaw Sprague, Psy.D., Consultant*
*Owner Managed Business Institute*

*The Balancing Act* is a must read for any CEO who wishes to deal more effectively and comfortably with today's diverse and volatile workplace. I have long endorsed the wisdom and unique leadership of Sharon Seivert to my clients—this latest gem should be on their reading list!

—*Suzanne Crow, CEO, Unemployment Tax Control Associates, Inc*

*The Balancing Act* is a tour de force with references to science, literature, music, religion, and mythology. Seivert guides her readers toward balance with a helpful, loving hand—a Virgil leading Dante through the Inferno. This book is impressive, supportive, educational, and self-enhancing—an extraordinary achievement.

—*Morton Newman, M.D. (Psychiatrist and Psychoanalyst)*

Sharon Seivert's Elements of Success workshop was spectacular. I felt lighter than air when I left. She is very powerful at helping people put their ideas into words and pictures. Discovering your real identity, vision, and mission is a must for anyone going into business. Without that connection to the heart of who we are, work is meaningless.

—*Suzanne Bates, President, Bates Communication*

Seivert's beautiful perspective on balancing life's often competing demands is theoretically rich and both practical and action oriented. *The Balancing Act* encourages us to carefully examine who we are at our core. When we act from this center, we end up both more effective and more satisfied.

—*Kevin Bourne, Executive Coach & Work/Life Consultant, Ceridian Corporation*

Sharon Seivert's Elements of Success process, really helped our organization focus on a common purpose. We want to be on the cutting edge in health care— and I feel that Seivert's message is our ticket to that end result.

—*Steven Kravetz, Owner, Center for Extended Care at Amherst and*
*The Arbors at Amherst*

Once again Sharon Seivert has hit the tap root on the tree of leadership. Synthesizing the wisdom of the ages with the challenges of modern, dot-com leadership, Sharon provides a valuable resource for coaches and leaders alike.

—*Kris Girrell, Executive Performance Coach, Camden Consulting Group*

The accelerated velocity of change over the past ten years has been extraordinary. Ultimate measures of success may remain, but if we are to be successful, our journey will require a fresh perspective and the courage to do honest self-analysis. I have found *The Balancing Act* to be tremendously helpful in facilitating my own journey. It serves as a roadmap, reminding me that how I get there is just as important as where I go.

—*Jeremiah White, Vice President, Fidelity Investments*

This book is a must-read for anyone in career or life transition. Finding your "center" is as important as finding the right job—and it's a big help in getting you there!

—*Frank Cullen, President, Keystone Partners (career counseling)*

The Elements of Success process helped our management team focus on our common values. Working through the elements, we identified areas that were out of alignment with our core values. Seivert's enthusiastic, no-nonsense leadership pushed us to develop a working mission statement that will provide us with motivation through the "tough times."

—*Karen Jackson, Director, Loomis Communities*

*The Balancing Act* succeeds where other self-help books falter because of Sharon Seivert's wisdom in emphasizing the importance of starting from the core of who we are in bringing balance to our lives—*all* aspects of our lives—from the personal to the planetary.

—*Louisa Mattson, Business Psychologist*

I have been through many strategic planning sessions over the past 25 years. What is different about the Elements of Success is that it is easy to understand and apply. I have watched this model work with everyone from CEO's to line staff, bringing them all together to improve their organizations.

—*Donna Clarke Salloom, Manager, ECCLI 2 Project (workplace education)*

*The Balancing Act*, presents an inspirational message underscoring the legitimacy and wisdom of balance as a goal, both for ourselves and our social institutions. An important and much needed work on the intersection between personal, interpersonal, and professional development.

—*Howard Seidel, Ed.D., Executive Career Consultant*

Sharon Seivert's presentation on *The Balancing Act* gave the members of my department a unique and insightful look at how they approach their work lives, what is important to them, and how to maximize their job success. It is a fun and interesting way to look at issues anyone in the business world wrestles with.

—*Bonnie Michelman, CPP, Director of Police, Security, and Outside Services*
*Massachusetts General Hospital*

The Elements of Success provides a holistic approach to customer service that combines both personal and organizational purpose.

—*David Crimmin, Senior Organizational Consultant, Bose Corporation*

The most important influence the Elements of Success had on me was that it helped to redefine my career goals based on who I am, rather than on the environment around me. With Sharon Seivert's system, I started my career search by defining my own identity and worked outward, knowing that in this way the end result would always be true to my self.

—*Neil Martin, Co-owner, White Magdelena House*

The Elements of Success process was very helpful to me and my partners in building a strong foundation for our new management consulting business. Working together in this way to explore our shared values, hopes, and fears and to get clear about our new vision and mission, was both exciting and bonding. From now on, I'll be enthusiastically recommending this work to my own clients.

—*Ken Estridge, Partner, CxO Management*

What I particularly like about Sharon Seivert's Elements of Success model is that it views learning as an essential process that emerges, in response to experience, from a person's core identity. Seivert translates complex concepts into an accessible framework that shows how individuals and corporations can learn, evolve, and adapt in a changing environment.

—*Steven Cavaleri, President, Knowledge Management Consortium International*

By using the Elements of Success process, the founding team at Avanti Solutions accomplished our stated objectives of defining and clearly articulating our corporation's key components. We also built closer relationships and gained insight into our individual motivators. Most importantly, we had fun!

—*Paul Gasparro, Partner, Avanti Solutions (a mergers & acquisitions advisory service)*

Through the Elements of Success process I was able to redefine my own life and work and set new, exciting, and personally rewarding goals. Having a true understanding of my own "elements of success" also provided me with a framework for helping my business clients succeed by gaining a better understanding of their full potential.

—*Patricia A. Campbell, Principal, Campbell Performance Strategies*

Sharon Seivert's approach to customer service is based on a key premise: individuals are happiest when they can align their values, motivation, and core assumptions about providing service with their actual delivery of service. In that context, customer service conflicts can be viewed as opportunities to realign their behavior with what they report to be most important in their lives.

—*Mike Halperin, Partner, Collaborative Action Technologies.*

Striking a delicate balance in the colliding worlds of personal and professional life requires constant reassessment. *The Balancing Act* challenges us to make the commitment to that assessment, and the attendant juggling of personal and professional lives. It has allowed me to make the periodic recalibrations required to afford a measure of success in all aspects of my life.

—*Kristen Alexander, veteran of the Retirement Plan Services industry*

*To Myra and Jack,*
*whose lives together were graced with*
*balance, love, and kindness*

# The
# Balancing
# Act

Mastering the Five Elements of Success
in Life, Relationships, and Work

## SHARON SEIVERT

PARK STREET PRESS
ROCHESTER, VERMONT

Park Street Press
One Park Street
Rochester, Vermont 05767
www.InnerTraditions.com

Park Street Press is a division of Inner Traditions International

Library of Congress Cataloging-in-Publication Data

Seivert, Sharon.
  The balancing act : mastering the five elements of success in life,
relationships, and work / Sharon Seivert.
      p. cm.
Includes bibliographical references and index.
  ISBN 0-89281-776-3
  1. Success—Psychological aspects. 2. Success in business. I. Title:
Mastering the five elements of success in life, relationships, and work.
II. Title.
  BF637.S8 .S426 2001
  158—dc21
                          2001003501


Printed and bound in the United States

10 9 8 7 6 5 4 3 2 1

Text design and layout by Priscilla Baker
This book was typeset in Aries, with Agenda as a display face

# CONTENTS

◆

*The Balancing Act* is arranged so that you can easily locate the material that is of most interest to you. The letters in parentheses following contents entries provide direction: **Personal Life (P); Relationships (R); Leadership (L); Organizations (O); World (W).** Uncoded entries are of general interest.

# ACKNOWLEDGMENTS

◆

To my family—my parents, Jack and Myra, and my siblings Irene, Tom, John, and Dorothy—for helping me keep my own balance throughout the years, for believing in me, and for giving me so much support and love.

To the many friends who graciously endured long periods of silence while I wrote this book.

To my new friends at Inner Traditions/Park Street Press: my editor Laura Schlivek, for her unrelenting enthusiasm for this project and her considerable competence in transforming *The Balancing Act* from a manuscript into the book you hold in your hands; to Priscilla Baker (interior designer) and Marek Antoniak (cover designer) for making it so beautiful; and to Rowan Jacobsen and Jon Graham, for first seeing the value of this material. Thanks also to Virginia Scott Bowman for all her tysetting assistance.

To the early readers of this manuscript, who gave me excellent feedback and considerable encouragement: Richard Burritt, Karen Speerstra, Dee Dee Majors, Louisa Mattson, Andrea Axelrod, Kathy Eckles, Kevin Bourne, Pat Campbell, Beth Kuykendall, and Jackie Gaudio.

To Lee Finkle Estridge, my business partner and co-founder of The Coreporation, for her focused intention and extraordinary wisdom; and to our associates and virtual partners, who share our dedication to fostering balanced organizations throughout the world.

To the many great writers and thinkers who are quoted within these pages.

To all the corporate executives and individual entrepreneurs who helped me finetune *The Elements of Success* within the real-life laboratories of their daily business.

And finally, to the Divine Harmony who sings throughout my life and who dances in these pages.

To all of you, thank you. You live in this book. You live in my heart.

# WELCOME!

◆

Dear Reader,

Does your life sometimes seem out of balance? Are there simply not enough hours in the day to get everything done? Do you feel that you lack the power to change things at work? Do you not have enough time to spend on important relationships? Do you have to struggle to keep all the diverse parts of your life together? Are you torn by conflicting demands or frustrated by the grind of this whole effort?

If you've answered "Yes" to any of the above questions, *The Balancing Act* may be of help to you.

In the pages that follow, I describe one tried-and-true method that can help you regain your balance and improve your work, relationships, or life in general. The kind of balance this book focuses on is balance within and among the five major *elements* of your life.

I have written *The Balancing Act* as a comprehensive approach with multiple applications not only for you as an individual, but also for couples, colleagues, groups, and whole systems (such as your workplace or community). For example, this book can prove helpful if you are a manager who needs to increase productivity or harmony in your organization; a busy parent who wants to reduce the stress resulting from so many demands on your time; a worker who feels that there's nothing you can do to improve things in your company; or someone who (like most of us) just wants healthier, happier relationships.

What is balance? According to *Webster's Dictionary*, balance is defined as a "State of equipoise, as between weights, different elements, or opposing forces; equilibrium; steadiness . . . act of balancing, as in weighing, judging, dancing. . . ."[1]
I think that balance is a state of inner and outer equilibrium, a highly desirable and exhilarating experience of life as being less fragmented and difficult. Feeling "in balance" reduces your tension and allows you to move more gracefully through life. The kind of balance I describe in this book is achieved by integrating five different elements of your life. I call these vital points of reference the "Elements of Success."

This five-faceted approach to balance results in much more stability than you can attain by simply reducing the tension between two opposing forces (such as weighing right versus wrong on the scales of justice, walking a tightrope or a balance beam, or resting at the midpoint of a teeter-totter). For this reason, I will not directly address the pull you may be feeling between your work life and family life. (There are many good books already available on this topic.) Instead, I will provide you with a powerful model, a set of user-friendly tools, and numerous hands-on techniques that will show you how to deal, step by step, with *all* the vital aspects of your life. I have found the Elements of Success very useful in my organizational consulting and executive coaching. I also have used this method myself—to improve my own personal Balancing Act—and it has helped me a great deal.

The goal of this book is to help you experience your life as a unified whole. This will significantly reduce the conflicting demands that sometimes put your stress level into the stratosphere. Between these two covers, then, you will discover the critical elements that can transform your life into what ancient people called "the miracles of one thing."

You may not think that such an ideal state of harmony is possible in your life. Indeed, many individuals I've met (no matter what their title or status) feel powerless to make the changes they want in their lives, relationships, or work. I have often been surprised by the people I've heard say, "But what can *I* do about it?" *The Balancing Act* is written as an answer to that question.

You may well ask: "But how can I possibly achieve a state of balance when nothing in my life stays the same, when everything around me changes so fast?" Rapid change is the sea we all swim in these days. Things change around you (or you create changes), and then you need to adjust to the new imbalance. And because this happens again and again (and again and again), your striving for balance becomes your own personal tango with the universal law of action and reaction—a dance in which life itself is your partner.

I find it instructive that *balance* is both a noun and a verb. Balancing is, above all, a process. Even if you manage to achieve what feels like a "perfect" state of equilibrium at some point, life will always demand that you move on to the next moment. *Actually, the perfect state of balance is the act of balancing itself!* This is because life is about learning—and learning demands that we move through periods of imbalance to new, more healthy points of balance if we are to successfully adapt and evolve. Life just won't allow us to park anywhere indefinitely because, especially in a rapidly changing environment, stasis results only in rapid decline and death.

The good news is that you are your own best teacher in this particular dance lesson. You know when you are in balance and when you are not. You can *feel* that sweet spot. You know when you're "on" and when you're "off," when you're sailing with the wind at your back and when you're stuck in the mud. Your sense of inner and outer balance, then, is a great teacher, an ongoing feedback loop that helps you adjust to shifting circumstances. This is no small matter. Quite simply, your sense of balance is an innate survival mechanism.

Interestingly, the kabbalah word for balance, *Lamed*, means "to teach." *The Balanc-*

*ing Act* then, can serve as a "teacher's aid" for you. Indeed, I have designed this book so that you can easily tailor the material in it to suit your particular personal and professional needs. For example, you can read *The Balancing Act*

- from cover to cover;

- by first taking the instruments in Part I, then focusing on the specific chapters in Part II that will help you improve given parts of your life, relationships, or work;

- by focusing only on the section of each chapter that is relevant to your particular interests (use the coding in the table of contents to find, for example, all the relationship material or all the organization material throughout the book); and,

- if you're already quite conversant with the properties of the five Elements of Success, you may want to move directly to Part III, where all the elements come together in a process called the Spiral of Synergy.

Finally, let me say that my hope in writing *The Balancing Act* was that it might assist you in affirming greater balance and harmony in every aspect of your life. This is important not only to you, but also to all those people whose lives and work will be positively affected by your increased happiness and well-being. After all, balance is your natural state. You deserve it.

Best wishes,
Sharon Seivert

# PART I

## Finding Your Balance in Life, Relationships, and Work

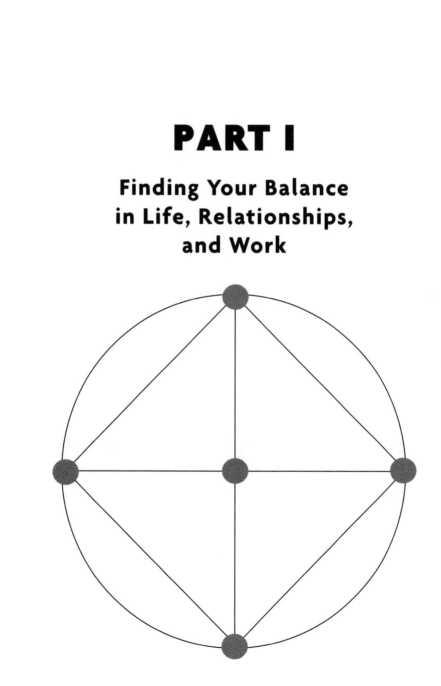

# FINDING YOUR BALANCE

## This Is How It All Began . . .

*There was only water . . .*
*but deep down in the water lived Kokomaht, the Creator . . .*
*he was bodiless, nameless,*
*breathless, motionless . . .*

*Then the waters stirred and rushed and thundered,*
*and out of the spray and foam [he] rose . . .*

*He stood upon the waters, opened his eyes, and saw.*
*There he named himself Kokomaht—All Father . . .*

*Then Kokomaht said: "Now I shall make the four directions."*

*He pointed with his finger and took four steps, walking on the water.*
*Then he stood still for a while and said, "Ho, this is north."*
*Then he went south and then east—*
*always taking four steps in each direction*
*and always returning to the center.*[1]
*—Pacific Coast Native American*
*creation story*

If you've read this far, you may have already decided that this book can be of some help to you. Like a great many other people, you may be fed up with the excessive demands on your time and may be seeking a life that is more harmonious.

The good news is that in much the same way as the Native American god Kokomaht created the world ("always taking four steps in each direction and always returning to the center"), you too can create a life that is more balanced and healthy. I chose to launch *The Balancing Act* with this creation myth because it illustrates that the life you make starts *within* you, then ripples outward in all directions.

But before I say any more, I ask that you please complete the three Balance Sheets that follow on the next few pages.

These instruments will help you assess the degree of balance you currently enjoy:

- in your life,
- in an important relationship, and
- in your workplace.

Please remember that there are no right or wrong answers, and no "perfect" scores. Just use these instruments as mirrors to reflect back to you what is true for you right now. It is a bit like marking a point of reference—"I am here"—on a road map before embarking on a journey. With this baseline of feedback, you can optimize your reading of the rest of *The Balancing Act*.

## The Personal Balance Sheet

Write a number from one (strongly disagree) to ten (strongly agree) in front of each statement to indicate the extent to which that statement is true of you.

And if you're feeling adventuresome, you may ask a good friend or colleague to give you a second opinion; i.e., another perspective on your state of balance. An extra score line is listed per item for this purpose. Be sure to cover your scores completely so as not to bias or distract the second test-taker.

| 1 | 2 | 3 | 4 | 5 | 6 | 7 | 8 | 9 | 10 |
|---|---|---|---|---|---|---|---|---|---|
| Strongly Disagree | | Disagree | | Neutral Don't Know Does Not Apply | | Agree | | Strongly Agree | |

### Element I

\_\_\_|\_\_\_ I manage stress well—as evidenced by a general sense of well-being and a lack of physical, mental, or emotional stress symptoms.

\_\_\_|\_\_\_ I feel calm, steady, and sure of myself most of the time.

\_\_\_|\_\_\_ I have a strong sense of who I am and what is most important to me.

\_\_\_|\_\_\_ Overall, I am happy and content with my life as it is right now.

\_\_\_|\_\_\_ I'm not easily rattled or thrown off balance when things get crazy around me.

\_\_\_|\_\_\_ I try to maintain a reasonable equilibrium between activity and quiet time in my life, including taking time off regularly to "do nothing."

\_\_\_|\_\_\_ To keep a good perspective, I often step out of the fray to watch the activity that goes on around me.

\_\_\_|\_\_\_ I have a strong code of personal values and ethics that guide my daily behavior and decision making.

\_\_\_|\_\_\_ I usually find that I have enough time to do the things that are important to me.

___|___ I feel strongly connected to something greater than myself (the source, God, a benevolent universe).

___|___ Total: Element I

## Element II

___|___ I am imaginative and innovative.

___|___ I have a clear vision of my future.

___|___ I'm eager to learn and am open to having new experiences.

___|___ Others would describe me as both positive and realistic, because I not only see possibilities but also potential obstacles.

___|___ I have a good sense of humor and enjoy "lightening things up" when they get too serious.

___|___ I am an optimistic person and know that I have a lot to offer the world.

___|___ I'm okay when my thoughts, ideas, or beliefs are challenged by other people or by new information.

___|___ I am an intelligent person with a strong, active mind.

___|___ I believe that my thoughts filter my current reality and help create my future.

___|___ I am aware of my existing beliefs, paradigms, and worldview—and how they influence my actions.

___|___ Total: Element II

## Element III

___|___ I know my life has a purpose; I have a strong sense of personal mission and a burning desire to make something of myself.

___|___ I am relatively consistent in action and productivity.

___|___ I have a lot of personal power and all the energy I need to accomplish the things that are important to me.

___|___ I am generally assertive (neither passive nor aggressive) in my interactions.

___|___ I work hard and enjoy what I do.

___|___ People would describe me as a self-starter: determined, self-disciplined, productive, and focused.

___|___ I have a strong will that is aligned with other people who have similar convictions.

___|___ I handle conflict well—neither avoiding it nor becoming aggressive.

___|___ It is easy for me to swing into action and turn good ideas into reality.

___|___ I take a lot of pride in what I accomplish.

___|___ Total: Element III

## Element IV

___|___ It's easy for me to access and clearly express what I am thinking or feeling.

___|___ I have good self-control of my feelings; that is, I am able to maintain a positive state and refrain from "dumping" my bad moods, anxiety, or anger on people around me.

___|___ I have healthy relationships at home, at work, and in my community that are supportive of the best parts of me.

___|___ Most of the people I know seem genuinely to respect and care for me.

___|___ I make certain that my communication with others is respectful, including listening actively when others speak.

___|___ I genuinely like, respect, and care for the people in my home, community, and work.

___|___ I appreciate and seek out diversity and difference of all kinds as a way to enrich my life.

___|___ People describe me as compassionate, kind, and considerate.

___|___ I am flexible and adaptable—I respond easily when situations or structures shift.

___|___ For the most part, I am aware of what's happening emotionally for other people and I can respond appropriately and with empathy.

___|___ Total: Element IV

## Element V

___|___ I take good care of my physical health.

___|___ I make my physical environments as attractive, neat, orderly, comfortable, and safe as possible.

___|___ I make a point of spending as much time as I can in nature.

___|___ I tend to move through my day in an unhurried, steady way.

___|___ I am skilled and competent in what I do.

___|___ I feel that my life is secure and stable.

___|___ My friends, family, and colleagues would describe me as solid, dependable, and reliable.

___|___ My finances are in excellent shape.

___|___ I have things organized well enough so that I usually have little trouble locating the items I need.

___|___ I have good habits that help me efficiently manage my personal, home, and work time so that I have a better chance of attaining my goals and making my dreams come true.

___|___ Total: Element V

Please note that the Personal Balance Sheet is protected by copyright law and may not be reproduced without the author's permission. To inquire about ordering copies, please contact: www.theCoreporation.com.

## Scoring the Personal Balance Sheet

**Directions:** Add up the scores you have per element and then transfer them to the table below. The highest possible score per element is 100, the lowest is 10.

| Element | Score #1 | Score #2 | Contributions to the Well-Being of Relationships |
|---------|----------|----------|---------------------------------------------------|
| I | | | A strong sense of personal identity and values; a feeling of being "centered," content, calm, and happy; awareness of a "spiritual" connection |
| II | | | A clear mind; hopefullness; a positive vision of the future; openness to new ideas; willingness to learn and innovate; awareness of personal paradigms and beliefs |
| III | | | Personal will, drive and pride; commitment and focus; excitement; desire; power and empowerment; a sense of personal mission; ability to assertively manage conflict |
| IV | | | Emotional intelligence; compassion; empathy; ease of communication; a feeling of connection to others; self-awareness; respectful relationships |
| V | | | Security, stability, order and reliability; financial or resource management; day-to-day habits and structures; physical health |

ANALYSIS: Scores in the 70–100 range indicate elements that are in good shape; scores less than 50 indicate elements needing more attention. Note that when you become stressed or encounter difficulties, you are likely to do more of what you already do well, rather than address and improve areas of chronic weakness.

Healthy elements (above 70):      Score #1_____

                                             Score #2_____

Elements needing attention (below 50):    Score #1_____

                                             Score #2_____

## Elemental Circle Graph
## (for Personal Life)

**Directions:** Transfer the score (or scores) you have per element to the circle graph below. The highest possible score per element is 100, the lowest is 10. Compare this graph with the relationship and organizational graphs on pages 13 and 18, once you have completed them.

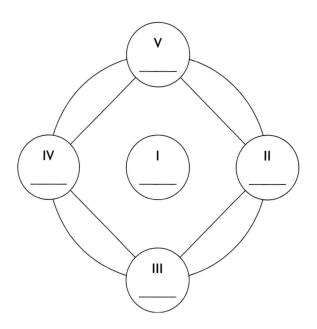

# The Relationship Balance Sheet

Write a number from one (strongly disagree) to ten (strongly agree) in front of each statement to indicate the extent to which that statement is true of a key relationship.

An extra score line is listed per item so that you have the option of evaluating two different relationships—or asking the other person in a significant relationship to complete the questions below. This will allow the two of you to compare scores easily, stimulate discussion, and improve the relationship. Take care to cover your scores completely so as not to bias or distract the second test-taker.

| 1 | 2 | 3 | 4 | 5 | 6 | 7 | 8 | 9 | 10 |
|---|---|---|---|---|---|---|---|---|---|
| Strongly Disagree | | Disagree | | Neutral Don't Know Does Not Apply | | Agree | | Strongly Agree | |

## Element I

\_\_\_|\_\_\_ We share many important values and have a strong spiritual connection.

\_\_\_|\_\_\_ We are very happy together and treat each other with genuine respect and love.

\_\_\_|\_\_\_ Neither of us gets lonely, agitated, jealous, or suspicious when we're apart.

\_\_\_|\_\_\_ We trust each other absolutely.

\_\_\_|\_\_\_ We can be completely "real" (no pretenses or masks) when we are together.

\_\_\_|\_\_\_ We know, treasure, and support the most essential and unique aspects of each other.

\_\_\_|\_\_\_ We bring out the best in each other, which helps make both of us better people (for example, happier, kinder, more self-aware or competent).

\_\_\_|\_\_\_ We know each other's strengths and weaknesses; i.e., neither one of us idealizes—or devalues—the other.

\_\_\_|\_\_\_ We have a good balance between activity and quiet time while together.

\_\_\_|\_\_\_ Each of us supports the other to a similar degree; i.e., we have a reasonably equal exchange of energy, resources, time, and commitment.

\_\_\_|\_\_\_ Total: Element I

## Element II

\_\_\_|\_\_\_ We share many common beliefs—and respect the differences we do have.

\_\_\_|\_\_\_ We find each other intellectually stimulating.

\_\_\_|\_\_\_ We have fun together and greatly enjoy each other's company.

\_\_\_|\_\_\_ Each of us encourages the other to learn and grow.

___|___ We have the ability to "lighten each other up" when we get too serious.

___|___ When we have different ideas or opinions, we take time to respectfully discuss our differences and try to learn from each other.

___|___ We believe we will share a good future, and we work together to make it happen.

___|___ Each of us thinks the other person has a good attitude and sense of humor.

___|___ Neither one of us projects our positive or negative traits onto the other person.

___|___ We are comfortable challenging, questioning, and thinking through issues with each other.

___|___ Total: Element II

## Element III

___|___ Our commitment to each other is strong, mutual, and steady.

___|___ Our relationship is exciting and highly energized. (This can be intellectually, emotionally, sexually, or because of a shared mission.)

___|___ When we have disagreements, we surface them quickly and "fight clean."

___|___ We are very attracted to each other. (This could be as a loyal friend, dedicated business partner, or passionate mate.)

___|___ We have compatible or complementary personalities.

___|___ We recognize and support each other's special gifts and talents.

___|___ We feel invigorated when we're together.

___|___ Neither of us dominates the other; we are comfortable with sharing power and decision making.

___|___ Our personal boundaries are clear and strong; we're careful not to step over any line that would make the other person feel uncomfortable.

___|___ We are independent people with our own distinct interests and lives.

___|___ Total: Element III

## Element IV

___|___ We know what's going on emotionally with ourselves and each other.

___|___ We talk freely, easily, and honestly—and listen fully to each other.

___|___ We love (or genuinely like) each other and neither of us hesitates to express our admiration or affection.

___|___ There is a good balance of giving and receiving in this relationship.

___|___ We trust each other absolutely.

___|___ When we have difficulties, we communicate and collaborate together to resolve them.

___|___ There is no emotional manipulation or ruling by moodiness in this relationship.

___|___ We respect and support the other person's individual identity, values, and dreams.

___|___ We have a deep, intimate connection—but are not merged or dependent.

___|___ We always consider the other person's needs and treat each other with kindness, empathy, and genuine respect.

___|___ Total: Element IV

## Element V

___|___ Each of us knows we can depend upon the other.

___|___ Our financial arrangements are clear and appropriate.

___|___ We feel secure and stable in this relationship.

___|___ Both of us can rely upon the other to keep the promises and agreements we've made.

___|___ By and large, we agree on how to spend our resources, time, energy, and efforts.

___|___ We have developed habits that create order, stability, and support for each other and our relationship.

___|___ We have clear parameters, understandings, and agreements in this relationship.

___|___ Neither of us would hesitate to help the other with whatever resources are at our command.

___|___ Both of us would agree that over time, there has been an equal exchange of value (time, effort, energy, or money) expended in this relationship by each of us.

___|___ We work well together to accomplish the tasks for which we're responsible and to take good care of our shared property.

___|___ Total: Element V

## Scoring the Relationship Balance Sheet

**Directions:** Add up the score (or scores) you have per element and then transfer them to the table below. The highest possible score per element is 100, the lowest is 10.

| Element | Score #1 | Score #2 | Contributions to the Well-Being of Relationships |
|---|---|---|---|
| I | | | A feeling of being "soul mates"; shared values; respect for each other's identity and worth |
| II | | | Compatible worldviews; intellectual stimulation; positive attitude and sense of future together; ability to "lighten up" each other |
| III | | | Strong commitment to each other; ability to handle conflict well; attraction and excitement; clear personal boundaries |
| IV | | | Love; respect; intimacy; empathy; companionship; understanding your own and each other's emotions; ease of communication; deep feeling of connection |
| V | | | Dependability; security; shared contributions to and management of joint resources; clear and fair financial arrangements |

**Analysis:** Scores in the 70–100 range indicate elements of this relationship that are in good shape; scores less than 50 indicate those needing more attention. Note that when you become stressed or encounter difficulties, you are likely to do more of what you already do well, rather than address and improve areas of chronic weakness.

Healthy elements (above 70):     Score #1 _____

                                 Score #2 _____

Elements needing attention (below 50):   Score #1 _____

                                 Score #2 _____

## Elemental Circle Graph
## (for Relationships)

**Directions:** Transfer the score (or scores) you have per element to the circle graph below. The highest possible score per element is 100, the lowest is 10. Compare your scores on this graph with the individual and organizational graphs on pages 8 and 18, once you have completed them.

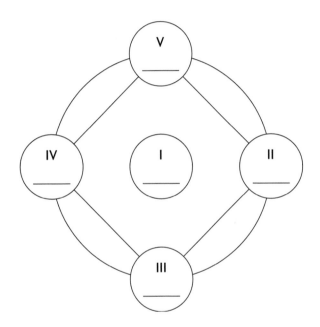

# The Organizational Balance Sheet

Write a number from one (strongly disagree) to ten (strongly agree) in front of each statement to indicate the extent to which that statement is true of your workplace.

Two scoring columns are listed so that you have the option of evaluating both your whole organization and your department—or, you can ask a colleague to evaluate your organization with you. Be careful to cover the first column completely so that you reduce the likelihood of bias or distraction while completing the second column.

| 1 | 2 | 3 | 4 | 5 | 6 | 7 | 8 | 9 | 10 |
|---|---|---|---|---|---|---|---|---|---|
| Strongly Disagree | | Disagree | | Neutral Don't Know Does Not Apply | | | Agree | Strongly Agree | |

## Element I

___|___ This organization demands that business is always conducted ethically.

___|___ It has a clearly articulated set of values that reflect what it's really like to work here.

___|___ This organization has a cohesive culture and a strong identity that unifies our activities.

___|___ This is a productive, but relatively stress-free and pleasant, place to work.

___|___ The work environment is usually productive yet calm.

___|___ People are rewarded for acting with integrity.

___|___ There's a minimum of wasted effort, busywork, and spinning of wheels.

___|___ Everyone here is treated well—fairly and consistently.

___|___ The way we work is aligned with our stated values (i.e. the way we say we want to be).

___|___ This business has a clear brand identity that accurately reflects who we are and what distinguishes us in the marketplace.

___|___ Our managers and leaders are very principled, honest individuals.

___|___ Total: Element I

## Element II

___|___ This organization has a clear vision that guides and unifies its activities.

___|___ New ideas, innovations, and creativity are encouraged and rewarded in this workplace.

___|___ This organization encourages and supports personal learning and growth.

___|___ Our leaders inspire us to do our very best.

___|___ People are vigilant for new ideas and information—inside and outside our organization—that can improve our possibilities for success.

___|___ Employees are optimistic about this organization's future—and their own future within it.

___|___ There is considerable laughter and good humor here.

___|___ This organization has demonstrated the ability to learn from its experience; it is highly adaptive, willing and able to change when necessary.

___|___ Knowledge and information are managed well in this workplace (that is, properly stored and transferred to increase organizational learning and minimize time wasted "reinventing the wheel").

___|___ The attitudes and beliefs held by most people here are supportive of the organization's best interests.

___|___ Total: Element II

## Element III

___|___ This organization has a clear mission.

___|___ There is a strong commitment to this mission at all levels of the organization, and people understand how their individual jobs further its accomplishment.

___|___ This workplace is characterized by high energy and excitement.

___|___ Honest, open disagreements are an accepted part of this work environment.

___|___ Leadership is consistent, strategically aligned, and well coordinated across the company.

___|___ People at all levels of the organization are highly motivated by the desire to do a good job; they feel pride in their work and have a strong sense of accomplishment.

___|___ Leadership prioritizes projects so workers can meet deadlines and stay on schedule without unduly stressing themselves.

___|___ Workers and leaders throughout the organization feel empowered to do their jobs.

___|___ People here are very committed to the organization and each other.

___|___ Work activity is steady and productivity high.

___|___ Total: Element III

## Element IV

___|___ This workplace has a strong sense of community and excellent morale.

___|___ The organization's customers are well-served.

___|___ Because knowledge flows easily throughout the organization, people can readily access whatever information they need to get their jobs done.

___|___ Employee retention and morale are high; turnover is low.

___|___ Communication is good within and across organizational lines; i.e., between work groups, departments, leaders, and workers at all levels.

___|___ Diversity of all kinds (race, gender, religion, opinion, and work style) is respected and encouraged in this organization.

___|___ People work well together and feel a strong sense of loyalty to each other and the organization.

___|___ Relationships and communication support our mission and reflect our values and vision.

___|___ The workplace environment is characterized by courtesy, respectful interactions, and genuine care.

___|___ It is safe to express what you're really feeling or thinking.

___|___ Total: Element IV

## Element V

___|___ This organization's structure is strong, flexible and a good design; i.e., it is highly supportive of the work that has to get done.

___|___ Organization's policies, procedures, and rules are clear, regularly updated, and facilitate its daily functioning.

___|___ Work habits and processes are efficient and orderly.

___|___ The financial health of the organization is excellent.

___|___ By and large, we have all the resources we need to meet our goals and objectives.

___|___ Things change in an appropriate, timely fashion; that is, they evolve when needed, and at a reasonable, steady pace, so as not to inadvertently cause other problems.

___|___ This organization has competent, well-trained managers and administrators.

___|___ The organization's structure, policies, and work processes guarantee the day-to-day implementation of its values, vision, mission, and good communication.

___|___ This workplace produces high-quality products or services.

___|___ We make steady progress toward our goals by monitoring feedback and by continually measuring and improving our performance.

___|___ Total: Element V

## Scoring the Organizational Balance Sheet

**Directions:** Add up the scores you have per element and then transfer them to the graph below. The highest possible score per element is 100, the lowest is 10.

| Element | Score #1 | Score #2 | Contributions to Workplace Health |
|---------|----------|----------|-----------------------------------|
| I | | | Cultural identity, shared values, a sense of corporate "soul"; the gravitational force that holds the organization together |
| II | | | A clear vision and sense of direction for the future; hope, optimism, good humor and attitudes unifying ideas and beliefs |
| III | | | A well-defined organizational mission and clear strategies that align and release the energy and pride in the worforce |
| IV | | | High morale and employee retention; fluid communication channels, easy flow of information to all parts of the organization; a feeling of community; respectful interactions; excellent customer service |
| V | | | Organizational structure; physical and financial resources; work processes, policies, and habits; managerial and administrative competence; steady productivity; products and services delivered |

**Analysis:** Scores in the 70–100 range indicate elements of the organization that are in good shape; scores less than 50 indicate elements needing improvement. Note that when your organization has problems, it will tend to do more of what it already does well, rather than address these areas of weakness.

Healthy elements (above 70):     Score #1 _____

                                 Score #2_____

Elements needing attention (below 50):     Score #1 _____

                                 Score #2_____

## Elemental Circle Graph
## (for Organizations)

**Directions:** Transfer the score (or scores) you have per element to the circle graph below. The highest possible score per element is 100, the lowest is 10. Compare your scores on this graph with the individual and relationship graphs on pages 8 and 13.

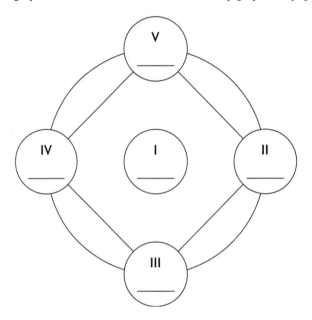

## Comparative Analysis of Scores

| Score Summary | Personal Score(s) | Relationship Score(s) | Organizational Score(s) |
|---|---|---|---|
| Element I | | | |
| Element II | | | |
| Element III | | | |
| Element IV | | | |
| Element V | | | |

| | Strongest Element | Least Strong Element |
|---|---|---|
| Personal Score(s) | | |
| Relationship Score(s) | | |
| Workplace Score(s) | | |

# INTRODUCING THE
# ELEMENTS OF SUCCESS

Your scores from the three Balance Sheets above can help you use the metaphor of the five classical elements to improve your balance in life, relationships, and work. Metaphors, images, and symbols are powerful tools because they provide us with a fresh perspective on complex problems that have been resistant to solution. In *The Balancing Act*, I use symbols that have proven useful to people from across the world and throughout the ages. The five Elements of Success are rooted in humanity's first speculations about, and understandings of, the real nature of our world. They represent truths that have withstood the test of thousands of years of human experience. For these reasons, then, they provide a powerful framework for rethinking how we can achieve health and balance today.

The five Elements of Success, which in classical thinking were the building blocks of all life, range from the most to the least subtle I. Essence, II. Air, III. Fire, IV. Water, and V. Earth.

I chose the five-element model for *The Balancing Act*, rather than the four-element model of some traditions, because the otherwise-absent element of Essence (*quintessence, the Center, Core, or "Ether"*) symbolizes the very quality that I think is most likely to be lacking in our lives and work today. Indeed, this vital point of reference serves as a gravitational force that keeps our lives from spinning totally out of control. This first Element is the center point of balance; hence, its indispensable role in *The Balancing Act*.

I also decided to describe five Elements of Success because when ancient scientists noticed that five was "dominant in the substructure of living forms" (such as the petals, flowers, and leaves of edible fruit),[2] they used this number to symbolize the "flowering of life,"[3] of rebirth and regeneration. Five also came to represent "Man, health, and love" (perhaps because the human form consists of a central trunk and four limbs) . . . and "the quintessence acting upon matter"[4] (the bringing together of heaven and earth). This is, after all, what most of us are really striving for in our daily balancing acts, isn't it? Regeneration, health, and love—just a little bit of heaven right here on earth.

The first of the five Elements of Success, *Essence*, is the most subtle of all the elements. It can't be seen or touched—but it is very real. The metaphor of Essence corresponds to your individual *soul* and *core identity*—the most essential and important part of you. When this first element is strong, you feel peaceful and calm, even in the midst of hectic activity. You have a sure sense of your personal identity, your values, and of who you are at your Core. In relationships, Essence provides a deep sense of connection, even of being "soul mates." And in organizations, this first element gives us a shared sense of values, ethics, and identity. It provides the "why" for our work together.

The second classical element, *Air*, corresponds to your *mind*. Air represents your beliefs and perceptual filters, which in turn create the world you actually live in. Air reveals your current hopes, ideals, fears, and worries. It is a vision of the future life, relationships, work, and world that you are already in the process of creating. In relationships, this element ensures that you and the other person share enough of the same beliefs about how the world works and also that you respect each other's opinions when you do disagree. In corporations, Air provides a shared vision of the future and often surfaces as leaders' and workers' hopes or fears about what lies ahead.

The element of *Fire* represents the power of your *will*. This third Element of Success propels you into action. It drives you. When your internal Fire is strong, you feel passionate about, and committed to, whatever you're doing. Focus and discipline come to you easily. You have all the energy and power you need. In relationships, it is often the passion of Fire that brings us together. This is true in personal as well as professional relationships, where shared energy and commitment form lasting bonds. The element of Fire in workplaces translates to a common mission and coordinated, effective, action.

The fourth element, *Water*, represents your fluid *emotions* and feelings. It connects you with others through empathy and the ability to listen well. It makes good interactions, communication, and enduring relationships much easier to attain. This element provides the "glue" between you and others. It builds trust, respect, collegiality, love, and loyalty. Clearly, this is a key element for lasting relationships of any kind. In businesses, this element contributes to staff morale, information flow, and good relationship building (among individuals, departments, and customers).

The element of *Earth* is the most tangible of all the Elements of Success. It corresponds to your physical *body*. Earth makes you practical. It "grounds" you—that is, it keeps you aware of physical realities and limitations. Earth is critical to being effective in the world. It is the element of implementation and physical resources, finances, health, and beauty. In relationships, the Earth element helps you share resources and build enduring structures that represent who you are together. In organizations, this element is evident as the physical structure of the workplace, the organizational chart, its financial resources, policies and proceedings, daily work processes, and the products and services that are the tangible results of the workforce's labor.

## The Elemental Circle—An Elegant Metaphor

These five elements are all contained in symbolic form in the Elemental Circle—an ancient, cross-cultural template that is a beautiful, compelling image. (You can see one form of the Elemental Circle on the cover of this book.) This elegantly simple metaphor encodes an easy-to-remember blueprint, a step-by-step map, for attaining balance in your life.

The Elemental Circle is, first and foremost, a practical tool, a healing technique long used across the world for the very purpose of achieving equilibrium among the five different elements of a person. This template is a structural *archetype* (a human instinct) that encodes a great deal of information about how you can achieve unity and integrity in your life, making it one seamless whole fabric. Indeed, by connecting these five points of reference, you can transform your life from the ordinary to the extraordinary.

The Elemental Circle is such a powerful template that it has been used extensively throughout time and by civilizations all across the globe. Consequently, it comes in many forms and is found in countless traditions. We see it today in such forms as the *compass* (which points you in the right direction) or a *baseball diamond* (which reminds you of what bases to touch as you round your way toward home).

Most North Americans know this image by its Native American name, the *medicine wheel*, used by tribal shamans for their healing rituals. The Wise Ones (European herbalists) called their version of this template the *magic circle*. They would cast the circle around themselves to draw down power from heaven while simultaneously protecting themselves from harm while they did their healing work.

Medieval European alchemists used the *squared circle* to represent the "divine marriage" of heaven (circle) and earth (square). When combined, these two universal forms contain exactly the same center point and intersect at each point of the four directions. The five points shared by the circle and square represent the five Elements of Success that are discussed throughout *The Balancing Act*. Indeed, this particular version of the Elemental Circle symbolizes my hope that this book will help you combine heaven and earth on a daily basis.

The squared circle is a very rich psychological and spiritual symbol. It contains codes for:

- the original Oneness (the Center),

- the way out to the manifest world (the four radii, or rivers, from the Tree of Life at the center), and

- the return to Oneness (the outer circle, which "smooths away" the sharp corners of the material world).[5]

Moreover, if you look at the squared circle as a three-dimensional object, it forms a *pyramid*, with the center as its apex, pointing our way to heaven and drawing down its power to improve our lives.

The five classical elements are also encoded in the Christian *cross*, where the heavenly axis (vertical line) crosses the earthly axis (horizontal line) resulting in the four directions, with Christ, the great healer, at its center. Many versions of the cross (for example, the Celtic cross) also contain circles at the center of the cross—using the language of symbolism to underscore the bringing of heaven to earth. The rich symbol of the combined circle and cross can be seen in exquisite stained-glass rosettes throughout the world's cathedrals, and remarkably enough, also in Celtic artworks that date back as far as 2000 B.C.

*Mandalas*, complex geometrical patterns long used in the East as tools to facilitate contemplation and meditation, are also forms of the Elemental Circle. Yogis say that the mandala represents the spiral journey you must take—first into the center of yourself (the psychological process of individuation), then back out again (merging with the absolute). The *labyrinth* was designed similarly. It is a walking contemplation, a way to journey into your quiet Center, away from the peripheral madness and distraction of your daily life. After you have been renewed in the center, you can return to your life, family, work, and community with the treasures you have discovered. The labyrinth was also used by some magical traditions to screen, weed out, train, and test initiates. The oldest evidence of magic circles are the *stone circles* of the Bronze Age. These are found throughout the world and are now believed to have been early (and remarkably accurate) astronomical tools for tracking time.

## Becoming Whole

The goal of the Elemental Circle is to create wholeness—a sense of easy coordination, integration, and unity. By using this template, you can make certain that all the key elements of your life are integrated within your daily balancing act. Indeed, this image can remind you how to maintain a center of gravity so that you don't spin out of control as you fly at breakneck speed through your day. And there's more!

When the Elemental Circle is complete, something truly wonderful happens: The whole becomes larger than the sum of its parts. This apparent miracle is called *synergy*. Synergy at work when things get easier for no apparent reason (much as traffic sometimes inexplicably clears after you've been stuck bumper to bumper). Theologians argue that synergy is "the cooperation of divine grace and human activity." *The Balancing Act* is designed to help you increase the experience of synergy throughout your whole life.

The template of the Elemental Circle also helps us become more "whole" by reminding us of how the key components of our lives (microcosm) fit within all the systems of which we are a part (macrocosm). Typically, both individuals and organizations try to "fix" things by addressing only one or two of the necessary Elements of Success. To make matters worse, these are usually the ones we already do well!

The perversity of this approach is that, under stress, an already out-of-balance situation spirals totally out of control.

For example, if you typically rely on the power of your mind (Air) to resolve problems, your first impulse is to analyze things rather than deal directly with a recurring communication problem (Water). A man who has always succeeded by forceful, committed action (Fire) may move forward without thinking about *why* he's acting (Essence) or designing the proper structure (Earth) to sustain his actions over time. When under financial pressure, a business may initiate a reorganization (Earth) that is not aligned with its values and corporate identity (Essence) or its long-range vision (Air).

The truth is that we generally leap into personal, relationship, or work cures without first doing anything more than a haphazard assessment of the nature of the problem. In this way, we are like the proverbial carpenter who has only a hammer and who therefore treats all problems as if they were nails. Happily, *The Balancing Act* adds a complete set of tools to our existing tool kits. By using the symbols, images, and metaphors in this book, you will be much more likely to gain the perspective you need to correctly evaluate your real-life problems and then choose the best remedy for a lasting cure.

The Elemental Circle and its five Elements of Success represent a holistic approach to perfect health and balance. Each human being is a unified, integrated, whole system—existing within the context of larger systems. Interestingly, the words *integrated* and *integrity* share the same Latin root word: *integer*, which means "whole," "complete," and "missing nothing." *Integrated* means "connected" (as in all the parts of your life), and *integrity* is defined as "moral soundness." The symbol of the Elemental Circle, then, encodes a systemic way for you to *thrive with integrity*; and achieve what Carl Jung called the "ultimate state of Oneness"[6] in your daily Balancing Act.

However, if you ignore any one of these five elements, they can ignite a war within you, creating significant imbalance. Indeed, some traditions of healing contend that such elemental imbalance is the source of all physical and mental disease. Happily, all the elements become stronger when they are unified and balanced within the Elemental Circle. The Whole really does become greater than the sum of its original parts. Thriving with integrity means that your life feels full and complete because you are welcoming home every aspect of yourself. This unification will give you tremendous energy and power—and lead you to personal and professional mastery.

◆

# THE GREAT ALLY INSIDE YOU

The Elemental Circle is the primary tool of one of your great Allies: the Magician. The Magician is a Core Type, one of many human archetypes that live within you.* It is a human instinct, a way of being, a lens for viewing the world, a useful model of behavior. The Magician is the internal guide who can show you how to cooperate with the forces of nature that create and transform the world. In this way, it serves as a terrific advisor for attaining health and balance. You and I, your friends, neighbors, and coworkers all have this particular human pattern (and a great many other patterns) available to us.

By working with the Elements of Success, you will gain the help of your internal Magician to achieve personal and professional mastery. The reasons for this are numerous:

- The Magician is the master of balance. This part of you believes that everything in the world is connected. It knows how to weave a whole seamless fabric from the diverse threads of your life. It can also integrate your day-to-day reality with your hopes and ideals.

- Using nature as its teacher, the Magician continuously learns and adapts to its environment. It also uses the secrets of nature to heal itself, others, and larger systems in natural, holistic (less invasive or traumatic) ways. The Magician heals by working with the energy of an individual or group.

- The Magician is practical, intense, powerful, and focused. It will work hard for you to make your ideal life a reality.

- It can show you how to develop mutually supportive, egalitarian relationships. Because the Magician believes we are all connected, it will urge you to simultaneously empower yourself and others, rather than attempt to gain control at anyone else's expense.

All these reasons make the Magician Core Type an especially good guide to help you navigate today's difficulties. In *Magic at Work: Camelot, Creative Leadership and Everyday Miracles*, coauthor Carol Pearson and I used the term "In-between" to describe the current transitional period in which we all live. In this In-between, we argued, humanity somewhat uncomfortably straddles the era of the Warrior (characterized by dualism, competition, debate, national economies, and Newtonian physics) and

---

*For more information on the Core Type advisors within you, please refer to my book, *Working from Your Core: Personal and Corporate Wisdom in a World of Change* (Newton, Mass.: Butterworth-Heinemann, 1998). You also may look to Appendix A for a summary description of the Core Types.

the age of the Magician (characterized by holism, cooperation, dialogue, global economy, and quantum physics). Change is occurring so fast now that it has been described as "discontinuous" (like a rocket taking off). As a result, the simple effort of living sometimes flattens us—almost as if we were trying to get a little drink of water from a full-force fire hose. Many of us feel that we have lost our moorings and are adrift in uncharted territory (what author Peter Vail so aptly called "permanent white water").

*We live in a moment of history where change is so speeded up that we begin to see the present only when it is already disappearing.*
—R. D. Laing, The Politics of Experience

The Magician is spontaneously awakening in many people these days because it can be of great help to us, our families, our workplaces, and our societies. "Magicians have always been masters of the space between—times like sunrise and sunset, when the boundaries between the worlds are not firm, when gods can walk the earth and humans can touch the sky."[7] Any in-between time makes us feel off balance and uncomfortable because our identity, dearly held beliefs, personal desires, ways of relating, and familiar structures are all being challenged by a world that suddenly demands new learning, and quick adaptation. The problem now is that we are all experiencing something within our individual lives that is actually much bigger than any one of us. We are being stretched between the conflicting realities of sharply different archetypal worldviews. The result is that we find ourselves trying to juggle all the normal parts of our lives while the band plays on—faster and faster and faster. No wonder we feel exhausted so much of the time! As my coauthor and I cautioned in *Magic at Work*, "Many of us have heard it said that when one door closes, another opens, but no one warns us that the hall between can be hell!"[8]

# Learning, Healing, Leadership, Power, and Change

**Learning.** Did you know that, in times long past, disciplines such as science, mathematics, philosophy, music, astronomy, psychology, and religion were not yet separate and distinct fields of inquiry? As a result the great thinkers of prior civilizations, in their attempts to understand the "essential nature of things," discovered an underlying unity in the universe that we can perhaps only fully appreciate today.[9] The early Magicians were students of nature, gathering its many secrets—the hidden knowledge that was helpful to (but not readily seen or understood by) others in their communities.[10]

The Magician Core Type believes that the purpose of your life is to evolve by learning. It also encourages you to pass on whatever you have discovered so it can benefit others. The kind of learning in which this Core Type excels is called *in-tuition*—a lifelong process of increasing knowledge by simultaneously observing inner and outer phenomena. I refer to this process as "Learning from the Core."[11]

*You must be the change you wish to see in the world.*
*—Mahatma Gandhi*

**Healing.** Another way the Magician can help you is in its role as healer—of our lives, relationships, work, and communities. In many cultures Magicians function as shamans or holistic healers, who maintain balance not only for seriously ill individuals but also for the whole tribe. Because Magicians believe that we have the power to heal ourselves, they typically act more as midwives than as doctors. They know that their healing power—"magic"—is to be used only "for the good of all" and "according to free will."[12] They also know that they are obligated, as it says in the Hippocratic Oath, to "do no harm" with these gifts from the gods. In many older cultures, shamans also helped heal their communities by rainmaking, mediating between disputing parties, predicting the future, and making certain that the group's actions were in harmony with nature.

**Leadership and Power.** As a result of their special powers, Magicians often had advisory relationships with the rulers of their tribes—as the legendary Merlin had with King Arthur. The Magician inside you has some nontraditional ideas about how leadership and power really work. This Core Type believes that today's problems are so complex that we need the input and perspective of everyone involved and that only in this way can we arrive at wise, enduring solutions. Neither the people at the top nor the people on the front lines of any organization, community, or nation have all the pieces that can make sense of these intricate, dynamic, living, puzzles. Only together can we clearly see the whole picture as it evolves.

The Magician Core Type treats leadership and power in ways that suit our times well. It believes that to do the most good, leadership and power must come from within, be shared, and empower both ourselves and others. The Magician's perspective is that wherever you stand becomes the center of the Circle, and that all your actions ripple out from this point to affect everyone around you. This paradigm encourages you (whether or not you have a leadership status, title, or assigned role) to claim your personal power and positively influence your community and workplace.

This internal guide knows how to move with the subtle energy of a system so that everyone within it experiences more alignment, ownership, and power. Paradoxically, by urging you to share power and knowledge with others, the Magician gives you more of both by weaving a strong network of interconnections and developing alternate support systems. And, because this part of you understands the underlying nature of systems (how systems exist within systems, each influencing the operations of the others), it can help you leverage leadership from any point in your organization to make the changes that are necessary for its survival.

**Change.** The Magician is the master of change. This is probably because this internal guide believes that lasting change first comes from within, then ripples outward, affecting your environment according to its receptivity and your ability. This internal Ally insists that if you want your life to improve, you need to start that improvement with yourself.

The Magician Core Type is relatively comfortable with change because it realizes that this is the natural, ongoing, "constant" state of the world. It also understands that there are many different kinds of transformation (creation, sustenance, destruction, concealment, and revealment). For this reason, your internal Ally is able to accurately perceive and appropriately cooperate with whichever form of change is active at a given time.

Both ancient Magicians and modern scientists agree that change is the underlying reality of the world. It is therefore vital that your individual Balancing Act remain *fluid* and *dynamic* and *whole*. Think of how you walk down a street. You move with little effort or conscious thought: falling forward with one step, finding the next point of equilibrium, and almost simultaneously springing

*The significant problems we face cannot be solved at the same level of thinking we were at when we created them.*
—*Albert Einstein*

forward with your next step. And on and on it goes. Interestingly, balance is often represented by the symbol of infinity, because it is dynamic change (an endless interplay between balance and imbalance) that allows for the possibility of infinity by preventing stagnation and therefore death.

Your great internal Ally can help you join in the natural, always-evolving dance of life that swirls all around you—and in this way, master *The Balancing Act.*

## New Ways of Thinking about Familiar Things

The five Elements of Success, the Elemental Circle, and the Magician Core Type are all powerful images that can reframe the way you look at the world and integrate the diverse parts of your own life so that they are no longer at odds with each other. As Charles Handy said in *The Age of Unreason:* "New ways of thinking about familiar things can release new energies and make all manner of things possible."[13] Even though *The Balancing Act* contains some of the oldest ideas under the sun, they (paradoxically) just might provide you with an entirely new lens through which you can more clearly see yourself, your relationships, your work, and the world in which you live.

Organizational expert E. W. Deming is reported to have said that all models were wrong—but some of them were useful. Because every model is a reduction of reality, a mind map, no model will perfectly fit all the circumstances you encounter. I chose the elemental metaphors and images for *The Balancing Act* precisely because their usefulness has been demonstrated throughout the ages.

Moreover, because the Elements of Success, the Elemental Circle, and the Magician are all archetypes, you will find them extremely easy to remember. (You already know them!) This in turn makes it more likely that you will be able to use *The Balancing Act* to make improvements in your life. You've probably already decided that doing more of what you've always done before—even at a faster pace—is not proving to be a particularly successful strategy for any aspect of your life. That's because what you are experiencing, both internally and all around you, is a changing of the archetypal guard. The new order always inherits, and must solve, the problems of the old order—but in its own special way. This is a good thing, because the new order may have a fresh perspective that will allow for innovative solutions.

The problems you face today are very real. You are not alone in your desire for a more balanced life. Indeed, there is a quiet revolution afoot. According to a recent study by the Radcliffe Public Policy Center, a full 80 percent of American men and women report that one of their top priorities is to have a work schedule that enables them to spend time with their families and have a better balanced lifestyle.[14] A prior corporate poll found that a startling number of workers would give up a day's pay each week for an extra day of free time.[15] I noticed the same phenomenon when I coached executives in career transition; i.e., a large percentage of these people were looking to trade off some salary for a more sane lifestyle.

I find it ironic that we live in an age when "life/work" balance is even a topic for discussion. When did work become separate from the rest of our lives? Unfortunately, a great many of us feel that we are forced to shoehorn our real lives somewhere around the edges of our paid workdays. Paradoxically, the industrialization of civilization has meant that we now spend more than *twice as many* hours working for a living (to supply food, clothing, and shelter) as did people in "primitive" societies. Indeed, the average North American today has one-third less free time per week than our parents did.[16] It is no wonder that there seems to be too few hours in the day to both earn a living and spend adequate time with loved ones.

The kinds of balance we seek are diverse. Not only do most of us want more unity between "life" and "work," we also would like to maintain our own physical and mental health while fulfilling the many demands put on our time. We seek a better balance between activity and rest, between being with others and having a bit of quiet time to restore ourselves. We also try to achieve a balance between different aspects of ourselves; for example, our "right brain" versus our "left brain," our emotional versus our logical selves, and our heads versus our hearts.

Not only do many of us juggle, as best we can, the often-conflicting demands of our children, spouses, and bosses, but a surprising number of people divide their time between the job that pays the bills and the art form, sport activity, or community service that makes them feel alive. Many of us also seek some kind of equilibrium between our material and spiritual lives and the amount of silence or sound in our days. And others among us strive to meet our own needs while guaranteeing the welfare of other people in our society and future generations as well.

My hope is that *The Balancing Act* will provide you not only with useful tools but also with a great deal of encouragement and some companionship as you pass through the labyrinth of this in-between time. Take heart. Even if you sometimes feel you are alone, realize that you are on the first wave of what promises eventually to become an international phenomenon.

For now, just use this book to help you with your own Balancing Act so that you feel more happy and sane. After all, you always have the power to change yourself— *and that is enough!* Fortunately, only a tiny percentage of people are needed to make a significant shift in any community, organization, or society. Physicists, chemists, biologists, and meditators alike have described a similar phenomenon of "phase transition or primary organizer"—that a mere *one percent* of a given population is required to affect a measurable change in the rest of the population![17]

I think that's very good news. Indeed, I believe that the time is fast approaching when we can make a quantum leap into a golden age in which our lives, relationships, and work will become "miracles of one thing."

# Introducing Parts II and III of *The Balancing Act*

The five chapters of Part II, "The Five Elements of Success" make up an Elemental Circle. Each chapter presents the contributions of that one particular element to your life, relationships, leadership, organization, and society. Part II is designed to give you the specific tools you need to promote your personal happiness and professional success. In addition, each chapter contains many practical exercises and colorful stories to help you develop that particular element in every aspect of your life.

Part II follows the same blueprint that Magicians from many traditions employ in their healing work; i.e., they start at the center and then call upon each of the four directions in turn. The spiral path that moves from the most subtle to the least subtle element (Essence through Earth) also traces the path that nature has designed as the cycle of creation and expansion. This organic process allows all living things to grow while staying healthy and remaining balanced—that is, by evolving from the inside out.

This is how it works.

Everything you see around you that was created by human hands came first from someone's identity; that is, who they were and what they valued (Essence). It then formed into an idea (Air). After some thinking, the person decided it was a good idea, so he or she put it into action (Fire). Next came the necessary interactions with other people (Water) to make the idea real. Eventually, what was ethereal and invisible became a tangible, concrete form (Earth). A new business was launched. A beautiful building now stands on a once-empty lot. The twinkling in your mother's eye became the child who grew up and turned into the adult you are today.

In the first chapter of Part II, "Moving from Your Center into a Rapidly Changing World," I look at the contribution of the first element to life, relationships, work, and the world. Essence is the center point of the Circle. It is the Core, soul, and identity, not only of individuals but also of the systems within which we live and work.

Chapter two, "Changing Your Mind, Changing Your Life," shows how the element of Air (the mind and the direction of east) contributes to a worldview and vision of the future that provide a strong, healthy context for all daily activities. This element is indispensible to creating a positive future and to staying mentally vigilant in the present.

"Acting on Your Passion," chapter three, describes the ways the element of Fire (will and the direction of south) helps you generate energy, strategize, and stay focused on and committed to a mission. Fire also alchemically transforms conflicts into forward-directed drive and power.

The fourth chapter, "Weaving a Web of Connection," shows how the Water element (emotions/west) can develop emotional intelligence and excellent communications, establish an enduring community, build good working teams, and foster healthy, honest relationships.

The final element of Earth (which corresponds to the body and north) manifests in all the structures, physical resources, policies, and habits that enable you and others to be capable, day to day, of "Creating New Realities."

After the Elemental Circle is completed in Part II, *The Balancing Act* moves on to Part III, "The Whole Is Greater Than the Sum of Its Parts." When all the Elements of Success are healthy and in good balance, you can move beyond balance to *synergy*. Your life, relationships, and work become Whole—and much greater than you could ever have imagined they would be.

In the sixth chapter, "The Spiral of Synergy and the Sacred Dance," I examine the creative Spiral of Synergy, the holographic nature of the world, and the primal silence and sound of the universe that still echo inside each one of us. I also put all the Elements of Success together in many step-by-step applications so that you can more easily use them to improve your life, relationships, and work.

I conclude *The Balancing Act* with a discussion of wealth. Chapter seven, "Increasing Your Wealth: The Natural Laws and Forms of Prosperity," begins by looking at the Magnum Opus (Great Work) of the medieval Alchemists; i.e., their attempts to make their lives "golden." Then it uses the Elemental Circle and Spiral of Synergy as templates for a comprehensive (and easily memorable) definition of the laws and forms of wealth—all to help you increase prosperity and happiness in your life!

And now, please turn to the next page to embark upon the great adventure of mastering the five Elements of Success.

◆

# PART II:

## The Five Elements of Success

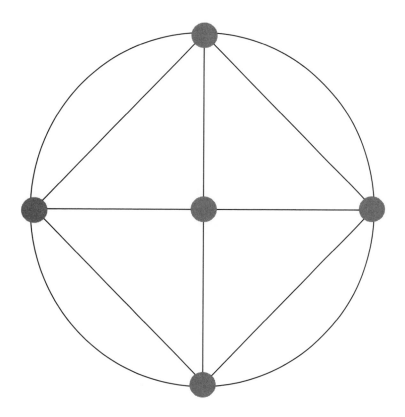

# 1

## MOVING FROM YOUR CENTER INTO A RAPIDLY CHANGING WORLD

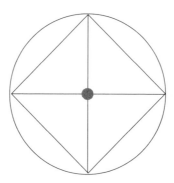

### A Web of Song

*In the Beginning the Earth was an infinite and murky plain, separated from
the sky and from the great salt sea and smothered in a shadowy twilight.
There were neither Sun nor Moon nor Stars. . . .
On the morning of the First Day, the Sun felt the urge to be born. . . .
The Sun burst through the surface, flooding the land with golden light,
warming the hollows under which each Ancestor lay sleeping. . .
So it was, on this First Morning, that each drowsing Ancestor felt the Sun's warmth
pressing on his eyelids. . . . They heaved their bodies upward through the mud.
Their eyelids cracked open. . . . Then, like the baby's first cry, each Ancestor
opened his mouth and called out, "I AM!" . . . And this first "I am," this
primordial act of naming, was held, then and forever after, as the most
secret and sacred couplet of the Ancestor's song.
Then the Ancestors took their first steps, saying, "I am—Snake . . . I am Cockatoo . . .
I am Honeysuckle . . .," calling to right and left, calling all things into being
and weaving their names into verses. The Ancients sang their way all over the
world . . . wherever their tracks led they left a trail of music. . . .
They wrapped the whole world in a web of song. . . .*[1]

—Australian creation myth

# The First Element

The first of the five Elements of Success is Essence. It is the center point of your Balancing Act. It symbolizes the "I am" that reverberates in the very Core of you. This internal point of reference contributes mightily to your own sense of balance by acting as a gravitational force that keeps all the disparate parts of your life from spinning out of control.

This first element has been described through the ages as your individual soul, a spark of the divine flame, and the temple of God within you. (If you do not believe in God or an individual soul, you can think of this first element as your Core biological identity, essential personality, individual life force, or unique nature that distiguishs you from everyone else.) This central element of success represents "quintessence . . . spirit . . . the Origin . . . the beginning of life."[2] It is also called *prana*, the animating force that connects you with the Source of your vitality. In this epicenter of yourself, you are able (when you are very quiet) to hear your own unique sound—the one that was birthed by, and is in perfect harmony with, the original sound of creation. This first element, then, represents your identity, your own special verse in the world's web of song, the "why" of your existence.

When Moses asks God His name (Exodus 3), the reply is: "I am that I am." This very same "I am" is the sound that was repeated by the Australian Ancestors to sing the world into existence. It is also the AUM of Hindu mythology and "the Word" of the Bible (John 1:1). All these creation stories describe the same primal sound, the causal word from which everything came into being, "the first truth-pregnant moment of creation."[3]

As mythologist Heinrich Zimmer says, Essence (which he refers to as Ether) was created directly from this original primal sound, making it the first of the five elements. Author Lise Vail concurs, saying, "Ether is the primary and most subtly pervasive manifestation of the divine Substance. Out of it unfolds, in the evolution of the universe, all the other elements, Air, Fire, Water, and Earth."[4]

You will find it easier to achieve and maintain a comfortable balance in your life, relationships, and work when you start from, and return to, your own Center. In this way, everything you do becomes more harmonious. It is only natural then that you will feel most happy, vital, and healthy when you stay "in tune" with this most essential part of yourself.

The First element lies at the middle of the Circle. It is the exact midpoint where "X marks the spot." The classic Rig Veda of India refers to the five directions as North, South, East, West, and *Here*. In *Mythic Ireland*, Michael Dames describes the "Here" as Mide—an invisible kingdom at the center of the Emerald Isle that united the four provinces and was held in common by everyone. Mide was a sacred spot where "an umbilical cord attached the country to the womb of the gods." In this magic in-between space, gods and people could easily meet. Legends say that the Tree of Life grew here at the dawn of time, and that the twelve kings of Ireland would meet at this site in peace. Today, on the Hill of Uisneach in the midlands of Ireland, a great glacial stone (Umbilicus Hiberniae) marks this supposed "navel" of Ireland—and the world.[5]

Essence encodes a secret for managing one of the greatest killers of our times—stress. If your Center is strong, you will always have a feeling of being "at home" in your own skin. You will feel more calm and less afraid. Not only you, but people around you will notice and be positively affected. One of my colleagues who is strong in this element was challenged recently by her tyrannical, and rather puzzled, boss: "Why do you still walk around here looking happy? Who do you think you are—the head of this department? Everybody else around here is smart enough to be scared for their jobs."

During those really crazy times, when you feel as if you're running around like a gerbil on a wheel, your Core is the calm "I" at the center of the hurricane. It serves as an internal beacon, a strong light in the fog. It shows you how to return to a safe harbor where you can "regroup," get your bearings, and regain your equilibrium. Then, when you're ready, you can start all over again—but this time free from fear, with a clear mind, and a renewed sense of purpose and direction.

You may find, however, that this first element is difficult to access and therefore in short supply whenever you are in perpetual motion, with little time left over for yourself. It is far too easy, even addictive, to get caught up in the external whirl of activity, the daily dramas, and forget your lifesaving internal point of reference. Due to the extreme subtlety of Essence (it is, after all, invisible), we tend to overlook its restorative and powerful nature when we are overly busy. We get distracted. We forget. We may start doubting the value—or even the existence—of this first element.

But, truth is, you really don't have to believe in anything. It is not your belief, but rather your first-hand *experience* of this internal balancing point that will make you want to return again and again to drink from this deep, refreshing source of vitality and boundless energy. Indeed, here is where your individual soul taps into the unlimited Source, allowing you to easily access creativity, intuition, and joy. Essence, then, is the gatekeeper for the very best part of yourself. And it is the statrting point of your own personal Balancing Act.

# PERSONAL LIFE

◆

## Finding Your Center of Balance

Very few of us have built sufficient quiet time into our lives so that we can stay "centered" as we rush through our days. We have come to consider such expenditure of

## You Have a Strong and Healthy Element of Essence When You:

- Are content (even happy) with your life

- Usually feel that you have all the time you need

- Have a strong sense of who you are

- Feel happy, calm, energized, steady, and confident most of the time

- Manage stress well (as indicated by a sense of well-being and a lack of physical, mental, or emotional stress symptoms)

- Maintain a reasonable balance between quiet time and activity; i.e., you are neither overly busy nor inactive

- Are not easily ruffled by changes and find it easy to be flexible

- Take "time out" from activity when you feel the need to do so

- Have good self-control of your mental and emotional state; i.e., you are not thrown off balance for long by anger, fear, self-doubt, envy, or depression

- Have easy access to your intuition (your inner knowing) and can rely on your hunches

- Regularly enjoy quiet time

- Have strong values and ethics that determine the way you act day to day and that guide you in your decision making

time to be a luxury rather than a necessity. As a result, we race about, getting a lot of "things" done—but really going nowhere. Take a moment now to pause and locate your central point of reference. Start by noticing your breath. You may find that it is quite shallow, cutting you off from your primary source of nourishment. Then pay attention to the thoughts that go through your mind. Look up from the book and try it. (Take just a moment. First notice your breath. Then notice your thoughts.)

Interestingly, when you do take a brief "time-out," nature has a chance to take over, slow down your mind's relentless activity, and relax your breath. I find that whenever I feel centered, things in my life tend to move much more naturally, at their own pace, in their own rhythm, and of their own accord; that is, I don't have to push and shove things into shape or leap into action to get things done.

There is a gap that exists in the small space of silence between your thoughts and also in the small pause between your outgoing and incoming breath. It is within this gap, this middle space, that the element of Essence resides. Here you can find the place where "the cosmic mind whispers to the individual mind."[6] Sages have said that there is a natural ongoing breath meditation that is common to all human beings; that is, as your breath comes into your body, it makes a sound described as *ham*. As you exhale, the sound is *sa*. The Sanskrit meaning of these two sounds is "I am That." In between these sounds is the gap, your internal still point of perfect balance.

Great artists and scientists have long known that their best work comes out of the quiet space between activities. Einstein once remarked many of his breakthrough ideas came to him while he was shaving. Mozart would have whole symphonies appear to him when he took his after-lunch walks. I too have found that creative ideas flood in when I spend even a little time in this "gap."

## Staying Centered

Finding and maintaining your center of balance is much like making music (which can be defined as a dynamic balance of sound and silence). Without appropriate, well-timed intervals of silence, music disintegrates into mere noise. It is the same with our lives, relationships, and work. To be or do our best, we need to find the right mix of action and inaction, activity and stillness, silence and sound—in every aspect of our lives. Unfortunately, most of us would say that our days are filled with excessive busyness and few intervals of restorative quiet. It is almost as if we are running around and around a deep, clear well and forgetting to drink from it.

Right now, in between writing these words, I sit quietly at my desk. As I think, I may pause to look out the window. If you were to pass by, it would appear that I am doing nothing. In this peaceful moment, however, I may have found exactly what I needed to say next. In other peaceful moments like this, I may make an important decision, calm down enough to talk civilly to a person with whom I was arguing, or break through on a project where I was stuck. What may look to the rest of the world like "down time" is actually of greater value than my just pushing ahead. And even though this powerful inner work is known only to me, it is the time I spend in this invisible space that makes all the difference in the quality and vitality of my life, relationships, and work. Therein lies the paradox of this first, and foremost, element: Sometimes, the less you "do," the more you accomplish.

You have probably experienced times when the harder you tried to do something, the *less* efficient and productive you became. Having insufficient intervals of rest and play prevents individuals, families, teams, and organizations from doing their best work. We foster "learning disabilities" when we do not plan, reflect upon, or integrate our activities. In short, being off center makes us a lot less smart. It prevents us from noticing problems in their early stages and winds up costing us significant amounts of time and money when they become full-blown crises. A good example of successfully combining activity and rest in the workplace comes from the highly productive West Germans. They have a 37.7-hour workweek and a whopping 42 vacation days and holidays per year.[7] It would appear then that work and play can make "beautiful music" together!

When we are always in motion, running around in circles (that is, living and working on the periphery of the Elemental Circle), we cannot possibly maintain our gravitational centers. We become weak from all this exertion. And then, in the words of William Butler Yeats:

> *Turning and turning in the widening gyre*
> *The Falcon cannot hear the Falconer;*
> *Things fall apart; the centre cannot hold;*
> *Mere anarchy is loosed upon the world . . ."*[8]

By taking regular time-outs, you will be able to see everything more clearly, rather than as a passing blur. You will make fewer mistakes, have fewer false starts, and need to expend less effort to get things done. Sailors refer to a point they call "the center of effort." It is the single point, the sweet spot, where all the forces of nature cooperate optimally with the sailor to drive the boat forward. Similarly, the Chinese sage Lao-Tzu assures us that when we move to Center, we get in touch with the Tao, the underlying order in nature. And "When there is order, there is little to do."[9]

The center point of Essence is where remarkable healing, insights, and creativity take place. Indeed, apparent miracles become possible when you act from your Core. The term *centering* comes from pottery. To throw a pot, you carefully center the clay on the potter's wheel; otherwise, it will quickly become lopsided and spin out of control. To successfully maintain conrol, the potter must remain calm and focused.

> *When you have found the center within yourself that is the counterpart of the sacred space, you do not have to go into the forest. . . . You can live from that center, even while you remain in relation to the world.*
> —Joseph Campbell

Similarly, the study of dance, music, yoga, or any of the martial arts can help you become better balanced physically, emotionally, and spiritually, so that your movements gain strength and grace. I have experienced the delight of using martial arts techniques to withstand the physical attack of a much larger, but off-balance, opponent. (I cannot tell you how much fun that is!) Indeed, all these disciplines are designed to help us attain a steady state of inner balance so that we can move more easily through otherwise insurmountable difficulties.

Below, I have listed several easy centering techniques, all extremely portable. You can use them covertly anywhere—home, work, or play—to help you with your Balancing Act as you go about your normal activities.

## Easy Centering Techniques

1. **Watch Your Breath**: Sit quietly. Close your eyes and turn your attention inward. Without attempting to make any changes in it, simply watch your breath. Notice how it moves naturally through your body. Feel the coolness of the air as it enters your nostrils and then its warmth as it leaves your body. Notice the easy movement of your rib cage. Feel the point at which the breath changes direction, like waves on the beach. In, then out. Out, then back in. Listen to the sound your breath makes as it passes gently in and out. Listen to your heart as it beats steadily. Whenever your mind wanders, just bring your attention back to your breath and return to your Core.

2. **Simple Breath Count**: Another easy method for quieting your mind is the four-count breath. You can do this anywhere—while working at your desk, walking (in time to your footsteps), at meetings, and as an all-purpose calming technique. Begin by taking a long deep, cleansing breath in. Then slowly let the breath out. After you have repeated this a few times, start a mental count. Set your own pace: slowly 1-2-3-4 in; slowly 1-2-3-4 out. When your mind wanders, bring it back to the breath and the count. Use the count to gently make your breath steady, even, deep, and long.

3. **Breath Count Plus Pause**: To the simple breath count, you can add a slight pause during the gap, the point at which the breath changes directions. For example, you may breathe in for four counts, pause for two counts, breathe out for four counts, and again pause for two counts. The variations on this theme are endless. Just set your own comfortable pace and count. It is most important that you do not tense or strain your face, neck, or chest muscles at any time, and particularly not during the pauses (when your initial tendency may be to "hold on" to the breath).

So let's take a moment to experiment right now. Please choose one of the above techniques to try. Put the book down for just a few moments as you use one of these methods to reconnect with your Essence. Whether you are already quite experienced in such techniques or this is relatively new to you, don't hurry on. Stop. Rest. *Breathe.* Move on only after you've given yourself the luxury of resting in that sweet spot. Here is your wonderful, yet elusive, island of sanity, your deep well of healing, the integral gravitational force that holds your life together, and the internal still point that is your little piece of heaven on earth.

## Everyday Ways to Find That Still, Small Voice

There are many ways to tap into your Core. For example, you can continue your chosen breathing technique while you are reading this book. Try it. A calming breath will focus your mind, lessen its normal, distracting chatter, and make you feel rested, even in the middle of activity.

Centering techniques include doing the things you particularly enjoy. After all, the quality that results from being connected with your Essence is happiness or joy. To stregthen your internal point of balance, just do what makes you feel happy, rested, content, or rejuvenated. This could include reading, painting, taking a nap, walking, dancing, watching the sunset, sitting quietly on your back porch, or talking with someone you love. Some people meditate, some pray, others write in journals or spend time in nature to regain their equilibrium. The important thing is that you find some reliable way to regularly listen to that "still, small voice" (I Kings 19:12) inside you.

I have found that singing, performing, listening to, or writing music is what brings me most quickly to my Core. Music, after all, is the most etheric of all the arts. In its highest and most powerful forms, music is uplifting. It allows us to experience the most vital parts of ourselves. Music can be inspiring, or it can act as a cool, healing balm to soothe fear and frustration. It might even reduce your blood pressure and ease other health problems. Indeed, the National Association for Music Therapy reports that music is being researched as a treatment modality for a wide range of disorders (including autism, brain damage, stress, Alzheimer's disease, surgical recovery, depression, learning disabilities, schizophrenia, and pain control) and also for the general care of patients ranging from newborns to the dying.

When you take the time to listen for your internal voice, you will be able to "hear" meaning resonate through you. In this way, you can gain understandings that would otherwise have eluded your more rational (and busy) self. Returning to your Core becomes particularly important whenever you are thrown off balance. If you find yourself beset by self-doubt, relentless worry, overwhelming sadness, anger, depression, envy, fear, or other disturbing states, stop action. Take a time-out. Choose one of the centering techniques in this chapter, or any other you prefer, until you feel back "at home" within yourself.

During difficult times, just return for a moment to your internal point of reference and observe what's going on both inside and outside yourself. Don't judge yourself. Just notice—and accept—this current imbalance. It may actually be a very good thing for you to be out of balance right now, because that discomfort will urge you on to a better place. From your calm internal center point, you identify what factors, inside and outside you, caused this disequilibrium. You will be able to adapt more appropriately to your evolving environment and determine what changes you need to make in your life, relationships, or work. You will also have a better idea of how to move from your Center into the next moment, increasing your odds of taking strong, positive action that will not damage yourself or others.

## The Treasure of Self-Inquiry

Centering techniques can also be helpful when you are facing something you don't know how to handle. Your "still, small voice" can lead you to buried treasure—solutions that come from your most intuitive self. These are also likely to be answers that are congruent with your life purpose and deepest core values, answers that you can live with over time. When you allow yourself to relax into your Essence, your mind becomes like a still pool, and solutions to issues with which you've been struggling are more likely to bubble up to the surface.

Sometimes you can access your Core by simply trusting your own intuition, or *gut* instincts. Interestingly, in some Chinese healing systems, your "gut" is the seat of wisdom in your body, a sort of second brain. It is where you take in information from the world around you and disseminate it to the rest of your body. I find it fascinating that this spot (the *hara*) is at the body's midpoint and center of balance.

Here is a good technique for accessing the wisdom of this second brain during your day-to-day activities. Lorna Catford and Michael Ray, in *The Path of the Everyday Hero*, suggest that if you're struggling to make a decision, just toss a coin. If you're satisfied with the way the coin falls, proceed accordingly. However, if you find yourself wishing the coin had fallen on its other side, your inner voice is telling you to proceed as if it had![10] Todd Waters, a friend from Minnesota who was at the time an advertising executive with his own firm, taught me this method many years ago. He used it to access his gut and prevent paralysis whenever he had to make a tough creative or administrative decision.

If you feel that tossing a coin is a bit too cavalier, for making a very important decision, try the self-inquiry method described on the next page. You will need to carve twenty minutes out of your day to do this process. Although this may seem like a large block of time, the self-inquiry method will take you right to your Core for the answer, thereby significantly reducing the time you would otherwise have spent spinning your wheels, rethinking the issue, and fretting. It also is likely to free up your mind so that you think more creatively. You can use this problem-solving method by yourself, or simultaneously with other people (friends, family, or co-workers) who are involved in a shared issue.

## A Self-Inquiry Method

**1. To begin,** you will need twenty uninterrupted minutes, a notebook or several sheets of paper, a writing implement, and a timer. Sit in a comfortable position. Become aware of your breath as it goes gently in and out. When you are ready, centered, and calm, you may proceed. If you wish, you can call upon what is Sacred to you. Focus on that and invoke its power.

**2. Ask your question.** (Write it down. Be clear and concise.)

**3. For *ten minutes* write down** whatever comes into your mind: possible answers, pros and cons. Try to keep the pen flowing.

**4. Stop.** Close your eyes. Sit in silence. Slow down your mind. If you wish, this is a good time to ask for help and inspiration from whatever you think of as the Source. Take a few deep breaths. Relax.

**5. For the next *five minutes,*** hold your mind steady. Meditate or use a breath technique to keep your mind open and receptive. If thoughts come, just move your attention back to your breath.

**6. Stop.** The answer may have come to you during this time. If so, write it down. If not, then you may repeat this procedure later. Do not use the self-inquiry method more than twice in one day.

**7. Keep yourself receptive.** The answer may come to you in the next few hours or days.[11]

A variation on the self-inquiry method above is to:

1. Write down your question.
2. Make a list of everything that comes to mind.
3. When you can't write anymore, stop.
4. Then forget the problem. (Take a walk or a nap, move on to another project, read a good book, make dinner. Do anything but think about the question. Let go.)
5. When you come back to the problem later, you will be refreshed, less tense, and more likely to hear any answer that bubbles up to the surface from your Essence.

## Claiming Your Power, Naming Your Self

Ancient Magicians believed that they gained their power by discovering their real names—that is, their Essence and own personal identities. For the purposes of *The Balancing Act*, you can claim your personal power by reflecting upon what is of most value to you. This is a way to "name" who you really are. If you don't take time to think about these essential things, it's easy to become "integrity challenged." Your espoused values and real-life behavior won't be aligned. People around you will see that something is "off": that the picture doesn't match the words; you don't "walk your talk"; you aren't at home in your own skin; and you seem fragmented, scattered.

You might think of your identity as being "a loving husband, father of two beautiful children, and a child of God." Your identity is how you would describe yourself to others, whatever is most important to you about yourself. If it changes, it will tend to do so slowly, overtime. You are not your job or vocation (for example, "a computer graphic designer" or "portrait painter"). That is subject to the whims of your employer or your own decision to switch to weaving. The identity that remains more stable underneath shifting careers might be "math and computer whiz" or "visual artist."*

Your Essence or core identity is the most vital and substantial part of you. The science of *autognomics* states that all living creatures have a core identity and that it is this identity (like a DNA blueprint) that determines how they evolve. For example, a tomato is designed to grow as a tomato. It cannot become a potato even if it sprouts in the potato patch and is told to shape up! On the surface, this analogy makes any attempt to change our core identity seem ridiculous. After all, what would make a tomato try to become a potato? When you think about, however, it's really not unlike many of us who waste a lot of time—sometimes large portions of our lives—trying to be someone other than who we really are. (I think this is the power of the fable of the ugly duckling—who never fit in because it was really a swan.)

We each have a reason for existing. Many people who report near-death experiences say they were told "it was not yet their time," and they had to return because they had not yet fulfilled their life purpose.[12] Upon their recovery, all these people altered their lives dramatically so they could act on what they had discovered in this heightened state of awareness.

The exercise on the following pages will help you discover the same sense of meaning with a lot less life-and-death drama. You already know what is important

---

* Some religious traditions insist that your Essence is whatever can never be taken from you. In one tradition, there is a contemplation practice called *neti, neti* ("not this, not this") that forces this issue. For example, you are not "a husband" at your Core, because your wife could sue for divorce, but you will always remain "a child of God." With this deeper definition of Essence in mind, however, please feel free to craft an identity statement that fits your life as it is right now and gives you a starting point for your Balancing Act. As things change (and they will), you will need to revisit and refine your identity statement.

to you; you just need to bring up this information from inside: This process is well worth any time you spend on it. When you are aware of, and act congruently with, your core identity and values, you will significantly increase your personal energy and vitality. When you do not honor who you really are, your energy will "leak out," making it very difficult for you to become who you believe yourself to be.

## Your Personal Identity and Core Values Statement

Begin this process by sitting down in a quiet place where you will not be disturbed. Take all the time you need. (If you have difficulty doing this exercise on your own, you may want to talk these questions through with a friend or coach.) And you may find it helpful to return to these questions over time, until you are comfortable with the answers that emerge.

### Personal Identity

After a few moments of silence, ask yourself the questions: "How would I describe myself to others?" "Who am I?" "What am I here to do?" and "What is the real purpose or meaning of my life?" Breathe. Listen. Wait for answers to emerge from your "gut," your intuition or deepest source of wisdom. Then try to write a brief identity statement here, defining your most essential self.

### Core Values

1. **Write a list of adjectives** that describe whatever it is you most value, what is most sacred to you. (If you get stuck, you can think of what makes you angry. Your values are the *opposite* of these items.) It may also help if you think of the qualities of people you admire and would like to emulate (or conversely, of people you dislike and don't want to resemble).

2. **When you have written** for a while, take a break so you can relax and allow your unconscious some time to reflect.

**3. Whenever you are ready,** come back to this list. Review it, adding or subtracting qualities.

**4. When you are done,** you can prioritize the qualities that remain. List them below in order of importance. This step is important because even excellent values can come into conflict when put to the test of daily life.

**5. After you prioritize your values,** you can complete this process by writing one or two sentences that capture your primary values, that is, what is most important to you. This is your personal values statement, a deliberate "naming" of your best self.

**6. As you go through the next few days,** observe how your values guide your behavior and decision making. Note other essential values that emerge.

The resulting brief identity statement and core values list will help you clarify, then commit to, the most "essential" you so that you can more readily experience your Core on a day-to-day basis. Moreover, this exercise permits you to review your own values regularly, alter them as your understanding evolves, and candidly examine the degree to which your actions are congruent with them. It can serve as your personal code of ethics, a touchstone that keeps you strong and clear in stressful situations when your integrity is under assault. And best of all, it will significantly increase your sense of balance, energy, personal power, and happiness to act from what you hold most dear.

## Magicians' Tools and Techniques (Essence)

Your great internal Ally has a number of remarkably useful tools and techniques to loan you. Have some fun with these images by trying them out as you go through your day.

**Magic Wand.** Ancient Magicians used their magic wands to transform hopeless situations into manageable ones. A magic wand is like a *point of leverage*—the still point at which a small intervention can create significant change. From the Center you can keep your perspective and see more clearly what needs to be moved and how to move it.

**Invoking the Gods.** In their tribes and courts, Magicians often had the function of keeping people in touch with the wishes of the gods and intervening when the kingdom needed assistance. Today you can invoke the gods by staying in touch with your own personal identity and values, and by helping your family, workplace, or community determine what is essential to them.

**Naming (Essence).** Naming is an ancient magical technique that increases the power of the Magician in you by helping you articulate the truth you see. It also helps you find your true Name. Naming from your Core can also help you discover not only the best parts of yourself, but also the essence of key relationships, your workplace, or the community in which you live.

**Book of Wisdom (Essence).** The Book of Wisdom is the place where you write down what you learn as you take your life's journey. It can help you remember any insights you gain along the way, and this will, in turn, help you adapt to future difficulties and shifts in your environment.

# RELATIONSHIPS

◆

## Uplifting Relationships

The first Element of Success in relationships represents the deepest possible connection you can have with another human being—a soul connection, in which you look into someone else's eyes and see your best self reflected back. No wonder we fall in love, or instantly admire someone, or hire that person, or decide we want to become better acquainted with that new neighbor. When you connect with someone else from your Essence, you feel as if you've known that person forever.

## Your Relationships Have a Strong and Healthy Element of Essence When You:

- Treat each other with genuine respect and love

- Come from the same, similar, or compatible cultures (or are very respectful of each other's culture)

- Feel energized, happy, and less stressed when you are together

- Share many common values and spiritual beliefs (or respect each other's differing values and beliefs)

- Are able to say what you think or feel without holding back or being guarded; i.e., you both can be your "real" selves when together

- Become better people—more self-aware, competent, loving, honest—by spending time together; you bring out the best in each other

- Feel completely content and "at home" with each other; experience each other as if you were "soul mates" or had known each other all your lives

- Each support the other to a similar degree; i.e., have an overall equal exchange of energy (as reflected in contributions of resources, time, emotional energy, and commitment to the relationship)

- Have a good mix of both activity and quiet time together

- Know each other's strengths and weaknesses, and neither idealize nor devalue each other

- Trust each other absolutely and have a strong spiritual connection

- Know and treasure the unique aspects of each other

- Do not feel lonely, agitated, suspicious, or jealous when apart

## When I Am with You

*It's not just for what you are yourself*
*that I love you as I do,*
*but for what I am*
*when I am with you.*[13]

As this wonderful old song hints, between you and everyone you meet there is an invisible yet palpable space that contains that relationship. We actually *are* better people in some relationships than in others. But why? In many ways, a relationship is almost like a mathematical equation; i.e., you + me = the relationship. This is why you are not exactly the same person with Sally as you are with Mom or as you are with Fred, because the chemistry of each relationship affects both you and the other person. Real friends call us "home" to ourselves. Other people keep us off balance and drain energy out of us. In truth, our relationships are "quantum"; the possibilities, endless.

The first element symbolizes the most essential quality and the real purpose of relationships. It is ultimately why we are drawn together and it determines how we treat each other. I only learned in recent years how valuable it is to evaluate my relationships candidly and on an ongoing basis. Indeed, I wound up expanding *The Balancing Act* because I needed to figure out for myself how to create a better balance in my own personal and professional relationships.

I learned a lot in this exploration. I began to pay closer attention to who made me feel happy, who didn't particularly affect me, and who dragged me down. I learned that relationships are all about energy: yours, mine, and ours. I started to ask myself if there was a relatively balanced, ongoing exchange between me and another person. If there was, we both felt better after we spent time together. If not, one—or both—of us felt worse. I also started to notice whether we were supportive of the best parts of each other or if we brought out the worst instead. I also learned a few things about what I now label "vampire love."

## Vampire Love?

Unfortunately, far too many people focus on attaining control or dominance in their relationships. This allows them to drain vital energy from others. People who go after your energy do so because they cannot (or choose not to) tap into their own Essence. It's a bit like someone secretly siphoning gasoline out of your car's tank rather than going to the gas station and paying for it themselves.

If you are in doubt as to whether a given relationship is okay or not, you can start paying attention to your body's signals. Some people are, for example, "a real pain in the neck." I have learned that a relationship is not good for me when I regularly experience stiffness in my body when I'm around that person, (especially increased tension in my neck or back). I also watch out for mental dullness or confusion, overcompliance in my behavior, free-floating fear or agitation, and the seductive exhilaration of being drawn into someone else's drama.

And, just as it takes two to tango, it takes two to play out the script for any negative relationship scenario. The "victim" in vampire love is seduced into turning over personal power and vital energy for the sake of holding onto a mate, job security, protection, or a (supposed) friend.

Any of us can participate in either role of a dysfunctional relationship. We are most in danger of draining someone else when we lose our own energy because we are not happy with our lives, are unclear about our life purpose, or are out of balance for other reasons. As a result, we begin looking around for whoever will allow us to tap into their personal store of energy. Unfortunately, much of what passes for relationships—from "falling in love" to choosing friends to signing business deals—is really just a barter of personal energy for some kind of external perks. These are rarely good deals, as both parties involved wind up losing. A good measuring stick for a positive relationship is that, over time, it has a relatively equal energy exchange between both parties. In the best interactions, the energy actually increases for both people. Another way to determine that a relationship has a strong Essence is that it helps both of you to experience your own joy.

Relationships can replenish our life force or they can deplete it. They can build us up or tear us down. We have to choose very carefully when, how, and to whom we give our time and energy. Yet I have noticed (and experienced) that most of us are quite cavalier about this vital part of our lives. We don't seem to realize the power that relationships have to lift us up or harm us—until we suffer the consequences of our bad choices.

The space between two people can easily become a container for our projections and illusions; i.e., whatever personal traits (positive or negative) we do not want to claim for ourselves. I once had a dispute with a business partner. He contended that our disagreement resulted because our "values" were different. (According to him, my values were bad and his were good.) But instinctively I felt that something much larger was at stake. Eventually I came to understand that it was nothing less than my Essence, my individual life force. Looking back, I realize that I had often felt off balance after our interactions—deflated, de-energized, more serious. I idealized this person and projected only positive traits onto him. Our relationship was doomed as soon as I noticed this pattern and stepped out of our dance. By reclaiming my personal power, I changed the unequal operating rules I had originally agreed to. As a result, the partnership quickly disintegrated. Over time I regained my balance by reclaiming the power and energy I had inappropriately given away to this other person.

Sometimes we find ourselves in relationships that have an uneven energy exchange that is *appropriate*. This includes serving people with real needs, such as children, ill friends, new staff members, even suffering strangers down the street or in far-off lands. In these cases make sure you replenish your energy so that you do not burn out. It is important that we "give back" to our communities and the world. It is an integral part of the Balancing Act, a way to show our gratitude for all the unknown others, past and present, who have contributed their efforts to support our lives. (The list of what we receive daily from unseen hands is mind boggling: just for starters, the farmers who grew the food you eat, the workers who constructed the roads you travel on, and the people who edited the book you're reading. We are carried through our days by these countless others.)

But whom we give to, and when, and how, has to remain our choice. I found that a good working rule for me is to simply pay attention—and allow no one to *take* energy from me. By using the the first Element of Success as the steady center point for all your relationships, you will be able to keep a healthy balance between the energy you need for yourself and what you happily give to others.

A friend of mine who is a hospital-based psychologist manages her own Balancing Act by taking a few moments of quiet time whenever she starts feeling drained. She says that her hospital colleagues frequently remark that patients are more cooperative with their treatment protocol after she returns from her brief time-out. Another friend, who is a member of a community organization with no small amount of internal disagreement, found a rather unique way to protect his own well-being while also supporting the good work of others.

> One day as Charles Dietrick was listening to a particularly contentious debate, he started doing a silent meditation technique. This relaxed him enough so that he could contribute to the group without losing his own temper. Charles continued this practice whenever meetings became chaotic. Over time, participants noticed that things went more smoothly whenever Charles attended the meetings. This was somewhat puzzling because he didn't seem to be doing anything special. When Charles's secret was finally pressed from him, the group good-naturedly assigned him the task of meditating during meetings to help them get their work done. (Whatever works!)

# LEADERSHIP

◆

## The New Leadership

Essence contributes authenticity and integrity to the role of leadership. Here, what matters most is who you are. In this new paradigm of leadership, you stand at the center of the Elemental Circle and move your organization from the reference point of your core identity and values. This provides your organization with the "constancy of purpose" that W. Edwards Deming listed as the first point in his management methodology.[14] A leader's constancy of purpose also reduces confusion and fear in the workplace because it provides an underlying, unifying field that becomes the subtle "reality" of the whole system. As a result, you are likely to discover that any change originating from your center of balance requires little effort on your part.

### Standing in the Center of the Circle

According to Taoist doctrine, the truly wise and great leader resides "invisible at the centre of the wheel, [moving it] without himself participating in movement and without having to bestir himself in any way."[15] Leadership from the Core provides a *point of leverage*—like a magic wand—with which you can more easily create system-wide change. Indeed, from the perspective of this essential first element, you can more clearly view your whole system. This is why your Core is the best possible vantage point from which to observe exactly what needs to be moved, how much, by whom, and when. A little bit of effort from this "center of influence" goes a long way.

Integral to the new leadership is the belief that we are all connected to each other, our fates and well-being intertwined. This is much like modern physicists' Theory of Everything; i.e., the belief that all matter is connected via invisible "threads." Hawaiian shamans see themselves as being similar to spiders at the center of a large web, "stretching out in all directions to every part of the universe." They believe that each Magician then can "send out vibrations along the web to consciously affect anything in the universe, according to the strength of his manna."[16]

The Magician Core Type believes that we claim leadership by thinking of ourselves as *central* to the systems in which we live and work (no matter what our position or role). Indeed, I've noticed that most people find this idea of leadership extremely empowering. This is particularly true for those individuals who work in organizations with weak management and unclear values. Keep in mind that you will not be seizing power from anyone else when you claim your own personal power. Rather, by leading from wherever you stand in the organization or community, you will be able to fill the *leadership vacuums* that exist in so many systems.

> *Ronnie Loesser was a management trainer in the Public Health Service's headquarters in Maryland. Although at that time there was no top-level support for Total Quality Management (TQM) efforts in PHS, Ronnie decided to offer a series of TQM awareness classes for anyone who wanted to attend. Because of my background in health care, she called me in to assist her.*
>
> *The classes were well received and filled quickly. People who attended became excited about the possibility of change. Participants learned ways to improve their work processes. They also benchmarked with each other, conferring across departmental lines. Soon other divisions within PHS, the Food and Drug Administration, and the Office of the Inspector General launched their own TQM efforts. Neither Ronnie nor all the people who attended these classes were in positions of authority. However, many of them decided to assume leadership from the Core. In this way, Ronnie and others affected significant change throughout this huge bureaucracy.*

You will gain real, lasting power if your leadership arises from the midpoint of the Elemental Circle. This is paradoxical because when we are at the center of a wheel, we are neither above nor below anyone else. This model of leadership is quite unlike the traditional leadership paradigm, where leaders rise to the top of a pyramid. (Interestingly, if you look at the Elemental Circle as if it represented a three-dimensional object you will see that the center point becomes the apex of a pyramid.)

When we believe that power is a scarce, limited commodity, leadership becomes a competition with designated winners and losers. But the truth is that people in the organization or society who supposedly have less power tend to project their frustration onto designated leaders, whom they then (passively or actively) resist. These leaders in turn often feel as if they are pulling dead weight. Who has the power then? Obviously, the line quickly blurs between those who have supposedly won and those who have lost control in the organization.

*One of my business associates spent some time advising managers in an automobile manufacturing plant. He reports that before he was called in to help them, labor-management relations had disintegrated to the point that angry workers, out of revenge for a heavy-handed management decision, put a handful of extra bolts in a difficult-to-locate section of every sixth car. This action cost the company incalculable losses in warranty repairs and damaged reputation. In turn, this tactic resulted in so much management anger that the warring sides could barely speak to each other.*

## Integrity and Leadership: The Only True Nobility

One of the key functions of leadership is to model behavior that reflects the organization's or community's identity and core values. Leaders are the keepers and guardians of the organization's "soul"—its *core culture* and *integrity.* The element of Essence teaches that *you change your environment more by who you are than by what you do.* (Or as Lao-Tzu said, "The way to do is to be.")

Whenever leaders act in ways that can be construed as unfair or "integrity challenged," their staff members will feel completely justified in following suit. When I consult in organizations that have problems with theft or workers not putting in full time and effort, I gently encourage managers to reexamine any policies they've put into place that might "justify" such behavior in their workers' minds. Typically, these workers feel that they have been "robbed" in some way.

Leaders also are well advised to establish hiring processes that help them attract, select, retain, and train staff members who are already aligned with the organization's identity and core values. This saves countless hours addressing "low morale," "personnel problems," and "bad fit." It also dramatically increases staff energy and productivity with minimum leadership intervention. It is so much easier and less costly for managers to get things right from the start, by leading from this first Element of Success.

Managers also can serve as models of integrity when they make certain that every decision is aligned with the identity of the organization.

*One manufacturing CEO I know had spent years developing a strong quality effort in his organization. On a weekend when he was away, his quality director of two years allowed a substandard order to be shipped to a valued customer. When the CEO returned on Monday, the place was in an uproar. Everyone wanted to know: What was he going to do about this breach of trust? He reports that he then had to make the most painful decision since starting his business: If he did not reprimand the quality director, the message would be that leadership did not really value this improvement effort. The CEO and the quality director spoke at length. Together they decided that the quality director had to step down, not as a punishment, but to ensure that the message would reverberate throughout the organization: No lack of integrity would be permitted, from anyone, at anytime.*

The truth is, everyone's behavior matters to the integrity of a system. And therefore *everyone* is integral to the well-being of a family, workplace, or society (much as your body needs every single internal organ to function properly). If you are a traditionally designated leader, you will gain loyal support when you treat others with dignity and respect. Leadership based upon hierarchical ranking is a vestige of a bygone era, when peoples' lives were dependent upon the whims of kings. Yet many of our workplaces are still run as if they were fiefdoms with ingrained caste systems.

*Ludwig van Beethoven was the first European musician to successfully break the caste barriers that had humbled musicians before his day. Even those lucky enough to have a patron were paid at a subsistence level. Beethoven was a fiercely independent maverick who refused a court appointment and was determined to make it on his own. Only a few years earlier, Mozart had tried to work independently, but died a pauper instead.*

*One day Beethoven and the great poet Johann Wolfgang von Goethe were taking a leisurely walk to discuss the song cycle on which they were collaborating. They noticed that the local duke and duchess were approaching in a carriage. Goethe and all others took their places at the side of the road, bowing low, in the manner of the day. But despite Goethe's tugging at his coat, Beethoven stood upright, refusing to budge. Much to Goethe's astonishment, when the royal couple stepped out of the carriage and recognized Beethoven standing straight up in a crowd of bowed heads, they simply nodded to him and continued on their way. Beethoven's explanation to the astonished Goethe was simple: "The only true nobility is that of the spirit. I bow to no one."*

By believing in his inherent inner nobility, Beethoven succeeded where others before him had failed. And he succeeded not only for himself. He also revolutionized the status of musicians in his and future societies. As you become increasingly confident of your real value, dignity, and the inner nobility of your spirit, you too will be able to exert leadership from the Core and attract the respect you deserve.

# ORGANIZATIONS

◆

## Creating Organizational Soul

The Magician Core Type believes in *immanence*—that everything is alive, that there is an indwelling spirit in all things. Therefore, from this perspective, your organization is also a living entity, a *human system*, with its own Essence or "soul."

The first Element of Success corresponds to a system's identity or core culture. This is an extraordinarily subtle aspect of any kind of organization (be it a workplace, neighborhood group, or political organization). However, this element has a pervasive influence throughout the corporation, holding everything together, giving it a sense of congruence, and having a profound impact on every decision.

Essence manifests as a business's identity, its purpose or reason for being. It is what is most unique about a corporation, what does not change. The equivalent of your individual "I am" is your organization's "who we are together." Essence, then, forms the Core of the organizational *culture*, what you and your colleagues have in common, the values you share that make your working together more meaningful.

The cultural identities of workplaces are as unique and different from each other as are the identities of individual people. In *Working from Your Core: Personal and Corporate Wisdom in a World of Change*, I described many distinct forms of corporate culture and how to use this understanding to make lasting organizational improvements. (See Appendix A for more details.) Moreover, achieving clarity about the cultural identity of your business is essential to branding, marketing, and distinguishing your organization in a competitive marketplace. You can get a good idea of an organization's culture from the *stories* it tells about itself, the lore of the system, and its moral parables.

For example, in one bank where I coached executives, the CEO intervened on behalf of someone who was having problems with her health insurance. The story went through the bank like wildfire. It reaffirmed its values of respect, fairness, and care for each other and customers. Such stories give color, dimension, and shape to our statements about who we say we are. They are extremely powerful. In fact, these stories tell us the truth about who we are—for good or ill. They show that we do (or do not) walk our talk, that our values are (or are not) real, that we really are (or are not) who we say we are.

## Systems in Search of a Soul

Even if you do not believe that it possible for organizations to have a "soul," acting *as if* that were true will have the pleasant outcome of making your workplace more "alive," vital, and happy. Morover, you will find that it's easier to make organizational changes when you act as if you were dealing with a living system that has its

## The Element of Essence Is Strong and Healthy in Your Organization When:

- The organization (community, workplace, association, committee, church group, or department) has a commonly understood and agreed-upon set of values
- Leaders and workers conduct business in a highly ethical way, treating each other and customers fairly; people are rewarded for integrity.
- There is an explicit values statement that reflects how business is really conducted
- People "identify" with the organization and are happy to work here
- Members feel that their work is "central" to the success of the business
- Your workplace has a strong, well-articulated identity and unifying sense of culture
- There are rewards built into your system for acting with integrity, even when such actions are unpopular
- Leaders and workers trust and respect each other
- There is a minimum of waste, rework, or busywork
- The environment is usually calm, pleasant, and productive
- People are active but do not feel overly stressed.

own inherent identity and strong roots. Indeed, if you honor the Essence of your business in these ways, you will greatly increase your likelihood of success.

Countless resources and hours of effort are wasted whenever organizations make changes that are not rooted in their true identity. Without due consideration for this first Element of Success, these attempts are doomed to failure. Ironically, even though most organizational changes take place for "bottom-line" reasons, few succeed—precisely because they are not in alignment with the organization's core identity and values.

The Center in systems is much like the Tree of Life in the Garden of Eden. Using the analogy of a tree, you can think of core values as being the roots of an organization that sustain its life at its source. The products or services are the natural fruit of these shared values. As Lawrence Miller, author of *American Spirit: Visions of a New Corporate Culture*, says, "An organization is much like a living organism. Its functions and structure are much like the body's. . . . Its adherence to a consistent set of beliefs, a 'good,' higher in scope and priority than any short-term decision or actions, which exerts overriding influence on all actions, is its soul."[17]

Soul is reflected in any corporation by the degree its core values are known, agreed upon, and practiced by its members. This can be a significant problem in organizations that have been thrown together by mergers or acquisitions. If inadequate attention is paid to the differing cultures of the two systems, the result is often chaos and confusion. And worse, by neglecting to form a new gravitational Center that integrates the best qualities of both cultures, the newly-formed business often winds up suffering from the *worst* common denominators of both systems.

Organizations with a strong Essence have a distinct character or personality. They have the reputation of being good places to work. Business is conducted ethically. People both inside and outside the organization are treated with dignity. A consistent code of ethics integrates the whole system. Lawrence Miller contends that more organizations these days are discovering their souls, which he defines as the "link between values, behavior, and productivity." He comments, and I heartily concur, that "we are fortunate to be living in an age in which this transition to maturity is being attained."[18]

Unfortunately, many workplaces are alienated from the best part of themselves. You will find that a lack of organizational soul makes you feel that something vitally important is missing from your work. You cannot do your best job, no matter how hard you try. A day at the office may leave you feeling feel drained, exhausted, or depressed. You can also see poorly developed organizational soul reflected in a lack of direction, inconsistent policies, and chronic stress or low morale in the workforce.

Actually, things can be worse if your corporation has a *negative* soul value. For example, a den of thieves could have a very strong—but extremely unpleasant—organizational culture. Another way to think of such systems is that they are similar to the voids described by astronomy that drain the life out of any stars, suns, or planets their gravitational pull can reach. A senior hospital manager told me that she and her colleagues used to joke that so much was demanded of them, they fully expected the next request to be: "Is that your last breath? Can I have it?" I've seen people so drained of their energy in such workplaces that they become physically ill. The first thing I noticed about one corporate client was how pale the workforce looked, how expressionless their faces, how their shoulders drooped as they walked, and the flatness of their conversations. Another place was such an unhealthy environment that I got physically ill upon entering the building and had to leave immediately. My body was the smartest part of me that day. This same place, I soon learned, cared so little about their employees that they gave them "pink-slip" notices en masse via e-mail.

Working in such environments is like being an extra in *Invasion of the Body Snatchers*, the classic science-fiction horror film in which aliens invade an unsuspecting town, then take over people's bodies, minds, and souls one by one. Those people who have had their bodies snatched look the same as they always did, but they've been turned into zombies. The really bad news is that many such "body-snatching" organizations are financially successful! Some pay their employees very well (in order to seduce them into overriding their instincts and staying on). Many of these vampirelike workplaces achieve a strong bottom line and good cash flow by draining the energy out of their people. Their financial reports may look good, but they are truly hazardous places to work.

> *I once had the unpleasant experience of consulting with such a corporation. Its CEO was a now-fearful man who had once been an effective, caring leader in another successful insitution. Caving in to the demands of his new board of directors that he act tougher, he hired an executive VP (a.k.a. "the hatchet man") to do his dirty work. This CEO felt so trapped and miserable that he once confessed to a colleague of mine that he desperately wanted to get out. He had a fantasy, he said, of becoming disabled—not horribly disfigured, "just a little disability," he said. That way he could quit with dignity, and without having to explain to anyone. That way, he said, he could get the hell out of this crazy place.*
>
> *I was always horrified to watch the senior management team huddle before board meetings when bad news had to be presented. Their goal was to determine which lower-level manager they could blame. "Who do we throw overboard to the sharks?" they would ask each other. That unlucky scapegoat would then be disciplined, demoted, or fired. Since this organization was always in crisis, this scenario was repeated with some regularity.*

## Identity and Core Values: Singing Off the Same Sheet of Music

Your company's values and core identity provide an unseen, but pervasive, structure: a "unifying field" that permeates your entire workplace. This invisible structure becomes visible in its effects, such as the behavior of employees or the quality of products and services. A corporation's culture results from "a few guiding formulae or principles . . . that express the system's overall identity. . . ."[19] Margaret Wheatley, in *Leadership and the New Science*, says that these guiding values are critical because, "What we lose when we fail to create consistent messages, when we fail to 'walk our talk,' is not just personal integrity. We lose the partnership of a field-rich space that can help bring form and order to the organization."[20]

I find that some businesses can beautifully state their identity (who they are and what they were created to do) and their values (what they hold dear and reward in their employees). But in far too many workplaces, organizational values statements are so incongruent with what really goes on that reading the statement out loud causes workers to roll their eyes. Identity and core values cannot be mandated or handed down from on high. *They already exist.* They simply have to be discovered and articulated. The process of discovering and naming an organization's Essence is critical to its success because it aligns everyone (in much the same way as a chorus sings off the same sheet of music).

You will be happy in your work to the degree that there is a good match between your own identity and that of your organization. Shared purpose and values within a system create *alignment*, a powerful gravitational pull that gives people a strong feeling of a unifying center. (This is much like the sense of stability we experience due to the force of the earth's gravity—despite the reality that we are hurling through space at extraordinary speeds!) Clearly stated workplace identity, purpose, and values are necessary for people to feel that they are in alignment with each other and their organization.

> *The senior officials in a division of a large state agency approached me because they were having trouble with several newly hired junior staff members. These people were asking for more empowerment and were starting to act out in inappropriate ways.*
>
> *A quick consultation showed that the problem was rooted in the significant gap between the values of the junior versus the senior staff members. This department was new and had grown very quickly. After the initial group of senior managers was in place, the department chief had told them all to go ahead and fill staff positions as they saw fit. Unfortunately, these managers did not clearly articulate the organization's values during the recruitment and selection processes.*
>
> *I recommended that the agency realign its staff on core values. Then it could stop spinning its wheels and get back on track. After the organizational identity and values were clarified, staff members could then determine for themselves whether or not these were congruent with their own personal values and identity. Each individual could then decide whether to get on board or stay behind at the dock.*
>
> *Although this process was difficult, the problem would only have worsened if ignored. Fortunately, this department did not make the mistake of empowering staff members before aligning them. If they had, the organization would have been ripped apart at its seams.*

A choir can be made up of the most diverse people in the world. They come together, however, to sing the same music in the same key and at the same tempo. Otherwise, we would have cacophony. Similarly, there can be great diversity in an organization, except around its reason for being. This first Element of Success, the Essence of any system, is not negotiable.

## Discovering Your Organization's Identity and Core Values

You cannot *make* an organizational identity or values statement. It is a process of discovery, a treasure hunt for the invisible field that already holds the corporation together, those few foundational, guiding principles that integrate it. You can discover a workplace's real reason for being and its core values by noticing what people spend their time doing, or, conversely, by listening to what people complain about. (They will complain about what they value but feel is missing in the organization.)

Begin by asking, then listening carefully to, what people have to say about the workplace (both positive and negative comments). Then list key words that surface to describe the character or culture of the organization, what people have in common, the "why and who we are together." By paying attention to what you hear and observe, you can describe the business's real identity and core values.

## Your Organization's Identity and Core Values Statements

Does your organization already have a values statement and an identity statement? If so, write them below. If not—or if you think they are inaccurate or incomplete—you can use the following spaces to describe your view of your business's core values and identity.

### Organizational Identity:

Ask yourself why your organization exists. What is its Essence? How does it describe itself to the rest of the world? What is it in business to do? (If you answer, "make money," a gong will sound and you will have to go back to the beginning of this chapter. Making money is the *result of*, not the *reason for* being.) Your workplace's identity has to do with purpose and meaning. It may be why you or your collegues chose to work here and what you believe makes this company special. (Example: a family-owned manufacturing firm that has been a good neighbor in its own community for seventy-five years.)

### Core Values:

1. **You can begin** by writing a list of adjectives that describe what is most valued and important in your organization. Or you can think of what makes people here most angry—your shared values will be the opposite of these qualities. (Examples: fairness, competence, honesty, caring.)

**2. Once you have** a reasonable list, prioritize the values that are most important to people.

**3. Then write** a sentence or two that reflects your workplace's primary values (i.e., a values statement).

**4. As you got through** the next few dats at work, observe the values by which people act and make decisions. Test your identity and values statements against the organization's behavior.

Drafting a short identity statement and a brief values statement (or a prioritized list of core values) for your organization would best occur *after* you have gathered input from everyone in the system so that you see what people really have in common. The brief statements that result from this effort provide a powerful way to increase awareness of what matters most to the whole group. With these core values clearly articulated, everyone in the workplace is more likely to act in an integrated fashion—and with integrity—according to this agreed-upon set of guiding principles.

Unfortunately, many corporate identity or values statements are blurred together with their vision or mission statements. To be most effective, each of the five Elements of Success need to be clearly and distinctly differentiated. If they are mixed together, the result will be confusion, a loss of energy, a dilution of your efforts, and perhaps an inability to achieve your goals. You can think of each of the Elements as a separate part of a bridge that you need to first build, then cross to reach your destination. If any piece of the bridge is missing, you won't be able to make it across the chasm. This is go one of the reasons it is so important to reflect upon your workplace's culture, identity, and values.

*I learned a lot about organizational culture when I consulted with various branches of the Department of Defense. I worked with U.S. Air Force Intelligence when they were suffering drastic reductions in staff. These people were excellent workers and dedicated officers. In military service, many of them had discovered what they were best suited to do, yet now they were being displaced. Their identity, their sense of who they were in the world, was badly shaken.*

*Those officers who left military service quickly discovered that, although their skills and capabilities translated well into corporate America, there were few other organizations that shared their personal values of loyalty, intelligence, and patriotism. These were just a few of the traits of the culture within which they had been immersed for years.*

For these people, as for most of us, the culture of our workplace is something we take for granted. It is as invisible as the Essence, yet everything we do within system is defined by it that. Because organizational cultures vary so much, it is important for you to articulate both your own and your workplace's key values so that you can determine the degree of fit between yourself and a potential or current employer.

## An Integrity Check for the Element of Essence

1. Compare the Personal Identity and Core Values statements you wrote earlier in this chapter with your organization's identity and core values. In what ways are they similar? In what ways are they different? If they are significantly different or seemingly incompatible, does this adversely affect you? In what ways?

2. How can you influence your system by assuming leadership at the center? Where might you begin?

3. If you do not feel that you are able to influence your organization, do you need to find a new "home" in a more compatible system? What workplaces do you think might have an identity and values that are more similar to yours?

## Helping to Create Core Values in an Organization

I sometimes encounter people who feel that their corporations have no strong ethics or are morally bankrupt. What can you do if this is the case for you? First, you need to remain true to yourself. You can bring out the best in colleagues or neighbors by modeling what it's like to live and work from your own Core, by reminding others of what is important to them, by acting on your values, and by supporting others when they do the same.

Occasionally, one person can shift a whole system's understanding and behavior. As the story that follows indicates, a breakthrough sometimes occurs only after a great deal of hard work. Fortunately for all of us, there are many people who are using this first Element of Success to make some surprising changes in our workplaces and in society.

*While working for an international beverage company, John Toomey proposed an antialcoholism educational campaign on college campuses in cooperation with Students Against Drunk Drivers and Mothers Against Drunk Drivers. He soon found that many of his colleagues and supervisors were not comfortable with the idea of publicly speaking out about teenage and college-age alcoholism and related deaths. For years, John persisted with his public education concept. During these same years, he was regularly passed over for promotions.*

*At long last, John was given the go-ahead to develop his program. Within a short time it was so successful in generating public awareness that other beverage companies quickly followed suit. Today, due to the efforts of this one courageous and persistent individual who insisted on acting from his individual values, a new standard of public responsibility has rippled through this entire industry.*

I am often asked by people. "What can I do? This place is impossible. Nothing will ever change here." Sometimes I advise these people to get out as quickly as they can because the environment is toxic for them. At other times it is clear that they need to move on to find a place where they're more at home.

But much more often my answer to this question is, "Just be true to yourself." If you remember that wherever you stand is the center point of the Elemental Circle, you'll be okay. This means simply doing what you can, where you can, and when you can. After all, the only thing you can ever do, really, is to change yourself. *This, in itself, is enough.*

## Essence in Action: Central Minnesota Group Health Plan

*It was my great fortune to have served as the first president of the board of directors and CEO of Central Minnesota Group Health Plan. This was a truly magical organization. It was successful because its founding members were clear from the outset about the values we wanted to see in health care.*

*Our purpose was to deliver comprehensive health care services that were respectful of our members and that treated them as full partners in their health care. We also valued the separation of finances from direct patient service.*

*The commitment of the organizing group magnetized a loan from Group Health Plan of St. Paul. The board and administrators of that successful plan not only had an identity that was similar to ours, they also compassionately remembered the difficulties of their own pioneering efforts. Capitalization was one significant difficulty. Attracting physicians who shared the group's values was another—and one that for a long time seemed insurmountable.*

*Years passed while the founding group, an extraordinarily talented and dedicated group of individuals, negotiated with local physicians and tried to draw new doctors to town. Finally, Gary Strandemo, an idealistic Harvard-educated family practitioner, answered the group's prayers. This was his idea of what a medical practice should be. But one doctor was not enough to launch a new medical center. Fortunately, Pat Lalley soon agreed to come on board with Gary. Other original top-notch core staff members included Jan White and Joy Barth (administrators), Barry Radin (PA), and fabulous, hard-working nurses, receptionists, lab assistants, medical transcriptionists, and many other talented individuals.*

*Soon the first members enrolled in CMGHP for their health care. In turn, they talked their friends, work colleagues, and relatives into joining us. The rest, as they say, became history, as this tiny organization catapulted to success.*

# WORLD

◆

## A Deeper Integrity

The lack of balance many of us feel in our personal and organizational lives is reflected in similar imbalances on the international stage. Indeed, in this In-between, it may sometimes appear that humanity has lost its center of gravity altogether, and that the world is spiraling completely out of control.

The chasms between the "haves" and "have nots" continue to grow, fueled by the very urbanization that allows the middle classes of many industrialized countries to live in a manner that would have been the envy of kings past. Yet not everyone shares in this wealth. Even in America, a staggering 8.3 percent of children under twelve years of age go to bed hungry at night!

While international politics continue with hot spots of upheaval, many of our social systems across the globe are experiencing a breakdown of traditional values. This process is disturbing to many people. In response to an apparent disintegration of social, family, and personal values, concerned individuals in societies the world over—community and business leaders, attorneys, scientists, politicians, educators, and other authorities—struggle to establish new ethical standards.

Corporations and workers alike suffer from the increased stress that is a by-product of the decades-long disintegration of a mutual commitment between employer and employee. Businesses have merged and downsized with such regularity that the resulting layoffs have spawned a booming "outplacement" industry.

Some days it seems that we've lost our center altogether.

I think that most people do care about the suffering of their fellow human beings. But they also feel paralyzed—at a complete loss for how to tackle these extremely complex social and world issues. How can we act in a way that is congruent with our values of caring and fairness, of love and respect for others? How can just one person make a difference in the face of such overwhelming difficulties? How do we enter this out-of-balance world from our Core?

"Think globally—act locally" is a phrase that springs into my mind. But to most effectively tap the first Element of Success and positively affect world issues, go just one more step "locally." That is, go inside. From your calm Center you are more likely to be able to clearly perceive the points of leverage that can have the most impact on our shared problems. By resting in your Essence, you can touch the connective webbing of which we are all an integral part. And when you and I move from our Essence, we are in a position to do some real, lasting good, (rather than mucking about like vigilantes).

I believe that what is happening now in our workplaces and the world actually does *not* bode ill for us in the long run. Go ahead, call me a Pollyanna, but here's my reasoning. In the past, standards of integrity and values were *externally* determined, and individuals often revolted at the uneven enforcement of these external mores. Policing was necessary. The privileged, the clever, the "integrity challenged," and the unscrupulous often lived by a different set of rules entirely. This fact was lost on no one.

As the Magician Core Type emerges in this In-between, a clearer sense of individual purpose and values will begin to arise more organically from within each one of us. In the future, I think that we all will be expected to access our personal power *and* to use it for the good of our communities, workplaces, and world. And I think that as a result (and quite paradoxically), we could arrive at the deepest level of integrity the world has experienced in recorded history.

We are definitely breaking down. But we may be breaking down in order to break through! The element of Essence can help us hold ourselves together as things continue to shake out around us. This will make it more likely that you and I will emerge, relatively unscathed, on the other side of this In-between.

And when we do, this first Element of Success can help us heal and unify the world with shared principles that bubble up from the Core of each one of us—principles that reflect the very best part, the quintessence, of humanity.

◆

# **2**

## CHANGING YOUR MIND, CHANGING YOUR WORLD

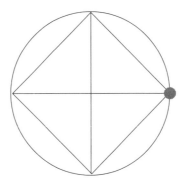

### Let There Be Light

*In the Beginning . . .*
*God created the heavens and the earth . . .*
*and the earth was without form, and void;*
*and darkness was upon the face of the deep.*
*And the Spirit of God moved upon the face of the water.*
*And God said, Let there be light;*
*and there was light.*
*And God saw that the light was good;*
*and God separated the light from the darkness.*
*And God called the light Day, and the darkness he called Night.*
*And there was evening and there was morning, the first day.[1]*
*. . . And the LORD God formed Adam out of the soil of the earth,*
*and breathed into his nostrils the breath of life;*
*and man became a living being.*
*And the LORD God planted a garden eastward in Eden;*
*and there he put the man whom he had formed.[2]*

—Hebrew and Christian creation story

# The Light of Awareness

The second Element of Success, referred to classically as "Air," arises directly from your Essence. It contains the invisible nourishment you take in with every breath and the light that illuminates your entire world. Air uplifts you by helping you *learn* and by giving you *clear sight*. This element represents *vision, inspiration*, and *humor*, all of which are critical to your personal Balancing Act. Vision helps you see clearly where you are right now, the next steps to success, and—off in the distance—where it is you want to be. Inspiration infuses your life with a sense of meaning, a guiding philosophy, creative ideas, new perspectives and possibilities. Humor is another invaluable gift of the Air element, one that has the effect of making you "light" enough so that you can see things from a fresh perspective.

Of the five aspects of every human being, it is your mind that corresponds to Air. Your mind is very powerful. It helps you cocreate your life. This is how it works: Whatever your mind shines attention on is enlivened, supported, and perpetuated for you. The attention of your mind acts much like a spotlight; whatever you focus your awareness on is illuminated and becomes your reality. Whatever is outside that spotlight might as well not exist. And in a very real way, for you, it does not.

To underscore how true this is, consider that your senses pass on eleven million bits of data to your brain *per second*. (Stunning, isn't it?) But from this onslaught of information, you consciously process a mere sixteen bits of data per second.[3] (Sobering, isn't it?) Your mind both filters *in* and filters *out* data and in this process significantly determines both your current and future realities. This is why sages have correctly contended throughout the millennia that *your world is what you think it is.*

Human beings are model makers. Your mental models allow you to function, moment to moment, by making sense out of an extraordinarily complex world. Clearly, we all need strong perceptual filters to help us navigate through the onslaught of information that bombards us every moment. Your personal worldview (*Weltanschauung*) helps you do just that. It is a combination of all the paradigms you find useful for daily life. Your worldview was initially handed to you by your society and family. Then you maintained it and, to a greater or lesser degree, revised it according to your own experiences. If you have consciously examined the strong perceptual filters you were initially given, you have been able to weave a worldview that, over time, has become increasingly a fabric of your own design.

This is a critical issue, because so much of what both you and I have been taught is likely to be outdated and no longer adaptive, if for no other reason than that it's been handed down, largely unchanged, for so many generations. We have to look very carefully at our beliefs. Where did they come from? Who taught us? And who taught our teachers? How did they know that their information was correct? How does it stand up against conflicting research and beliefs?

By and large, we do not examine why we think the way we do. This is a form of mental laziness that is *normal* but not *healthy*. Indeed, such inattention and automatic acceptance of others' ideas is how our minds—these marvelous instruments—become dulled. For example, we rarely scrutinize the information we receive to see how much it has already been filtered by institutions and individuals who would benefit if our beliefs supported their goals and needs. I say this not to suggest any conspiracy theories but rather to encourage you to stay alert. Just continue to use your natural critical faculties to observe the information that is presented to you. This will guarantee that other people's perceptual filters do not automatically become your own.

Such alertness is vital because your worldview is a way of *naming*, and therefore constructing, your day-to-day reality. Such naming acts much like an *enchantment* or *magic spell*, changing everything you see according to that filter. The only problem is that, as you go about your busy days, it is extremely hard to remember you are living within the enchantments that you or others have cast!

Learning is the best way to lift an enchantment and change your paradigms. Learning is both the food for, and the fruit of, the mind. It is also the key to adaptation. If you are ever to achieve the balance you want in your life, you need to first learn what does and doesn't really work for you—and then change accordingly.

Unfortunately, the ability you and I have to learn is sometimes sabotaged by inertia or by our attempts to hold on to cherished beliefs about ourselves, others, or the world. Indeed, what tends to happen is that we spend our lives selectively gathering data to support our already existing beliefs. It is a form of daily "self-hypnosis." If, for example, I think the world is a dangerous place and someone is a despicable person (or, conversely, that the world is a wonderful place and this same person is a saint), I will act accordingly because my attention selects the "right" information.

We tend to wake up and see our mental boundaries only when we bump into them, either because they no longer serve us or because someone challenges them. When we are overly comfortable with these mental ceilings and walls, they tend to confine and shape our growth. But when we step out from the shadow of their influence, even for a moment, to illuminate and examine them anew, we can suddenly have a fresh-air, long-distance view of our lives—where the possibilities are endless.

Unfortunately, all of us tend to gather people around us who will support our existing beliefs. This serves to support the shared enchantment, making it quite unlikely that our ideas will ever be challenged. But this insularity is not in our best interests. We are actually better off—at home, at work, and in society—when what we think is prodded enough to encourage both individual and collective adaptation and survival.

Perhaps the best way to test and choose your beliefs is to examine them from your calm Center. When your mind is strongly connected to your Essence, you have two stable points of reference to begin your Balancing Act. You are much less likely to go awry when you use these two beacons to illuminate your path and help you navigate safely through your life. Clearly, the optimal way of learning is to direct your mind to process all information through your Core identity and values. By combining the light of your mind and the deep resources of your inner knowing, you will greatly increase your odds of arriving at wise choices. In fact, you can't go wrong.

# PERSONAL LIFE

◆

## Lightening Up Your Life

This in-between transition time is similar to the moments of sunrise and sunset, when the rapidly shifting angle of light plays tricks on us, changing our perceptions, opening us to new insights, and showing us what is just ahead on the horizon. Today, the air practically crackles with a wealth of information and changing ideas. It is almost as if we simply need to "tune in" to retrieve all the myriad data that is now floating on these invisible airwaves.

In the Native American medicine wheel, eagles or hawks often represent the Air element because they have expansive vision that allows them to scan the environment for miles around. These days it is particularly important that you and I scan the horizon for all the possibilities that are emerging. Inevitably, any new data we pay attention to will change the way we see ourselves and the world we live in.

In *New World, New Mind*, authors Robert Ornstein and Paul Ehrlich argue that because the world changes more in a decade now than it used to change in millennia, whatever you learn today will soon become obsolete. The only thing constant in life anymore, they argue, is change itself, so "Adapting to change must be the center of any new kind of teaching."[4] In that context, what you and I most need to learn is *how to learn* so that we can constantly evolve with our rapidly changing environment!

### Learning = Adapting to a Changing Environment

You can use the flow of new information to continually monitor how well your current beliefs and mental maps are helping you adapt to shifting circumstances. With every new piece of information, you will have to determine whether your current worldview comfortably permits this data within its borders. If not, you'll have to decide whether to discard the information, put it on hold until you know more ("bracket" it temporarily), or expand your worldview. What is important is to continually review whether your beliefs support you in living a happy, productive, and balanced life.

**You Have a Strong and Healthy Air Element When You:**

- Are both positive and realistic about the future (that is, you simultaneously see the exciting possibilities and potential difficulties)

- Have a long-view vision of your future or a strong sense of your next steps

- Are open to new ideas

- Encourage questions about your existing ideas and beliefs and are comfortable examining the accepted ideas and beliefs of others

- See clearly what your own paradigms are now—and how they affect your behavior

- Are aware that your thoughts create both your current and future reality

- Demonstrate creativity, innovation, imagination

- Know how to transform your ideas into reality

- See what you have to offer the world and don't "hide your light under a basket"

- Freely share your thoughts with others

- Enjoy learning and are willing to experience new things

- Have a strong intellect and an inquiring mind

- Easily see the humor in life and don't take yourself or your opinions too seriously

- Like to "lighten things up" and have fun

- Generally have an optimistic, positive, cheerful attitude

According to the science of autognomics, *learning is what we do to act effectively and adapt successfully to a changing environment.* Typically, we protect our identity by filtering what we perceive. This process forms a self-perpetuating, habitual loop in which we select the information we want from our complex surroundings. However, this is not real learning. Learning starts when we are faced with what American philosopher Charles Pierce called an *irritant of doubt*—something that doesn't quite fit our ideas about the world. This is annoying; it makes us uncomfortable. However, these challenges are much like grains of sand that adjust over time into valuable "pearls" of understanding that force us to and survive.[5]

In this in-between time, our beliefs are constantly being challenged, thereby giving us golden opportunities to break through existing mental barriers. Futurist Joel Barker calls this kind of attention *paradigm-vigilance*; it allows us to see new ideas and surprising information as opportunities rather than as threats. Most of us tend to react with anxiety, defensiveness, or panic when any of our dearly held beliefs are threatened. We then respond by dismissing the challenge, denigrating the challenger, or vehemently defending our point of view. Unfortunately all these responses make it much more difficult for us to transform our lives.

## The Learning Zone

This model of learning refers to three potential zones of differing readiness to learn. They are the comfort zone, the learning zone, and the panic zone.

The *comfort zone* is the inner ring of your learning. It contains your existing skills, abilities, and accepted ideas.

The *learning zone* is the middle ring, where learning occurs. You do not necessarily find this zone comfortable; there is always anxiety (and sometimes excitement) involved in venturing into unknown territory. Each time you go into the learning zone, you learn more. Once you overcome that tempoary imbalance to master the new knowledge or skill, it becomes part of your comfort zone (which enlarges with each new understanding).

The third zone, the outer circle, is the *panic zone*. When you are confronted with new ideas or previously unknown concepts that shatter cherished beliefs, you may slip over the line into the panic zone. Or you may find yourself in the panic zone because you are overwhelmed by a deluge of new information. Obviously, it is difficult to learn when you are anxious and stressed.[6]

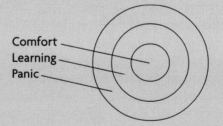

Comfort
Learning
Panic

Unfortunately, too many of us live and work at such a fast pace that we are too stressed to gather and process new information—and therefore learn. Sometimes this means that we hunker down in our comfort zones and accept whatever information we're fed. And at other times it means that we live in the panic zone, where we also are not able to learn and adapt. Both nonlearning zones result in avoidable costly errors.

Great thinkers from all times and places have taken it upon themselves to test, and expand, the borders of our shared knowledge—despite humanity's well-established tradition of punishing heretics. Every new discovery pushes the boundaries of what our species knows, until our accumulated knowledge can no longer fit within the existing collectively agreed-upon framework (e.g., "the earth is flat"). Then we are all forced to move on to a larger structure that can accommodate both the old *and* the new knowledge. This is how the shared mind of humanity evolves. Air is, after all, a gaseous element. It expands our understanding so that we can take in seemingly contradictory information: for example, that electrons are both particle (matter) and wave (energy).

When we do not learn, we are like shut-ins who inhale the same stale air day after day. You can stimulate your learning by seeking out people who will question you; by looking at issues from different perspectives; by reading; by sitting quietly to think; and by seeking new knowledge in your profession or in other fields that interest you. Cross-disciplinary exploration often produces healthy hybrids of learning. Indeed, significant contributions to fields of knowledge frequently come from people *outside* them; that is, people who are not content experts and who therefore are not blinded by that system's current mental maps.

## Who Is in Charge of Your Mind?

You are what you think. Moreover, what you think is how you feel. Your mind paints your world and creates your life within it. Your thoughts make you happy or miserable because they instantaneously alter your entire body chemistry. Psychoneuroimmunologists have discovered that your brain and immune system communicate via hormonal messengers that translate your thoughts and feelings into chemical events in your body. Your mind is not housed only in your brain. It actually is a "delicate web of intelligence that binds the body together."[7] Your mind is the home in which you live.

The question then arises: Who is in control of your mind? Your mind can be your best friend and your worst enemy; it can make you healthy or ill, happy or miserable. It has extraordinary power. However, a mind with no one in charge is much like a car without a driver behind the wheel. The car goes anywhere it wants, careering out of control, causing untold damage! Too often, our minds act like the child in the movie *Home Alone*, who runs wildly from room to room, thrilled to be left behind to do whatever he wants. However, as even the child in this movie fable eventually learns, survival requires mental discipline. This is not surprising, because *discipline* comes from *disciple*, which in turn comes from the word *"to learn."* Therefore, the *way to learn is to discipline your mind.*

*Make your mind large, as the Universe is large, so there is room enough for paradox.*
—*Maxine Hong Kingston*

Your Essence is the trustworthy "driver" of your mind. When your mind is connected to your Core it has direction, and the best part of you has control of your life. A detached intellectualism results if the mind is cut off from the Center. Indeed, the mind then becauses a "small" and is capable of considerable harm. However, by assuming full responsibility for staying in the driver's seat, you'll be able to easily navigate through your life. However, if you don't focus, your mind, it can flit from hopes to fears and back again at an alarming rate. The effect on your body (and your present and future life) is much like slamming your feet simultaneously on both the brake pedal and the gas pedal.

Maintaining a strong connection between these first two Elements of Success can also help free you from the agitation of repetitive, negative, and self-defeating thoughts. Your mind has great powers of enchantment: It can quickly brew "a tempest in a teapot" with just one recurring thought, thereby ruining even the most beautiful of days. Conversely, it can transform prison cells into contemplation rooms where genius flourishes. This is how World War II concentration-camp survivor Jakow Trachtenberg invented his unique speed system for mathematics, American labor organizer Saul Alinsky wrote his books, Anwar Sadat decided to work for peace between Arabs and Israelis, and Mahatma Gandhi discovered the power of passive resistance.

To gain the full gifts of your mind, just remember that you are in charge of this exquisite instrument that projects your inner reality outward onto a big, blank screen and calls it Life. To paraphrase Abbott and Costello's most famous skit, "Who" really is on first base, and "What" (is on your mind) really is on second.

In the wonderful Italian film *Life Is Beautiful*, director Roberto Benigni tells the tale of how a father saves his son's life by ingeniously reframing the horrific experiences of a concentration camp into a child's game. Benigni based this film on his own father's stories of how humor and a determinedly positive attitude kept him alive in the camps. My Minnesota neighbor, Bill Cusack, had similar stories about how attitude and humor helped him and the rest of the downed crew of the 8th Air Force "Dorothy D" first survive one and one-half years in the infamous Stalag 17-B prison camp in Krems, Austria—and then the long walk (at half their former weights) from Krems to Paris after they were freed.

You and I are the directors of our own life movies. We write the scripts and cast the parts. Our attitudes have the ability to paint the world black or white or gray or pink. The exercises that follow will help you control your attitude (and experience) by quieting your mind and connecting it more strongly to your Essence. They will help you direct your thoughts and clear them of clutter. After all, you are in charge of your mind—you don't have to tag along behind, following it wherever it wants to go.

## Exercises for Changing Your Mind

1. **Connect your mind with your Center.** Begin with a simple breath count (see exercises in chapter one). Watch your breath for a short time. Then begin noticing the activity of your mind as it tries to distract you. Every time a new thought or worry grabs your attention, just observe it for what it is. Don't judge or resist it. After noting it, simply return your attention to the count and your breath. You can use this exercise to reconnect with your Center and also to become more aware of what's really going on in your mind.

2. **Shine the spotlight of awareness.** Sit quietly. Watch your thoughts as they arise. Note how your body responds to these thoughts (for example, how an angry thought causes your jaw to tighten or a worry upsets your stomach). Then, after noting your mental and feeling states, shine your awareness, on each thought. Acknowledge the information or feedback it has for you, then allow it to dissolve into this light. Self-defeating thoughts prefer to go about their business in the shadows of your mind and will tend to run for cover whenever you focus attention on them.

3. **Observe self-talk.** When you find yourself agitated, angry, afraid, or in a difficult situation, stop a moment to observe what is going on. First notice your breath. If it is shallow, begin to deepen it so you can think more clearly. Then watch your thoughts. What sort of conversation are you carrying on with yourself? Are you repeating defensive, angry, or fearful phrases? If so, first do a "reality-check" to observe what is causing your distress. If there is little truth to these phrases, then you are doing negative programming and setting yourself up for increased difficulty. Take a time-out to reconnect your mind with your Center, thereby bringing yourself back into better balance.

4. **Affirmation.** After acknowledging what's on your mind, return to the breath. This time, instead of the simple breath count, repeat a positive affirmation on the in-breath and out-breath. It could be "I am calm" or "I am happy." By the way, you don't have to believe these statements are true at the start. You may not be at all calm or happy. Pay attention to how resistant your mind is to positive programming. This is because you have been doing *negative* programming while fretting, worrying, and complaining. By temporarily shifting your internal messages from negative to positive, you can create both a

better present experience and future reality.* Just envision yourself in this improved state until you can *feel it* inside, until it becomes your new internal experience.

**5. Focus your mind to improve communication**. When in conversation with another person, first note what you are saying to yourself. After that observation, put your own thoughts on temporary hold and direct your mind to listen very carefully to what he or she is saying. Instruct your mind to gather data at many different levels—not just the words, but also the vocal tone, emotions expressed, what is left unsaid, and body movements. This should keep you fully engaged. You also will be more likely to understand the other person, interact with empathy, and take appropriate action thereafter.

**6. Change your mind, your body chemistry, and your reality**. Begin by remembering the last time you were thoroughly happy. Bring all the details into your mind: who was there, what kind of day it was, how old you were what you were wearing. Hear the sounds. See the colors. Let yourself relax into this prior experience for several moments. Then, when you are done, notice how dramatically your mind, body, and emotions have changed. Quite literally, you have just reexperienced that same event. You can easily transport yourself to such happy states in the future, just by directing your mind there.

## Seeing the Light Inside

The second element in *The Balancing Act* has the effect of lightening us up. It frees us from mental limitations that blind us to our own internal light and that prevent us from sharing it with the world. Educational researchers (such as Joseph Chilton Pearce and Howard Gardner) argue that we *all* are potential geniuses. If you were lucky, you had parents, friends, or mentors who told you not to hide your light under a basket. If not, you may be blinded to your own brilliance—and this learned disability will severely limit your contributions to the world.

Our minds can play tricks on us, making us feel unworthy or not good enough. We hold back. We put aside the dreams of our childhood and construct adult lives that are too small for us. Consequently, few of us ever recognize or achieve our potential. The story below encourages us to see who we really are so that we, like the great sun goddess Amaterasu, can bring our shining gifts out into the world.

---

*Repeated phrases, such as positive affirmations, are a good start when your intent is to replace negative programming with positive programming. However, it is vital to remember that these are just stepping stones—a sort of "halfway house"—and not the goal. *Any* form of self-hypnosis causes stagnation in your mind and blocks off your access to your own wisdom and soul.

*Amaterasu is the chief deity of the Shinto religion. One day Amaterasu decided to retreat from the world into a cave. Without the sun, the world was covered with darkness and cold. Nothing could grow. All the other gods and goddesses begged Amaterasu to return, but she would not.*

*Finally, Uzume, the goddess of laughter and merriment, took action. She climbed on top of a washtub and began dancing, singing, screaming bawdy remarks—and doing a strip-tease! All the gods and goddesses made such a commotion that a curious Amaterasu finally opened the door to her cave—just a crack—to see what was going on.*

*Fortunately, the gods and goddesses had, with great foresight, installed a mirror directly outside the cave. Amaterasu, who had never seen her own beauty before, was dazzled. While she stood in front of the mirror, dazed with delight, the other deities grabbed the door and pulled it open.*

*And this is how the sun returned to warm the winter-weary earth.*[8]

This wonderful legend also illustrates that we can improve the quality of our minds through laughter. Laughter can break our mental bonds. Cheerfulness is often considered a necessary companion for learning or enlightenment. Tricksters throughout the world have used humor to reveal truths and give inspiration. Indeed, many great teachers use a variety of techniques, such as koans, paradoxes, and parables, to trick (distract, overwhelm, confuse) their students so that new information has a better chance of getting past their mental barriers. Laughter heals broken bodies and bruised relationships. And, in the workplace, laughter is a necessary component of inventiveness and brainstorming. In a way, then (to rephrase the old DuPont motto), laughter results in "Better Things For Better Living . . . through *mental* chemistry"!

## Ways to Lightening Up

1. **See the light inside.** Find a place where you will not be disturbed for a few moments. In a systematic way, fill yourself with light, from head to toe and back again. Choose a color of light that feels energizing or soothing to you. See yourself, first filling up with this light, then radiating it through every cell of your body. Feel the waves of light pass through you. This exercise is particularly helpful when you are tired or not feeling well.

2. **Laugh out loud.** Read the comics or a humorous article, rent a funny video, go to a card store and browse. Spend time with someone who has a great sense of humor, or do something that makes you laugh out loud. If all else fails, just go to a place where no one can throw a net over you, and start laughing for no reason. You can even try different kinds of laughs, imitating those of people you know. Pretty soon you'll be rolling on the ground with

tears streaming down your face. Laughter is a charm that alters your body's chemistry, changing your mind and body for the better.

**3. Be irreverent.** If someone is giving you a tough time, imagine him or her in a clown outfit or pink tutu. If you are mentally stuck in a painful situation, run a repeated mind film of this scenario backwards or at high-speed forward. Add the Marx Brothers to certain particularly difficult scenes, or dub in the voices of your favorite comics. If you have a problem that's stumping you, find a way to turn it inside out or upside down in your mind.

**4. Try plerking!** Some people say play and work *do* mix. They call this combination *plerking*. Try it. Urge your mind to reframe some troublesome aspect of your life, a relationship, or work as if it were a game. Dive into it as if you were a child at play. Look at it in the least serious manner possible, as if you had nothing to lose.

**5. Brainstorm with others.** Use brainstorming techniques with your friends, family, or colleagues to generate new ideas in areas where you may be stuck. Set aside 15 to 20 minutes. First clarify the topic upon which you'll all brainstorm. Then set down the rules: Make certain everyone agrees that during the five "brainstorming" minutes there will be no commenting on or criticizing of anyone's ideas and that everyone will speak whatever comes into his or her mind. Have someone else keep time and shout out the minutes as they wind down. Quickly write down each idea on newsprint, where everyone can see it. Above all, enjoy the process. (If you're doing this right, there should be lots of laughter.) Stop at five minutes. Then use the remaining time to discuss and prioritize all the great ideas you've generated.

**5. Contemplation: Lightness is your nature.** Consider the space that exists in your body. Even your bones, the most dense part of you, are made of molecules that are almost entirely empty space, with microscopic electrons rapidly swirling around a tiny nucleus. The following analogy illustrates how light you really are. *The proportion of space to matter in each atom of each molecule of every cell in your body is the same ratio as a nickel (the nucleus) to a penny (the orbiting electron) two miles away!* Whenever you catch yourself feeling overly "heavy" and serious, contemplate the dancing lightness that is your true nature.

**6. Fill yourself with air.** Imagine yourself filling up, like a balloon, with pure air. Then, in your mind's eye, see yourself gently lifting off the ground. Make certain that mentally you attach a strong, silver string to a solid object, so that you can quickly return to "reality" at any time. This way you can go as high and far as you wish. Look at your life, or a particular problem, from this clear perspective. Experience how different everything looks and feels from this height. When you are ready, return slowly to where you began. Take this sense of lightness and clearer perspective with you throughout the rest of your day. And if you notice yourself getting extra-serious again, just turn your mind back to what you felt in this experience.

## Visioning a Brave New World

You are already creating tomorrow with the thoughts and attitudes you have today. What are you choosing for your own future? Will it be born from your *hopes*? From your *fears*? Or from a confused, jumbled mix of both? What are you now pouring your attention and energy into—what are you now carrying into the future?

Each one of us has the option of creating the brave new world we see in our mind's eye. These future possibilities range from Shakespeare's magical island to Orwell's desperate visions of cannibalism. We have a tendency to either rise *or* sink toward whatever we believe is possible. The good news is that we can actually learn the attitudes of optimism or pessimism.

Noted psychologist Martin Seligman states that *learned optimism* is how you think and react when you suffer a setback; that is, how you use the power of "nonnegative thinking" to change the destructive things you say to yourself. *Learned pessimism* is "the giving-up reaction, the quitting response," the helplessness that follows from the belief that whatever you do won't matter.[9] The stakes are very high here. According to Seligman's research, optimists have stronger immune systems, catch fewer infectious diseases, have better health habits, and actually live longer![10]

If you and I follow our fears, we cannot sustain our hopes, and we will unwittingly sabotage ourselves. When we lack hope, we sink into despair or become jaded. We no longer believe that a good life, relationships, neighborhood, workplace, or world is possible. With this belief as a base, we filter in data that supports our pessimism. We will even attack and discount opposing information, thereby discouraging others' hopeful visions, all in the name of making them face "reality." The problem with a pessimistic attitude is that it determines what we "settle for" right now and in the future.

Visioning acts much like a *crystal ball*: It cuts through the fog so that you more clearly see the potential realities that are available to you, right now. And in so doing it helps you shape a better future. Visioning something helps make it real. In fact, what you vision you actually *experience* in your mind and body *as if* it were real.

Successful athletes have long known about this phenomenon. In one experiment, a college basketball team was divided evenly into three groups to find out what made for the most effective practice. Group A was told not to practice their free throws at all. Group B was instructed to practice free throws regularly. Group C was told to just *imagine* they were practicing free throws (for the same amount of time as Group B physically practiced them). Researchers were stunned by the results. Group C, those who practiced only in their minds, improved their free throws the most![11]

> *O, wonder!*
> *How many goodly creatures are there here!*
> *How beauteous mankind is!*
> *O brave new world,*
> *That has such people in 't!*
> —*William Shakespeare,*
> The Tempest

You can begin the visioning process for the future you want to create by trying to imagine what it would look like if it were "perfect." (This is *your* ideal, so it can be any way you want it to be.) By stretching your mind to consider the possibility of an ideal world, you force yourself to look at everything anew. This is a dialectical process that moves you from:

- where you are now (your current reality) to

- the image of your future, and then to

- a better life than you have now, in the direction of your "perfect" world.

If visioning a future is difficult for you, you can try looking at your present life, relationships, and work as if you have never seen them before. Have some fun. Step outside yourself to get an entirely new view. This is called "beginner's mind," and it can spark remarkable, fresh insights. Like Shakespeare's Miranda in *The Tempest*, you and I can use beginner's mind to see the brave new world that waits for us, looming somewhere on the horizon, just within our reach.

---

### Creating a Personal Vision

1. **Review your core identity** and list of personal values (from chapter one).

2. **Imagine what your life would look like** if it reflected your identity and values, if it were everything you hoped for. Write some notes below or on a separate sheet of paper.

**3. Identify your fears** and the obstacles you believe are in the way of accomplishing your ideal life. Be candid. Pay particular attention to recurring self-defeating thoughts. Make notes below or on a separate piece of paper.

**4. Note the difference** in your feeling states between #2 and #3—your hopes versus your fears. Realize that you are currently creating your future with your thoughts, just as you helped create today with your prior hopes and fears. Make your choice about the brave new world you want to create.

**5. Return to Step #2** and refine your vision in any way you choose. Now think about this future of your choosing until you can *feel* it and *see* it. Really get inside it. Experience it until you can see and feel and touch it as if it were already real, as if you were already there. You know you've got it when you feel uplifted, inspired, hopeful. Have some fun. Let go. Imagine you are on the hologram deck of *Star Trek* where anything can magically come true.

**6. You may find it helpful** to take a separate piece of paper and *draw* the vision you see. You can illustrate your vision in any way that is meaningful to you; that is, you can draw it, make a collage, write a song, or choreograph an interpretive dance. (Any of these methods will activate your right brain and free up your full intelligence.) Remember, this is *your* vision—and it only needs to have meaning for you.

**7. Now, from this experience** write your personal vision statement in the space below. The purpose of your vision statement is to serve as a beacon of light that leads you into a future of your own design.

Come back to revisit your vision on a regular, even daily, basis so that it serves as a bridge to the future of your choosing. Keep it firmly in mind so that it changes your current reality and transports you eventually to your ideal world. The purpose of a clear vision is to align your daily actions and decisions with your Essence so that you are progressively drawn closer and closer to the life you choose. Keep your vision in a place where you can look at it regularly or recall it easily. It will light your path during dark times and keep you moving in the right direction.

*Vision is the art of seeing things invisible.*
*—Jonathan Swift*

Make certain your vision is sufficiently "inspiring." It should make you feel hopeful and optimistic—less worried and tense. This is, after all, the future into which you are traveling, a future that is completely congruent with your core values and identity. A great way to increase your commitment to making your hopes real is by giving your vision "a voice"; that is, by gathering up your courage and speaking it out loud to someone you trust, someone who will support you. By bringing your vision into the light of day, you can hold it more steadily in your mind and give it all the attention it needs to become your next reality.

## Magicians' Tools and Techniques (Air)

**Crystal Ball.** A tool used to foretell the future and see the present more clearly. It gives you new perspectives and shows you things in a different light. The crystal ball also can help you scan the environment for new information, keeping you paradigm-vigilant.

**Magic Dust.** Helps you dissolve obstacles and problems by using "mind over matter" (actually mind-*with*-matter). Your attitude affects reality; you already know how to make problems larger or smaller, more or less difficult. Magic dust represents the kind of learned optimism that transforms difficulties into treasures of learning.

**Riddles, Koans, Paradoxes.** These tools have been used by sages to challenge outdated worldviews by creating obstacles to normal assumptions and ingrained patterns of mind. They can create the kind of mental tension that will help you break through to new understandings and move from duality to a dialectic.

**Thought-Control Techniques.** Affirmations, contemplations, creative visualizations, meditation, prayer, relaxation exercises. These methods are used to calm, focus, and direct your mind so you can eliminate negative self-programming.

**Naming (Air).** A way of determining what you are doing to create your reality. It includes examining your worldview with all its concepts, ideas, and metaphors. Naming also includes verbalizing your hopes and fears, naming your preferred future, admitting to yourself what you really want, and declaring your personal vision to others.

**Book of Wisdom (Air).** This could be a journal in which you write down your vision, hopes, fears, dreams, new ideas, insights, and components of your belief system. It can be used as a skyhook to remind you of your learnings, insights, and visions during times when your hope, and inspiration are low. The Book of Wisdom can also be used to note what you're currently thinking and feeling (and therefore what you're creating for the future). It also can be used to track mental chatter and expose negative thinking.

# RELATIONSHIPS

◆

## A Meeting of the Minds

When you think about it, it's actually amazing that relationships work at all. Remember the data about our perceptual filters: that each of us takes in *eleven million* bits of data per second from our senses, but consciously processes a mere sixteen bits of that data? In relationships, as in every other aspect of our lives, we each cast our own enchantment upon the world and then mistake it for the one-and-only objective reality. All of your friends, colleagues, relatives, and neighbors have their distinctly different lenses through which they perceive and experience you and the rest of the world. To a staggering degree, each one of us lives in a completely different "enchanted" world of our own making.

*Some enchanted evening*
*You may see a stranger,*
*You may see a stranger*
*Across a crowded room. . . .*
*—Richard Rodgers and*
*Oscar Hammerstein,*
*"Some Enchanted Evening"*

## Enchantment and Learning

Knowing that we relate to everyone through the filters of our own mental constructs can actually help us interact better with others. We tend to think someone else is good or bad, interesting or boring, attractive or not, all based upon our ingrained existing beliefs. You and the other person in any given relationship are constantly selecting which data to process about each other. Clearly, someone else can find fault with you, if that

## Your Relationships Have a Strong and Healthy Air Element When You:

- Greatly enjoy each other's company and have fun together

- Share many common beliefs about the way the world works

- Are respectful of each other's differing thoughts, feelings, ideas, opinions, and beliefs

- Laugh a great deal together; enjoy each other's sense of humor

- Appreciate the other person's attitude toward most things

- Believe you have a good future together and work together to shape that future

- Feel "light" when you're with each other; have the ability to lighten each other up when either of you gets overly serious

- Have many interests in common

- Find each other intellectually stimulating and respect each other's learning style

- Feel comfortable questioning or challenging each other's ideas and enjoy thinking through problems together

- Are open to trying new experiences that the other person suggests

- Enjoy learning more about what makes the other person tick

- Encourage each other to continually learn and grow

- Discuss what you think and feel about issues and difficulties as they arise

- Are careful not to project your (negative or positive) traits onto the other person

is what he or she is looking for. Conversely, other people can see your finest qualities if they choose to—*and* if their own filters give them the ability to perceive what's best about you.

In the healthiest relationships each person sees and respects what's best in the other without denying or ignoring shortcomings, differences, and difficulties. With this kind of sharply focused awareness, you will always have the option of shining a spotlight upon and thereby bringing out the best qualities of the other person, be it your employee, spouse, child, or neighbor.

> *The story is told of the country grocery-store clerk who was asked by someone passing though town what the people there were like. It was a pretty place, the visitor said, and he wondered if he would enjoy living here. The clerk asked, "Well, tell me: What are the people like where you live now?" The man replied, "Oh, that's why I want to leave. They're really nasty—not only unfriendly, but also terrible gossips!"*

*"Gosh, that's too bad," replied the grocery clerk, "'cause that's just how folks are here, too."*

*Only a few minutes later, another visitor came into the store. He asked the same question, and the clerk replied, in turn, with the same question he had asked of the first man. The second man answered, "Well, actually, they are great—would give you the shirt off their backs. Couldn't ask for better neighbors."*

*To which the clerk replied, "Well . . . that's just how folks are here, too."*

*When queried by an incredulous bystander who had witnessed both conversations, the clerk said, "Both those guys would have had the same experiences they'd had before 'cause they'll carry their attitudes with them wherever they go."*

## Blue Smoke and Mirrors

Your relationships provide a powerful way to learn about yourself because you can use them as mirrors. As the fable above indicates, we carry our attitudes with us wherever we go, including into each new relationship. This is why we tend to have similar patterns (and problems) of interaction, whether we are at home, at work, or in our communities. If you take this perspective into your relationships, everyone you meet becomes your teacher, and daily life becomes a full-time school.

Relationships can be quite tricky. Consider the common game of mutual projection. It is not unusual for us to attribute to others whatever it is we do not want to "own" in ourselves. For example, if you don't recognize your own anger, you will tend to notice it (and react adversely to it) in others. This can also happen if you "idealize" someone—assigning your own positive traits to him or her but not seeing these same traits in yourself. When a lack of self-esteem causes us to project our good qualities onto others, our sense of unworthiness is likely to be reflected back in how shabbily they treat us.

You can shine light on your relationships by staying alert and by discussing difficulties as they arise. By articulating what you really think and feel, you can continually revitalize a relationship. Moreover, by staying aware of what's happening in your interactions, you can sometimes discover what's really going on inside *you.* Knowing that everyone enters relationships with a fully equipped worldview can prepare you to respect the other person's differing beliefs while agreeing to disagree. Although beliefs are important in any relationship, they are not a person's Essence. Our ideas about ourselves, each other, and the world do change as we learn and grow.

A lack of tolerance for someone else's beliefs is a death knell to any personal or professional relationship. Although you can use disagreement to stimulate learning about each other, you must do so with considerable care and respect. If a dispute is disrespectful, it signals a lack of security or understanding in the attacker (and, not infrequently, a projection of negative traits onto the other person). It is easy for disagreement and criticism to result in a defensive reaction that backslides into debate rather than moving forward into dialogue. However, if during disagreements you exhibit tolerance of other people's opinions, an honest curiosity, and a desire to learn more about them, you will be able to develop wonderful relationships that bridge all kinds of human differences.

Mental gamesmanship occurs in relationships when people try to "psych-out," manipulate, or gain power over each other. This behavior arises from fear, a need to control, or a mutual protection pact. If the participants stay within the lines they've drawn, then interactions continue as before and both worldviews remain intact. However, in this kind of setup the relationship is over if either person changes.

Another issue to watch out for is when people speak one thing but do another; that is, they don't walk their talk. If you believe what someone says rather than what he or she does, you will be easily taken advantage of. Although this statement seems quite obvious on its face, it's really not as easy as it appears. In fact, it can drive you a crazy to have to continually sort through conflicting data (what someone says is true versus what you feel or see). Some people have developed great skill in creating a smoke screen about who they are—a bit like the Wizard of Oz. And if they've done it long enough and have built sufficient protection around this image, they sometimes even believe the mirage themselves. This makes them very convincing. Be forewarned: Such people will go to great lengths to protect this illusion, and they can easily harm anyone who naively assumes that the smoke screen is the real person.

## Happily Ever After

This second Element of Success contributes to healthy relationships in many ways. It helps you learn about yourself, know your own mind, and see things more clearly. Your primary relationship, of course, will always be with yourself. That is the one constant factor in all your other interactions. You carry your attitudes, thoughts, and beliefs with you to greet everyone you meet. Therefore, it is only when you or I are "happy in our own skin" that we have the possibility of living happily ever after with somebody else.

You create your world with your beliefs about what is possible, what is right, what is true. Then you select people to play the roles you cast them in. If you are unaware of your role as director, you will wind up playing the same dramas over and over again. But if you understand how relationships really work, you are more likely to find others who have this same awareness. And with them you can enjoy a true meeting of the minds.

Once you have the people that you treasure in your life, the second Element of Success can help you envision and build a shared future together. This element also encourages you to have fun together, lighten each other up, enjoy the time you spend with each other, and laugh out loud. In a high-pressure world of constant motion and stress levels that kill, these are extraordinary gifts for any relationship.

# LEADERSHIP
◆
## Inspirational Leadership

We expect leaders to speak clearly about their dreams of the future. We want decision makers who can articulate a collective vision that unifies us, that cuts through the fog, thereby helping us create the best possible future together. Indeed, we classify as "great" those leaders who are so inspiring that others happily take up their vision as their own. Such inspiration is a property of the Air element. According to *A Dictionary of Symbols*, Air is related to the breath of life (speech), the stormy wind (creation), and also space for movement and the emergence of life processes.[12]

But inspirational leadership is not confined to the top of the organizational or political hierarchy. *Au contraire!* Think of the great social, political, scientific, and artistic leaders of the past century. Many of them emerged into their roles by the conviction of their brilliant ideas or uplifting ideals. Knowledge, good ideas, inventiveness, astute observations, and truth telling are a huge part of the wealth of humanity. So, no matter what your title, you can be an inspirational leader because you are integral to the *mind* of your system. Your function is similar to the intelligent cells that make up the human mind and are spread throughout the entire body. Clearly, our human systems need their full intelligence if they are to function optimally.

By actively learning, then freely sharing your experiences, you can serve as a model for how your organization's "mind" works best. And if you are a designated manager in your workplace, you can breathe new life into it and increase its intelligence by soliciting and rewarding everyone's participation in team learning, idea generation, and paradigm-vigilance. You can also encourage people to speak their minds, thereby creating new knowledge.

## A Philosophy of Management

Good leaders have an overriding *philosophy of management*, a paradigm or framework for everything they do. Quality guru W. Edwards Deming underscored the importance of such a unifying paradigm when he said that a business executive's philosophy should not be bound by "retroactive management" (such as management by objectives or results-oriented management). In arguing for a future-oriented philosophy, Deming quipped on the PBS special, "The Deming of America," that "you can't drive a car by looking in the rearview mirror!"

You have probably noticed, however, that managers are often thrust into positions of leadership rather than being prepared for them. Indeed, executives are rarely taught *how to learn*—that is, how to stay open to new ideas and knowledge. Our systems often cut decision-makers off from vital feedback and other critical sources of information. Many managers' days are so busy that they can't take time to think clearly, plan for the future, or reflect on the present. Another problem is that most organizations tend to reward action-oriented behavior only. This makes it difficult for business leaders to read a thought-provoking new book, think quietly for a few moments, envision the future, or develop a forward-directed philosophy to help their systems. In all these ways, leaders are removed from access to the second Element of Success.

## Moving through Resistance to Renewal

Leadership is as much an art as a science. This may be the most true when executives are charged with bringing their organizations through a difficult transition period. The art of leadership lies in knowing when (and whether) a paradigm readiness exists in your system; that is, when your coworkers or community members are also arriving at the conclusion that a particular way of working together is no longer productive and must change.

You will move through organizational transitions most easily if you seek the involvement of everyone and take care to not make people feel that what they did in the past was wrong or wasted effort. This approach will reduce foot dragging and subtle sabotage. Resistance to change is natural. Our old habits, opinions, and fear of the unknown are often deeply rooted. (Many psychologists say that any significant change, any major letting go, is experienced as if it were a "little death.")

According to author Marvin Weisbord, leaders need to help their corporations go through four phases when letting go of the past and moving into the future. These phases are cyclical. They are *contentment, denial, confusion,* and *renewal.* Little change is possible during either *contentment* or *denial.* In the *confusion* phase there is anxiety, a "blocked excitement" that signifies a readiness to learn. Weisbord advises that "the seeds of success are sown in confusion and sprout in renewal."[13]

A good leader keeps the best of the old knowledge as a benchmark for the new. We do not have to abandon the ideas of the past while we are growing into the future. After all, these concepts and ways of working were successful in getting us to this point. To ignore the past (or colleagues with "old" ideas or a department with a different point of view) is folly. It can result in dilettantism, when leaders move from one theory of management to the next. This sends confusing messages throughout the system and prevents the integration of new learning. It also can surface as poor knowledge management: not storing, transferring, or passing on information to colleagues and the next generation of leaders and workers, who will therefore have to reinvent the wheel. In such cases, we lose the advantage of standing on the shoulders of those who've come before us, and a wealth of knowledge is lost.

# ORGANIZATIONS

◆

## Creating a Bright Future for Your Workplace

The second Element of Success is critical to the development of *learning organizations*— systems that know how to learn from experience and adapt successfully to change. Indeed, a learning organization sees itself as a *whole system* in which a shift in one part will create motion (intended or not) elsewhere. The model of the Elemental Circle is a comprehensive systemic template that can greatly support the development of more intelligent workplaces.

### Learning Organizations

A learning organization can be recognized, in part, by the fact that it rewards new ideas, constantly trains and retrains staff, and allows its people sufficient time to plan and reflect. This creates a dynamic, highly responsive action-learning environment in which thinking, action, reflection, and implementation are integrated. In this way the whole system is able to "think about itself" while simultaneously doing its work in the world. Its assumptions and paradigms can be tested, new inventions born, adaptations quickly made—all of which goes a long way toward increasing shared intelligence and ensuring a bright future for your business.

The great enemy of organizational learning (actually, of any kind of learning) is fear. Fear of making a mistake. Fear of being punished for making that mistake. Fear of authority. Fear of looking ignorant in front of colleagues. Fear of admitting we don't know something. Fear that if we share information we will lose power. Fear that if we tell others our ideas they will laugh at us. All these fears conspire to keep us constricted within our current limitations. Over time, these fears build up until they calcify into the solid, impenetrable wall that separates people in an organization, preventing them from learning, adapting, and succeeding together. Fear not only cuts us off from each other, it also detaches our thinking from our Essence, clouds our vision, and draws the worst possible future right to us. As W. Edwards Deming said, "The economic loss from fear is appalling."[14]

Another way a corporation learns is by the creation of knowledge and then the careful stewardship of that new information and understanding. The burgeoning field of knowledge management supports the development of learning organizations by creating infrastructures that store and transfer information so that other

## The Air Element Is Strong and Healthy in Your Organization When:

- Your organization has a strong unifying vision toward which it is moving and that guides its daily activities

- There is an explicit vision statement that accurately reflects people's shared ideas (hopes and fears) for the future of the organization

- Leaders and workers feel optimistic about the corporation's future—and their futures within it

- The organization is creative and innovative; new knowledge is constantly being generated

- There is a free flow of ideas, and people are "tuned in" to new ideas or possibilities

- Rewards are built into the system for the generation and implementation of new ideas

- New knowledge is managed well, i.e., transferred to those who need it to increase shared learning and minimize wasted time

- The work environment is cheerful; people are good humored and enjoy their work; there is a fair amount of laughter

- The organization encourages and supports learning; it trains its people and allows them time for thinking, planning, and reflection

- The system is highly adaptive; it regularly learns from its experience and changes accordingly

- Leaders inspire people to do their very best

- There is a general paradigm-vigilance; people at all levels stay alert for new ideas that could improve the likelihood of the business's success

- You are on the cutting edge in your industry

- Most workers and leaders have positive attitudes that are supportive of the organization and each other's work

people within the system are able to pass on vital data and insights that will make one anothers' jobs easier. Clearly, this saves time, money, and energy.

You can increase your own and your workplace's intelligence by making certain that the information you have is appropriately disseminated. In this way, other people in your organization will learn what they need to know so they can work optimally. By freely sharing your expertise and experience, you can serve as a model for how the system's "mind" is supposed to work. And, if you are a designated leader in the organization, you can expand its collective mind by soliciting everyone's participation in idea generation and paradigm-vigilance.

## Creating an Organization's Vision: A Field of Dreams

Most companies have a vision statement. Very few of them are effective. To make an organization's vision useful, we first need to think about the reason for having one. A corporate vision has been described in many ways, including:

- a constant beacon, like the North Star, that helps us navigate through darkness;[15]

- a declaration that "forces us to take a stand for a preferred future" and "channels our deepest values into the workplace";[16]

- not a destination, but rather an already existing field permeating organizational space, a field of ideas, a force of unseen connections that influences employees' behavior.[17]

Whether we consider an organization's vision to be a destination, a declaration of a preferred future, or an already unified field of dreams and ideas, it must inspire, uplift, and align people so they act in a congruent fashion. Creating a shared vision is a way of ensuring that the organization's Essence will be brought forward into the future. It also illuminates the disparity between "what is" and "what can be," thereby creating a positive tension that motivates individuals to act as one mind in closing the gap between the system's current state and its preferred future. It casts a bright light on our shared dreams and values. It also brings our shared fears into the light of day, so we can see obstacles are now in our way. The process of visioning forces us to find our collective voice and speak out loud about what we're really thinking. In an organization, vision is like the sun that rises in the east. It is an expression of our hope—and it simultaneously gives us hope by making us cast our vote for a brighter future of our own design.

*When John F. Kennedy launched the American space program, he captured the American imagination. The workers directly involved with that NASA effort report it as the best working experience of their lives. People gave much more of themselves than they thought possible. Indeed, NASA's clear vision of putting a man on the moon served to create shared dream among its workforce.*

*One journalist reported that he was visiting the NASA headquarters near Baltimore just before the successful launch. There, late one night, he passed a cleaning woman who was scrubbing a hallway floor. He asked her what her job was, wondering what her daily responsibilities entailed. She surprised him by answering proudly, "I'm helping to put a man on the moon."*

## Writing an Organizational Vision Statement

Having a clearly stated, collectively crafted vision statement breathes life into an organization because it helps people become "of one mind" about things. A corporate vision statement can be very simple, just a sentence or two. Begin the visioning process by having everyone review your company's list of core values and its identity statement. With that as your touchstone, you can proceed to build the next phase of your bridge to the future.

Next, envision what your workplace would look like if it functioned in a way that reflected those core values and was true to its identity. This vision is your ideal, your picture of what is "perfect." (This is not some expert's idea of a perfect system. It can be whatever you and your colleagues wish it to be.)

---

### Your Organization's Vision

Does your workplace already have a vision statement? If so, write it below. If not, or if it does not embody the best qualities of the second Element of Success, you can use the space below to write a sentence or two that describes your vision for your business. You can also use this process to help shape the future for your department, work team, or community group.

1. **Review your organization's core identity** and list of core values (from chapter one).

2. **Note the organization's major hopes and positive beliefs.** Imagine what your workplace would look like if it reflected its stated identity and values, if it was everything you hoped for. This is an ideal. It doesn't have to be at all real. You're on the right track when you're coming up with ideas that are inspiring and uplifting. Write some notes below or on a separate sheet of paper.

---

**3. Identify the fears and the obstacles** you believe are in the way of your organization's attaining this state. Pay attention to the discouragement and complaints you've regularly heard. Make notes.

**4. Note the difference between #2 and #3**—the system's hopes versus its fears. Your workplace is currently creating its future with its dominant thoughts. Discuss with others the future you want to create together.

**5. Return to Step #2** and refine your organization's vision in any way you choose. Now sit quietly. Think about this future until you can *feel* it and *see* it and *experience* it as if it was already real, as if you were already there in your new workplace. Activate your right brain and access your full intelligence by using a separate sheet of paper to *draw* your vision for your organization. If you are visioning with others, have papers, crayons, paints, or other materials ready so that members of your work team can create their own visions of the future. You know you've got it when you feel uplifted, inspired, hopeful, happy. Let go and have some fun with this process. If you find that you or your work group are getting serious, you're going in the wrong direction. The purpose of the Air element is to lift you up to new heights. Don't worry. You'll get to hammering out the details and making this "real" at a later stage in the Elements of Success.

**6. When everyone is done,** have them "show and tell" their visions to the rest of the group. This is usually an exhilarating experience.

**7. Now from this experience** write your (brief, easy-to-remember) corporate vision statement in the space below. Its purpose is to serve as a beacon of light that leads you and your coworkers into an ideal future.

Do whatever you can to keep your organization's vision firmly in mind. Revisiting your corporate vision on a regular basis will help you coordinate your system's day-to-day behavior and keep it moving in the right direction, thereby building that bridge to the future you so clearly see. In this way, everyone involved can start to experience this future as you all are being drawn closer and closer to it.

In order to have the full mind of the organization reflected and aligned, it is preferable to have everyone in the system participate in this visioning process. In large organizations, this can be done by using the Elements of Success process throughout the organization. Another a good way to accomplish this in a short period of time is to have a "future-search conference" or an "open space" meeting where people from all parts of the corporation, and perhaps important customers and stakeholders, are brought together in one place so that the organization can think out loud about itself and its future. An extraordinary number of ideas are generated quickly, people are galvanized so that the change process can be jump-started, and the business gets everyone fully on board to move into into its chosen future.

Management consultant Peter Block provides the following formula for writing "visions of greatness": 1) Forget about being number one; 2) Don't be practical; 3) Begin with your customers; 4) You can't treat your customers any better than you treat each other; and 5) If your vision statement sounds like motherhood and apple pie and is somewhat embarrassing, you are on the right track.[18]

The best organizational vision statements I've ever seen clearly stated the ideal and were uplifting, inspiring, compellingly stated—and mercifully brief. Every worker in the system could repeat this succinct phrase. A corporate vision is often a lofty ideal that you may not reach in the near future, and it is not easily measurable. (Leave that to the mission—and its goals—in the third Element of Success.) You can also do a vision statement for your department, church group, school board, quality team, or community arts council. All these would benefit from the shining "beacon" that a vision statement can provide the group.

## An Integrity Check for the Air Element

Now compare your organization's vision with the personal vision statement you wrote earlier in this chapter. Ask yourself: Are these two visions compatible? Can you fulfill your personal vision within the context of your workplace's vision? Write your thoughts here.

Another excellent way for people to envision the ideal workplace is to fantasize what it would be like if they woke up, Rip Van Winkle–style, ten years from now. My experience is that this allows the organization's current hopes and dreams to surface more easily. Indeed, I have found this exercise to be a humorous, nonthreatening, way to approach the visioning process. (This is especially true for individuals who've not previously participated in a visioning exercise.) Sometimes workers report to me that it hurts too much to hope. They feel that the gap between what is and what could be is too large and therefore too painful for them to examine. The Rip Van Winkle guided fantasy is an easy way for many people to let go of their current limitations, lighten up, and let their creativity soar.

Another exercise I've found useful is to have participants list the qualities of their "ideal" organization. Then I proceed to give them a firsthand classroom experience of developing such a working environment, while simultaneously teaching them some of the tools they will need to transform their own systems. It has been delightful to watch participants in the process of creating ideal work environments. As what is possible dawns on them, their faces light up, their eyes shine, their interactions become less guarded. They laugh, play, and learn together.

The voicing of an ideal, then experiencing it (even in small degrees), opens our eyes to the way workplaces can be. As our worldviews expand to include more and more possibilities, our visions for ourselves and for our organizations will expand significantly.

One caution here: When you design a corporate vision, it is important to envision the ideal *without identifying with it* (that is, don't confuse the first two Elements of Success). The more we feel compelled or under pressure to achieve an ideal, the more likely we are to delude ourselves (and others) and to sacrifice anything to that ideal. History is littered with examples of theoretically perfect visions that caused terrible side effects the architects of change did not anticipate. This "law of unintended consequences" is why it's so important to stay vigilant and observe the results of our actions. When we are moving toward our vision, we need to maintain a bifocal perspective; that is, we need to keep our eyes on the ideal, while continually scanning the environment for ripple effects and for new information about better ways of doing things. This dual perspective will guarantee your company a very bright future, indeed.

One of the reasons I have so much hope for the future of the workplace is my observation that people learn very quickly. Indeed, once people have experienced a more ideal business environment, they find it difficult to settle for less and often move on to help create new systems that meet or exceed their revised standards of what is possible.

## Air in Action MIT's Media Laboratory

*In the middle of the Massachusetts Institute of Technology's sprawling campus, there is a four-story, white-tiled, modernistic building designed by the famous architect I. M. Pei. It houses one of the most innovative—and well-funded—think tanks in the world. Stepping off the elevator into the hallways of this bustling center is a bit like walking into the next century. The Media Lab's "mind" consists of distinguished scholars, highly innovative and curious professionals, and brilliant graduate students who play/work day and night. At the time of this writing, there were 259 separate research projects proceeding in the laboratory.*

*The lab's experiments may seem at first blush to be a bit esoteric, but many have had practical applications. For instance, the workers here have invented computer graphic innovations for motion pictures and television; discovered a way to use holography to show how radiation treatment of a brain tumor will affect the rest of the brain; gained remarkable insights into the ways we learn; developed high-resolution satellite weather mapping and defense monitoring; and found a way to change cartoon characters from flat drawings into multidimensional characters. And these are just a few examples.*

*The Media Lab has been called a Disneyland of multimedia. Indeed, it felt a bit like being at a carnival, with the sound of laughter and blaring radios floating from work areas into the hallway.*

*I was told by my guide that representatives from corporations all over the world tour here. In fact, while I was visiting a small group of foreign businessmen passed my guide and me, then went into a conference room to discuss possible cooperative ventures with the lab. Interestingly, although business people come to the Media Lab for its innovative technology, many leave wondering out loud how they can duplicate its exciting "spirit" and creativity in their own work environments.*

*The Media Lab has a long-standing tradition of freely offering its ideas and the results of its experiments to anyone who can use them. Consequently, it has been very successful in attracting large sums of money from private donors to fund its experimentation. According to my next-door neighbor, David Boor, a visiting scientist at the lab, 170 companies invest in the Media Lab's research. These include Fortune 100 giants, major universities, the U.S. Army, technology industry leaders, and toy companies. Another friend, Bradley Horowitz, who worked at the lab while a doctoral candidate, reports that a dean once said to him in a pique, "I just can't understand why you get so much money. All you ever do over there is play!"*

# WORLD

◆

## When There Is No Vision, the People Perish

In *New World, New Mind,* Robert Ornstein and Paul Ehrlich argue that "Our species is now at its most important turning point since the Agricultural Revolution. For the first time humanity has the knowledge to destroy itself quickly, and for the first time humanity also has the knowledge to take its own evolution into its hands and change now, change the way people comprehend and think."[19]

We now have a better understanding of the power of our minds to control our individual and shared destinies. Our collective hopes and fears have created the world we live in today, and continue to create the world we will live in tomorrow. One way that we can make our future more Shakespearean and less Orwellian is to stay mentally alert; that is, to watch what we feed our minds as part of our daily fare. As Ornstein and Ehrlich argue, we need to replace our *old minds* (that respond to abrupt physical changes) with *new minds* (that can perceive the slow stimuli now threatening to upset our balance and well-being). They add that, "the time has come to take our own evolution into our hands and create a *new* evolutionary process, a process of conscious evolution."[20]

*Any sufficiently advanced technology is indistinguishable from magic.*
—Arthur C. Clarke

We also can help create a better future by developing the magnificent instrument of our minds right now. We need to critically evaluate what is real and what is not. Unfortunately, our perceptions are often shaped by others. For example, American children may see tens of thousands of murders on TV while growing up. Because their minds absorb this stimuli in an undifferentiated fashion—*and they experience it as if it were real*—they cannot help but come to the conclusion that the world is a very dangerous place indeed. This establishes a paradigm that further filters the information they receive, causing them to scan continually for potential attack. In summary, this bombardment of biased information sets up a vicious cycle of fear, and this, in turn, creates more fear. We need to teach our children (and ourselves) how to evaluate the "realities" that are prepackaged for us.

The evening news is another good example of how information can be biased in a way that does not help us create a collective future built on hope or ideals. Whenever there's a fire, armed robbery, kidnapping, rape, or murder in the area, or a massacre in another corner of the world, these events headline the news. Our minds then process this information and create subtle, undifferentiated impressions that make us feel as if we were under the very same threat! I think that the Dalai Lama's comment on this phenomenon cuts to the chase. He states that it is the nature of human beings to be gentle and compassionate. In support of his argument, he points to news coverage. Indeed, he says, the reason all these sensational acts of violence lead the news is precisely because *they* are the aberrations. The millions of kind acts that occurred that very same day are taken for granted, he says, because compassion and love are the true nature of humanity.

We now know a great deal more about how we learn. This gives us a newfound ability to *choose to learn in ways that increase the ability of our species to adapt and survive*. More and more of us are coming to understand that indeed the world is as we think it is and that our future is as we hope or fear it will be. This being the case, we can take our own, and our world's, destiny into our own hands and create a glorious future.

To do our part, you and I need to carefully choose the beliefs and understandings for projection into the future. We also must continually monitor and eliminate our negative self-programming. By becoming more aware of what we feed our minds, we can make better choices about how to nurture this amazing faculty. And when we master our own minds, we will be in a position to teach future generations how to do the same.

In the Bible it says, "When there is no vision, the people perish" (Prov. 12:18). As we move into our collective future, we need to assume clear-sighted, inspiring leadership in every aspect of our lives, relationships, and work. This will help us articulate and sustain a compelling vision of the best possible future for ourselves and our children. I encourage you to take up leadership wherever you are so that together we can move confidently out of the old world and into this newly emerging world.

Truly, you and I will suffer or thrive according to our shared perceptions of today and our shared visions of tomorrow.

◆

# 3

# ACTING ON YOUR PASSION

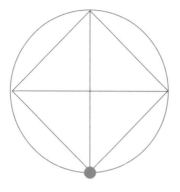

## The Primal Furnace

*In the Beginning there was nothing, neither time nor space, neither stars nor planets, neither rocks nor plants, neither animals nor human beings. Everything came out of the void. It all began with space and time and a very hot plasma composed of quarks, electrons, and other particles. . . .*

*Our starting point is the primal explosion, the zero point of our time scale, when the prevailing temperatures were infinite. . . . Basically, the early universe was a rather simple object, whose condition essentially can be summed up by a single parameter: temperature. . . .*

*In the first fraction of a second after the Big Bang, the temperature of the universe exceeded $10^{32}$ degrees. In the next fraction of a second, matter was produced from this primal stew. It consisted of "all sorts of particles, including quarks, electrons, neutrinos, photons, gluons, X particles, and their corresponding antiparticles." The temperature fell precipitously. The X particles decayed and more quarks than antiquarks were left behind in the hot plasma.*

*As this primal furnace cooled off, "protons, neutrons, atomic particles, atoms, stars, galaxies, and planets formed [from the excess quarks]. Finally life sprang up in many solar systems of the universe—in one case, on a planet of a most ordinary star situated on a spiral arm of a galaxy at the rim of a large cluster of galaxies. There, in the course of four billion years, plants and animals, and eventually human beings, developed out of the simplest organisms."[1]*

—The creation story of science

# Fire in the Belly

The third Element of Success (Fire) provides the drive and passion you need to sustain your Balancing Act so that you can create the life, relationships, and work you most desire. It gives you extraordinary power by taking the raw energy contained in your values (Essence) and ideas (Air), and then transforming them into forward-directed, focused action. Human beings ranging from ancient cave dwellers (who used Fire for cooking and making tools) to modern scientists (who harnessed electricity and split the atom) have employed this alchemical element to transform other kinds of raw natural power into more easily used energy.

Fire symbolizes your unique gifts, your particular piece of the puzzle, your contribution to the Whole. It propels you to find your bliss and then act on it. Sages throughout human history have likened our lives to a "hero's journey." The journey you need to take, they say, is to discover your purpose in life, your mission, what you are here to do—and then act on what you discover. And, they add, if you do not, both you and the world will suffer for its lack.

Even if what you have to offer is small in your own eyes, it is significant in the scheme of things because, truly, no one else can do it. I repeat, for whatever reasons—talent, timing, associates, friends geography, knowledge, or understanding— no one else can make your special contribution. And chaos theorists would agree that everything you or I do has both seen and unseen ripple effects, contributing to a chain of events beyond our observation or comprehension.

I know that it is difficult for many people to believe that what they do really matters that much. And yet, something in all of us burns to "make a difference." This is the *fire in the belly* that fuels us. The third Element of Success gives you and me the drive we need to create lives full of passion, zest, and pizzazz. Lives that are less gray and more colorful—lives that can make a real difference for ourselves, our loved ones, our communities, our workplaces, and the world.

Unfortunately, our personal lives sometimes seem too small for us, our relationships unfulfilling, our work not a particularly good "fit" for our talents and abilities. So what can you do if any of these things is true for you? How do you discover your gifts? How do you find out what you are to contribute to the world? This third point of reference in the Elemental Circle can provide you with these answers.

The element of Fire corresponds to the power of your *will*. You need a strong personal will, with its accompanying drive, passion, and commitment, to be successful in your Balancing Act. It is your will that marks you as a self-starter. Fire sustains you with discipline and a can-do attitude. It also gives you pride in whatever you accomplish, a feeling of commitment in your relationships, and a sense of ownership in your work.

If you do not have enough of this third Element of Success, you will have a difficult time getting things done. You may avoid committing to your relationships or your work. You will tend to avoid conflict and feel somewhat passive and lackluster. It may be hard for you to get out of bed in the morning, because there's nothing really exciting that lies ahead of you during the day. You also may find yourself spending an inordinate amount of time doing things (such as watching TV, hanging out, surfing the Net, or reading the paper) that leave you feeling vaguely unsatisfied, as if you're just "killing" time. As a result, you sometimes wonder if life is passing you by.

Conversely, if you have too much Fire it may make you overly active, hyperbusy. Other people are likely to find your behavior aggressive. Fire then becomes a consuming passion that can rage out of control. However, by staying mindful of the other points of reference in the Elemental Circle, you can channel even a very strong Fire in beneficial directions. If your personal will is aligned with the other Elements of Success you really can't go far wrong. And if you have the opportunity to align your will in a common purpose with other like-minded individuals, you can accomplish just about anything together.

# PERSONAL LIFE

◆

## Discovering Your Personal Mission

Your will is an internal fire that supplies you with the motivation to take action. That drive can show up as excitement, commitment, enthusiasm, boundless energy, or even anger about some "wrong" that needs to be "righted." The Fire element yearns to have something to burn for, some purpose that will fuel and sustain you through all your activity. And, much as your body needs good food to convert to internal fuel, any activity that is not supportive of your personal mission or congruent with your values and vision will be like junk food—bereft of nutrients.

### Harnessing the Will of Fire

Agni was the Vedic god of fire who guarded hearths and received sacrifices, "which he carried in his mouth of flame to the gods."[2] Agni is referred to in the Ayurvedic tradition of healing as "the fire in the stomach" that cooks the food we eat so that it can be digested and used by the whole body. Similarly, the Fire element acts to "digest" (i.e., to alchemically transform) all your actions into something meaningful for your whole life. A strong, healthy internal fire can change even the most menial, mundane task into a valuable learning experience. Conversely, all action loses its potential for

**INNER TRADITIONS** • **BEAR & CO.** • **HEALING ARTS PRESS** • **DESTINY BOOKS** • **Park Street Press** • **BINDU BOOKS** • **BEAR CUB BOOKS**

Please send us this card to receive our latest catalog.

☐ Check here if you would like to receive our catalog via e-mail.

E-mail address _____

Name _____ Company _____

Address _____ Phone _____

City _____ State ___ Zip ___ Country _____

Order at 1-800-246-8648 • Fax (802) 767-3726

E-mail: orders@InnerTraditions.com • Web site: www.InnerTraditions.com

Inner Traditions • Bear & Company
P.O. Box 388
Rochester, VT 05767-0388
U.S.A.

## You Have a Strong and Healthy Fire Element When You:

- Are fully committed to the activities you undertake; they have meaning and value for you

- Believe that your life and work are moving in a direction you want

- Have plenty of energy to do the things you want to do

- Are relatively consistent in action and constant in productivity

- Work hard and enjoy your job but are not a workaholic (i.e., you have a full life)

- Have a clear purpose, a personal mission, and a burning desire to make something of yourself

- Move easily from an idea or plan to acting on it with determination and confidence

- Are able to focus on whatever you're doing at a given moment

- Feel strongly, even passionately, about certain things or people

- Neither shrink from conflict nor are combative

- Have a strong will that is aligned with other people of similar convictions

- Are a "self-starter"—self-disciplined, focused, productive, determined, and committed to a course of action

- Take pride in who you are and what you've accomplished

good if this third Element of Success is weak. When Fire is not directed toward some focused end, it can:

- burn you up in meaningless activity ("signifying nothing");

- burn you up with frustration (because you are not moving toward your goals);

- burn others up (because they get in your way); or

- dissipate unused (which will leave you feeling frustrated and exhausted, because an untended fire slowly dies out).

## When You Commit to Something

Commitment and discipline are the keys to keeping your internal fire alive. This is why sages have said, *When you commit to something, the gods line up behind you.*

Discipline is the constant companion, the daily manifestation, of commitment. Discipline shows up in your self-effort and self-control. It contains the thousand small actions that move you from point A to point B. Indeed, you need ongoing discipline to accomplish anything worthwhile: to eat properly, to see a project through to completion, or to control your temper when someone is rude to you. Commitment is how you channel the element of Fire so that you can make steady progress toward your goals and ensure that your actions bear fruit.

Commitment and discipline are reinforced when you have a clear sense of personal mission. A personal mission is exciting enough to make you want to leap out of bed in the morning (okay—to make you want to roll out of bed when the alarm goes off). It also must make good use of your special talents and gifts, so that you feel "fired up" about contributing these pieces of the puzzle to the world.

## Discovering Your Gifts and Crafting a Personal Mission Statement

Before trying to craft a personal mission statement, it's a good idea to articulate your special "gifts." To help you find these, Cheryl Gilman, author of *Doing Work You Love*, recommends that you reflect upon what you enjoyed doing as a child. Research indicates that our brains are hardwired at birth with what we have to offer the world. The result is that although we may be quite competent doing other things, we will always feel vaguely dissatisfied unless we are making use of our special gifts in some part of our lives. Your gifts are likely to be something you did effortlessly as a child or teenager and that you might dismiss as being something "anyone" can do.

For example, I always believed that anyone could perform music, if they just put their minds to it. This is because music—singing, playing, and composing—was easy for me, and it gave me so much joy. Then I read Gilman's book and reconsidered my assumptions. My parents tell the story that when I was only two years old, I toddled over to the crib where my just-born sister, Irene, was crying. In an apparent effort to soothe her, I sang in my little-child voice the same lullaby I'd heard my Mom and Dad sing to her: "Goodnight, Irene, goodnight." They were stunned.

Clearly, I was hardwired to make music. That is also borne out by the fact that I am miserable when music is not significantly in my life. During these times, I wind up feeling as if there is a hole inside me so large that the wind could blow through it.

Bringing your gifts out into the world is vital to your Balancing Act. This is probably why Buddha is reported to have said that the real work for each of us is to *discover our work and then with all our heart to give ourselves to it!*

## Finding Your Gifts

**1. What did you most enjoy doing as a child?** If you can't remember, ask your parents, siblings, or childhood friends. What activities give you the most joy and satisfaction now? These may be related to your special gifts. What do you think you have to offer the world? (Make notes below.)

**2. One way to gain insights into your gifts** is to write twenty stories about the accomplishments of which you're most proud. These can be from any part of your life. Pay particular attention to patterns that emerge. (Note: Write these stories on separate paper. You can make them a mere sentence, a full paragraph, or even pages long.)

Having a list of your special talents will support you in writing a personal mission statement. A mission makes whatever you do more effective, because your actions are consistent, your efforts aligned. This focus reduces false starts, tangents, and wasted time. For all these reasons, you will find it very helpful to write down your mission (and then the goals that support the accomplishment of that mission).

Your mission is something you feel passionate about. A personal mission statement is a way to declare to yourself exactly what you intend to do; i.e., what you are going to accomplish, how, and by when. It keeps the Fire element inside you stoked. Your mission statement will help you concentrate on one aspect of your vision in order to bring it into reality *within a specified time period*. The mission, in contrast to an ideal, lofty vision, is something that is doable. It is measurable and clear—you will know whether or not you've accomplished it. It is a declaration of your intention, something you commit to without equivocation.

Therefore, if your vision is of a peaceful world where disease and hunger are completely eradicated, your own personal mission could read something like this: "My personal mission is to work in the field of international health to alleviate the suffering of others." You can then draw up specific goals and timelines that are like subsets of the mission and support its accomplishment. For example: "Next year I will travel abroad at least two times to participate in eye camps in third world countries" or "I will complete my application to medical school by next month."

And one more thing: Remember to look at the *whole* of your life when crafting a personal mission statement. People often create significant imbalance when they direct the Fire element to just one part of their lives. You will find that when you align this third Element of Success with the others, you'll have plenty of energy to sustain the balance you seek in your life, relationships, and work.

## Your Personal Mission Statement

**1. Note a key aspect of your life for which you'd like to write a mission statement.** This should be something you feel passionate about, something that is very important to you and that you have a strong desire to accomplish.

**2. Review your core values and identity statements (chapter one) and your personal vision statement (chapter two)** so that your mission will be congruent with these other points of reference. Also review the gifts you listed on the previous page.

**3. With these first two Elements of Success and your personal gifts** in mind, draft a one- or two-sentence statement that reflects your mission for this aspect of your life. For example, if a significant part of your identity is connected to being a "loving mother," and your vision is of a perfectly happy home, your personal mission may be "to raise two healthy, happy children who treat themselves, their parents, and other people with respect and kindness." (You may need separate statements for different parts of your life. If so, make certain each statement is congruent with the others.) Remember that a mission statement is doable and measurable and has a specific time line.

**4. In support of your personal mission,** note a few goals that will facilitate its accomplishment, a reasonable time frame for getting these done, and some ways to monitor whether you're staying on track. (To continue with the prior example, one of your immediate goals may be to "establish ground rules by next week for how to settle the children's arguments more fairly.")

A clear sense of mission can help you keep the fire burning inside, even when work, relationships, or other life circumstances are discouraging. A personal mission "lights a fire" under you. If you feel that your internal fire is low, it's probably time to do something about it. Don't let life pass you by! Many people spend their time wishing for a better job, a nicer house, a more supportive community, or a perfect mate. But because they haven't sufficiently engaged the help of this third Element of Success, they don't have the drive they need to change their circumstances. When you claim your personal power, a great deal can change in your life.

Your internal yearning gives you the energy necessary to attain your desires—to start your own business; to raise healthy, happy children; to save lives with your surgical skills; to make a difference in your community; or to design a first-class product. Fire is what propels you to get from here to there, no matter what obstacles are in your path. A clear personal mission focuses the Fire element in a direction that is positive for you and others. Undirected, your desires work at cross-purposes with your fears, causing agitation and distress to build up inside you, much as steam builds up in a pressure cooker.

Obviously, stress is not all bad. Without some stress, you wouldn't have the energy to get your work done. But too much stress can burn you up. An excessive Fire element (i.e., one that is out of balance with the other Elements of Success) can cause sleeplessness, worry, compulsive activity, aggressiveness, angry outbursts, and a host of physical problems.

Another caution: Your mission is not "you." This may seem too obvious to even mention, but I've noticed that a lot of people confuse their personal mission (Fire) with their personal identity (Essence). Indeed, this is such a common cause of imbalance these days that it has given rise to a frequently repeated put-down: "Get a life."

The one-pointedness of a mission, if not held in check by the other points of reference in the Elemental Circle, can turn into an obsession. Sometimes we become so focused on achieving our goals that nothing else matters. We may say that another part of our life is important to us, but our behavior and time allotment belies this claim. As a result, we wind up missing out on precious time with family and friends or abandoning cherished projects. Indeed, such separation and alienation (from loved ones, other parts of our lives, and our own Core) is very similar to the way philosophers have described the experience of hellfire.

## Exercises to Strengthen and Direct the Fire Element

1. **Physical exercise** of all kinds increases internal fire and will by getting the blood moving. Aerobic and anaerobic exercises, for example, have been found to assist in digestion, decrease depression, and increase energy and strength. And, researchers now say that daily fresh-air, low-tech walking is actually one of the best possible exercises.

2. **Candle contemplation.** Before going into a personal conversation or a business meeting for which you need great resolve, you may wish to sit in front of a burning fireplace or light a candle. Take that image with you as a symbol of your fiery commitment to your mission.

3. **Burn the barriers.** You can also dedicate a few moments to imagining the element of Fire burning up barriers, both internal and external, that stand in the way of accomplishing your personal mission.

4. **Have your own fire ceremony.** Many cultures have fire ceremonies of purification. In this adaptation, you can create a fire in which you burn all your destructive habits and tendencies. You could replicate this ancient ritual by writing down self-destructive thoughts on a sheet of paper, tossing them into a fireplace, and "letting go" of them mentally and emotionally as you watch the paper go up in flames.

5. **The ax exercise** is a great release for anger or fear. Stand with your feet firmly on the ground, your legs slightly apart, your body in good balance. Bend over to pick up an imaginary heavy ax. Get a firm grip on it, then slowly lift it above your head with both hands. As if to split a piece of wood for a fireplace, swing the ax down to the ground, moving your full spine from the tailbone (take great care not to strain your back with this exercise). If you are

far away from others (or if you have *really* tolerant people about you), you can let out a loud yell with this swinging movement. This exercise is designed to release the pent-up toxic residue of anger and fear, thereby reducing the likelihood that you will act inappropriately during any tense situations.

**6. Drumming.** An ancient technique for fanning your internal Fire is to play the drums. If you lack the actual instrument, you can "drum" your belly or chest instead, making loud Tarzan-like sounds. (This can be a lot of fun. Again, be respectful of others around you so that you don't disturb them—and so they don't come after you with a net.)

**7. Turn off the TV.** One of the great energy drains the world over is watching TV. We spend countless hours here (studies indicate up to dozens of hours per week in America).[3] The Barbara Bush Foundation for Family Literacy discovered that although 27 percent of all American adults are functionally illiterate, fewer than 1 percent of homeowners lack a TV set![4] Sitting in front of the TV actually exhausts already-tired individuals. This is primarily due to overstimulation of the eyes and the disruption of sleeping patterns. Flopping on the couch after work does nothing to accomplish your personal mission and only extinguishes your internal fire. TV is a "distillation" of real life, a shadow substitute for it. Unfortunately, it is a widespread intoxicant of choice, one that shapes our behavior and expectations and isolates us within our communities.

## Purification and Prioritization

As you increase your internal Fire, you will find that it is a great purifier. This third Element of Success burns away whatever is no longer vital in your life. Fire destroys your negativity and illusions. Your mission, commitment, and discipline will help you with this "weeding-out" process by prioritizing your time and giving you the criteria you need to make other tough decisions. Fire clears up your thinking and propels your actions. It is so strong that even metal bends to its will.

The Fire element shows us not only our gifts, but also our limitations. It forces us to choose carefully how we allocate our time and resources so that we waste neither. Fire forces us to make choices about what (and who) is most important to us. Although this process of letting go may be painful, it eventually results in clarity, fulfillment, and joy.

*In the now-classic movie* City Slickers, *Mitch Robbins, (the character played by Billy Crystal) has lost all his joy in life. At the prodding of his friends and concerned wife (who admonishes him to "find the smile" he's lost), Mitch goes off to a cowboy ranch for a vacation. There he is instructed by the trail boss of the cattle drive in the Secret of Life. It is "One Thing," the boss says. The One Thing, it turns out, is different for each of the newly initiated cowboys (and, by inference, for each one of us).*

*Mitch's awakening begins when his heart opens as he helps birth Norman (a calf), whom he also nurses, saves from drowning, and eventually takes home with him. As the story unfolds, the city slickers wind up having to bring the cattle herd home for real when the trail boss dies suddenly and the hired hands run off. In deciding to complete their journey (by bringing the herd home so that the cattle wouldn't die in the wilds), the city slickers become real-life heroes. Each experiences the joy of first finding, then focusing on and committing to, "one thing"—his own personal mission.*

I actually learned this same lesson from Sharon Voss, a Minnesota friend and colleague from my political organizing days. I will never forget Sharon's admonition to a group of us who had just finished writing a very long list of what we wanted to get done, ASAP. She urged us to choose "one thing" to accomplish that coming year. If we made that our mission and put our combined full force behind it, it had a much better chance of happening. Then, we could then move on to the next thing. Otherwise, she said, this time next year we would probably be looking back, wondering why we had so little to show for all our effort.

## Magicians' Tools and Techniques (Fire)

**Magic Shield.** A protection from distractions, difficulties, and harm, so that you can bring your gifts into the world. This is a powerful technique by which the Magician in you imagines a shield of any kind (the Elemental Circle, a brick wall, a body-length metal shield, a transparent breathing membrane that filters out negativity before it affects you). You can use the magic shield when you are around people who drain your energy; in conflict situations; and as a way to boost your confidence and reduce your own fear.

**Magic Sword.** A truth-telling technique that helps you cut through confusion, conflict, and difficulty or through layers of a problem until the root is exposed. The magic sword helps eliminate or stave off the *internal* enemies (fear, doubt, confusion, poor boundaries, low self-esteem) that sometimes hold you captive, and also the real-life external adversaries who confront you.

**Lightning Rod.** Ancient Magicians often served as lightning rods for their tribes, helping to safely channel Fire from heaven to earth. This tool can help you ignite the Fire element in yourself and others via empowerment and alignment.

**Golden Thread.** The purpose of this tool is focus, one-pointedness, prioritization, keeping you on track. It leads you out of the confusing labyrinth of day-to-day work and life. Your personal mission acts as a golden thread that weaves all your activities together into one seamless fabric.

**Naming (Fire).** Articulating your personal mission, goals, and strategies—where you want to go, by when, and the way to get from here to there.

**Book of Wisdom (Fire).** A tool used to write down your personal mission and the goals that will help you accomplish it—that is, exactly what you're going to do to make your dreams come true.

# RELATIONSHIPS

◆

## When Sparks Fly

The quality that most distinguishes romantic ties from other kinds of relationships is the element of Fire. If "sparks fly" between people, they say things like, "He's so hot." If not, they might say, "We're just friends." (As if a friend was not a priceless commodity!) And if a romance is ending, the partners are likely to feel that, "The fire we once had has died."

But the third Element of Success is not restricted to romance. You will notice that many other important relationships rely on the passion of Fire to first ignite, then continuously fuel them. These include political causes or religious alliances (in which Fire supports a shared mission), an intellectual attraction between academic colleagues, or a business partnership in which Fire is channeled into the development of an exciting product. These relationships can be as intense as any marriage. Here, the element of Fire provides the vitality that first draws you together. And as the initial fever transmutes over time into a steady heat, the third Element of Success will help you sustain the relationship and make you feel happy to be alive.

*You give me fever,*
*Fever when you hold me tight,*
*Fever in the morning,*
*Fever all through the night.*
*—John Davenport and*
*Eddie Cooley, "Fever"*

In relationships of any kind, the Fire that attracted you to each other needs to be tended by both parties, or else it will go out. It is

## Your Relationships Have a Strong and Healthy Fire Element When You:

- Have a strong mutual commitment to each other (or to a shared cause)
- Ignite energy, passion, and intensity when together (the reasons for this could be intellectual, emotional, sexual, political, or a shared goal)
- Are attracted to each other and want to spend time together
- Manage conflict well; i.e., you feel free to have disagreements, surface problems quickly, and "fight clean"
- Have compatible personalities
- Are relatively well matched in energy and activity level
- Appreciate each other's distinctions, differences, and unique qualities
- Recognize and support the special gifts and talents you each have
- Are happy to be together despite your differences and may even find these differences stimulating
- Feel energized when you spend time together
- Share power and decision making equally
- Are respectful of each other's personal, relationship, and professional boundaries; give each other the "space" you need and don't inappropriately step over lines
- Share many common interests
- Have personal missions and goals that are compatible
- Don't let either person dominate; have strong personal wills that are well matched
- Are independent people with distinct interests; are not "symbiotic," "merged," overly dependent, jealous, or possessive of each other

crucial that both you and your partner support the Fire element *in each other*. This is not always easy. Sometimes people close to you do not understand or appreciate your unique gifts and will actually discourage you from acting on your passion. Perhaps they don't want you to get hurt, or maybe they prefer to keep your attention focused on them. This is a significant danger to the relationship and to your personal Balancing Act because the Fire in you can go out if it is snuffed in this way. A good rule is not to take advice from anyone whose own Fire is weak in that particular area. For example, the best friend who has stayed in a job for reasons of security is not likely to encourage you to risk changing careers, no matter how right that would be for you.

No matter how much you love or admire someone, it is vital that both of you keep clear boundaries. This is a critical aspect of your Balancing Act. Somehow, a lot of us have gotten the idea (as expressed in our popular love songs, novels, and magazines) that the ideal relationship is one in which we merge with each other. We've become a bit too literal about "two becoming one." I think the mathematical equation in really good relationships is that the two remain two, while simultaneously becoming "more" when we are with each other than when we are alone. If the boundary of a cell is breached, the cell dies. If the protective boundary of our skin is cut, a resulting infection can kill us. And if we "lose ourselves" in each other, we really can lose ourselves. This is why the third Element of Success is so vital for shoring up our protective, life-enhancing emotional, physical, spiritual, and mental boundaries.

The Fire element reminds us that we are separate, distinct individuals. It shows us our differences, our unique and distinct qualities. Paradoxically, the qualities that distinguish you from someone else are often the very reasons you were drawn to each other in the first place. And after the "honeymoon" is over (the relationship is through its initial phase), these same differences can cause sparks to fly again whenever you disagree with each other.

## When Wills Collide: Managing Conflict in Relationships

When two people become angry with each other, the potential exists both for destruction and for positively redirecting this fiery energy. When you strike two stones together, you create sparks that can ignite either a raging forest fire or a controlled campfire. The question then is, how can you capture those sparks and use them for good?

There are five principal reasons for conflict: disagreement about information, strategy, goals, norms, or beliefs and values. According to the Thomas-Kilman model of conflict management, there are five possible ways for you to handle disputes when they arise.[5] Each method for managing conflict is appropriate in some situations, but not in others. Clearly, relying on any of these approaches exclusively will only create more problems for you.

The big secret in managing personal strife is to understand that *all conflicts start inside you*. Old legends of courageous knights and Magicians encode the secret that the monsters these heroes fought were actually inside them! There was no easy way out: these internal demons could not be killed, conquered, or escaped from. Instead, the hero had to transform them. This doesn't mean that there are no real dangers or bad guys out there. What it does mean is that because we help create our lives, the best way for us to reduce discord is to start with a candid assessment of ourselves before embarking on a crusade to change somebody else or save the world.

## Five Strategies for Managing Conflict

**Avoidance:** Not addressing the conflict by sidestepping the issue, postponing talking about it, or withdrawing from the interaction.
Q: If there's no apparent disagreement in your relationship, is it being avoided, deferred, or repressed? Is conflict smoldering just below the surface?

**Accommodation:** Neglecting your own concerns to satisfy someone else's. This ranges from selfless generosity to yielding to someone's demands out of fear.
Q: Does one person in your relationship usually defer to the other?

**Confrontation:** Standing up for your own rights, defending your side of an issue, or using your power and will to "win." Remember that anger may be an instinctual way of protecting yourself against real aggression.
Q: Does one person regularly confront the other, or do you both? Do these confrontations tend to clarify and reduce the problem or do they accelerate it?

**Compromise:** Finding a middle ground that partially satisfies both parties; splitting the difference. (Watch out. Sometimes with fifty-fifty solutions both people feel they've lost and are just waiting for the next go-around.)
Q: How easy is it for the two of you to compromise? Do both of you feel that the solutions you come to are "fair?"

**Collaboration:** Working in partnership to explore the reasons for the disagreement, learn from each other, and come to optimum solutions for both parties. This method usually helps you arrive at the most enduring solutions. (However, beware of collaborating with someone who has a hidden agenda. In World War II, the "collaborators" were the local officials who worked with the Nazis.)
Q: How well do you work together to come up with long-term solutions?

An example of how conflict can be transformed comes from aikido, a martial art that uses the force of the attacker to render a physical attack harmless to *both* parties. Below is a remarkable story of an aikido master who transformed conflicts that were much more difficult to resolve than any you or I are ever likely to encounter.

*Koichi Tohei was a young man who was put in command of a unit of Japanese troops in China during World War II. He determined that his primary responsibility was to bring the men in his care home safely. To accomplish this, he decided upon a very unorthodox approach: to bring into battle the essence of what he had learned as a student of aikido ("that we should have peaceful, loving attitudes toward all beings").*

*In his first battle, he centered himself in the way he had been taught, then stood up in the trenches, facing the enemy's bullets. From that extremely precarious position, he gave orders to his troops.*

*During the entire time Koichi Tohei was in China, none of his men were killed. Even though they were frequently fired upon, they themselves never injured an enemy. Tohei says, "When we did capture an enemy, instead of sending him back to our headquarters I would untie his hands at night and tell him to leave. We did not wish to harm him. There were times during the war when we would be moving along a road and the enemy would recognize us from a hill in the distance. Instead of firing at us, it was as if they were waving at us to go on in peace, which we did. . . . It may sound crazy to most people, but I never lost a man. It worked."[6]*

You too can transform conflict when you use the Elemental Circle to move from your Center to Fire and back, smoothly into and out of the fray. This is much like moving into the external turbulence of a hurricane, then back again into its calm center. Thomas Crum has adapted the aikido approach to improve personnel and work relationships. As he says in *The Magic of Conflict*: "The daily struggles and conflicts are still there. It is our relationship to them that can be totally different. Instead of seeing the rug being pulled out from under us, we can learn to dance on a shifting carpet. The stumbling blocks of the past magically become the stepping stones to the future."[7]

## The High Price of Avoiding Conflict

Neither the Magician nor the Warrior Core Type inside you is likely to avoid conflict. (See description of Core Types in Appendix A.) For the Warrior, conflict is an opportunity to test your personal mettle, to demonstrate power and fine-tune your skills. For the Magician, it is an opportunity to transform misdirected or pent-up energy in ways that are helpful to everyone involved. You may find yourself avoiding clashes because in the past you have hurt people you valued, or your "win" was only temporary, or you were soundly beaten. However, when you avoid conflict, even for the most noble of reasons, no one wins.

The ancient motto of Western healers was to "do no harm." This includes not allowing *yourself* to be harmed. The price of avoiding a fight is often quite a bit higher than you could imagine; i.e., it often includes some "hidden" costs such as:

- the harm you cause yourself by allowing someone to abuse you,

- the harm you cause others by allowing them to get away with patterns of abuse, and

- an almost-inevitable escalation of conflict.

The underlying reasons for disputes tend not to go away of their own accord. The ostrich technique simply is not an advisable long-term strategy. Not only do problems remain, they usually get worse over time. What could have been handled in its early stages as a skirmish can sometimes wind up resulting in full-scale warfare. If you try to repress the Fire element inside you in order to stay in a relationship, it will burn you up or be released later in totally inappropriate ways (much as a lid blows off a pressure cooker). Well-managed conflict can actually serve both you and the other person: It surfaces important issues so that you can deal with them more appropriately; it releases (rather than represses) energy; and it channels emotion in constructive directions.

# LEADERSHIP

◆

## Power, Motivation, and Empowerment

More than any other Element of Success, Fire has traditionally defined good leadership. Organizational leaders are typically chosen from those people who evidence "fire in the belly." They are self-starters who manage to succeed by the sheer force of their strong wills or who rise to positions of authority because they'd rather be in charge than have someone else tell them what to do. Whatever the reason, good leadership requires the proper use of this third element.

One of the issues leaders have to face early on is how to keep their workforce "fired up." The motivation for work varies from person to person. Some of us work just to keep a roof over our heads or to feed our children. Others of us really love the work we do, take pride in it, and enjoy being with colleagues. Unfortunately, the Fire element has been extinguished in many workers due to lack of use. If employees are called upon to act decisively by a manager who is consistent, fair, and trustworthy, most of them will eagerly rise to the occasion. Much as our bodies need to convert food to internal fuel, employees will starve without "meaningful work" (i.e., work they can be proud of that is congruent with their personal values, vision, and mission). This issue is a critical one for worker satisfaction, productivity, and retention. One of the principal tasks of leader-

*Anything of value in my experience has happened because of a monomaniac with a mission.*
—Peter Drucker

ship, then, is to call employees to their own heroic quest by reminding them of their personal missions and by providing avenues for them to put their individual gifts to good use for themselves, the work group, and the organization.

## The Natural Motivator: A Desire to Do Good Work

The Magician in you believes that an internal fire burns in all people as a strong desire to excel at their work. If this is true, you do not need to "motivate" employees. Rather, all you have to do is *allow* workers to act on their passion and do the good work they naturally want to do.

The third Element of Success manifests as an innate human hunger to achieve something meaningful in life, to do work that makes a difference and allows us to be proud of what we've accomplished. Almost all the people I've met in the workplace truly want to do an excellent job, and they become very frustrated when they cannot. As W. Edwards Deming argues, although leaders tend to blame their employees when things go wrong, a full *85 percent of organizational problems are due to systemic, rather than worker, difficulties*.[8] When managers blame employees for systemic problems, they inadvertently extinguish the natural motivation in those workers. And then leaders have to replace it with external motivators that are far less effective (and usually much more costly).

When most of us start a new job, we are energized, raring to go. Then, little by little, we get discouraged as we hit resistance and apathy in the workplace. We lose our spark. One of the best things you can do as a leader is to carefully tend the natural fire in the people you supervise. In addition to aligning them around a common mission, you can keep the Fire element stoked by giving them sufficient autonomy and authority to do their best work. (Micromanagement is akin to smothering a campfire by pouring dirt on it.) Precious few leaders allow workers this level of freedom, but when they do, the results are spectacular. Indeed, passion is the best possible fuel to propel us through our day-to-day work. As Naval Commander John T. Oliver of TRANSCOM once told me, "I get up every morning, bicycle to work, sit down at my desk, look around my office, and hear myself say: 'There's no place I'd rather be!'"

> *Two hundred years ago Johann Sebastian Bach was writing the rules of harmony for all time. Why did he do it? Pride of workmanship.*
> —W. Edwards Deming

## Bringing Fire from Heaven: Empowerment

Ancient Magicians were often pictured with one hand pointing toward heaven, the other toward earth so that they could act as *lightning rods* for their communities. Just as lightning is created when equal electrical forces from the sky and the earth are explosively drawn together, you can release tremendous power in your workforce by aligning people with this Element of Success. There is a law of physics that states: "Any mass already has large quantities of energy stored in it . . . [and] small applications of energy, properly administered, can liberate much greater units of energy from this mass."[9] The workers in your care have a large, stored, ready quantity of energy just waiting to be liberated. You can release this energy by:

- helping people clarify their own personal missions,

- aligning workers so that their jobs are congruent with the organization's mission,

- employing their individual gifts in ways that support both their own and the organization's missions,

- helping to set priorities (individually and for your group),

- giving clear, consistent directions,

- allowing people the authority to act and make decisions, and

- rewarding individuals and work teams for behaviors that are supportive of the group's mission.

The Fire element helps you claim your power so that you are able to shape your own destiny and champion those in your care. This is a leadership issue that can sometimes put you in conflict with higher authorities, as the story of Prometheus so colorfully illustrates.

*It is said that Prometheus created man by taking clay from a river bank, then artfully molding it "into the likeness of the gods." The goddess Athena helped him by breathing life into his creations. However, the ancestors of humanity "were only half alive. They still did not know how to employ their bodies' strength or how to direct their spirits."[10] The lot of the first human beings was quite difficult; they lived in caves or wandered the earth. Zeus was jealous that he now had to share his earthly playground with these pathetic creatures, and he decided that he would not allow them to have the gods' property of Fire.*

*However, out of compassion, Prometheus "determined on a dangerous course in order to benefit mankind. Stealing fire from heaven, he hid it in a stalk of fennel and carried it secretly to earth." An enraged Zeus "ordered Prometheus to be nailed to a cliff in the Caucasus Mountains, where he hung for thirty thousand years."[11]*

I often hear people complain bitterly about management's misuse and hoarding of power. Like Prometheus, they believe that they too must "steal fire from heaven" if they are to have any power at all. Legends about stealing the power of Fire are common to humanity. The Jicarilla Apaches tell a similar story, saying that the fox tricked the fireflies into giving him the secret of Fire by teaching them to dance, lulling them into a trance, then bringing their fire ("his tail burning like a torch") to human beings.[12]

The caution contained in the Prometheus myth is that he was severely punished for taking power from the top of the hierarchy. In organizations this kind of conflict most often arises when leaders have not properly aligned their employees before empowering them. The system's survival demands that people inside it do not work at cross-purposes. The individual work we do must be aligned with the organization's mission, each other, and other departments. Otherwise, the Fire element will burn ineffectively, unevenly, or out of control, causing severe imbalance in our systems.

If Prometheus had understood the Elements of Success, he likely would not have focused on stealing the gods' fire. Instead he would have realized that he could claim his own personal power to ignite the fire of those in his care. Each of us already has all the Fire element we need, right inside us. Just as it is an act of leadership to consider yourself central to your workplace and an indispensable part of your organization's mind, it is an act of leadership to keep your own internal fire burning. Although higher level managers can change your title or alter your external power, no one (not even Zeus!) has the ability to give or take away your internal Fire. It is yours and yours alone. Now, *that* is real power!

The Magician's use of the Fire element provides a significant advantage over traditional leadership. When you notice that energy is decreasing in the workplace, you can share your own sense of commitment with others, much as one candle lights another or as a hearth keeps you warm. And, best of all, as you pass the flame along throughout all levels of the organization, other people in turn can "rekindle" your fire when it is running low. The beauty of this approach to leadership is twofold: *you no longer have the responsibility of carrying the torch alone; the fire of passion will always burn brightly wherever you are.*

# ORGANIZATIONS

◆

## Lighting the Torch

At the start of the international Olympic games, a huge torch is ignited that continues to burn for the duration of the games. Your organization's mission is much like that torch. It is what you are in business to do—the "One Thing" your corporation

## The Fire Element Is Strong and Healthy
## in Your Organization When:

- Its mission is clear
- The mission statement accurately reflects its real mission
- The mission is congruent with the organization's vision, core values, and identity
- Individuals within the system are aligned by a strong, common sense of purpose that they can clearly articulate
- Leaders are consistent, aligned, and well coordinated in the messages they send, and the directions they give, to workers
- Employees are committed to the corporation and each other
- The workplace is highly energized; there is a lot of excitement in the air
- Both workers and leaders are empowered; they have the authority and decision-making ability they need to get their jobs done
- People have pride in their work and a sense of "ownership"
- Leaders are clear about priorities, and use those priorities to organize work and set attainable deadlines
- All employees are aware of the part their jobs play in achieving the organization's mission
- Activity is steady and productivity is high
- Most of the people in the workplace are self-starters
- The organization rewards those behaviors that are aligned with its mission
- Conflict is addressed immediately and is used to surface underlying problems
- Honest, open disagreements, within and among all levels of the system, are an accepted part of this workplace

has dedicated itself to accomplishing so that it can move a crucial step closer to its ideal vision.

The mission is tangible, measurable, and doable. Because it is just within grasp, the mission sets the workplace "on fire." This third Element of Success transforms the more abstract elements of system identity and vision into an alchemical fuel, a boundless source of energy that aligns everyone in the system and compels them to move forward with incredible determination.

## Defining Your Workplace's Mission

A clearly stated mission engenders commitment, passion, discipline, and focus in employees. And when the shared mission is congruent with individual missions, people become eager not only to get their own work done, but also to contribute wherever possible to the good of the whole. The third Element of Success turns an organization's values and vision into a real-life crusade, or, to quote from the classic *Blues Brothers* movie, "a mission from God."

Your organization's mission needs to be *clear* enough for everyone to see and *consistent* (so people are not pushed and pulled in different directions when trying to accomplish it). The mission sustains the system and everyone in it, as did the ancient Roman Vestal Fire, the perpetual fire that was the mystic hearth of the empire."[13] Vesta was the Mother Goddess of the city's founders, and her fire was kept burning for more than six hundred years in the heart of Rome. It was said that "As long as the flame was live, any man or woman inhabiting the city felt secure. . . ."[14]

The third Element of Success provides the way for a business to act on its vision and core values. It must be exciting enough to set workers and leaders "on fire," then align them into coordinated activity. Because an organization's mission is measurable, it needs to include not only a clear succinct statement, but also, once that's written, the details necessary to accomplish it. This includes specific goals and objectives, timetables, the budget, a marketing strategy, new product development, etc. It also should include evaluation criteria for monitoring the progress of plans, testing of pilot programs, comprehensive feedback systems, and what the rewards will be for behavior that furthers the mission.

Many an organizational "mission statement" is actually a hodgepodge of its values, vision, and mission—an overly long, fire-stomping jumble of words that forces these distinct energies into the same container, where they blend together, which dilutes their effectiveness. By keeping these different aspects of the organization's strategy distinct and separate, you can better clarify exactly which Elements of Success are—and are not—being sufficiently tended to for the system's optimum health.

## Your Organization's Mission Statement

Does your organization have a mission statement? If so, can you paraphrase it in a sentence or two? Does it make you eager to go to work? Is your workplace highly energized? These are signs of a strong organizational mission. If you are able to briefly paraphrase your organization's mission statement, write it down here.

If your organization does not have a mission statement, use the steps below to write one or two sentences describing *your* impression of your workplace's real mission.

1. **Begin by reviewing** your organization's core identity, values, and vision from the prior two chapters so that your organizational mission will be congruent with the first two Elements of Success.

2. **Remember that a mission statement** is doable and measurable. It also has to be "fiery," passionate—something that people will really care about and want to accomplish.

3. **Write one or two sentences** that capture your organization's real mission.

4. **Your next step** is to note some key goals that support this mission. Eventually, these goals will need to include strategic details such as reasonable timelines, budgets, and measurements that will support the accomplishment of your mission.

It is your responsibility, not your boss's, not your workplace's, to develop a strategy and find the work that brings your gifts out into the world. You may or may not ever be paid for doing so. Many writers, artists, musicians, inventors, and entrepreneurs, for example, have a "day job" that covers the rent and allows them to use their talents during off-hours. The key is to have a life and work strategy that supports your personal mission so that it continues to fuel you. In the best of all worlds, however, your own and your workplace's mission are compatible. And that, I assure you, is an exhilarating way to live.

## An Integrity Check for the Fire Element

1. Compare the personal mission statement you wrote earlier in this chapter with your organization's mission statement. In what ways are they similar? In what ways are they different?

2. If the two missions are compatible, determine the work you can fully commit to within your organization. Decide what work best suits your talents and abilities.

3. If the two missions are significantly different, does this adversely affect you in any way? If yes, you may need to draw up a strategy that will bring you step-by-step to a more suitable place of work. Jot some notes below on how you might proceed.

## Burning Away the Unnecessary

You can use your corporate mission as a litmus test to determine how tasks need to be prioritized. In this way, you can greatly reduce superfluous or wasted effort throughout the organization. The mission helps burn away everything that is unnecessary. In *The Seven Habits of Highly Effective People*, Stephen Covey recommends a four-quadrant time management model (see below) to help prioritize your daily workload. The third Element of Success dictates that the items listed as "important" in the first two quadrants be completely congruent with the workplace's stated mission, vision, and values.

| Time-Management Matrix | Urgent | Not Urgent |
|---|---|---|
| Important | I. Crises; pressing problems; deadline-driven projects | II. Prevention; "production capacity" activities; relationship building; recognizing new opportunities; planning |
| Not Important | III. Interruptions; some calls, mail, reports, and meetings; popular activities | IV. Trivia, busy work; some mail and phone calls; time wasters; pleasant activities[15] |

Covey contends that if you spend more time on activities in Quadrant II (important/not urgent), you will incrementally reduce Quadrant I (crises) over time. Many leaders are drawn to crisis management because it makes them feel heroic. Quadrant I is similar to *fighting* forest fires, whereas Quadrant II is the equivalent of *preventing* forest fires. (Unfortunately, crisis management is much more visible and often provides the criteria by which leaders are rewarded.) By focusing on Quadrant II you will not be as easily distracted by interruptions and busywork activities, neither of which contributes to productivity over time. Covey contends that by focusing your work in this way, your effectiveness will take quantum leaps.

You are probably painfully aware that the clutter of workplace activity tends to obscure its real work. The question that needs to be applied to everything screaming for your attention is: "Does this task further the organization's mission?" The following story was told by Jerry Tureski, at the time the director of the Government Service Agency's Federal Supply Service in New York State. It clearly illustrates the power of this one-pointed question.

*The Federal Supply Service is responsible for providing paper, packaging, office supplies, and a host of miscellaneous items to government offices, including many branches of the military. At the time of this story, the New York branch of the FSS had an annual sales volume of $600 million. It* also had a huge backlog, many unhappy customers, and a terrible reputation for service. The leaders in this branch decided to correct the situation by instituting a rigorous quality improvement effort. They had all workers focus on one question regarding their organizational mission (their version of it was "Does this activity provide service to our customers?").

They then completely eliminated all activities to which the answer was "No." In eighteen months, this branch of the FSS had significantly cut their late delivery rate (from 20 percent to 2 percent) and radically slashed their back order rate by 93 percent (from $400 million to $1 million)!

This is not the end of the story. This Federal Supply Service center accomplished their organizational miracle just in time to supply the highly specialized and increased demands of Operation Desert Storm. They would never have been able to deliver in this crisis had they not already accomplished their dramatic organizational turnaround.

## Mission and Strategy: More Thread Than Sword

Traditionally, an organization's mission is supposed to serve as a clarion call to duty, a battle cry, a sword that cuts through confusion and points the way to victory (e.g., winning more market share). The strategic details necessary to accomplish it constitute a battle plan that was designed by generals—and that the foot soldiers are to carry out with precision and without question. The purpose of this kind of mission is to rally and point the way for the troops, and the strategy is designed to leverage all available resources to win the war.

In the Elements of Success, however, the mission (and its accompanying strategy) has a somewhat different purpose. It provides a road map that you are to follow from this moment into the future. In many ways, a corporate mission statement acts much as a *golden thread* by weaving a common thread of purpose throughout our diverse, daily tasks. (According to a famous Greek myth the golden thread was a magical gift from Ariadne that brought Theseus safely out of the Cretan labyrinth.) Furthermore, the mission can:

- provide a link between the sky (vision) and the earth (reality), moving the organization a step closer to the world it envisions;

- align the collective will of all employees in order to generate commitment and cooperation throughout the workforce;

- serve as a call to action, then focus and direct that activity;

- provide a meaningful context and compelling reason for the business plan, thereby winning the hearts and minds of all involved;

- increase energy while reducing resistance and the likelihood of working at cross-purposes; and

- help people stay focused on their part of accomplishing the mission and strategy, the goals and tasks for which they are individually responsible.

Many students of military history argue that generals often are fighting the previous war, and that only after much bloodshed do they adjust their overall strategy. (For example, generals maintained Napoleonic battle strategies throughout the Civil War and even into World War I, thereby sending countless soldiers to certain death in the face of improved weaponry.) Today's workplace leaders often function similarly by persisting with fear-based management techniques that have long since been proven counterproductive. (As quality expert Deming insisted, fear must be "driven out" of organizations.)

*The best business strategies will be those that rely upon and release the internal fire in all workers so that they are free to act on their passion.* To tap this phenomenal energy reserve, organizational strategies must be flexible, easily adaptable, and available for constant review and renewal. They also will need to allow employees maximum autonomy, the power to self-motivate, and the ability to self-organize. In many cases this will require some adjustments to how we've delivered products and services in the past. We will have to reexamine our road maps, continually making certain we're on track, rather than just pushing ahead harder and faster in the same predetermined direction.

Systems theorist Steven Cavaleri, one of my long-time colleagues and current president of the Knowledge Management Consortium International, suggests that we free workers' potential by *decoupling* work processes; i.e., making the components of a work process less dependent on each other.[16] Then if one key employee is absent, or a "bug" shuts down the computer, productivity does not completely stop. Steve cites a brilliant example of a decoupling strategy used by car manufacturing factories. Here teams of workers bring their parts of the car to a central location whenever they are ready, rather than having to wait for the people before them in the process to complete their tasks. A decoupling strategy minimizes the potentially catastrophic effect of a weak link in the chain. I would also argue that, by removing interruptions to their work, it allows individuals to accomplish their own personal mission and excel at their jobs.

## Using Conflict to Release Energy in the Workforce

It has been my experience that very few businesses handle conflict well. In most cases, conflict tends to be repressed. Honest, open discussions are rarely encouraged. People fear losing their jobs or being punished in other ways for expressing differences of opinion, especially if they disagree with their bosses. On the other hand, bosses all too often feel justified in saying whatever they want to those they supervise. The results are devastating for the organization: Mistakes are covered up, brilliant insights are not captured, knowledge is lost, employees lose their internal motivation, and productivity slows. It is very difficult to rekindle the Fire element in these circumstances.

Very few organizations in the world know more about dealing with conflict than our designated Warrior institutions. While consulting for several branches of the United States Department of Defense, I've had my eyes opened to the many gifts the Warrior has for the Magician in this in-between era. One lesson the Warrior teaches us is that strong boundaries are necessary for survival. The Warrior also teaches that good fences make good neighbors; that the way to peace and harmony (in our homes, our workplaces, and the world) is not through "peace at any price," but through immediately and honestly addressing disputes as they arise. (This is a painful lesson the Europeans learned from their pre–World War II accommodation policies. Hitler later confessed that he would not have pressed forward at several critical points had he encountered early resistance.)

> *Pick battles big enough to matter, small enough to win.*
> —*Jonathan Kozol*

In my work with Department of Defense (DoD) employees, I have been impressed by the degree to which this Warrior institution has been meeting the challenges of the In-between. For example, a cross section of DoD employees in one of my workshops beautifully articulated the combined strengths of the Warrior and Magician Core Types when they defined their shared values, vision, and mission as follows:

**Values:** Peace, freedom

**Vision:** A world where every human being lives in peace and has the freedom to live as he or she chooses

**Mission:** A strong defense of America's and its allies' borders

In this in-between era, even the United States armed forces are expanding the methods by which they can accomplish their mission and achieve their vision. This includes using their strength and skills to take care of victims of natural disasters in this country and to alleviate starvation in foreign lands.

I feel that there is great reason for hope if the Warrior and the Magician Core Types work together to transform the ways we handle conflict in our workplaces and throughout the world. And surely, if so many real-life Warriors in the Department of Defense can embrace the emerging Magician with such remarkable grace, our workplace Warriors can certainly learn how to follow their lead.

●

## A Case Study: Lynnette Yount Associates

*Lynnette Yount Associates is a small, successful consulting firm that specializes in providing quality improvement and change management services to government agencies. Its early days were even more difficult than most entrepreneurial ventures due to an unusual circumstance: the sudden death of Ms. Yount's fiancé, Kenny.*

*At Kenny's death, Lynnette went into shock. Her family and friends gathered around her for support. As days turned into weeks and weeks into months, she grieved and grieved.*

*Meanwhile, the world was continuing with business as usual. Her clients were understandably concerned about whether Lynnette could meet her contractual obligations. Ms. Yount and her associates finally had to decide whether to abandon their business efforts. They were in the middle of several course designs that required both student and instructor manuals. Lynnette and her colleagues were already scheduled for seminars and consultations. Ms. Yount consulted with her colleagues, advisors, friends, and family. After a great deal of discussion, the general concurrence was that she should proceed, as long as she had the strength and the health to do so.*

*Lynnette called up all the willpower she could muster. She dug into work during the day and cried herself to sleep at night. She had long been convinced that her team-oriented quality-improvement techniques could greatly benefit the beleaguered government workers she encountered. She committed to that passionate personal mission to maintain her focus and keep the fire burning inside. For a solid six months there was no letup in the work that was required to get this new venture off the ground.*

*Today Lynnette and her associates look back with disbelief that she made it through the ordeal at all. Her organization, meanwhile, has provided tens of thousands of grateful government employees with high-quality services. None of this would have happened if not for the thread of meaning and purpose that her business mission provided her during this time of intense personal grief.*

# WORLD

◆

## Burning Across the World

As you know from reading the international news, the element of Fire is very active across the globe today. Not only has the irrepressible human desire for freedom toppled oppressive governments; long-repressed hatreds are being fanned into flames. Hot spots of "ethnic cleansing" continue to erupt. Irreplaceable rain forests are scorched to clear the acreage for faster cash crops. Border disputes flare into wars as the old order crumbles and whole peoples redefine who they are in the new world.

Here in America racial strife still sim- mers, occasionally erupting to burn portions of cities to the ground. Land- mark buildings have endured terrorist explosions, public servants have been bombed, and charismatic religious and separatist fanatics have fulfilled their own prophecies of the Apocalypse with deadly shoot-outs or by burning their fol- lowers to death. Now more than ever, you and I need our great Ally, the Magician, to help us courageously face and transform these fiery dragons, these unresolved conflicts and fears that we have suppressed and carried within us, smoldering, for far too long.

*We have met the enemy
and he is us.*
—*Walt Kelly, "Pogo"*

The danger is that unless fire is carefully tended, it can burn out of control and become insatiable. The element of Fire separates us. This is critical to our develop- ment as healthy individuals; however, if our evolution (as individuals or as a society) is "arrested," in the fire element, we will cause problems for all the people and creatures around us. An unaligned will is insatiable, and its impact can be devastating. Indeed, if not kept in balance with the other Elements of Success, Fire can torch the house while we are still inside it. Indeed, we can see evidence of this phenomenon not only in our sometimes shabby treatment of each other, but also in the rapid burning up of our natural resources and our failure to see our connection to the world's diverse plant and animal species.

The ancient Romans named Vulcan as the deity of the destructive aspect of the Fire element. He was the "god of fire in its uncontrolled manifestations, such as the volcanoes that perpetuate his name."[17] Fire destroys the fabric of society or the world whenever charismatic leaders convince others of the necessity of *their* mission and *their* needs without honoring the different, and equally important, missions and needs of others in that social and economic system.

Overly fiery leaders draw to themselves, like moths to the flame, people who are in search of meaning in their lives and who allow others to define that meaning for them. The wills of such followers are then subjugated to the leader they choose. Human history is full of accounts of the damage done in the name of causes. Indeed, the destructive effects of unleashing this Vulcan form of fire are often handed down through generations as people deify their leaders and carry on the torch of unholy ethnic, religious, or political causes.

Our national and international political, social, economic, and ecological problems are so serious that they cannot be ignored any longer. Like a smoldering volcano, they threaten to erupt at any time. What the Magician Core Type teaches us is that:

- our problems, fears, anger, and hostilities will not go away of their own accord, and ignoring them is not likely to be a successful strategy;

- it takes at least as much energy to ignore problems as it does to deal with them;

- we tend to carry our problems with us wherever we go; and,

- the only way out is *through*.

Therefore, the route to international peace and prosperity is, paradoxically, to *embrace* the Fire element and the transformative aspects of conflict. We must acknowledge our problems, find their root causes, and assertively and honestly address our differences. It has never been possible, after all, to sweep real or metaphorical fire under a rug!

The dilemma then is how to make a difference in the In-between without each of us embarking on our own personal crusade to save the world. (Trying to impose our wills on others actually *creates* many of the problems listed above.) The solution appears to be that we must do as much as we can without burning ourselves out or torching those who differ from us. A good way to begin may be for each of us to keep the Fire element within our own hearth, home, and workplace until we are in better command of our own Balancing Acts. If we try to tame the world's monsters before we've conquered our own, odds are that we'll make a mess of things; i.e., we'll project our unresolved issues outward. Pride will then precede a fall.

You can start the healing of your society and the world by acting on your own passion, i.e., by contributing your personal gifts to your home, relationships, work, and community. You can—and must—make a difference! By taking care of your own backyard first, you'll gain the skills and mastery you need to act on a larger stage. Then, as each of us develops a clearer sense of personal purpose and a genuine respect for the gifts of others, we can work together to blaze a path into a more magical future.

# 4

# WEAVING A WEB OF CONNECTION

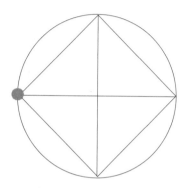

## The Infinite, Primordial Ocean

*In the beginning everything was like a sea without light.*
*There was only Kali, the Original of all manifestations,*
*the infinite, primordial Ocean.*
*From the vast formless waters of the Supreme Kali all things rose and*
*disappeared again, in endless cycles. Her womb was the birthplace of*
*even the gods, who addressed her as the beginning of all . . .*
*Creatrix, Protectress, and Destructress.*
*Legends say that Kali is the primordial Shakti, and that from a part of her only*
*"arises Brahma, from a part only arises Vishnu, and from a part only arises Shiva."*
*It is also said that "just as rivers and lakes are unable to traverse*
*a vast sea, so Brahma and other gods lose their separate existence on*
*entering the uncrossable and infinite being" of the Great Kali.*
*"Compared with the vast sea of the being of Kali,*
*the existence of Brahma and the other gods is nothing but such a little*
*water as is contained in the hollow made by a cow's hoof."* [1]

—A Hindu creation myth

# The Treasure House of Compassion

The Fourth Element of Success is Water. It helps you feel your desires, express your purpose, and form the relationships necessary to project your gifts into the world (Fire). Water also allows you to eloquently communicate your ideas (Air) and articulate your indentity and values (Essence). This point of reference connects you with your own internal workings and helps you understand the workings of others. In this way, it weaves strong, enduring bonds with all those people who support you in your daily Balancing Act. In addition, this fluid element links us in subtle, but very real ways to other individuals, creatures, and the world in which we live.

Indeed, field-theory physicists say that our universe resembles an ocean that is "filled with interpenetrating influences and invisible structures that connect."[2] Interestingly, ancient Egyptians called this all-encompassing vibrational field *Nun*, the primal ocean.[3] The Chinese considered the element of Water to be the "abode of the dragon," from which all life comes. Many ancient cultures thought of water as the original fountain that preceded all form and creation.[4] In India, Water is referred to as *matritamah*, the most maternal of elements, which preserves life by circulating throughout the whole of nature in the form of rain, sap, milk, and blood. And, because the mother births the child, it was believed that these primeval waters "contained all solid bodies before they acquired form and rigidity."[5] Medical researchers echo these ancient myths. They say that your body is composed primarily of the ancient seawater from which all of humanity evolved. Although you and I may appear and feel solid, our bodies are very much like rivers with a constant flow of changing cells.

Because Water connects you and me to what we're feeling inside, and simultaneously to all other living creatures, it is the element of respect, empathy,compassion, and love. Indeed, the primal goddess Kali is described as the "Treasure-House of Compassion" and "the fount of every kind of love."[6] Venus, the Roman goddess of love, arose fully formed from the sea. Compassion is the natural effect of experiencing our ties to each other and the world. This connection is neither an academic theory nor a fond hope. It is the reality of life—our vital link to the primordial force that swims within, through, and without us, sustaining every moment of our existence. Water teaches us that we are an integral part of the world in which we live and that at a cellular level, it is an integral part of us.

Native Americans believe that we are all "related." Indeed, we exist in an ocean of relationships that comprise our daily lives and work. Water bonds you with your family, friends, and coworkers, making you a vital link in your communities. It is indispensible to honest communication, excellent teamwork, and the flow of information. It makes you more considerate in your interactions and shows you how to more effectively serve others.

Systems theorists also say that we are all related, that we exist as systems within systems. For example, our cells dwell within our bodies; we live within our communities; these are necessary components of our nations; those exist as part of our ecosystem; Earth rotates within our solar system, and it within the galaxy. As superstring and other unified-field theorists argue, we swim within an "ocean" where we are tied to everyone and everything via thin, invisible "strings." Yet, on a day-to-day basis, we can easily forget these pervasive, all-encompassing connections of which both the ancient sages and modern scientists speak. Indeed, often we feel quite separate from each other and nature.

The fourth Element of Success serves as a point of reference for making certain you stay connected to yourself. It lives inside you as your emotions. This includes not only your changing feelings and moods but also the "emotional intelligence" that is pivotal to your success in the world.

Without a strong Water element, your life, relationships, and work become dry, brittle, lacking life. You start feeling detached and inflexible. Inevitably, your tenuous Balancing Act will shatter. If, on the other hand, your Water element is excessive, it can lead to a breakdown in your personal boundaries; a symbiotic merging or identification with others; or a submission of your will, beliefs, or identity to someone else. Too much of this fourth element can overflow the banks of its structures, as happens with information overload, a lack of impulse control, or emotional outbursts.

# PERSONAL LIFE

◆

## Feeling Fully Connected

The word *emotion* comes from the Latin *movere* (to move) + *e* (out). E-motion, then, contains within it the seeds of action. It is your feelings that give wings to your thoughts and provide you with the energy to act. For example, I may know I need to make that important phone call, but other matters intervene. I think about it some more. Finally, I feel a surge of energy and make the call. (What propels me to act could range from fear of missing a deadline to feeling confident that the moment is right.)

Our emotions often cause us to behave *instinctively* from our pure feelings, even before we realize what we've done. For example, you could leap without thinking to save a child from an oncoming car, hurling your own body into grave danger. At other times you could yell at an astonished spouse, just because you had a difficult day at work. In both cases, you wonder incredulously afterwards: "What happened?" Our feelings are not logical. But they are very fast and powerful. Our emotions are

## You Have a Strong and Healthy Water Element When You:

- Feel connected to, and genuinely like, family, friends, and coworkers
- Treat others respectfully
- Feel appreciated by others
- Find it easy to collaborate with others at home, in your community, and at work
- Have excellent communication skills find interactions easy—effective, fluid, respectful
- Enjoy listening to other people
- Feel and demonstrate empathy and compassion
- Are flexible; find it relatively easy to change with shifting structures and new situations
- Have a strong supportive community in your life with relationships that support your personal values, vision, and mission
- Seek out and encourage differences and diversity
- Enjoy being with people of other cultures, races, religions, politics, gender, and opinions
- Are comfortable with dialogue and have respectful discussions with others about important issues
- Understand what you're really thinking and feeling and are able to articulate it (without blame or projection)
- Manage your emotions appropriately; i.e., maintain a relatively positive even keel and don't "dump" your bad moods, pessimism, anger, or fear on others around you

ruled by the Water element—and they are a mighty force to be reckoned with.

You and I are likely to experience a wide range of emotions (sometimes even conflicting emotions) as we go about our daily Balancing Acts. It is helpful to pay attention to what you're really feeling, because emotions can cause you to go quickly in and out of balance, stabilizing or destabilizing you. As you make the emotional assessment below, keep in mind that no emotion is either good or bad—truly. Emotions that are not socially sanctioned (like anger or fear) can sometimes protect us from real harm. Similarly, confusion may be the prelude to a creative breakthrough.

After all, emotions are just manifestations of raw energy. Like waves on a sea, they change form, flowing into and out of each other. One moment you're happy; the next you're really annoyed. What's important is to use your emotions as a point of reference in your Balancing Act. Just pay attention to what you're feeling—and why. In this way, you can greatly increase your moment-to-moment equilibrium.

## An Emotional Inventory

Using the list of emotions below, make an assessment of the dominant feelings/ emotions you regularly experience. That is, which of the emotions listed below do you most frequently feel? Circle all the ones that come to mind, then go back and rank the top three that most significantly (positively or negatively) affect your daily Balancing Act.

**Fear** (anxious or nervous; apprehensive; worried; panicky)

**Anger** (irritated or annoyed; frustrated; furious; enraged)

**Confusion** (undecided; unsure; bewildered; lost)

**Sadness** (feeling "low" or depressed; disappointed; pessimistic; grieving)

**Envy** (jealous; disappointed with what you have versus what others have; spiteful)

**Flat-lining** (not feeling much of anything; feeling dull; bored; lacking a range of emotions)

**Excitement** (energetic; lively; fired up; interested and eager)

**Joy** (happy; optimistic; cheerful; elated; ecstatic)

**Contentment** (feeling safe; satisfied; the sense that things are in good order and in balance)

**Love** (feeling accepted; cared for; respected; trusted; affectionate)

**Other emotions:**

Medical research on the brain explains why you may sometimes experience conflicting signals between your "head" (the logical part of you) and your "heart" (your "feeling" side). It appears that this all-too-common conflict has a real foundation in physiology—we have both a "rational brain" and an "emotional brain."

Most neuroscientists today believe that the limbic system and prefrontal lobes of the brain are integral to the workings of what they have dubbed the "emotional brain." Moreover, the research of neuroscientist Joseph LeDoux on the circuitry of the brain has demonstrated the pivotal role of the amygdala (a small almond-shaped part of the brain that stores emotional memory). It is this emotional "sentinel" that mobilizes your entire body into immediate action while your thinking brain (the neocortex) is still mulling things over. Thanks to this tiny part of the brain in our childhood caretakers, many of us are still walking around alive today.

LeDoux contends that "Anatomically, the emotional system can act independently of the neocortex." I think that this is a common experience for many of us—our emotional and thinking selves often do act independently. And LeDoux adds, "Some emotional reactions and emotional memories can be formed without any conscious cognitive participation at all."[7] We know this, too. Our emotions can cause us to act in ways we do not understand. Sometimes these responses are instinctive, adaptive, and lifesaving. (You might distrust someone for no apparent reason and find out later that you were right—he turned out to be a crook.) At other times your emotions may be based on outdated memories that, upon reflection and further investigation, do not apply well to the current situation or individual.

Researchers continue to delve into the mysteries surrounding the nature of emotions. Interestingly, there is mounting evidence that "there is not one single emotional brain, but rather several systems of circuits that disperse the regulation of a given emotion to far-flung, but coordinated, parts of the brain."[8] Scientists speculate that in the not-too-distant future we will be able to trace the different brain maps of each major emotion.

Clearly, emotions can help each of us to act more (or less) intelligently. When you understand your own and others' emotions, you will be able to act more appropriately for each situation you encounter. This is why emotional intelligence can enhance the quality of your whole life.

## Developing Emotional Intelligence

Whereas wisdom is a property of Essence, and standard "rational" intelligence is a property of the Air element, *emotional intelligence* belongs to the Water element. Although it is a relatively recent concept, emotional intelligence has gained considerable attention in the past few decades as we try to unravel the secrets of what makes us "tick."

Emotional intelligence has been studied extensively by psychologists and educational researchers who wanted to understand why some people are so much more successful than others. As David McClelland discovered in the 1970s, the competency of such "stars" has more to do with "empathy, self-discipline, and initiative" than with academic aptitude, grades, or advanced credentials.[9] And, as Howard Gardner postulated in the landmark book *Frames of Mind*, human beings have not one kind of intelligence, but actually *multiple intelligences*. (Gardner described seven forms of intelligence that were located in specific, identifiable parts of the brain. These were verbal, math, spatial, kinesthetic, music, interpersonal, and intrapersonal intelligences.)[10]

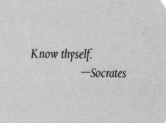

*Know thyself.*

—*Socrates*

Clearly, having a high IQ doesn't mean that someone would behave intelligently. We all know incredibly bright people who can't get along well with others or who make unbelievably bad decisions that adversely affect their lives and work. Conversely, we all know people who couldn't be described as geniuses but who are very "smart" and successful in many facets of their lives. Interestingly, the IQ measurement was developed in World War I, when the United States Army "needed a quick measure of the capabilities of its unknown, untrained, and untried soldiers."[11] The military borrowed French psychologist Alfred Binet's tests for determining the "mental age" of children for schooling. An advantage of this test was that it could be administered to the large groups of young men being drafted for service. Unfortunately, after World War I, the IQ test took on a life of its own, and the scores became more important than Binet originally considered them.

Clearly, the best of all possible worlds is when our emotional and rational minds act in concert, neither one dominating the other. The most intelligent people I know are those who navigate through their lives with a balance—rather than a war—between "head" and "heart." This highly desirable state of equilibrium is one way to define emotional intelligence.

And the really good news about emotional intelligence is that it can be developed! Please see Appendix B for a list of the measurable traits of this form of intelligence (which include interpersonal and intrapersonal skills, adaptability, stress management, and general mood). Appendix B also includes a description of how to use the Core Types to improve your capabilities in this area. If you (or perhaps more to the point, your family, friends, colleagues, and neighbors) believe you are lacking in a given area of emotional intelligence, this methodology can help you actually do something about it.

## Techniques for Increasing the Strength and Health of the Water Element

**1. "I am connected to . . ."**
This is a powerful contemplation in which you fill in the blank, thereby reinforcing your ties to others. It can be done any number of ways. For example: Repeat it when you are walking quietly by yourself. You can also do this exercise when you are talking with a coworker, when you notice people who are physically different from yourself, when you gaze into the eyes of a child and see a fine intelligence looking back at you, when you are petting a dog and feel a deep kindness surge through you, or when you sit on the bank of a river and watch it meander.

You can also move your attention to a larger stage by contemplating, "I am connected to everyone" . . . "I am linked to everything." Let the reality of that fill you. Feel your invisible, "superstring" ties to the world around you.

**2. Is that you, Mom?!?**
This exercise may be a big stretch, but it can make you feel much more connected to the people around you. The philosophy of Tibetan Buddhism, which incorporates the principle of reincarnation, argues that we need to treat all people, those we like and those we dislike, with equanimity and respect because we have likely been together in prior lives and have had other (good or bad) relationships. For example, any one of the people you meet could have been the mother who took care of you ages ago and who is therefore still deserving of your kindness, love, and respect. Try on this completely different perspective and feel how dramatically it expands your mind and heart.

## Weaving a Web of Connection

The fourth Element of Success is vital to your Balancing Act in part because your interactions weave a network that can keep you from coming unglued when you're under excessive pressure. They also form the safety net into which you can fall when you occasionally do lose your equilibrium. Relationships are links that vary greatly in strength, durability, and support.

With some people, you can really "be yourself"; with others you may find yourself (wisely) guarded. Some individuals I've met have a great capacity for intimacy and honesty. Most people enjoy being with them and can relax completely, because they know they won't be judged or demeaned. This kind of acceptance affects us

like a soft rain and encourages us to blossom. And yet other of our associations
enrich us by filling necessary, more
traditional roles in our lives.

Your very first "community"
was your family. The kinships you
formed there significantly affected
the development of your internal
emotional state and also, in part,
determined the relationships you
went on to form outside that first, primary group. Your workplace community is another form of "family." Indeed,
you may see a great deal more of coworkers
than you do of your family of origin. Workplaces
can house an extremely wide range of relationships—from people we'd like to
strangle, to those who matter-of-factly get their work done so we can do ours, to
people we greatly admire. And, lastly, it's not just other human beings who "people"
our communities. We have ongoing interdependent interactions with all the other
animal and plant life "communities" within our ecosystem.

As you develop this fourth Element, it can contribute mightily to your success in
life, relationships, and work. For example, your web of connection makes all the
difference if you have lost your job, because 70 percent of people find their new
livelihood through their personal networks; i.e., friends and acquaintances of friends.

> *The rainstorm and the river
> are my brothers,
> The heron and the otter are my friends.
> And we are all connected to each other,
> In a circle, in a hoop that
> never ends.*
> —*Alan Menken and
> Stephen Schwartz, "The
> Colors of the Wind"*

## Identifying Your Community

1. **List the most important people** in your life. Particularly note family members, key friends, or colleagues with whom you can share the best and worst
parts of yourself.

**2. Note your major communities.** These could include extended family, your work colleagues, neighbors, church members, a support group, or people with whom you share a hobby. To what degree do your communities overlap? How strongly connected do you feel to people within these different groups?

**3. What is it you receive from and give** to each of these groups?

**4. Note members of these communities** with whom you have the most in common, and who most support your own Balancing Act.

People whose values I share:

People with whom I have a common vision and beliefs:

People who most support me and encourage me in accomplishing my personal mission:

## Empathy and Compassion

In *The Power of Compassion*, the Dalai Lama maintains that "Every human action that is without human feeling becomes dangerous."[12] Empathy is the fountain from which emotional intelligence flows. Cross-cultural studies with thousands of subjects have shown that people with strong empathy (in particular, the ability to read feelings from nonverbal clues) were "better adjusted emotionally, more popular, more outgoing . . . [and] also had better relations with the opposite sex."[13]

The word *empathy* is derived from the Greek *empatheia* which means "feeling into." Empathy, your ability to understand what others are feeling, is a natural part of childhood development. It comes when you begin to differentiate between your own suffering and someone else's. Interestingly, with this new awareness, you are better able to comfort another human being. Researchers think that the development of empathy may hinge on parental discipline styles, especially having had our attention called to any distress that we may have caused someone else.[14]

Compassion is rooted psychologically in our understanding of our *own* suffering. In other words, a disconnection from ourselves results in a disconnection from other people. Unless we understand our own internal workings, we cannot possibly comprehend, nor connect to, others. The compassionate impulse many people have to serve others is deeply rooted in the realization that, in truth, we all are "related." I believe that such a realization is the cornerstone, not only of emotional intelligence, but also of a life well lived.

Christ commanded his followers to treat others with respect and dignity: that is, as you treated "the least of these my brethren," so you were treating him (Matt. 25:40). His words were echoed only a few years back by Mother Theresa when she stated that it was a joy, not a hardship at all, for her to care for the lepers in Calcutta because she saw God in each one of them. Buddhists believe that compassion is the highest of all the virtues. The Dalai Lama once said that his religion needed no temples or complicated philosophy—it was simply "kindness." Indeed, Buddhism urges people to go through life with the attitude that they have the responsibility to free *all* living beings (not just people) from suffering and help them to attain happiness. (No small order!) Interestingly, when I have experimented with trying on these different lenses of relatedness from the world's great spiritual traditions, it has had the effect of making me more patient and kind in my treatment of others.

## Magicians' Tools and Techniques (Water)

**Magic Words.** These constitute the spoken and unspoken language of the heart. They are used to connect deeply with others, to communicate within and between the worlds, between species, and at great distance. They translate your thoughts to people who do not speak your language and even allow you to speak directly, without the possibility of deceit, heart to heart.

**Magic Cloak**. Used by ancient Magicians to change their form, to become invisible, to shape-shift, and to travel to other worlds. Today's equivalent is active listening, when your personal agenda and needs temporarily become "invisible" enough so that you can truly hear others when they speak; i.e., when you can comprehend the meaning that lies within and between their words.

**Healing Herbs and Love Potions**. These were organic medicines gathered and tested by ancient Magicians, who used them to heal wounds, remove barriers between people, and balance the elements in people's bodies. The greatest of these healing potions are *love* and *respect* (for yourself and others).

**Divining Rod**. Used by shamans around the world to find hidden, underground sources of water. Today the Magician Core Type encourages *dialogue* to access the deep pool of common meaning, unconscious wisdom, and subtle understandings that exist (like an underground spring) between individuals and among members of a group.

**Magic Boat**. Sometimes used by legendary Magicians to transport the dead back from the underworld. You can do roughly the same thing for yourself or others who are discouraged and "dispirited" in relationships that have gone "dead," at work when morale is low, or in communities when people have become apathetic or hopeless.

**Community Building Rituals**. A common function of ancient Magicians was creating rituals that defined the community and served to bind its members together. In our homes, neighborhoods, and workplaces, a revitalized community is created when there is a spirit of togetherness, despite differences of opinion and the degree of diversity.

**Covens**. The Wise Ones we call "witches" were actually rural healers who gathered in small groups. In these covens, the wise ones learned from each other, did their healing work, and kept each other "in line"; i.e., tied to each other, the community, and the Sacred.

**Naming (Water)**. Magicians often knew the real name and nature of everything and everyone around them. Today you can gain similar power for yourself when you dialogue with others so that you can identify their best gifts and encourage their development.

**Book of Wisdom (Water)**. In ancient days, Magicians would write down whatever they learned in their Books of Wisdom. This included insights into the real names and diverse gifts of others, or community-building rituals that worked well. In this way, this knowledge could easily be passed on to others within the group.

## Your Relationships Have a Strong and Healthy Water Element When You:

- Genuinely like (or love) each other—and don't hesitate to express that sentiment

- Listen attentively and respectfully to each other

- Honestly share your feelings and thoughts

- Both stay alert to what the other person feels; i.e., there is a great deal of empathy in this relationship

- Do not project your positive or negative traits onto each other

- Have no emotional manipulation, moodiness, or blaming between you

- Treat each other with affection, kindness, and respect

- Always take the other person's needs into consideration

- Have a close, intimate relationship but are not "merged," symbiotic, or overly dependent

- Support the other person in expressing his or her individual identity and "living" the values, vision, and mission

- Collaborate well and dialogue together to solve problems

- Have a deep sense of trust, intimacy, and mutual respect

- Are very supportive of each other and have a good balance of giving and receiving

- For the most part, like each other's friends and family (and when you don't, you still treat them respectfully and courteously)

- Greatly enjoy each other's company

# RELATIONSHIPS

◆

## We Are All Related

Each of the five elements contributes to the success of our relationship Balancing Acts, but Water is the "stuff" of connectivity. It is the deep well of love that makes our lives feel worth living, the glue that holds us together, and the kindness that soothes us when we're hurting. Whereas the love of self is the quality of the Center, it is love of others that is the quality of Water. The fourth element allows our marriages to be intimate, our business dealings to be respectful, our interactions with siblings to be kind, and our conversations with strangers to be courteous.

In the Bible, Christ says, "This is my command: Love one another" (John 15:17). The element of Water connects us to the best part of ourselves through each other. This is why we fall in love—we look into each other's eyes and feel the exhilaration of touching the Sacred. Our mistake is that if we think this other individual makes us feel this way, rather than understanding that it is the relationship itself, the act of loving, that does it.

Interactions form a field between two people, and we are forever changed. The unseen connections that you feel with someone else may be more real than you ever imagined. Quantum physics demonstrates that once two electrons have been paired, they will continue to exactly mirror each other's spinning axis, even after they are separated![15] Similarly, we all carry the effects of prior relationships with us, even when those people are no longer in our lives. Both common sense and science caution us to take great care in selecting the people with whom we spend time, because our influence on each other goes well beyond the boundaries of those original connections. This is why the sages from all traditions encourage us to keep the company of good people. In *Leadership and the New Science*, Margaret Wheatly shows how modern science provides a new rationale for this old advice: "Different settings and people evoke some qualities from us and leave others dormant. In each of these relationships, we are different, new in some way. . . . This doesn't make us inauthentic, it merely makes us quantum."[16]

These insights underscore the importance of carefully choosing friends, partners, and a community that will acknowledge our separate identity, respect our values, believe in our vision, and support us in accomplishing our mission. Truly, these are the kinds of relationships that will help us be all that we can be.

## Good Communication—From Basics to Dialogue and Beyond

One of the keys to good communication is learning how to remove internal and external blocks to the natural flow of information between you and others. Most of us assume that we know how to communicate. Unfortunately, even though communication is basic to human interaction, it is often not done well. Some common communication problems to be alert for are:

- making assumptions about what the other person is saying;
- leaping immediately into "helping" someone solve a problem;
- carrying on a conversation with yourself while the other person is talking;
- interrupting;
- asking probing (rather than clarifying) questions;
- inserting something in the conversation that you want to talk about, or offering unsolicited opinions and advice.

Miscommunication is often the result of incorrect, unchecked assumptions, misinformation, or insufficient data. Communication is simple—but not easy. It requires ongoing attention to other people and genuine care for them. This is really hard to fake, no matter how many "communications" courses you take. Indeed, I've noticed that most people can sense when someone doesn't really like them or when they're not being told the whole truth.

Communication ranges from basic discussion to debate to dialogue to unspoken communication. The purpose of *discussion* is to increase your understanding of others—and theirs of you—through speaking, listening, and asking or answering questions. Discussion also can help us clarify what we think and feel about something. *Debate* is a form of discussion in which you and I challenge each other's beliefs. This can help us rethink important matters. It does, however, tend to be adversarial and therefore can increase conflict because whatever we say is seen by the other person as either "right" or "wrong."

In intimate relationships, including with friends, family members, and close business colleagues, the two kinds of communication that most strengthen our connections with each other are dialogue and empathic nonverbal communication. The word *dialogue* comes from the Greek root word *logos*, meaning "spirit."[17] Dialogue means to "pass through spirit" by connecting with each another. Dialogue allows us to hear not only what others say but also the meaning that lies underneath those words. Dialogue acts as a *divining rod* that searches for the deep pools of understanding, insights, and experience that lie within and between us. And there's more. When you and I dialogue, we increase our odds of tapping into a much greater pool of understanding; i.e., what Carl Jung labeled the collective unconscious.

The other form of communication that is vital to successful relationships is *nonverbal communication*. Sometimes we feel so close to another person that we seem able to read each other's minds, to know and anticipate each other's needs. According to a classic study conducted by Professor Emeritus Albert Mehrabian at the University of California in Los Angeles, words constitute only 7 percent of one-to-one personal communication, whereas a whopping 55 percent of communication is contained in body language and 38 percent in vocal tone.

It is no wonder, then, that emotional intelligence skills (such as the ability to read nonverbal cues) are so critical to your success in relationships. Very little of what you and I are trying to say to each other can ever be successfully

*All you need is love, love.*
*Love is all you need.*
*—John Lennon and*
*Paul McCartney,*
*"All You Need Is Love"*

captured by words. When you think about it, it's almost a miracle that we ever manage to successfully communicate at all!

*Call it a clan, call it a network, call it a tribe, call it a family. Whatever you call it, whoever you are, you need one.*
*—Jane Howard*

Impulse control is another aspect of emotional intelligence that is critical to good communication. In our interactions with each other and the world, we need to manage our emotions and delay gratification (the fulfillment of our fiery desires). All relationships demand impulse control. If you're in a marriage, you have vows to honor. If you're in a friendship, you need to know when to "bite your tongue" and take a walk so you can cool down. If you're a child, you have to learn not to hit your brother, even if you really, really think he deserves it. And if you have an incompetent boss or an insolent employee, well . . . don't even go there.

Impulse control also factors into your interactions when you deliberately put other people's needs before your own. Relationship implies a mutual responsibility to serve and care for each other. With your spouse, for example, you need to collaborate on decisions, finances, and personal plans. Not infrequently, you may need to put your mate's needs before your own. In a good marriage, this giving and receiving will have a balance and fluidity to it, and this, in turn, will strengthen ties while allowing each person to blossom. In far too many cases, however, impulse control lasts only through the "honeymoon" phase, and what started out as a gentle give-and-take winds up becoming a one-up/one-down relationship with an ongoing emotional tug-of-war.

## Creating Community

*I have perceiv'd that to be with those I like is enough,*
*To stop in company with the rest at evening is enough . . .*
*I do not ask any more delight,*
*I swim in it as in a sea.[18]*
—Walt Whitman

Many of us seek a strong, supportive community: good like-minded people with whom we can regularly interact. Today, especially with the rush of our daily demands, it is difficult for us to make time to create the kind of friendships that sustained our parents, their parents, and generations before them. Many of us feel isolated, cut off from our families of origin and each other. This is a critical issue for us as individuals and for our entire society. Too often we get home late from work, make supper, then flop down in front of the TV or log onto the Internet. Others of us spend our off-hours helping our children with their homework or going to the gym. But, by and large, we don't interact regularly with people outside the small boxes we call home and work.

> It was Karen Speerstra, editor of Working from Your Core, who first called "the Sophias" together. This group of amazingly talented women loved each other almost immediately. We met monthly for several years. The purpose of our gatherings was to speak from the heart about whatever was going on in our lives, to support and challenge each other in our spiritual development and creative efforts—and to eat! The members of the group produced several published books, art shows, new business ventures, and a musical play.
>
> But those were just the tangible results of our constant encouragement of each other. We also helped each other keep our lives together as we grieved the loss of family members and mates, debated significant moves, and celebrated all the holidays—and each other's successes—with great joy. I always looked forward to our times together as an oasis of sanity and love in an often-crazy world. To paraphrase Whitman, I swam in it, as in a sea.

Those of us who have a strong community should count ourselves fortunate. It takes considerable time and effort to build friendships, but it's well worth it. Your community provides connections that support your Balancing Act and external points of reference that act as mirrors to keep you honest. And, in very real ways, it sustains not only our lives but also the lives of those in our care. To create community requires active, and ongoing, participation. You have to give of yourself on many levels. Some of us create community through our children and their school, athletic, musical, or scouting activities. Others of us form community through our churches, causes, interests, or the classes we take. If you have a group of people who are a source of friendship and nourishment, life is a daily pleasure.

## Welcoming Others into Community

One way to create community and strengthen your connection to others is by practicing *welcoming*. For example, you can warmly greet newcomers to your neighborhood, treat people who come into your home as if they were honored guests, or warmly welcome colleagues when they arrive in the morning; i.e., make a point of saying hello to them.

I find it ironic that many people consider themselves to be outsiders (even those whom everyone else thinks are the "insiders"!) To a greater or lesser degree, *we all tend to feel our differences* more than our similarities. Realizing this can help you dissolve some of the real barriers that this misperception creates. For example, you can act as a gracious host to the people you encounter. This could consist of such simple acts as making introductions, giving a new colleague a tour of your department, or treating a long-time neighbor to lunch. The practice of welcoming not only makes others feel more connected to your communities, it does the same for you.

> When I first met Marianne Hughes, she was a veteran political lobbyist in Massachusetts. Marianne has a talent for making people feel welcome. I "connected" with her immediately. At the end of our first meeting, I walked with her to pick up a book she needed at the nearby Dominican Brothers bookstore on Boston's Beacon Hill.
>
> While we were at the counter, an elderly man asked the clerk if he could see a counselor (who turned out to be away on vacation). Sensing that the man needed immediate help, Marianne stopped midstride and struck up an unhurried conversation with him. A half hour later, Marianne hailed a taxi, put a twenty-dollar bill in the cabby's hand, and sent the man off to a veteran's hospital for alcohol treatment.
>
> The man referred to Marianne's being there at his moment of great need as "a miracle." Her reply was: "Someday you'll be able to help someone else out, just as I had the chance to help you out today. In the meantime, it's important that you not throw this miracle away. Your job is to get well—that's how you can repay me. Call me when you're out and dry. Your life will be full of miracles from now on."

# LEADERSHIP

> The wise leader is like water . . .
> Water is fluid, soft, and yielding.
> But water will wear away rock,
> which is rigid and cannot yield.
>
> —John Heider,
> The Tao of Leadership

## Dissolving the Barriers That Separate Us

The fourth Element of Success helps you in your leadership Balancing Act by dissolving the rocklike barriers that sometimes separate individuals from different departments, classes, or races. Your internal Ally, the Magician, knows how to use the unspoken language of the heart—love and respect—to communicate between the diverse worlds that exist in most companies. I find it amusing that "love" is treated in most workplaces as if it was a "four-letter word." Many leaders would shudder and run for cover to hear it spoken out loud. However, love is the most powerful of all communication tools. It is tragic that it is in such short supply in today's workplace.

Respect is a good backup tool if love is banished from your office. You can call upon respect as an aid when you don't particularly like a colleague, yet you need to build a cordial working relationship. Over time, mutual respect can create a durable connection. In concert, however, the two magical tools of love and respect can create miracles—dissolve barriers, allow you to speak and hear without words, help you see the best in others. As you gain skill with these magical techniques, you can show others their best selves by reflecting what *you* see back to them. This is the same wonderful experience you have when you see yourself reflected in the eyes of someone who accepts, admires, or loves you.

In order to communicate between the worlds, you will need to pay attention to subtle messages; for example, both what is and is *not* being said. You can ask yourself questions such as: What's really happening here? What are the underlying emotions? How is morale? What are people *not* saying? How can I build trust so that people feel free to say what's on their minds? How can I give constructive feedback to improve performance? In this way, you can begin the dissolution of barriers that separate people in your organization.

## Preparation for Leadership: Developing Personal Mastery

Unfortunately, we are rarely prepared for organizational leadership, a position that requires self-knowledge, an understanding of others, and excellent social skills. These attributes of emotional intelligence are gifts of the Water element to leadership. Corporate decision-makers are rarely given the training or coaching that will support their development of personal mastery. (See Appendix B for an outline of the Core Type methodology for increasing emotional intelligence in executives.)

Rather, leaders tend to be thrown into positions of power—often due to content competency—then allowed to sink or swim. In ancient days, knights who wanted to become the king had to first:

- venture into the woods (their inner selves);

- find a way through it to face terrifying dragons (their internal monsters);

- tame, kill, or transform these monsters (address their fears, wounds, and questions);

- save the damsel in distress (integrate their opposite male or female side);

- claim the treasure (all the wisdom they have gained); and then

- return with their newfound wealth to the kingdom.

In other words, the knights first had to become emotional grown-ups before they would be considered for the role of king. What a refreshing concept! Mythology recommends this level of personal mastery because managers significantly affect the happiness, productivity, and well-being of everyone in their charge. Leaders who lack emotional intelligence—self-awareness, understanding, care, or compassion—make everyone around them miserable. And this form of executive incompetence adversely affects the bottom line. In contrast, leaders who have done their own inner work facilitate the good work of those they supervise. People want to work for bosses like this because high morale, trust, and success follow them wherever they go.

> *My uncle Kenneth Merry is a manager for the Water Department in Tacoma, Washington. One day he told me about the first time he met Billy Frank, a Native American environmental activist and a recipient of the Albert Schweitzer Humanitarian Award. Billy, who was then in his seventies, spent much of his youth in jail for acts of civil disobedience while trying to secure rights for his tribe. Ken and Billy met on a panel to discuss water issues for the Tacoma area. Billy Frank emphasized that "we all have to work together"—Indians and whites, the private and public sectors—to find enough water for everyone, while still honoring the earth. Ken told me how much he was looking forward to working with Billy Frank again. "Billy has a special way about him," said Ken. "He made me feel as if I had known him all my life."*

The fourth Element of Success provides a full range of emotions, a strong inner life, and a sense comfort with yourself and others. This helps you deal more competently with the very human problems of colleagues and employees, who, let's face it, do not always behave rationally or predictably. You can direct the Water element in your organization to create a fluid information flow, establish good channels of communication, and develop honest, trusting relationships. Water also can help you improve emotional intelligence among staff members, attract and retain the top talent, encourage teamwork, and build a strong, diverse, productive corporate community.

When leaders try to control their employees, they often find it as frustrating as attempting to hold water in their hands. Intimidation-based management techniques (such as command-and-control or micromanagement) often wind up first generating, then acting as dams for, employee resentment and anger. Of course, these dams often threaten to burst open with repressed emotions that are submerged in a backed-up lake of poor morale. Ironically, the managers themselves often become their own prisoners. Like the legendary Dutch boy who saved his town by keeping his finger in the dike, they cannot move far because they have to spend so much time and energy holding back the floodgates. As leaders bring the Water element into better balance, they can happily give up the illusion of control over others.

## Diversity: Accessing the Gifts of All

Claiming diversity is a hallmark of great leadership. Nobel prize winner Edward O. Wilson argues in *The Diversity of Life* that evolution has created all its myriad differences for some very good reasons. He says that we humans need to be stewards of our biological wealth because such diversity enhances the quality of life on earth. Similarly, diversity of race, creed, culture, gender, opinion, work style, and learning modality is vital to the evolution of an organization, and it greatly affects the quality of life in that system (as reflected in its morale and productivity).

One of your major functions as a manager is to *name*, then utilize, the gifts of all the diverse people in your workplace. As John Redtail Freesoul would say, all people are worthy of respect—even if only for the *potential* that is inside them—because "Knowledge of the Creator and the great mystery of life is hidden in everything created. . . . Every person, animal, plant, or rock has a message or lesson, its Medicine Power."[19] It is your responsibility, then, to establish and maintain an environment of respect for all those in your charge.

The wise leader champions and fully supports his people in their contributions of diverse gifts to the workplace. This doesn't happen by encouraging workers to aspire to the same externally defined "high" standard. As a senior manager in a Fortune 500 company once told a colleague of mine, "I just got it. I've thought I was for diversity. But what I meant is that I would hire any woman, minority, or foreign-born person who thought and acted just like me!"

Social theorists have suggested that instead of thinking of diversity as a *melting pot* (in which differences are assimilated and homogenized), we should use the analogy of a *stew*. In a stew, all the different ingredients retain their individual character, yet add to the flavor and texture of the whole. The advantage of the stew metaphor is that we can still "taste" the unique flavors of all the ingredients. The overall effect is that of increased richness. As our organizations increasingly become international companies within a global marketplace, they will benefit most from leaders who encourage ethnic, cultural, and other forms of diversity.

Managers will also need to capitalize upon the different gifts of men and women for the workplace. As more men and women share leadership positions, they can learn from one another's native strengths and weaknesses. In this way, they can collectively approach the alchemical ideal of the *androgynous monarch*. This perfect leader of mythology

> To the extent that this world
> surrenders its richness and diversity,
> it surrenders its poetry.
> To the extent that it relinquishes
> its capacity to surprise, it relinquishes its magic.
> To the extent that it loses its ability
> to tolerate ridiculous and even dangerous
> exceptions, it loses its grace. As its options
> (no matter how absurd or unlikely) diminish,
> so do its chances for the future.
> —*Tom Robbins*, Even
> Cowgirls Get the Blues

was typically pictured as a ruler who was half male, half female. In support of this ancient ideal, psychologist Sandra Bem found that the most successful managers had balanced male and female traits rather than being either strongly "masculine" or "feminine."[20]

The Core Type of the Magician has traditionally been pictured as an androgynous person, dressed in long, flowing robes (or as being very old and wizened), so that gender is difficult to determine at a glance. Also, Magicians sometimes were required to change form, appearance, or even their gender to do their healing work. There is inside you, then, a diversity of internal male and female wisdom that you can call upon to make you a better leader. (Jung called this opposite-gender wisdom your *animus* or *anima*.) Your great internal Ally can help you heal your organization by integrating your male and female traits. (This is represented in the image of the male and female snakes intertwined in the medical symbol for healing.) Fortunately, there are many excellent books that can help both men and women dissolve the barriers that separate us; for example, Deborah Tannen's *You Just Don't Understand* or Carol Gilligan's *In a Different Voice*.

# ORGANIZATIONS

◆

## It's All About People

The Water element in organizations—interactions, communication, information flow—is indispensible to the accomplishment of its mission and the realization of vision. And, the way a business treats its people demonstates who it really is and whether or not it is living according to its values. The health of the Water element in organizations is reflected in employee morale and its manifestations; e.g., recruitment, retention, and turnover. Corporations have to pay attention to their relationships, just as individuals do, in order to sustain them. In fact, it might be argued that most of the "work" in the workplace consists of keeping these relationships together. Management consultant Lynnette Yount says it this way: "All work *is* relationships." Another friend, David Bouchet, formerly of Digital, described his team's successful efforts as follows: "All our efforts eventually came back to the same thing. It's all about getting people to work together. It's all about people."

## All Work Is Relationships

Most of us tend to think of our job as the executive report we're writing, the truck we're unloading, or the department we manage. However, you have *no work* without your colleagues, employees, and customers. Your work activities are linked in a human chain that runs continuously from one person to the next. It is through such

## The Water Element Is Strong and Healthy in Your Organization When:

- Your workplace has a strong sense of community

- Morale and trust are high

- Communication is excellent between individuals and departments

- Information is easily accessible when you need it

- People work well together; there is good teamwork, and the workplace environment is characterized by courtesy, respect, and care

- Your corporation has superlative customer service and a clear definition of its customers

- Workers and leaders strive for consensus on all items of importance

- People support each other, especially during times of stress

- There is a strong sense of loyalty, respect, and trust among leaders and workers

- Employee retention is high, and turnover is low

- Your system supports its workers with good wages, benefits, and working conditions

- Employee assistance programs and other supports are available for personal crises

- People feel safe in expressing whatever they're feeling or thinking

- Life/work balance issues are openly addressed

- Diversity of people (race, gender, age, talent, and opinion) is strongly encouraged

channels, like streams emptying into a river, that your efforts join others and flow out into the world. You could also consider the tasks you do to be part of a complex web, a fabric woven from the threads of many relationships. Or, as Margaret Wheatley suggests, your work is part of interconnecting lines, "reaction channels"[21] through which energy is transferred throughout the organization.

One way to understand how your work processes flow into and out of others' efforts is by doing a work flow analysis. This can help you more clearly perceive the processes that already exist: the way information flows, how long it takes to get data from point A to point B, and where there are obstacles in the work flow (nonvalue-added tasks or barriers) that need to be removed.

## Seeing Relationships in a Work Flow Analysis

A work flow analysis is a tool you can use to diagram "the flow" of a given work process. It clarifies all the relationships and interactions, including the communication and information flow channels, that are necessary to complete your jobs.

A work flow analysis includes all the steps in a specific activity (such as "how our office handles written correspondence"). Diagramming what really happens in a work process can help you and others identify exactly what you do together, improve communications, eliminate redundancies, and make sure steps aren't skipped so that work activities flow smoothly from one person to the next. See the sample flow chart below that details all the steps a company must take in the process of receiving inventory. Then see if you can design work flow diagrams that apply to the functions of your workplace.

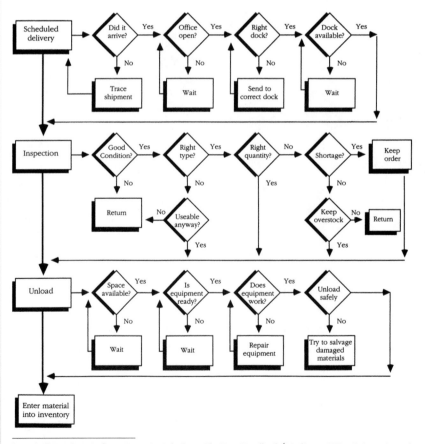

---

*Work flow chart is from Peter R. Scholtes, *The Team Handbook* (Madison, Wis.: Joiner Associates, 1998).

## Creating a Work Community through Teamwork

Most people have friends and families who support them through thick and thin. But the workplace is frequently a different story. Many of us are thrown together with people not of our choosing. It is a great thing to work with people you respect and genuinely like. If not, building teams is a proven way to develop a stronger sense of community in the work environment.

Creating and supporting teams can help you dissolve barriers between individuals or departments. One reason for this is that teams tend to foster dialogue, as opposed to the normal workplace communication patterns of discussion and debate. Dialogue allows you to hear not only the spoken words, but also the real meaning of what is being said. This is the way to arrive at solutions that are, in Stephen Covey's words, "win/win or no deal."

I have often heard participants in team-building courses spontaneously use the word "magic" to describe the new kind of interactions they are experiencing. Dialogue helps create the synergy of which so many teams speak. Workplace barriers prevent synergy by obstructing the flow of the Water element.

You can develop extraordinary work teams when you rely upon your great Ally to help you create *round tables* where power and work roles are shared; where team members are supported in taking a specific task through to its completion; and where the team's recommendations are implemented. There are many excellent techniques for developing group cohesion. For example, I have found that teaching people their Core Types or Myers-Briggs personality types or Enneagram points are fun, nonthreatening ways to promote understanding and facilitate interactions.

> One management group I worked with was already well into their quality improvement efforts and had begun to see some significant positive results. The head of this organization was determined to break down existing barriers and drive fear out of his system. He wanted his group to move on to an entirely new level of functioning together. During an executive retreat, we used the Core Type methodology to provide senior managers with professional and personal insights, an understanding of individual diversity in supervisory styles, and an analysis of the whole team's strengths and weaknesses.
>
> Many months after the retreat, the leader reported that he was still seeing results from this intervention. For example, whereas people used to be afraid to approach their boss, they now did not hesitate. He stated that people seemed more tolerant of each other. Subtle barriers had been dissolved, and people were working together much better than before.

Unfortunately, some leaders still believe that teamwork is an overly soft way of doing business. They fear that their people will get mired in a swamp of "warm and fuzzy" group meetings in which they waste time and money. However, it is this fourth Element of Success that provides the glue necessary to keep diverse individuals working together until they break through on resistant problems that would have been impossible to solve alone.

## Setting Up Teams to Ensure Success

It is the *process* of teamwork that eventually produces great *results*. Experts recommend that work groups allot approximately 25 percent of their time to maintenance functions. As a team leader, you need to make certain that group members: spend time getting to know each other; check in with each other when starting a meeting; evaluate the meeting at its conclusion; give everyone a chance to speak; settle disputes as they arise; and talk things through until everyone comes to a consensus about decisions. (Consensus doesn't mean that everyone on the team agrees 100 percent on every detail but rather that all group members are sufficiently satisfied with the decision to give it a try.)

Although spending one-fourth of a team's time on maintenance functions may seem excessive at first blush, it is exactly the kind of preventive medicine necessary to keep work groups from bogging down, breaking down, or having to do costly rework. Some characteristics of the most successful teams I've facilitated include having specific, clearly defined tasks—plus the authority to carry them out. It also helps if group members are given basic team training. (This makes sure you don't waste your time or theirs.) It also ensures the likelihood of success if groups are walked through their forming stage with facilitators who can make certain that all the Elements of Success are attended to.

High-functioning teams generally consist of a leader (the keeper of the content), a facilitator (the keeper of the process), and team members (who include a time-keeper and a scribe). I have found that it works best to regularly rotate these roles. This ensures more equal participation: It keeps the talkers or those with a hidden agenda from taking over, and it also encourages the shy members to come forward and take full responsibility. Work groups tend to be most productive when they consist of four to eight individuals. (This appears to be a natural human grouping. If the group is any larger than that, it bifurcates, much as a living organism subdivides. If the team is any smaller, it lacks synergy.)

One of the first steps for a work team is to draw up its own ground rules and operating procedures. Then it can use the Elements of Success to establish a strong foundation by clarifying the team's identity, shared values, vision, mission, and lines of communication and authority (and make certain these are aligned within the organization). Setting up an agenda is an excellent first item of business for each meeting. Even if a tentative agenda is drafted beforehand, it has to be agreed to by all the participants, adjusted, then posted on newsprint for all to see, with estimated times assigned to each item.

As the meeting progresses, business items can be checked off as they are completed. If need be, discussion items and times can be renegotiated by the whole team. Although this process initially seems time-consuming, it soon makes for great efficiency because everyone in the group is completely aligned. There is no pushing and pulling, no working at cross-purposes.

Of course, forming teams is not the solution to all work problems. Unless they are already in place, up and operating, teams are not great at generating quick solutions. Teams are most useful when your business needs long-lasting solutions to complex problems. They also can be a big help when you need different viewpoints or "buy-in" from other parts of the organization. Teams also are an excellent vehicle when a variety of expertise is required to resolve a difficult issue.

I have facilitated the establishment and development of many teams, working with them from the beginning to the completion of their tasks. Often members are skeptical at the outset about the value of the team maintenance functions I insist upon. However, I can predict with considerable accuracy the degree to which a group will succeed or fail. As deadlines approach, conflicts (Fire element) tend to arise in all work groups. Universally, it is the teams that have paid attention to the Water element who retain their balance, stay together, and produce exciting results. Those that shortchanged their maintenance will fall apart as soon as the road gets bumpy. The rewards are high for corporations that develop good work teams. I have seen such groups, even in the space of a few days, break through on problems that have plagued their organizations for years, wasting untold resources and time.

## The Flow of Information in an Open System

In recent years, there has been an increase in attention to "knowledge management." The fourth Element of Success has a significant impact on the flow and generation of knowledge in an organization. When the Water element is unhealthy, information is hoarded, blocked, or diverted in its natural flow (and therefore does not get to all parts of the system). Worse yet, this vital element can be poisoned by fear and lack of trust. When information is allowed to flow freely throughout a corporation, it increases knowledge by fostering learning, sparking creativity, breaking down barriers, and dissolving fear.

Unfortunately, many workplaces I've seen have considerable trouble with the Water element. Mismanagement of organizational knowledge is likely to occur whenever the following circumstances exist: Employees don't feel that they're being heard; there is underlying resentment regarding issues that were never dealt with properly; employee fear and anger are repressed; customer service problems are unresolved; morale is low; employee turnover is high; or there is a general lack of trust. If the Water element is ignored for a long time, it will either a) stagnate and cause the organization to rot from the inside due to lack of cooperation and productivity, or b) overflow its banks and uncontrollably flood the system, resulting in outbursts (such as labor strikes) or covert revolution (that is; passive-aggressive behavior).

Communication competence, which is vital to the smooth flow of information, is often underdeveloped in the workplace. The interaction patterns of senior managers set the tone for the whole organization. Too often, however these are directives and commands that rely on workers' fear of job loss to ensure compliance. The problem is that fear poisons the Water element in a corporation, infecting everyone as it circulates throughout the system. Much as your body needs fresh, clean water to survive, organizational systems need nourishing, efficient communication for knowledge to flow. Unfortunately, despite the sea of memos, e-mails, faxes, and meetings that we all swim through daily, most of us could lament as did Samuel Taylor Coleridge in *The Rime of the Ancient Mariner* that there is:

> *Water, water, everywhere,*
> *And all the boards did shrink;*
> *Water, water, everywhere,*
> *Nor any drop to drink.*[22]

One of the most beautifully designed organizations in the world, your body, contains many lessons for optimizing systemwide information flow. An intricate yet highly efficient communication system operates via fast-acting fluids to pass necessary information on to every cell in your body. This is without your giving it a thought, without your needing to control or command it. Furthermore, your internal communication system has many cross-connections that serve as fail-safe mechanisms to sustain your life, just in case any part of you is temporarily or permanently damaged. When your corporation is a healthy community, it acts just like a human body or like any aggregate of cells that has evolved a membrane: i.e., it serves as a physical a container that sustains the interactions of you and your colleagues.

Fluid communication and easy information flow are necessary to create a corporation that is an *open system* rather than a *closed system*. Closed systems, such as machines, tend to run down as *entropy* (decay, wear and tear) increases. Open systems allow additional information, ideas, and energy to flow into them; in this way they continually renew themselves. This openness counters the cyclical pattern in which a closed system's growth slows down, then turns into decline, and finally results in death.

The secret to the long-term survival and vitality of a business, then, is constant renewal, change, and adaptation; i.e., constantly being "in-formation." You can even think of the element of Water as "pre"-structure; indeed, *it is the reason for organizational structure*. Optimally, your company's form is designed to support an easy flow of the Water element—communication, information, interactions—throughout the entirety of it. (Indeed, this is why Water precedes Earth in the Elemental Circle.)

Open systems are alive. They grow and evolve in full cooperation with the community and world around them. In this way they can continuously renew themselves while still maintaining their own distinct identity, boundaries, and integrity within their surrounding environment.

## Defining Your Workplace's Community

Your organization is a web of relationships. It functions as an open system within a larger network of relationships that constitute your industry and society. Clearly, the development of community is good for any business.

In many ways, the wider the circle is cast, the more inclusive it is, the more people who feel they belong to your business community—the better it will be for your company. As Peter Block says, "We treat all people who come in contact with us as members of our organization."[23] A business community includes employees, their families and friends, your customers and suppliers. Moreover, your workplace exists within an infrastructure that includes the political, educational, and other structures that support you. You may wish to think of layers or circles of community, with the inner rings being more immediate relationships than the others.

### Key Organizational Relationships

In the space below, you can list key members of your organization's community. These can be individuals and other organizations vital to your business's success. Or you can use this exercise to define only the organizational community with which you personally interact. Or you can work with team members to define the key people who form your more immediate workplace community.

1. **Staff members (employees, departments, jobs functions, partners):**

2. **Customers** (current and prospective):

3. **Stakeholders/investors:**

4. Vendors/suppliers:


5. Families of staff members:


6. **Community** in which your organization lives; physical environment, neighborhood, schools affected:


7. **Industry members** (current and potential competitors and allies):


8. **Others:**


## An Integrity Check for the Water Element

1. Do you feel comfortable in your work community? Do you have friends there? Note the people you particularly like, trust, respect, admire, or feel connected to.


2. To what degree do your work and personal communities overlap? Note where.


3. In what specific ways does your work community share and support your personal identity, values, vision, and mission?

## Building Relationships within the Economic Community

In order to survive, your workplace needs a constant flow of the Water element into and out of it. This can be accomplished by participating fully in the larger economic community so that money and other resources flow into and throughout your business to nurture every corner of it. When organizations offer their products in the marketplace, they are reaching out to connect with others, offering to provide them with resources and services they need. This ongoing exchange benefits everyone.

When an interchange of resources and services is fluid and honest, everyone prospers and grows. Your economic community expands. When we think of marketing as a way to develop a thriving economic community, we are more likely to treat other members of that community well. The fourth Element of Success encourages us to nurture long-term relationships with vendors, customers, and employees, rather than trying to make a quick profit or get the best deal. Stable, mutually beneficial, long-term relationships are very good business. They provide us with the support of concerned neighbors who feel interdependent and look out for each other's best interests.

However, now that the whole world is the marketplace for many of us, we sometimes forget to "think locally," to pay attention to and take good care of our own neighborhoods. In the old days, it was easier for people to see their mutual dependence. Our grandparents were an integral part of their communities. They has to rely upon the good will of their neighbors if their businesses were to survive.

Fortunately, increasing numbers of corporations are becoming better neighbors within their immediate communities. In many cities, restaurants and hotel chains contribute food to homeless shelters on a daily basis. Some large corporations make it a policy to build in neighborhoods and towns that other businesses shun. Such organizational behavior bodes well for the collective health and well-being of our communities.

●

## The Fourth Element in Action: Healthy Communities Massachusetts

*Healthy Communities Massachusetts (HCM) is a coalition of twelve hundred individuals, private organizations, businesses, and public institutions who have banded together to develop seventy-one initiatives for improving the quality of life in towns and cities throughout the state of Massachusetts. HCM was launched in 1994 as an outgrowth of the World Health Organization's Healthy Cities project, an attempt to completely redefine and approach the issue of public health.*

*The World Health Organization argues that public health is related to economic health, and in turn, the economic health of our neighborhoods is related to education, and that to politics, and so on. In Healthy Community initiatives, every part of the town or city is seen as interdependent and critical to its overall health.*

*HCM and organizations like it throughout the world look at the myriad, complicated problems of their communities with the perspective and cooperation of insiders—people who live and work in the neighborhood. HCM believes that by first owning our collective problems, then dialoguing about them, we are more likely to arrive at solutions that will be meaningful, effective, and long-lasting.*

# WORLD

## An Inescapable Network of Mutuality

*Each organization is . . . a system within a system, within a system,*
*within a system. The universe [is] one fabric. . . . There are no*
*resource problems—only relationship problems.*
—Leland Kaiser, Managing at the Ninth Level

It is the element of Water that connects us within the body of humanity. It shows us that we individuals are actually systems that exist within systems—and that the boundaries we see are much more fluid than we can imagine, more like permeable membranes than brick walls. The well-being of our neighborhoods, homes, schools, workplaces, economies, nations, and the ecosystems we all share are inextricably linked. Each of these

*A human being is a part of the whole*
*[but he] experiences himself . . . as something*
*separated from the rest. . . . This delusion is a kind*
*of prison, restricting us . . . to affection for a*
*few persons nearest to us. Our task must be to*
*free from this prison by widening our circle of*
*compassion to embrace all living creatures*
*and the whole nature in its beauty.*
—Albert Einstein

systems is an inseparable part of its larger community. Together they form a complex web of subtle, but powerful, ties.

The gift of this fourth Element of Success is the understanding—and experience—of our connection to all people (and, some would argue, every creature) in every part of the world. The task before you and me is to widen our circle of compassion so we can claim kinship with all our "relations."

*Almost anything you do will seem insignificant, but it is very important that you do it.*
*—Mahatma Gandhi*

When we truly understand that we are all connected, we are more likely to remember that the effects of our actions ripple out in all directions, like the waves caused by a small stone thrown into a pond. Our actions echo throughout our systems, causing echos in yet other interlinked systems. To quote the chaos theorists, "a butterfly stirring the air today in Peking can transform storm systems next month in New York."[24] In this vast sea in which we all swim daily, what each of us does with our lives really does matter and has effects beyond our comprehension.

One of the problems we now face is that most of us are too exhausted from work, too isolated by our individual concerns, too dulled by TV, or too consumed by child care to create local community—much less to connect with the larger circle of humanity. This is one reason W. Edwards Deming (in the PBS special "The Deming of America") urged workplace leaders to make certain that their employees had time and energy left over at the end of the day. In this way, they could contribute to other systems (school boards, church groups, volunteer organizations) that form the seamless fabric of the community. He argued that these other organizations, in turn, nourished the workplace.

In a society in which loneliness and alienation are severe problems, many of us can help create *networks of responsibility*—people who care for one another. Building community can happen in countless simple ways, including treating a troublesome customer with respect, offering directions to a lost stranger, or attending PTA meetings. We connect not only with others, but also with our best selves when we go out of our way to say hello to a shy person, do some community service, stop by an elderly acquaintance's home for a visit, or intervene when somebody needs help. Indeed, the ways we can build community are endless.

*I sought my own soul—but my soul I could not see,*
*I sought my God—but my God eluded me.*
*I sought my brother—and found all three.*
*—Anonymous*

*It really boils down to this: that all life is interrelated. We are all caught in an inescapable network of mutuality, tied into a single garment of destiny. Whatever affects one directly, affects all indirectly.*
—*Martin Luther King Jr.*

After connecting with our more immediate "brothers and sisters" within our own neighborhoods, it is only a few short, logical steps to expand this paradigm of relationship to include people within our national boundaries and eventually others in the world. Indeed one of the Water elements gifts is its ability to dissolve the formidable barriers that have separated and suppressed people in the past.

But we now seem to be wavering between warring impulses—old habits versus new understandings. Will the systems within systems, our neighborhoods and nations, become even more separate, or will we form lasting bonds with one another? This is a critical question before us today. And there is another vital question regarding our network of mutuality: how are we to develop a more sustainable relationship with "the infinite, primordial ocean" of our own ecosystem, this all-encompassing, delicate system within which we live, work, love, and breathe?

One answer to all these questions, I believe, is for us to develop our emotional intelligence as a species. The evolution of humanity has not been an easy or an even-paced journey. But now it is high time that we "grow up."

The truth is, we must learn how to share our world as if we were all members of the same family who sit down to dine and converse with each other at the end of a long day. Actually, we have little choice in the matter; we affect one another whether or not we intend to.

To ensure our collective survival, we need to develop, one person at a time, the emotional intelligence that will enable us to communicate and collaborate more skillfully on shared problems. In this way we can learn how to speak the language of the heart and return to a state of pre-Babel. And when we have empathy and compassion for others, we will become more capable of serving them and the world. I think that our own lives, and the lives of future generations, depend on it.

# 5

# CREATING NEW REALITIES

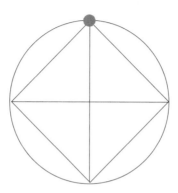

## The Goddess Earth

*In the beginning, Gaea, the Goddess Earth,*
*"brought forth of herself, without consort,*
*Heaven . . . the Hills . . . and the Sea."[1]*
*In this way Mother Earth, the universal parent,*
*gave birth to everything that we know.*
*The Romans say that Gaea "was born from Chaos"*
*and that, without a mate, she bore*
*Uranus (the Sky), Ourea (Mountains), and Pontus (the Sea).[2]*
*American Indians tell how, in the beginning,*
*all people and animals*
*"emerged from the Earth's uonic hole,*
*and it was just like a child being born from its mother."[3]*
*Indeed, from time immemorial,*
*people have recognized that the Earth is the womb of all that lives,*
*that it "produces all things*
*and then enfolds them again . . .*
*[it] is the beginning and end of all life."[4]*
—from Roman and Native American creation myths

## All That Matters

The last of the five Elements of Success is Earth. As the tangible, visible "house" for all the other elements, it provides the concrete structures that allow you to implement them in your daily life. Earth forms the channels through which your interactions and and communications flow (Water). It carries your activity to fruition in strong, reliable vehicles (Fire). It also helps you materialize your hopes and dreams (Air), and puts your values to repeated test in daily life (Essence). The Earth element corresponds to the physical body that serves as a container for your soul, mind, will, and emotions. Earth, then, is where the rubber meets the road, It is the reality-testing part of the Balancing Act.

You and I rely upon the generosity and beneficence of our Mother Earth. She is matter (from the Latin word for "Mother"). As her children, we receive her *material wealth*—all the bounty of the earth with its extraordinary physical resources that translate into our food, shelter, money, possessions, beauty, the pleasures of the five senses, and good health.

Earth represents both the continually unfolding miracle of life and also the considerable daily effort you expend to harvest nature's bounty. It sustains your life, relationships, and work by helping you master your craft, take good care of your body, make enough money ("daily bread") so that you are financially secure, stay at a task until you complete it, and create the right channels for your talents. Earth is solid, concrete, measurable. It sometimes constricts and limits us, forcing us to make difficult choices. No one denies the existence of this final Element of Success. Conse-

*Magic isn't the fuzzy, fragile, abstract and ephemeral quality you think it is. In fact, magic is distinguished from mysticism by its very concreteness and practicality . . . magic demands a steady naturalistic base. . . . Magic makes something permanent out of the transitory, coaxes drama from the colloquial . . . magic [can] be made, wholly and willfully, from the most obvious and mundane . . . it is a matter of cause and effect.*
—Tom Robbins, Even
Cowgirls Get the Blues

quently, it tends to be the one we first attend to in our lives, that is most obvious in our relationships, and that is most understood in workplaces. Paradoxically, because we rely on the Earth Element so heavily, it may become something we take for granted, as when we push our bodies to exhaustion or treat the earth's resources as if they were limitless. However, it is this fifth element that teaches us how to renew our physical selves and how to replenish our natural resources. Earth is contained in all the small, daily ways you take care of yourself, tend to your relationships, and get your work done. Earth makes real magic possible. It completes the Elemental Circle with its practicality, its ability to transform ideas into matter. This last Element of Success demands that you remain fully of this earth, that you pay attention to the details. Without it, all your efforts up to this point—your cherished values, lofty ideals, passionate mission, and supportive connections—will come to naught.

Earth is the element of manifestation. It is the solid vessel that brings all the other aspects of yourself into reality. Remember that ancient Magicians are often pictured as having one hand pointing to the heavens (to draw down inspiration) and the other pointing to Earth (to "ground" that inspiration). Earth not only provides you and me with the tools we need to make our heart's desires come true, it also grounds us (keeps us in the present moment) by displaying and making us face the limitations of our current reality.

If we have too little of the Earth element, our lives lack order and security. We have a hard time accomplishing what we want to do. We may wind up in dead-end jobs that underutilize or underpay us. We have difficulty managing our finances or other vital resources, including our physical health. We eat erratically, or we gulp down foods with insufficient nutrients. On the other hand if we have too much of the Earth element, we tend to "calcify" (as Rudolph Steiner said); that is, we become rigid, inflexible, emotionally hard, or get stuck in overly comfortable ways of doing things.

This last Element of Success also represents the process of implementing everything we've learned so far. It is only by integrating the insights you've gained from experience that you can make change happen in your life. Your great Ally, the Magician, helps you gain the skills you need slowly, so you can mature over time and gain solid mastery in your chosen craft. The Earth element cautions that there are no straight lines in nature, that the route to personal mastery and wisdom is often a winding road. And one with no shortcuts.

In this fast-paced, instant-messaging world, Earth slows us down. This tends to make many of us impatient. When we see the potential of the future as clearly as if it were already happening, we don't want to waste time doing "administrivia" details that make us feel hopelessly bogged down. Instead of just rolling up our sleeves and doing the work required by the Earth element, we tend to push ahead, hoping beyond hope that it is a straight pathway from point A to point B. However, in reality, our life journeys tend to be winding, indirect, often seemingly inefficient. Earth cautions us that if we desire the quick path or the straight line, we are doomed to frustration.

The Magician Core Type maintains that our life processes, although often apparently chaotic, have their own order, that the journey itself is at least as important as the destinations we envision. Mary Catherine Bateson illustrates this truth beautifully in *Composing a Life* when she says, "Life is an improvisational art form . . . the interruptions, conflicted priorities and exigencies that are a part of all our lives can, and should, be seen as a source of wisdom."[5]

# PERSONAL LIFE

◆

## Crafting Your Life

The Earth element contains a paradox that can help you greatly with your personal Balancing Act; i.e., *the Earth appears solid but is not.* It is constantly changing.

It is alive.

The Romans believed that the goddess Gaea was born from the god *Chaos*—and modern science would concur, saying that this is still the reality of our earth. The true nature of the world, so chaos theoreticians tell us, is hidden beyond the ability of our senses to see, hear, smell, touch, or feel it. This is most disconcerting: The very ground on which we walk is actually swirling energy!

This underlying nature of the Earth element can help you craft your life, providing living models from which you can design better structures for every aspect of your life. All such structures must be *solid* enough to contain your activities and carry them out into the world, yet they must also be *flexible*, easily adaptable to changing circumstances. Ironically, the only real stability available to you and me these days is to become comfortable with the natural chaos that surrounds us, and in this way, to work *with* nature, rather than struggle against her. After all, nature only *appears* chaotic. There is a profound, underlying order to nature, which is why many scientists are now referring to this phenomenon as *complexity* rather than chaos.

Because the Earth element is always evolving and changing, it requires our constant attention. For example, such things as maintaining our homes, possessions, and health all need to be done regularly, little bit by little bit, over time. We cannot exercise, clean the house, discipline our children, hire staff, or go to work just this one time—get it all done and then forget about it. (Would that it were so. . . .) We will have to do these chores again and again, because that is the nature of the Earth Element.

Fortunately for all of us, not only is this last Element of Success very demanding of regular attention, it also is quite forgiving. If we don't tend to a particular matter today (e.g., buy groceries), we probably can still do it tomorrow. However, we get into trouble with the Earth element when we procrastinate excessively, much as

## You Have a Strong and Healthy Earth Element When You:

- Take good care of your physical health (take time to eat well, exercise regularly, get enough sleep, and don't work yourself into exhaustion)

- Stay on top of all aspects of your financial resources; maintain a sufficient cash flow, and do not find it difficult to draft a budget or live within it

- Feel secure in your life, relationships, and work

- Make certain that your home and work environments are attractive, well organized, pleasant—not only neat, clean, and orderly but also physically safe and comfortable

- Tend to move through your day in an unhurried, steady way

- Are consistently productive

- Make certain that whatever you do is done well (so that you don't have to redo it)

- Pay attention to detail; check out the facts and collect data before proceeding

- Have no trouble setting (and keeping) realistic personal and professional deadlines

- Develop strong competency and skills in your chosen field

- Are considered by others to be "solid"—reliable, steady, dependable even in crises

- Are well enough organized to find the items you need when you need them

- Treat day-to-day chores in a matter-of-fact manner or as a welcome break

- Have efficient life and work habits that help you attain your goals and realize your dreams

- Do regular "reality testing"; i.e., seeking feedback from family, friends, or colleagues so that you can make necessary life, work, or relationship improvements

- Keep your nose to the grindstone—and still make it a point to take time out for yourself

- Are drawn to physical beauty and Nature

- Dress attractively and appropriately, maintaining a good physical appearance

farmers can lose their whole crops if they wait too long to plant or harvest them.

The earth we live on goes about its business in such a matter-of-fact way that it is easy to forget the magic of this complex life that swirls all around us. This is not surprising, as our human perceptual system developed instead to notice those things that change very suddenly (that is, those things that most threatened our ancestors' lives). Like the archetypal Good Mother, the earth supports and sustains us, without calling any undue attention to herself. Gaea is generous, full of countless daily miracles that we tend to overlook: trees budding in spring, then turning color in fall; children mastering complex language and coordination tasks; animals that can stand and run only hours after birth; rich soil that grows the grains we eat; or sudden rains that make the city air sparkling clean again.

Our own bodies act much as Gaea does, silently keeping us healthy. If we cut a finger, our bodies rush internal "emergency crews" to the site before we can consciously think of what to do. In fact, our bodies are self-healing constantly, daily warding off thousands of invading microorganisms. You can feel more magic in your life just by paying attention to the everyday splendor of the Earth element, including the joy of having a human body and being able to feel life pulsing through your veins. As Walt Whitman said in *I Sing the Body Electric*:

> *The love of the body of man or woman balks account,*
> *the body itself balks account.*
> *That of the male is perfect,*
> *and that of the female is perfect. . . .*
> *For it the globe lay preparing quintillions of years*
> *without one animal or plant,*
> *For it the revolving cycles truly and steadily roll'd.*
> *In this head the all-baffling brain,*
> *In it and below it the makings of heroes.*[6]

## Grounding Techniques to Strengthen the Earth Element

*Grounding* includes staying in touch with reality, dealing with physical limitations, becoming more practical, taking care of details and allowing this final Element of Success to sustain us. There are numerous everyday ways you can stay grounded. A few are listed below.

**1. Take a physical break.** Walk outside on your lunch break or whenever you feel agitated or tired, or when you need to clear your mind. Just for that short time, let all your senses focus on what's around you. Delight in nature, the changing seasons, the beauty of the gardens you pass. Remember that there is natural healing available in reconnecting with the earth.

**2. Indulge your five senses.** Quite literally, stop and take some time to smell the roses. Linger over a delicious meal. Set aside a quiet hour in the evening to do nothing but listen to your favorite music. Sit under a tree with your back against the trunk. Watch the sun rise or set. Lie on the ground and watch the clouds go by. Cuddle your child. Embrace your spouse. Go dancing. Get a massage. Experience the joy of living in this body.

**3. The mountain pose:** Stand as tall as a mountain with your feet positioned directly below your hips and your toes pointing straight ahead. Evenly distribute your weight on the four points at the bottom of each foot (the inside and outside of both the heel and ball). Taking a deep breath in, draw yourself up to your full height: head, neck, and back straight but not rigid, hands loose at your sides. Slowly breathe in and out. Feel your strength, your steadiness—you are a mountain, rising from the earth. (You can do the mountain pose without attracting attention to yourself, for example, while talking with others at work, or while waiting in line at the grocery store.)

**4. The tree of life contemplation:** Stand with your feet firmly planted on the ground. Imagine that your spine is the trunk of a tree and that your feet have roots. With each breath, feel your roots growing—through the floor, into the ground, and deeper yet into the center of the earth. As the roots go down, draw up the strength of the earth. Feel its energy enter your whole body, like sap rising through the trunk of the tree. When you are ready, imagine that you are growing branches that reach from the crown of your head to the sky. Continue breathing. Feel yourself as a tall, regal tree that simultaneously touches the sky with its branches and the center of the earth with its deep roots. To complete this exercise, imagine your "branches" sweeping back down to touch the earth again. This completes the circle, returning any overflowing energy back to the earth. (If you wish, you can actually gently bend over and touch the ground.) Then sit quietly for awhile, until you feel sufficiently grounded to return to your activities.

**5. Go ahead—hug a tree.** Or at least thank one. Trees are the main source of the oxygen you breathe. They act as our planet's lungs. Not only that, trees cycle water up from the soil and release it into the air, creating a beneficial cycle that creates more rain and prevents the land downwind from becoming desert wasteland.

**6. Body contemplation:** Sit quietly. Allow your breath to ease gently in and out. When your mind slows down, turn your attention to the miraculous workings of your own body. Notice how your breath causes the lungs to expand and contract, lifting the chest slightly up and down, and gently moving your rib cage slightly in and out. Listen to the beating of your heart. Feel the pulse it sends throughout your body. Know that blood is coursing through your veins, carrying vital nutrients throughout. In this way, turn your attention to every part of your body. Express gratitude as you become aware of the silent workings of this exquisite container for your life force.

## Moving from the Mundane to the Magical: Using Habits to Craft Your Life

Although great dancers, gifted artisans, and other highly skilled professionals make what they do *look* easy, there is always hard work involved. This is why students in ancient guilds spent so many years learning the details of their craft under the watchful eyes of their teachers. You probably had to expend significant effort mastering the basics of your profession before you could experience those exhilarating break-through moments. The Earth element teaches us that practice makes perfect, that there are no shortcuts to competence. When it comes to gaining the gifts of Earth, we must roll up our sleeves, plant the right seeds at the right time in fertile ground, till the soil, pray for good weather, and harvest the crops when the moment is right. This is why it is said that "God is in the details."

In fact, many spiritual traditions treat grounding practices as a direct way to experience the Sacred right here and now. As Zen teachers say, "When you wash your bowl, wash your bowl!" That is, don't let your attention wander; focus on whatever you've doing at any given moment, and do it as well as you can. The Earth element supplies old-fashioned elbow grease to get the work done. Only with hands-on applications are we able to test our theories against real-life experience and turn our daily work into a scientific laboratory. Earth embodies the brass tacks of trans-forming our lives from the mundane into the magical, in much the same way as a skilled blacksmith transforms a slab of metal into an intricate work of art.

Habits are the way we "craft" our lives. They help us implement and integrate change in every part of our Balancing Acts. Habits are the structures of time and activity, all the details necessary for organizing and managing our lives and work. They are patterns of behavior repeated frequently enough so that they become "crystallized" into recognizable forms. Habits make our daily tasks more efficient by linking discrete and varied activities into cohesive patterns that are easier to re-member and accomplish.

Habits are the *rituals* of our lives, relationships, and work. All traditions are made up of rituals designed to increase the group's memory, make sense of life, and re-mind the group's members about each one's connection to each other and to a deeper purpose. By the force of repetition and experience, rituals make life feel safer, more stable. They give us a deep sense of security. Rituals are, by their nature, predictable. They tend to be done exactly the same way, over and over again.

The difficulty comes if rituals take on a life of their own and lose their original meaning in the sands of time. Such habits can become empty containers, no longer carrying anything of value. When this happens, rituals can actually become counter-productive *ruts*—habits that are cast in stone, no longer alive and relevant. Unfortunately, we often are emotionally attached to the ruts we get ourselves into (because they make us feel safe). In many cases, we have used these habits for so long that they now define the borders of our lives.

Habits help us with their efficiency; that is, we don't have to reinvent the wheel every time we turn around. They make it easy (eventually automatic) to remember what to do next. A similar sort of memory serves in the human body "so that we do not collapse into a heap of bricks."[7] In much the same way as memory holds your body together, habits hold your life, relationships, and work together. Furthermore, the shared, overlapping habits of you, your family members, your neighbors, and your colleagues hold your systems together.

Rituals are often seasonal, with a natural life of their own that comes and goes. It takes a while to get habits in place, then they function well—then circumstances change, and they no longer are appropriate. If you continue with a ritualized habit much beyond its natural life span, you will feel as if you are banging your head against a brick wall. Habits in any part of your Balancing Act must be assessed regularly to make certain that they still have meaning and purpose; otherwise their weight will crush, rather than support, you.

## Identifying and Changing Your Habits

The purpose of learning is to alter any habits that prevent you from successfully adapting to a changing environment. Therefore, it is critical to regularly review your life rituals so that you can make certain they are working optimally for you.

A good way to change your habits is to start small. Make a goal of examining just one habit that no longer works well for you (or is not congruent with the other Elements of Success). Then make that goal more "concrete" by writing it down. For example, if your goal is to take better care of your finances, begin by analyzing your financial habits. How do you work with money? Write down your current patterns. Then break down your goal into discrete, manageable tasks with realistic times attached. (For example: "I will subtract the amount from my checkbook immediately after writing a check.") Write down specific tasks under your goal. This technique of analyzing your habits and crystallizing your goals is like making a promise to yourself. It makes your goals more real, more tangible. And, in turn, this process dramatically increases the likelihood that you will be able to draw down the power of this inspiration to Earth.

Answering the following questions can help you determine if any of your current life and work habits need to be changed.

## Making an Inventory of Your Personal Habits

**1. Review your personal values, vision, mission, and assessments** from prior chapters so that you can note habits that need to be changed to support your Balancing Act.

**2. What habits do you have in place** that seem to be working well for you, that are efficient and still have a purpose?

**3. What habits are not working** as well as they have in the past?

**4. Where are there inefficiencies** in your life? Where do you waste excessive amounts of time, or find yourself doing the same things over again?

**5. What could you reorganize,** systematize, streamline, or delegate so that you optimize your time and effort?

**6. In what way might your current habits be tweaked,** improved, or modified to be more supportive of what you want to accomplish?

**7. Choose one area of your life,** relationships, or work in which your Balancing Act needs improvement. Then choose one habit to change in order to implement that improvement.

*The key is to stop doing the things that no longer work for you!* By starting to change them now, you can revitalize and rebalance your whole life.

When you take stock of your habitual processes, simply note if there are any activities within them that do not add value, that are superfluous, or that take too much time. You may benefit by checking with friends, relatives, or colleagues about alternate ways of doing activities that they have discovered. One technique for analyzing and changing habits is to diagram a flow chart for one of your life or work activities. (See the example in chapter 4.) As an example, you might want to look at all the steps you normally take to get to work in the morning. When I first did this analysis, I noticed that I could lose as much as a half hour vacillating about, then preparing, what I was going to wear! From that point on, I set out my clothes the night before. This analysis of my habits resulted in an immediate alteration of an unproductive habit. This new habit, in turn, resulted in a more efficient process of getting to work.

## Magicians' Tools and Techniques (Earth)

**Rituals.** Repeated patterns of behavior that are used to remind the community of their connection to each other and the Sacred. Rituals are also the life, relationship, and work habits you use to accomplish your daily activities.

**Grounding.** Ancient Magicians often brought inspiration to Earth and helped manifest it. Grounding includes the many practical ways you bring your values, ideas, and mission into reality.

**Magic Mirror.** A tool for seeing what's true, so that you don't delude yourself. The Magic Mirror is a feedback mechanism that shows you how you are measuring up to standards you have set for yourself. Using the Magic Mirror can also help you ask the right questions and see how to make necessary course corrections.

**Magic Formulas.** These were secret codes by which Magicians passed on information, such as healing cures. Magic formulas, including habits analysis and statistical processes can point to the roots of problems, provide standards for benchmarking, and help you make decisions based on data rather than hunches.

**The Study and Imitation of Nature.** Magic is the study of nature. By imitating the natural forms that exist on earth, you can create more organic and life-enhancing habits and structures for your life, relationships, and work.

**Naming (Earth).** Saying what is true—right here and now. (As Sergeant Friday of "Dragnet" advised, "Just the facts, ma'am, just the facts.") Naming includes checking the data, looking at labels on food, researching information on the Internet, putting simple or complex feedback systems in place, or using process control measures at work.

**Book of Wisdom (Earth).** Writing down what you've learned. Listing the how-tos, what did and did not work, any data that would provide a basis for continuous improvement of your habits and goals. Also include the questions you used to unearth deeply rooted underlying problems.

# RELATIONSHIPS
◆
## Making Love Real

*Don't talk of stars
Shining above,
If you're in love,
show me.*[8]

In *My Fair Lady*, an exasperated Eliza Doolittle tells her loquacious suitor to stop with the words—"If you're in love, show me." That same aspect of the Earth element was echoed in recent years during a hilarious scene from *Jerry Maguire*, when Cuba Gooding's character chants over and over to his sports agent, "Show me the money." These characters made the point colorfully—without this Element of Success, you and I have no relationship.

Earth makes love real. It asks love to be here now so that it can nurture and sustain us day to day. As Woody Allen once said, "Showing up is 80 percent of the job." That is true also of relationships; they require us to "show up" for each other. Earth provides us with the life-enhancing gifts of security and stability. Someone may sing to you, "I will love you until the end of time," but the Earth element interjects, asking a question the Beatles made famous: "Will you still need me, will you still feed me, when I'm sixty-four?"

### Show Me You Love Me

Love, after all, is in the details. Earth supports and sustains our physical experience of love; it is where we plant love so that it can be nourished and grow strong. The fifth Element of Success is reflected in all the small, often mundane, ways we maintain our relationships and take care of each other. It helps us put food on the table, bring home flowers, remember the anniversary, do the laundry, send cards to a friend, visit a neighbor at the hospital, and pick up the phone to ask, "How are you?" Earth is the outward manifestation of our feelings for each other. Without this element, love rings hollow.

Because Earth is the tangible demonstration of our relationships, it is always critical to their success. I may say that you are a great employee, but if I pay you poorly, it doesn't count for much, does it? Earth demands that you put your money,

## You Have a Strong and Healthy Earth Element in Your Relationships When You:

- Have agreement, clarity, respect, and a sense of equality about what each other contributes to the relationship (e.g., finances, work, time, talent, resources)

- Cooperate to take good care of joint resources (e.g., money, property, home, office space) and agree, by and large, on how to use them

- Have financial arrangements that are clear, fair, and appropriate

- Both feel secure, stable, and solid in your relationship

- Would not hesitate to use the resources at your command to help each other in times of need

- Do not "discount" the other person's worth or contributions or claim that yours are of greater value

- Are comfortable demonstrating how you feel about each other

- Have developed day-to-day habits that create order and stability in your lives, that are supportive of each other and the relationship, and that do not significantly annoy the other person

- Have clearly and cooperatively defined the parameters, boundaries, structures, and "rules" of the relationship. If you are friends, business partners, or lovers, this could mean agreements about shared property. If mates, it could be about where you live and work; if parents, how you raise the children; if colleagues, who is in charge of what tasks

- Can be relied upon to keep the promises you make to each other

- Manage together to take care of all the tasks for which you both are responsible

- Are comfortable with the other person's physical presence and appearance

- Support each other in staying physically healthy

- Work together to make your home or other shared property attractive, functional, pleasant, orderly, physically safe, and comfortable

time, and energy where your mouth is. Earth results in clear, fair contracts; promises that are honored; relatively equal exchanges of energy and favors between friends; and spending unhurried time with your children. It is the function of Earth to translate our values, words, and desires into repeated, reliable behaviors that are sustainable over time. Earth also demands that we act appropriately and in accordance with the expectations of a relationship; that is, that we stay within appropriate and agreed-upon boundaries.

Earth also defines limitations and mutual responsibilities. It demands that you select from among infinite possibilities and then pour your time and effort into the vessel you have chosen. For example, by selecting a mate, you choose a channel for the marriage relationship and accept not only its joys, but its responsibilities as well. When you have a child, you embrace both the delight and limitations that come with being a parent. When you hire an employee the two of you enter into a contract of mutual responsibilities: an honest day's labor for an honest day's pay.

After you enter into a relationship, the Earth element encourages you to do the required maintenance work; that is, establish positive rituals that support your interactions. For example, perhaps you have developed a habit of visiting your mother every Sunday night. Maybe you and your children look forward to your nightly quiet time together when you read to them before bedtime. Perhaps you and your spouse have a standing Friday night date where the two of you can be alone, enjoy each other's company, and remember why you got married in the first place. All of these are examples of rituals that serve to nurture the relationship and keep it growing over time.

This Element of Success also demands that we keep the implicit and explicit promises we make. Explicit promises are intentions we have "crystallized" by verbalizing them to ourselves or each other. This is both good and bad news. By writing down an intention or speaking it out loud, we put it into a more earthen form, thereby increasing the likelihood we will accomplish it. However, if we become careless, overwhelmed by too many promises, or actually make conflicting committments, we are setting ourselves up for big trouble. I once heard it said that our broken committments never go away. They just gather like deadwood, cluttering the shores of our lives.

The promises you make in relationships include such things as arriving at the appointed time to meet a friend, getting the agreed-upon papers to a colleague, or paying bills in a timely fashion. There are also implicit promises you make when you enter relationships: for example, to give your children the physical, mental, and emotional food that most nourishes them; to honor your parents; to be kind to those you call friends; to love your mate; and to do the best job you possibly can for your employees and employer.

## Reality Check

The Earth element provides you and me with an ongoing reality check in relationships. It shows us that handsome is as handsome does, that words are transitory and appearances often illusory. Earth shows us, in very tangible ways, how we truly value each other and what our real priorities are.

Earth demands that we have genuine respect for what each of us contributes to the relationship and that neither of us discounts the time or energy the other person expends. This Element of Success cautions that we are in trouble if one of us believes that our part of a friendship or a work project is "worth more." Relationships are tricky in this regard because each of us brings our unique talents, beliefs, and capabilities to the interaction. It is only when we value the contributions of the other person that a relationship can endure.

Conflicting valuations often take place in battles over money. A critical reality check for relationships is to look carefully at what each person provides, not only financially, but also in the equivalents of time and energy. In many traditional marriages, the husband commutes into the city to earn a paycheck while the wife stays at home to care for the children. This economic arrangement is typically agreed upon for the stability of the family unit. However, unless both people acknowledge these very tangible contributions, each will come to resent the "fact" that his or her spouse is not giving enough to the relationship. Unfortunately, it is almost a cliché in Western society that money comes to be seen by *both* parties as a greater contribution to the family than the home labor and time. (This is despite all the research that calculates how much money would be needed to replace that "free" labor.) When devaluation of any kind occurs, the wars soon begin and the earthen structures of the relationship disintegrate.

The fifth Element of Success is the final link in your relationship Balancing Act. It provides the bedrock of endurance, stability, and solidity for all your interactions. It is the secure hearth that contains the fire of love so that you can be warmed on cold days. It is the solid vessel that holds the nourishing water of life for the times you are dry and thirsty. It is the field you build where your dreams of wonderful relationships can finally come true.

# LEADERSHIP

## Managing Form and Function

The Earth element contributes management and administrative skills to your Balancing Act as a leader. All leaders, no matter how senior, have management responsibilities, because their proper handling of details is critical to their company's success. Moreover, one of the best ways you can serve your workplace is by developing viable organizational rituals and strong structures that serve as reliable vehicles to get the system's work out into the world.

### Assisting in the Evolution of Organizational Rituals

The fifth Element of Success requires all of us to assume leadership in areas where we have particular skill, expertise, relevant work experience, or training. It also calls upon every worker to exercise leadership by giving feedback about the efficiency of work processes and the quality of products and services delivered to customers. Those people designated as decision-makers are responsible for initiating changes in work rituals and structures whenever environmental or internal circumstances demand a systemic shift. Since most of us are resistant to change, managers need to help everyone learn new habits while simultaneously providing support during difficult transitions.

Good leaders prioritize training and education, which are indispensable tools for altering ingrained habits. Unfortunately, only one in fourteen American workers has ever received formal training from an employer. Instead, most of our corporations have subscribed to the "follow-Joe-around" school of job training. Obviously, this results in a steady *erosion* of our skill and knowledge base, because what Joe manages to teach another person is always going to be less than the total of what Joe knows. In turn, what that person is able to teach the next person will always be only a part of what he or she learned. This results in an inadequate investment in knowledge generation and management, and does not lend itself to organizational learning or adaptation. When executives have to root out old habits that are deeply embedded in the system's memory, training becomes especially critical. The Earth element shows us why we need so much patience to move through significant organizational change. People evolve organically, too, only when they are ready. Unfortunately, work and life habits can become like bricks that are held in place with cement—so resistant to movement that they will cause significant damage if a leader tries to blast through them forcibly.

Old habits, rules, and procedures are best dismantled piece by piece, with respect for those who built them and for the structure they have held in place so long. After all, they have served a good purpose. The underlying meaning and reason for each (new and old) ritual needs to be scrutinized. In this way, change can proceed carefully, intelligently, scientifically. The Earth element urges us to move slowly and systematically—to make just one change at a time, then watch for repercussions and unintended consequences throughout the whole system. It argues against surgical procedures, unless survival necessitates it.

However, in real crisis situations, emergency measures may be required. If workers believe that these extreme efforts are necessary for survival, they are more likely to support them. When leaders and workers act in concert, even at these late stages, miracles can occur. As in real life-and-death situations, organizational systems can mobilize their internal resources and transform even the most resistant of habits overnight. The deeply imbedded desire to cling to life puts everything into perspective. It provides a great impetus for quickly modifying deeply entrenched, counterproductive habits.

## Asking the Right Questions

It is said that when author Gertrude Stein was on her deathbed, she asked over and over again, apparently puzzled, "What is the answer?" Then, quite suddenly, Stein sat bolt upright. Her last words were, "No—what is the *question!?*"

Good leaders ask questions. Indeed, success lies not so much in finding the right answers but rather in asking questions that will lead us to new knowledge and revitalize our workplaces. Questions uncover the facts that can help us with our reality checks. They serve as magic mirrors, revealing truths that are currently obscured from plain sight. For example, a problem can be delved into more deeply by systematically asking these six questions: *What?*, *When?*, *Why?*, *Where?*, *Who?*, and *How?* Another magic formula for finding the root cause of any problem is simply to ask the question *Why?* five times. (For example, Q: "Why did the machine shut down?" A: "Because the fuse blew." Q: "Why did the fuse blow?" And so on.) These questioning techniques lead us step by step, like detectives following a trail of evidence, until we discover the real culprit.

## Using the Magic Mirror of Feedback

*Mirror, mirror, on the wall,*
*who's the fairest of them all?*

The Magician Core Type uses the *magic mirror* to see truths about the present and the future that are concealed from others. Feedback systems act as magic mirrors for leaders, clearly reflecting the reality of what is happening in the organization. Feedback is necessary for an individual or system to learn, adapt, and survive.

A good feedback system has many components. For example, it includes *benchmarking*. This is what Snow White's stepmother was doing when she asked her famous question of the magic mirror. The *benchmark* in this case was a standard by which she compared her beauty to that of other women in the kingdom. When you benchmark, you look both outside and inside your system to arrive at new standards of quality. You can even benchmark with corporations outside your industry to find ways to improve your work processes, expand your perspective, and keep yourself alert so you can grow with the times.

Benchmarking helps determine the standards you wish to meet. Once you set these standards, you can use the *magic formulas* of measurement and statistical process control to achieve the quality you desire. The beauty of such techniques is that anyone in the organization can exert leadership by using these tangible tools to improve the work he or she does.

Fortunately, statistical techniques are much more user friendly than they used to be. Now people at all levels of corporations can use checklists, control charts, cause-and-effect diagrams or histograms to collect feedback and measure progress toward goals. Such tools help leaders manage the *whole system* rather than micromanaging individual workers. The techniques support the search for truth, often leading us deep inside the Earth element to find buried gold: counterintuitive insights about the reasons for chronic problems.

## Making Course Corrections

Problems are a natural part of organizational life. However, the first difficulties that surface are likely to be symptomatic of hidden underlying issues, much as a dog's annoying bark wakes its owners to the presence of an intruder. Similarly, leaders need to follow the trail of these first presenting problems, then make course corrections based upon what they find.

In *Peak Performers: The New Heroes of American Business*, Charles Garfield states that one of the common traits of his "new heroes" was their assumption that they would make errors. After these inevitable mistakes, they would quickly decide upon *course corrections* and continue in the right direction. Garfield notes that the first moon launch was perfectly on course only *10 percent* of the time and that the other *90 percent* of the time was spent adjusting the course. He argues that (as in the moon launch) what matters to great leaders is results and that it is more important to produce the "critical path" than any theoretically perfect path. This involves constant questioning: Are we on track? If not, where are we off—and why?

The other Elements of Success helped you determine your course: the theoretically perfect path. Now you can use the Earth element's monitoring techniques to measure the degree to which your business is on or off course. Such feedback tools serve as a compass—and they work best if they are put in place at the start of the journey. Unfortunately, many organizations are not so proactive, and find themselves having to make radical course corrections just to survive.

A good feedback system serves as a health-maintainence mechanism for an organization. It not only includes benchmarking, setting of standards, and using measurements, but also:

- asking direct questions,

- setting up easy ways for workers to give opinions and ideas,

- making sure people know they will not be blamed for mistakes,

- treating mistakes and problems as clues that lead to the underlying root causes, and

- redesigning the corporate structure as necessary so that it remains vital.

What is clearly implied here is that *good leaders manage the system, rather than individuals*. In most workplaces, when mistakes are made, the culprits need to be captured and punished. First, blame must be assigned. Then the offenders are fired, disciplined, or "managed" differently (i.e., motivated, cajoled, or threatened in an attempt to prevent the problem from reappearing). This approach only buries the underlying issues more deeply. As the Gertrude Stein story illustrates, these are "answers," but they are not likely ever to unearth the vital questions we need to ask.

Biologists say that there is "a delicate web of intelligence" that binds any body together.[9] A similar web of "body" intelligence also pervades your business: It is the hands-on experience of every worker. Managers have the responsibility to gather and use this extraordinary wealth of feedback for the good of the whole organization. Because front-line employees actually deliver the services or products to customers, executives need to constantly gather data about what the customers are saying—and how the system can be improved. (This is like your fingers letting you know whether the water you're touching is tepid—or boiling!) When a feedback system is constructed that taps the full intelligence of the organization, leaders will always know what fine-tuning needs to be done day to day. In this way, early warning signals can replace the eruption of severe crises.

## Designing Organizational Structure

In *The Fifth Discipline*, Peter Senge contends that managers often neglect their role as *designer* of the organizational structure and that "it's fruitless to be the leader in an organization that is poorly designed."[10] You need to be proactive when it comes to the issue of organizational structure, because a strong, flexible, and well-designed system will make everyone's job easier.

The rituals or work habits shared by a group of people solidify over time into protocols, rules, procedures, and lines of authority. Indeed, this is how the structure of a business evolves. In many ways, an organization is formed from behaviors that developed to reflect, perpetuate, and *house* its values, vision, mission, and interactions. Although the tail should not wag the dog, this is precisely what often happens once an organizational design gets set in place. Structure needs to provide stability and security for its leaders and workers. But it also needs to be flexible enough to facilitate—not get in the way of—the work that needs to be done.

The fifth Element of Success provides the organization's "earthen" vessel. Poorly designed systems are like sieves through which the wealth, energy, and resources of corporations are lost. Such workplaces tend to unintentionally reward dysfunctional behaviors and in this way dissipate rather than augment organizational efforts. According to Steven Cavaleri and Krzysztof Obloj: "Structure is the primary determinant of behavior in systems." They contend that if leaders want to create any long-lasting behavioral change, they must change their system's underlying structure.[11]

It is generally easier to build good institutions from the ground up, rather than overhauling old ones. Although very few of us have the opportunity to start a new business of our own, many of us will have ample opportunity to use the real crises in our organizations to implement structural transformation. If survival issues force your workplace to abandon old ways of doing things, you may be able to call upon the phoenix to rise from the ashes. Our current global marketplace is an excellent illustration of this phenomenon. After the destruction caused by World War II, Japanese and German industries were forced to construct new buildings. This led to more rapid industrial expansion than that of the Allies, who simply refurbished their old, intact buildings.

As a leader, you need to work within the confines of your organization's design. This simultaneously provides limitations to and channels for your work—an obstacle here, an opening there. Structure is the manifestation of prior decisions. When it no longer works, it must be adjusted in thoughtful ways, or the system will malfunction. Clearly, we are undergoing a sea change in how we configure our workplaces. Charles Handy predicted many of these changes in *The Age of Unreason*, in which he described newly emerging structures such as:

- the shamrock organization—in which the three leaves are core workers, specialist contract workers, and a flexible labor force;

- the federal organization—allied individual groups with some shared identity;

- the triple "I" organization—knowledge-creating organizations that add value via intelligence, information, and ideas.[12]

I am fascinated by the experimentation in workplace structures. People in substantial numbers are telecommuting from home or trading pay for a shorter work-week. As Handy says, thanks to these massive shifts, more of us will become what he labels "portfolio people." That is good news, he contends, because *it will bring better balance into our lives.* The "portfolio" of our work may be some combination of two forms of paid work (for wages or for fees) and three forms of unpaid work (homework; gift work; and study.)[13]

Still, many of our workplace containers are cumbersome and overly complicated. They are so rigid that they tend to crush the life out of the people within them. The example below comes from a sector of the federal government with which I have worked. Too often work processes, once established for good reason, are left in place even after that reason no longer exists. After a while, these processes become boulders in the paths of workers who only want to do a good job.

> *One group within the Public Health Service told me of the time they invited a dignitary to visit their office. For a variety of historical reasons, this part of the PHS required many officials to sign any document that left the agency. Consequently, this letter of invitation went up and down the chain of command for many months, a few revisions here, a word changed there. Eventually the invitation returned to its originators, finally approved for release. This, however, turned out to be an embarrassment for everyone involved. The dignitary had long since come and gone.*

One last caution: Many leaders respond to all crises by automatically moving around the furniture; that is, by reorganizing or reengineering their systems. Often this only makes things worse—sometimes much worse. Any systems design or redesign needs to serve the values, vision, mission, and interactions of the organization; that is, Earth needs to house the other four elements. *Always, form is to follow function.* Structure needs to be flexible enough to easily transport the organization's knowledge throughout the whole system and smoothly deliver products to the world. Far too often, however, this is not the case. Because the Earth element is so easy to see and manipulate, leaders can throw up a temporary emergency structure (like a tarpaper shack) that provides a roof for the night. Too often, however, these temporary systems stay in place and actually perpetuate the very problems they were meant to ease. Leaders wind up creating this tangible, temporary change so as not to really change.

# ORGANIZATIONS

◆

## Building Systems That Work

An organization's structure is the *body* that houses its ideas and values, giving them shape and allowing them to take form in the world. It is the hearth that contains the fire of mission, keeps it burning, and puts it to good use. It is the channel through which information flows. It is the container that we use to bring into the world the results of all our work, the fruit of our labors—our products and services.

The structure of a business directly reflects the metaphors used by its architects to describe it. Just as the Magician Core Type uses the technique of *naming* to reveal the real nature of something, you can "name" your organization via the metaphors you choose. These metaphors will shape your perception so that you more easily see, then emphasize, that particular aspect of your workplace's reality. Common metaphors used to describe organizations range from machines to living systems, from prisons to family groups, from battlefields to playgrounds. In truth, our corporations are actually *multiple realities*, many things at once.

In the Industrial Age, organizations were usually seen as machines that had replaceable parts. Today more people think of businesses as analogous to organic, living systems. Corporations have even been compared with trees, where "the trunk and major limbs are core products; the smaller branches are business units; the leaves, flowers, and fruit are end products. The root system that provides nourishment, sustenance, and stability is the core competence."[14]

Unfortunately, most organizations today still tend to use the same workplace structure—the hierarchy—whether or not it suits the particular functions and needs of that system. The hierarchy is the workplace form that most of us know and have grown up in. It is modeled on the military: the classic, time-tested, successful Warrior institution. Although the hierarchy is a strong structure, it is not very flexible, nor is it particularly "alive." In fact, *the hierarchy was designed to deal efficiently with death*: that is, to facilitate the clear, immediate, and uncontested replacement of superiors who fall in battle. In military hierarchies there is no question as to who is next in command and whose orders are to be followed in these life-and-death moments. Clearly, the hierarchical structure is not an appropriate design for all workplaces. Although many companies are harried much of the time, they are (one hopes) not active battlefields with dead bodies lying about!

Another problem with the hierarchical structure is that it goes out of balance rather easily. Steven Cavaleri says that rigid organizations, in efforts to protect themselves from competitors, expend their energy outward. This is not even good military strategy. No general worth his salt would do what many corporate leaders do: send a predominance of their resources out into battle and keep so few resources to guard the internal workings of the fort, leaving it unprotected, weakened. And, like a tree with dry rot, a system that is weak inside will eventually collapse on itself.

Our future organizational forms must be strong and flexible enough to accommodate new growth and to adapt quickly to changing circumstances, much as a seed has to break out of its shell so that it can bloom. Indeed, the most vital systems I've seen—startups, entrepreneurial efforts, or organizations with very strong missions—are often somewhat chaotic. This In-between is a time of new beginnings, a springtime of experimentation with structures, not only in the workplace but also in art, music, literature, and governments. These are times for us to be bursting out of our old shells and creating new forms within which we can all more easily balance our lives, relationships, and work.

## The Earth Element Is Strong and Healthy in Your Organization When:

- The organization's structure supports its values, vision, mission, and relationships and is an effective, efficient vehicle for bringing the organization's products and services out into the world

- The system is flexible (capable of changing and reforming as necessary), but it does not change unnecessarily or too fast (thereby avoiding the creation of other problems)

- The business is in excellent financial health and has a stable bottom line

- Managers and administrators are competent and well trained

- The organization's policies, procedures, and rules are clear, regularly updated, and supportive of the tasks that need to be done

- Habits and processes are efficient and orderly

- The workplace has a steady pace that is highly productive

- The organization has the resources it needs to meet its goals in a timely manner

- The fruit of its labor is the production of high-quality products and services

- Employees feel secure and are well taken care of

- The workplace itself is comfortable, neat, physically attractive, safe, and conducive to efficient working

- The organization has excellent feedback systems; course corrections and other changes are determined by constant monitoring of feedback

- Individuals are not blamed or punished for errors; instead the mistakes are treated as clues that can lead to the solving of deeper root problems

- The organization uses quality tools to gather data and to constantly review work habits so that they add value and are efficient

- There are ongoing improvement efforts to support long-lasting, incremental changes

- The corporation's products or services are a good value for the money; they are reliable and trustworthy; standards of quality are determined by customers

## How Your Organization's Structure Really Works

1. **Does your workplace have an organizational chart?** If so, draw it below. If not, draw your impression of your organization's design. Be sure to note where you are within this structure.

2. **How does this structure work** for—and against—the well-being of the whole system? How does it support the other Elements of Success?

3. **If you have ideas for redesigning** your workplace in any ways that would better support its activity, list them below.

4. **List work processes** (organizational habits) that you believe need improvement. Note any suggestions you have for improving them.

## An Integrity Check for the Earth Element

Use the spaces below to answer the following questions.

1. Think about the congruence of your personal and workplace habits and structures. Are they of a piece, or do you have to completely shift gears when you move from one to the other?

2. How similar or different is your pace of completing tasks? Are you efficient and effective in both your home and work? Are there ways you can transfer skills or effective habits from one aspect of your life to another?

3. Do you have supportive structures in both your home and workplace that help you complete your entire "portfolio" of work? Are there any outdated, ineffective habits at home or work that you need to rethink or any skills you need to retool?

## The Organization as a Living System

Because your Ally the Magician believes that everything is alive, the living systems metaphor for organizations fits most comfortably within its worldview. You could even think of your organization as being somewhat like a human being. For example, your corporation has a self-contained body similar to your own. The structure that holds everything together is like the connective tissue that defines your physical boundaries and supports all the swirling life that exists within those boundaries. Departments are similar to internal organs (both contribute to, and are dependent upon, the life of the entire system). Energy and money pulse through your workplace, much as blood and nutrients move through your veins. Your organization's products or services are the fruits of its hands, heart, and mind. You and your colleagues are like the cells that do all the day-to-day work. And, as we have explored in the other Elements of Success, your organization has its own distinct personality, mind, will, and even soul.

When you imagine an organization as being similar to other living organisms, it is easier to understand why layoffs or hostile takeovers send devastating shock waves throughout the whole system—they are like a serious accident or major surgery. Treating an organization as if it was a living system encourages us to take preventive measures before it becomes fat or overgrown. If you eat excessively and do not exercise regularly, odds are that you will gain weight. Businesses also grow in inappropriate ways. A colleague of mine once consulted with a large government agency that had hired three thousand more staff than its budget allowed! When a congressional committee called them on the carpet, radical surgery was the only option available.

## Birthing and Caring for an Organization

Gaea gives birth to the whole world through her body. The carrying and birth of a child is a long, often uncomfortable, and ultimately painful process, but, as any mother will tell you, well worth all the trouble. So it is with the birthing of a corporation, a new department, or new products and services. Rarely does anything spring forth into the world fully grown, as did Athena from Zeus's head. Your organization, its departments and products, probably all developed in a way similar to the human gestation process. It is no surprise then that *labor* is a requirement for moving from *conception* to successful *delivery* in all significant creative actions.

After a child's birth we must immediately move on to a new stage: the nurturing of this beautiful, fragile creature, its daily care and feeding. Similarly, the Earth element insists that we give constant care and attention to new products, organizations, or departments. The continuous nurturing that is required for child care is not a bad analogy for the ongoing attention that is required for any business to succeed.

## Continuous Improvement as a Way of Life

Business author Tom Peters once said, "The most efficient and effective route to bold change is the participation of everyone, every day in incremental steps." This is referred to as continuous quality improvement (or *kaizen* in Japanese). A Japanese participant in one of my seminars defined kaizen as *a way of life* that combines "study, practice, and faith." Continuous improvement is an aspect of the fifth Element of Success. It is a one-step-at-a-time approach to problem solving. Kaizen could also be described as a combination of patience, determination, and applied innovation. It is an inch-by-inch approach to improving the status quo by making a small improvement, then moving on to the next small step.

Kaizen is perhaps better suited temperamentally to the traditional work culture of Eastern nations, whereas in America we have historically preferred to make quantum leaps. If that first attempt fails, we tend to move on rather quickly to something else. This difference in approaches to quality improvement is a bit like the legendary race between the tortoise and the hare. One Food and Drug Administration (FDA) manager, upon learning about the concept of continuous improvement, commented to me: "I've often thought that the way we work is like the way some teams play baseball. Everyone who gets up to bat tries to hit a home run, but all they have to do is get on first base!"

*The magical potential of kaizen can be illustrated by a story told to me by Frieda Sohn, a sculptress who was my seatmate on a flight from Baltimore to Boston. While looking together through a book with beautiful art plates, we came across one that had a quote by Albert Einstein in its border. Frieda, who was eighty-two at the time, paused and looked out the window. When she spoke softly a few moments later, I could hardly believe my ears: "I knew him, you know."*

*For the rest of the flight, I listened in rapt attention to Mrs. Sohn's delightful stories. Frieda had been a Lithuanian refugee whose family lost everything in their flight from Hitler's troops. Once in America, she obtained a scholarship to Columbia University, where her roommate was Margaret Einstein. Frieda soon became a frequent guest at the family's home in Princeton and a favorite of Margaret's famous father, who nicknamed her "Friedel."*

*One day when they were talking, Professor Einstein stunned Frieda by remarking, with great humility, "You know, my dear Friedel, I'm not nearly as smart as everyone thinks I am. I just stay at a problem longer than anyone else."*

I found it most interesting that Albert Einstein described his own thinking process as being much more like kaizen than breakthrough quantum leaps. I think the truth to making lasting change in our organizartions lies somewhere between these two approaches. I suggest that enduring transformation takes place when we use kaizen daily to prepare ourselves for any window of opportunity that suddenly opens. Both magic and genius, it appears, come from bringing the tortoise and the hare together at last!

## The Fifth Element in Action: An Alive Congregation

*I once attended an Episcopalian church in Maryland to hear my brother Tom sing for a baptism. Tom and I were welcomed warmly by people who went out of their way to introduce themselves. This congregation consisted of all ages, many races, and similar numbers of men and women. I found it somewhat startling that the members of the church felt quite comfortable walking in or out of the service whenever the spirit moved them. The scene was nothing short of chaotic.*

*When the time came for the baptism, the female pastor took the crying baby in her arms, kissing and cuddling it. The congregation laughed at her unsuccessful attempts to pacify the screaming baby when water was poured on his head. When the pastor gave the baby back to his parents, she declared triumphantly above the cacophony, "I always said I wanted an alive congregation!" People burst into laughter. This parish was thriving financially, growing rapidly in size, and obviously generating great loyalty and love in the process.*

# WORLD

## May You Inherit the Earth

*Don't it always seem to go
That you don't know what you've got
Till it's gone.
They paved paradise
And put up a parking lot.*

—Joni Mitchell

Thanks to the research of many scientists, we now know much more about the real nature of our earth than we used to. We understand better its delicate, complex fragility and the ways we have inadvertently hurt it. It now appears that humanity has been living out of balance with the earth for some time, by consuming too rapidly our shared "capital" of nonrenewable natural resources. According to Robert Ornstein and Paul Ehrlich, "our total inheritance took billions of years to assemble; it is being squandered in decades."[15]

In *The Last Hours of Ancient Sunlight*, Thom Hartmann eloquently describes the consequences of our disregard for earth. Below are some of "the facts, ma'am, just the facts."

**Dwindling "Ancient Sunlight."** This is the term Hartmann gives to our oil, coal, and gas resources, all of which were produced from sunlight by vegetation 300 million years ago. We have been spending down so rapidly on this precious savings account that at our current rate of consumption, these supplies will last less than forty-five years.[16] In our own or our children's lifetime, we will have reached the bottom of the barrel! Since so much of our current food production and distribution depends upon technology fueled by oil, the ramifications of depleting these resources are disturbing.

**Population Explosion.** While it took the first two hundred thousand years of human existence to reach one billion people, the second billion took only a hundred and thirty years, and the third billion a mere thirty years more. And the escalation has continued, reaching six billion human beings in 1999. By 1987 we were the most populous species on the planet (in terms of biomass). No one disputes that the current growth rate cannot continue. The only question is how it will stop—and most of the possible scenarios are not pretty. They include widespread famine (because we are outstripping our food supply), wars over limited resources, plagues, natural disasters (due to climate disruptions), and scientific solutions (such as birth control.)[17]

**Pollution.** We're currently pouring more than six billion tons of carbon into the air annually from our burning of trees, coal, and oil. This released carbon forms a "greenhouse" shield that results in global warming and the wild weather extremes that many of us have already observed in our own regions. These, in turn, cause "natural" disasters and adversely affect the food supply. For example, Hartmann notes that temperatures in Antarctica, "relatively stable since the dawn of time," have risen sufficiently to melt large portions of its ice shelves. These contain 70 percent of the earth's fresh water, and such melting will cause severe flooding as oceans rise significantly around the world.[18] And that's just air pollution. Our water supply is almost undrinkable in many parts of the world, and more than 75 percent of the topsoil that existed worldwide just a few centuries years ago is now gone.[19]

**Species Extinction.** The rate of extinction for the past three hundred million years was approximately twenty-five species of animal or plant life per century. Until now. Today we are losing up to 100,000 species per year! In the past century, we have lost nearly one-fourth of all the species of plant and animal life that were present when humanity first appeared. The last time there was such a mass extinction was the death of the dinosaurs.[20] Our own destiny, our own survival, is tied in subtle ways to the lives of all other creatures in our fragile ecosystem. Indeed, if the earth's diversity continues to decline at this rate, the extinction of the creature at the top of the evolutionary pyramid may be just around the corner.

**Trees, Water, and Desertification.** Trees are our major source of recycled oxygen—they are the earth's lungs. Trees discharge water into the air to create rains and then draw the water up from the soil to release it again. When a land is denuded of its trees, the area downwind of it lacks rain and a vicious process called *desertification* begins. The soil becomes salty; remaining trees are more vulnerable to parasites and disease; crops fail. Camelot quickly becomes the barren Wasteland Kingdom. Forests all over the world are being destroyed—a staggering seventy-two acres of rain forest are cut down *per minute*. Even if saplings are planted in their place (more often the acreage is cleared for housing, crops, or grazing), it will be several decades before these tiny trees can supply the atmospheric moisture of the trees they replaced.[21]

That's the bad news. So what can we do? How can we honor Gaea who births and sustains us? Hartmann suggests that we remember how to live in harmony with nature by revisiting the stories of Older Cultures, the First Peoples who lived sustainably for millennia. Simultaneously, we need to rethink the paradigms of our Younger Cultures, which have created these problems in the first place. And we can start this global transformation with ourselves. "The most important part of personal transformation—leading to planetary transformation and/or sowing the seeds for a brighter future," he says, "is to become fully alive, alert, aware, conscious of our surroundings and the divinity everywhere."[22]

To bring ourselves and our ecosystem into greater balance, it is vital that we start changing our technology so that we can use our remaining oil to develop alternate energy solutions. It would also be wise for us to decrease our dependence on centralized power utilities and corporate farming. Don't worry—you and I don't need to return to life as it was in primitive societies; we just need to more intelligently conserve our current resources. We also need to think about what is "enough," what will actually increase our (felt and real) security. Sustainable agriculture techniques are actually capable of replenishing the earth while it feeds us, and "intentional communities" are springing up that could provide us and our children with new, supportive living situations.

If you and I connect with others to think through these issues of survival, we can solve our shared problems and reduce our numbness to the crises surrounding us. Although earth has remarkable strength and a truly magical capacity for self-healing, we must do our part. Like good children everywhere, we must help Mom out when she needs us. That would be now.

Gaea holds the keys to unlocking the secret truths of nature, the mysteries of the ages, which people throughout the millennia have sought to understand. Our sciences have contributed not only to the problems listed above but also to our understanding of the underlying magic that is the earth's reality. Everything and everyone is interconnected, conscious, alive. Even our small personal actions have a positive or negative effect. These understandings encourage us to assume stewardship of the earth's wealth so that many generations from now—even until the end of time—we will continue to inherit the earth.

◆

# PART III:

## The Whole Is Greater Than the Sum of Its Parts

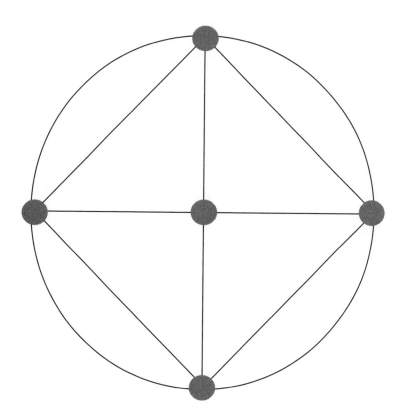

# 6

# THE SPIRAL OF SYNERGY
# AND THE SACRED DANCE

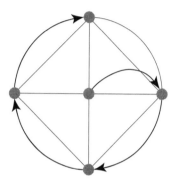

### The Divine Music

*Listen to the melodious music of the divine poet.*
*He plays upon the flute of love—*
*the notes soar to heaven*
*and reach the distant stars*
*and dance on the raging waves of the sea.*
*The earth, the sea, the sky, the stars*
*are all woven together*
*by the soft strains of the divine music.*
*Its vibrations echo through the corridors of time*
*in the endless canopy of the sky.[1]*

—from the *Sama Veda*

# The Spiral of Synergy

The whole of the Elemental Circle is greater than the sum of its parts. When you bring the five Elements of Success into a dynamic balance, miracles can start to occur. This phenomenon is called *synergy*—"the cooperation of divine grace and human activity." As you link the Elements of Success from the first element to the last in your daily Balancing Act, you create the spiral diagrammed below.

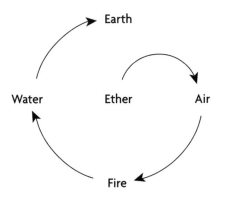

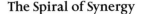

**The Spiral of Synergy**

I call this form the Spiral of Synergy because *synergy is both the* result *of your Balancing Act and a* proof *that you are moving along the right track.* Synergy is what you experience when your life, relationships, or work seem to "sing." When a musician sounds a note in its very center, not only do you hear that one tone, you also hear the overtones, the harmonics, the natural sympathetic sounding of a series of notes around it. Its vibrations cause ripple effects that make other notes vibrate, sometimes audibly. The more "in tune" the note is, the more rich and full it sounds. Similarly, the more "in tune" you feel because the Elements of Success are congruent and "vibrate sympathetically," the more in balance and synergistic your life will become.

The Spiral of Synergy, then, is the goal of *The Balancing Act*. It is one of the secrets contained within the Elemental Circle. This dynamic, constantly evolving spiral provides a well-tested working blueprint for how you can *experience* more of a sense of oneness and unity in every aspect of your life. From this point on, I will refer to this exhilarating experience of Oneness as the "Sacred." It is the beginning point and the end point—the Source and the result—of *The Balancing Act*. Symbolically, the Sacred is the Whole of the Elemental Circle that contains all of the five separate elements. The Sacred is also spoken of as the greater Circle that encompasses and provides the container for all our individual circles. Or as Hermes Trismegistus, a great Alchemist, once said: "God is a Circle whose center is everywhere and circumference is nowhere."[2]

For success in your own Balancing Act, you need to define "the Sacred" in a way that is meaningful for you. Many scientists refer to the Sacred as the *unifying field* or the *cosmos* or the *universe*. Christians pray to *God the Father*, Muslims to *Allah*, the *Supreme Being* who comprises all the attributes of perfection. Kabbalists—the early Jewish mystics—did not speak the full name of the Divine, instead calling it *G-d*. Ancient Hindus worshipped *Kali, the great Mother*. Some people think of the Sacred as *Creation*, the *Source* of all life, or *Life* itself. Others refer to a *Higher Consciousness*. Buddhists call this Oneness *Emptiness* or *No-thing*. Atheists think of this phenomenon as the *Void*. Taoist sages describe the great, incomprehensible *Tao*, where yin and yang cease to be opposites and come into unity. Zen practitioners believe that there are no words that can possibly capture this *ultimate reality*. Many Native Americans refer to the *Great Spirit*, which is the animating force in every form of nature. Even our workplaces today are being affected by humanity's desire to name and connect with the Sacred. The July 2001 edition of *Fortune* magazine headlined an article on "God and Business." In it were numerous stories of corporate leaders, business owners, management consultants, and others, who are quietly weaving their lives into a unified, whole fabric and infusing their jobs with meaning by unobtrusively bringing their spirituality to work.

The Source has countless names from which you can choose. But however you define it, the Sacred will give you an experience of profound oneness, a deep sense of meaning, and the conviction that your life is an integral part of one seamless fabric. The Sacred is the unifying context for your Balancing Act.

## The Gift of Each Element of Success to the Whole

The Elements of Success, the Elemental Circle, and the Spiral of Synergy are powerful tools that allow you to touch the Sacred in many ways:

- When you rest in your quiet Center, you can hear the Universe pulsing within and without you.

- Air inspires you to touch the Mind of God.

- It is said that passion, Fire, "is God's way of saying hello" and making you feel alive.

- Water connects you to the Divinity in others.

- Earth is how you manifest the Sacred, making it "real" in your daily life.

By bringing all the Elements of Success together, you and I can experience increased balance and synergy, thereby making us realize that we are much more than we think we are. Truly, we are One.

# The Gift of Each Element

Each of the five Elements of Success provides a vital link to creating synergy in your life, relationships, and work. Below is a summary of some of the key points of Part II.

*Element #1: Essence* (Soul) contributes contentment, calmness, equanimity, and a sense of identity (who you really are) to your life. It gives relationships trust; honesty; the ability to be your genuine, full selves with each other; and sometimes even a feeling that you are "soul mates." Essence adds the qualities of integrity and natural nobility to leadership. Your workplace benefits from the element of Essence with strong clear identity, values, ethics, and respect and fair treatment for all its members.

*Element #2: Air* (Mind) gives you optimism, a sense of the future, the enjoyment of learning, a clear mind, and the worldview through which you filter information from your senses. In relationships, the element of Air translates into "a meeting of the minds"—shared beliefs and interests, laughter, a positive attitude, and intellectual stimulation. The gifts to leadership from Air include inspiration and a forward-directed philosophy of management. And this second Element of Success gives organizations a unifying vision, the willingness to learn, and the ability to generate new knowledge.

*Element #3:* The *Fire* element (Will) contributes intensity, focus, and a sense of unique purpose to your life. Relationships benefit from Fire's passion, commitment, personal boundaries, and ability to handle the conflict sparked by differences. Fire marks leadership with the self-starting power of "fire in the belly," consistency, and the ability to empower others. Businesses benefit from the aligning mission of Fire, its energy, its excitement, and the shared pride in a job well done.

*Element #4: Water* (Emotions) gives you emotional intelligence, empathy, compassion, good communication skills, and a sense of connection with others. It is indispensable in relationships, contributing true intimacy, genuine affection, and the willingness to share what you are thinking with each other. Leaders benefit from the element of Water by developing self-awareness and social skills. This element also helps managers access the wealth of diversity in their organizations and dissolve barriers that separate people. Water benefits systems by contributing a strong sense of community, high morale, an easy flow of information through excellent communication channels, and both employee and customer loyalty.

*Element #5: Earth* (Body) helps you implement the other Elements of Success. It gives you security and stability in your life, good physical and financial health, productive habits, and mastery of the skills you need to do your work. Earth makes the love in relationships more "real." It transmutes affection into solid agreements about how to manage shared resources and accomplish day-to-day mundane tasks. Earth gives leaders the ability to design optimum organizational structure, ask the right questions, build feedback systems to catch mistakes earlier, and reinvent organizational habits and processes as necessary. In organizations, Earth is not just structure and established work processes but also tangible products and services, the fruit of all its labors.

## Using the Spiral of Synergy to Improve Your Life, Relationships, and Work

In the first pages of *The Balancing Act* I tell the Native American story of the god Kokomaht who created the world: "always taking four steps in each direction and always returning to the center."[3] Whenever you are having difficulty with a given Element of Success, you can retreat along the evolutionary spiral pathway (or return directly to your Center) to regain your balance.

All of the five Elements of Success are integrally linked in this way, each one "informs" and supports the others. The Spiral of Synergy acts as a map that can pinpoint where you are now and where you may need to go in the cycle to rebalance your life. For example, if you're having a dispute in a relationship about money management (Earth), you may need to look to the prior element (Water) and examine your communications. You may also want to take yet another step back and get some agreement about how to better handle conflict when it arises (Fire). And so on. If you discover that the Element of Success you're having difficulty with is Essence, the "step back" you'll need to take in the evolutionary/creative cycle is to invoke whatever is Sacred to you.

Take the time now to refer back to the scores of the three Balance Sheets you completed in Part I. Use the space below to list the elements that are the strongest and least strong in each aspect of your life. This information points out where your likely strengths and weaknesses will be as you use the Spiral of Synergy to attain mastery in every part of your life.

|  | Strongest Element | Least Strong Element |
|---|---|---|
| Personal Life |  |  |
| Relationships |  |  |
| Organization |  |  |

The material that follows provides the theoretical context and scientific and mythological underpinnings for the Spiral of Synergy. If you'd rather just leap into action, you can skip ahead in this chapter to the exercises that will help you use the Spiral of Synergy and all the Elements of Success to improve your personal life, career, relationships, leadership, and workplace.

## Creating Your Life from the Core

In *Working from Your Core: Personal and Corporate Mastery in a World of Change*, I described an early spiral of synergy that I called the "Core Learning Model."[4] What I have since discovered is that the Spiral of Synergy reflects not only the way you and I learn but also the way we create our lives *and* the path of continual evolution.

But allow me to back up a bit. The Core Learning Model borrowed from the work of many learning theorists and researchers, including Walter Shewhart (his "Plan-Do-Check-Act cycle"[*5]) and David Kolb (his "action-learning cycle"[**6]). Although it has many variations, the standard action-learning cycle can be summarized as having four key components, including thinking, acting, reflecting, and integrating (or implementation).

### The Action-Learning Cycle

One day, as I was looking at the action-learning cycle for another writing project, I noted that these four points mirrored the outer ring of the Elemental Circle: Thinking (Air)—Acting (Fire)—Reflecting (Water)—Integrating (Earth)! But it was missing the

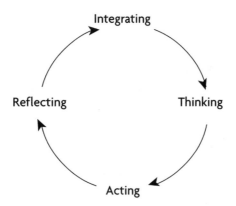

vital element at the Center of the Circle. Essence represents the core of all learning, the "in-tuition" that connects us with the infinite wisdom of the Sacred by having us first self-reference our own core identity.

Your center, then, acts as a gravitational pull that keeps you from falling apart. This principle is called *self-referencing*, a learning trait that is "fundamental to all self-

---

*Shewhart's PDCA cycle translates directly to the order of the traditional Elemental Circle: Plan (thinking), Do (acting), Check (reflecting), Act (which he defines as implementation or integration).

**Although the Kolb action-learning cycle does not follow the same order as the Elements of Success, it does have all the elemental parts: abstract conceptualization (thinking), active experimentation (acting), concrete experience (implementing), and reflective observation (reflecting).

organizing systems."[7] I like to think of the principle of self-referencing as the biological imperative of William Shakespeare's famous and oft-quoted advice: "To thine own self be true." As I stated in *Working from Your Core*:

> *Self-referencing is a survival mechanism that organizes our lives, that literally keeps us from falling apart. It allows us to maintain our integrity, to stay who we are by responding to changes only in ways that are congruent with our core identity. It prevents us from changing randomly. Thanks to self-referencing, princes become frogs (and vice versa) only in fairy tales.[8]*

Interestingly, the addition of the first Element of Success at the center of the standard action-learning cycle has the elegant effect of transforming the circle into *a spiral* that moves clockwise from the center and outward to greater learning and adaptation. The *cycle* of learning then becomes the *spiral* of learning. I think this is actually a truer reflection of reality. We do not spend our lives on the same flat circle, going 'round and 'round. Instead, by and large, we evolve over time by building on each new thing we learn.

The spiral that results when the Center is added as the beginning point of the learning cycle traces not only the path of how you learn and grow but also (in reverse) the path by which you retreat and regroup when you're under stress. It outlines the natural path of evolution and adaptation (and, in reverse, healing and repair) for all living organisms (and organizations). The spiral also provides a map for cocreation (i.e., how you can best participate in the creation of your own life and other masterpieces). The center point of the circle, therefore, is an essential and indispensable part of learning—its beginning and its end. Interestingly, many ancient people thought the Center symbolized "the intersection of macrocosm and

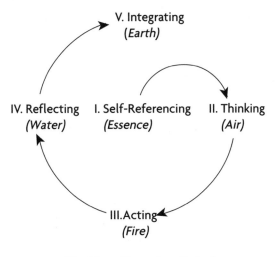

**The Core Learning Spiral**

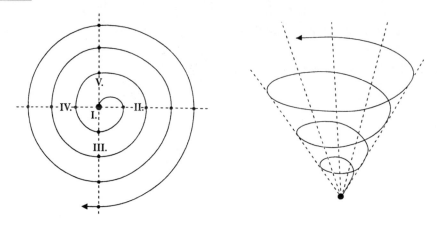

**The Spiral illustrates how learning evolves.**

microcosm." It was also " . . . the point of origin of departure and the point of return . . . moving from the center to the circumference is the journey into manifestation and multiplicity, while the journey back is to the spiritual centre, unity, the One."⁹

The *Spiral of Synergy* is congruent not only with ancient cosmologies (who held that the "higher" [more subtle] elements always precede the "lower" [more visible] in creation) but also with many of the new sciences. One of those new sciences is *autognomics*, which means "self-knowing." Autognomics is the study of how all intelligent systems learn. It defines learning as your ability to adapt to a changing environment while self-referencing; that is, maintaining your core identity. Autognomics theory supports the model of the Core Learning Spiral by asserting that you and I learn and adapt *from our identity*—we move into the world from who we are. Whenever we are faced with anything out of the ordinary—stress, an attraction, or what Charles Sanders Pierce referred to as an "irritation of doubt"—our instinctive response is first to tap into our Core; that is, we return to our identity.

Modern biologists concur. They refer to a phenomenon called *autopoiesis*, which Erich Jantsch describes as the ability of all living systems (these "never resting structures") to continuously renew themselves. Whenever an organism does change, Jantsch argues, it first "refers" to itself. Any future form it takes will be completely consistent with its identity. A living system's instinct for integrity is so strong that it "keeps the memory of its evolutionary path" and when under sufficient stress retreats along the same pathway.¹⁰ That is, it spirals back to its Center.

## Changing from the Core

Even though your Core is the most stable part of you, it too can change over time. Indeed, your very Essence evolves as you learn and adapt. Conversely, it stagnates or contracts if you close yourself off from learning. This learning can come from an *outside* stimulus (that comes into your Core as an "irritation of doubt" from your environment) or from *inside* stimuli (your connection to the Sacred). You will expand and grow—or conversely, contract and decline—depending upon how you handle this input.

On a daily basis, you receive feedback from your environment. In a great many cases, this information never reaches your Core because it is screened by your perceptual filters. If you are alert, however, some of the information from your environment will travel all the way back to the Center of yourself and demand your attention. An evolutionary response is to expand your comfort zone, to learn from the feedback and adapt. Initially you will do this according to the core identity and values you already have in place. But sometimes you may need to rethink your values and identity in the light of these challenges from your environment. Similarly, you may receive internal challenges that demand changing your Core. That is, you will likely arrive at points in your life when you decide that you need to re-create yourself in order to increase your direct connection to, and experience of, the Sacred.

For example, I used to keep myself very busy. I was always on the go. Finally (due to both external and internal challenges), I decided to completely regroup. I carefully reviewed every aspect of my life, every habit and relationship, with the criteria of how it affected my general energy, health, and life force. If I felt it brought me closer to an experience of God, it stayed. If not, I let it go. The result was that, little by little, I redefined who I really was—carefully choosing beliefs, behaviors, work, relationships, communities, and activities that were more life-enhancing. I consciously reprioritized my values and redefined my identity. For a solid year, I lived outside my comfort zone. Although this was a very disorienting, lonely, and sometimes painful process, I now am able to move into every aspect of my life from a "new-and-improved" Core. The tangible outcomes are that on a daily basis, I experience more clarity, less fear, better boundaries—and enjoy greater balance, calm, and ease.

Relationship and organizations can also change their Essence in similar ways. In relationships, when either of you changes (evolves or contracts), the other has a choice about how to respond. Unfortunately, too many relationships are "death pacts" in which people stay together as their individual and shared life force declines. They both become smaller. In ideal relationships, however, the love we share grows. This helps us evolve and change from the Core by giving us a stronger experience of our best nature (expanding our identity and bringing us closer to the Sacred). We each become more than we were before—and the Core of the relationship expands.

Although the Core is the most essential part of an organization, it too can change and evolve over time. The difficulty is that far too many workplaces "lose" their

Center. The system forgets who it is, who it started out to be. This weakens values, identity, and effectiveness. However, when an organization consciously shifts its identity and values in positive, evolutionary ways (either from internal or external stimuli), it too can increase its life force.

In summary, then, the Core Learning Model and the Spiral of Synergy are dynamic, highly versatile models that encode vital truths about change, learning and adaptation, the evolution and healing of all living organisms, the fundamental process of creativity, and even the development of leadership and success of our organizations. Now let's take a look at what scientists say about how these dynamic models can help you in your own daily Balancing Act.

## Your World Is Alive

Many scientists now believe that our universe is alive. It acts much like a "hologram," ever changing, constantly in motion. A hologram is a three-dimensional laser image that looks like the actual object. Remember our first glimpse of Princess Lea in *Star Wars*? She appeared to Luke Skywalker as a hologram urgently begging for assistance.

Holograms look completely real. For example, you can walk around a hologram of a maple tree and view it from all sides, looking at the details of the leaves, just as you would with a tree in your own backyard. But if you try to touch the hologram, you'll find that it is an illusion; your hand will go right through it. Another remarkable aspect of holograms is that no matter how many times you cut up a piece of holographic film, when you shine a laser through it, the whole image will still be there! No matter how small, no matter how many times the film has been divided, the hologram always contains the whole picture within it. Neurophysiologist Karl Pribram used the metaphor of the hologram to describe what he had discovered about how our brains function: that memories seem to be stored throughout the entire brain. Similarly, Einstein's great student, the quantum physicist David Bohm, used the concept of the hologram to explain his discoveries about quantum phenomena.

In his master work, *Wholeness and the Implicate Order*, Bohm asserted that what we see as reality in our daily lives is actually an illusion. He contended that the universe consists of a deep, underlying level of order. This includes both the *implicate* order (that which is hidden from us or "enfolded") and the *explicate* order (that which is now "unfolded" and is therefore perceptible to us). What we see around us, Bohm said, is the result of continual movement between these two orders: electrons that "shape shift from one kind of particle to another," quantums that "manifest as either a particle or a wave."[11] He called this phenomenon "holomovement."

Holomovement is the nature of the universe. It is the Sacred Dance of Life. In the

East, the holomovement has for millennia been called the *Tao*, the "cosmic process" in which all things in the cosmos continuously flow and shapeshift, the cycle of "ceaseless motion and change."[12] In *The Tao of Physics*, Fritjof Capra states that it is not surprising that physicists today are returning to the mystics' (and your Ally the Magicians') idea of the immanence of an alive universe. After all, the roots of physics come from the sixth century B.C. Greece, a time when science, philosophy, and religion were not separate disci-

> But I know every rock
> and tree and creature
> Has a life, has a spirit,
> has a name.
> —Alan Menken and
> Stephen Schwartz,
> "The Colors of the Wind"

plines. These ancient scientists believed that all matter was alive. They saw no distinction between animate and inanimate objects, or between spirit and matter. Their goal was to discover "the essential nature of things," which they called *physis*.[13]

Bohm believed that the potential to be one thing or another was encoded in the implicate order of the electron, creature, or person. We all are, it seems, an "ensemble of possibilities." There is an implicate order contained in the DNA in every cell of our body; for example, the possibility of having black hair or red, brown eyes or green. No matter what part of our bodies we examine, the whole of ourselves (including this almost infinite ensemble of possibilities) is contained within each and every cell, just like a hologram! The same could be said of an organization; that is, a wealth of information about that system's ensemble of possibilities is carried by every single person in it.

To paraphrase David Bohm, your Balancing Act is a holomovement—a dynamic, fluid, ever-changing dance among the Elements of Success. This is the Sacred Dance that causes you and I to experience our lives as whole, one, unified—the "miracles of one thing."

## The Miracles of One Thing

Bohm believed that everything in the cosmos (including you) is made out of "the seamless holographic fabric." Therefore, he concluded, it is meaningless for us to think of the universe as composed of "parts."[14] Bohm's mentor, Albert Einstein, had stunned the world by proving that space and time were not really separate but what he called a "space-time continuum." Bohm went even further than Einstein, stating that *everything* in the universe is an integral part of an interconnected continuum. He echoes the legendary father of alchemy, Hermes Trismegistus, who said: "It is true without lie, certain and most veritable, that what is below is like what is above and that what is above is like what is below, to perpetrate the miracles of one thing."[15]

Astrophysicists today describe the universe as an "integrated, incomprehensibly vast vibrating field of ionized, pregaseous plasma."[16] This is not to say that everything around you is an undifferentiated mass but rather that whatever you see as distinct and separate is really part of an undivided Whole. A profound energy-and-matter unity lies just below the apparent diversity of your world and life. It appears that modern science has now verified an esoteric truth that was considered by sages from all times and places to be the Great Secret of the Ages:

*We are all One.*

You and I are "miracles of one thing." We all come from the One and return to the One. Ancient Magicians known as Alchemists believed that a small spark of the infinite exists within each one of us (that what is below is like what is above, and what is within is like what is without). They encoded this belief by representing gold with the same icon as the sun (because Alchemists considered gold to be the "miniature sun").[17] Interestingly, this symbol is a circle (the macrocosm of infinity) with a dot at its center (the microcosm). ⊙ It is a *hologram* that represents the Sacred dwelling both inside and outside you!

This symbol is remarkably similar to other Elemental Circles found throughout the world, to the natural sound forms of circles within circles discovered by Hans Jenny, and to the visions of Older Culture shamans such as Black Elk, who said: "And I saw that the sacred hoop of my people was one of many hoops that made one circle, wide as daylight and as starlight, and in the center grew one mighty flowering tree to shelter all the children of one mother and one father. And I saw that it was holy."[18]

## Sacred Geometry

The Elemental Circle is a masterpiece of *sacred geometry*. It contains the Sacred Circle itself, the Mystic Center, the icon of gold, the square, the cross, the alchemists' *squared circle*, the four radii and directions, four triangles, and, by inference, the pyramid and the spiral.

Sacred geometry uses such images to symbolize universal order. These cross-cultural metaphors may predate language. They encode archetypal information that schools us via "in-tuition" and elicits from us a deep resonance of truth. Sacred geometry uses the shapes of such symbols to remind us of the truths of nature that form the foundation of ancient wisdom. For example, the spiral reflects the movement of galaxies. The circle recalls the orb of the sun and moon, the rings of trees, and the starlit dome of the night sky.

*When I was a child, my parents had a circular brass plate that they hung above a fireplace. On it was a scene that captivated me. A group of eighteenth-century European men were standing around, having what appeared to be an animated discussion. The remarkable thing about this plate was that in the picture itself was a circular plate hung above a fireplace. And it contained the very same scene! I would stare at my parents' circular brass plate, delving into the circles contained within its circles, until I was completely lost somewhere inside it. Perhaps this was my earliest clue as to the real nature of the world.*

In many healing and magical traditions, the directions of "above" and "below" are added to the Elemental Circle. These two extra directions emphasize the multidimensional, all-encompassing nature of reality. Adding these two directions to the other five in the Elemental Circle gives us the number seven, which is a number symbolic of "perfect order, a complete period or cycle."[19] In *Lake of Memory Rising: Return of the Five Ancient Truths at the Heart of Religion*, William Fix states that the cosmologies describing five or seven elements of humanity are "related systems." He adds:

*The sevenfold structure of man is part of a universal pattern of sevenfold manifestation, as the seven colors in the rainbow and spectrum; the seven notes in music . . . the seven days of creation . . . and so on. . . . This is one reflection of the many ways in which man is a microcosm of the macrocosm, wherein he comprises all the elements and patterns of the world.[20]*

And there's more. If you look at the *squared circle* of the alchemists as if it were a three-dimensional object with the center as its top point (apex), you will suddenly see a pyramid leap out toward you from the flat page. Fix argues that the Great Pyramid was elegantly designed millennia ago according to mathematical equations that reflect what ancient people knew about the nature of the universe—information that humanity has long since lost.

Much of what our ancestors believed about nature is encoded in the numerous forms that are contained within the Elemental Circle. The question that stumps me is: How did these ancient scientists, mathematicians, Magicians, and sages arrive at their extensive knowledge? They didn't have our spaceships, our telescopes, computers, or microscopes. How did they manage to figure out all these things? Fix argues that early humanity was more capable than we are today of doing magical or shamanistic travel. Indeed, records indicate that some of our ancestors had the power to leave their bodies temporarily and "travel" such distances that they could actually *observe* events in far-off lands and, in some cases, the planets rotating in their orbits. When these seers returned from their extraordinary experiences, they reported with great accuracy the same phenomena that we have only in recent centuries been able to scientifically verify.

With all that the ancients were able to observe, they formed a seamless fabric of wisdom that embraced music, mathematics, geometry, architecture, chemistry— indeed, all the arts and sciences. They believed that they and the world around them were cut from the same divine cloth, and they treated all fields of inquiry as an integrated, natural whole. All knowledge, wisdom, magic, and synergy, they believed, came from the study of nature.

## The Sacred Dance of Silence and Sound

Music can be defined as a holomovement of silence and sound, a sonic dance of activity and rest. Both silence and sound are integral to music. The same could be said for all of Life. Many of the creation stories quoted in *The Balancing Act* begin with a state of precreation: a void. One myth states that in the beginning was silence— and then the silence "moved." As these stories tell us, silence existed before the primordial sound. As Joachim-Ernst Berendt says in *The Third Ear: On Listening to the World*, "If the world is sound, and God is more than His creation, then He is Silence."[21] This supports the Bible's advice to "Be still and know that I am God" (Psalms 46:10).

Debate has raged for centuries about the real nature of the silent void. Some cosmologies insist that it is emptiness. Others argue that it is pulsing with life. Depending on which point of view you take, the primal silence corresponds either to the *zero* (emptiness) or the *circle* (all of life). The zero is a form of the circle that has a particular meaning and carries with it a whole philosophy. According to *A Dictionary of Symbols*, zero is "symbolic of the latent and potential."[22] Zero also represents emptiness, no-thing, the void, and nonbeing.[23] Interestingly, zero is "a completely mental entity" that arose sometime between 500 and 800 A.D. *Zero does not exist in the natural world.*[24] And although the zero did great things for mathematics, it also provided a theoretical foundation for the negation of the spiritual. The concept of zero led many philosophers, scientists, writers, and intellectuals to disconnect from their personal experience of the Sacred. This detachment resulted, in many cases, in an arid and fragmented intellectualism. And because these prominent thinkers have so influenced the way we view our own world, the culmination of their philosophies over the centuries has created a serious imbalance in the way many of us experience our lives even today.

### The Great Circle of Silence

From this point on, I will use the Circle (rather than a zero) as the beginning point and the end point of all the Spiral of Synergy exercises. My rationale follows:

- I agree with those scientists and philosophers who say that the universe is not empty but rather very much alive

- *The Balancing Act* uses the study of nature for its philosophical underpinnings—and zero does not exist in nature

- Nature (I'm told) abhors a vacuum.

On the other hand, if you disagree with my working definition, please feel free to use your own in all the exercises that follow. Personally, I like to think of the Sacred as the divine music of pulsing silence and sound to which all of creation dances. The great Circle of Silence enfolds and unfolds all the sounds we hear. All reverberations arise from and return to stillness. The sounds we hear, then, correspond to David Bohm's unfolded, explicate, or visible order, whereas silence is the enfolded state that contains the ensemble of all possible sounds. And, as many creation stories tell us, the very first of these unfolded sounds was the primordial "Word" or OM.

## The Primordial Sacred Sound

The primordial "I Am" (OM or AUM) is said to be the Sacred Word that created the Cosmos. Sufis call OM *the eternal primordial sound*. Sikhs define it as *Naam*. Indians refer to *Nada*, the divine music. In Genesis it says that *the voice of the Creator* moved over the waters to form the world; and in St. John's gospel, it was *the Logos* (the Word) that brought the world into existence.[25]

Humanity now has the technology to track the echo of this primal sound that occurred an estimated twelve to fifteen billion years ago. In 1965 two American communication engineers, Arno Penzias and Robert Wilson, heard "interference" on their radio equipment. This same background noise was later identified as the primal sound that had been calculated and predicted previously by physicist Robert Dicke.[26]

There are those who argue that the Big Bang could be thought of as a sound or vibration, rather than a huge explosion. It appears that the Creation sound was not a one-time-only occurrence. Indeed, it appears that the universe continues to form itself through an ongoing, echoing song that has intervals (as does all music) of stillness and resonance. As Peter Guy Manners says in his introduction to a video of Hans Jenny's dramatic sound experiments (*Cymatics III: Bringing Matter to Life and Sound*), "Everything holds its existence, solely and completely, to Sound. Sound is the factor that holds it together. Sound is the basis of form and shape. In the beginning was the Word and the Word was God. . . into the great Voids of Space came a Sound, and matter took shape."[27]

Hans Jenny's remarkable experiments have contributed mightily to our understanding of how life unfolds by demonstrating how sound creates form out of unformed matter. Jenny projected a variety of sounds through sand, metal filings,

> *Nothing in the Universe is so like God as Silence.*
> —Meister Eckhart

*Prayer involves becoming silent, and being silent, and waiting until God is heard.*
—Søren Kierkegaard

liquid, and other materials. *These then vibrated into organized shapes*, including spinning spirals (like the galaxies); the many different forms we see in nature (billowing clouds, sand dunes, seashells, leaves, flowers, even vertebrae); beautiful, mandalalike forms. When Jenny had the human voice chant OM into water, the sound created the vibrations of dynamically shifting circles within circles! [28] Interestingly, in a great many traditions the sacred sound of OM corresponds to the One, the Whole, the outer Circle, and perfection itself.

Sound vibration appears to be the path that connects the seen and unseen worlds, form and energy. Scientists who support the Theory of Everything concur, arguing that everything in the world is composed of and interconnected by invisible, infinitely small, "vibrating strings." It appears that the Australian creation myth I quoted at the beginning of chapter one captures a profound truth: Our world is indeed "a web of song."

Echoing this theme in a video about music and vibrational healing, Jeff Volk says "We live in a vast ocean of sound whose infinite waves ripple the shores of our awareness in myriad patterns of intricate design and immeasurably complex vibrations . . . Permeating our bodies—our psyches, to the very core of our being."[29]

Twenty-five hundred years ago, the great mathematician, scientist, and philosopher Pythagoras described this vast ocean of sound as being the "harmony of the spheres." Pythagoras made an extraordinary contribution to human knowledge when he discovered that all natural phenomena in the universe could be described in the same terms as the numbers and mathematical ratios found in music. Pythagoras said that the planets in our solar system make certain tones in their orbits, and he then codified these into the musical scale and overtone series that still determines today whether music is considered "harmonious" or "dissonant." Physicist Werner Heisenberg declared that Pythagoras's definition of rational numerical relationships as the source of all harmony was "one of the most momentous discoveries in the history of humanity." He also argued that "the entire programme of today's precision sciences was thus basically anticipated by Pythagoras."[30]

When I was studying music in college, I learned that the pitch by which Western musicians tune their instruments has risen significantly since the 1800s to give European orchestras a more exciting, sharp, or "brilliant" tone. This is one of the reasons that music of Eastern nations sounds so flat and dull to Western ears. Indian music, for example, is tuned to "Sa," the exact note used for thousands of years for the sacred mantra OM. In this musical tradition "Sa" has always been considered the frequency that reflects the earth's orbit around the Sun;[31] that is, it is the earth's special tone in the cosmic "harmony of the spheres" described by Pythagoras. Classical Indian musicians are trained for years until they internalize this tone by which they are able to tune their own voices and instruments. And in extraordinary experiments, biologists demonstrated that plants preferred music tuned in this ancient system so much that "in their effort to reach the source of this music, they lay almost horizontally, forming angles of up to sixty degrees so as to twine around the loudspeakers."[32]

I think that a significant reason for the imbalance so many of us feel these days is that, in a very real way, we are "out of tune." For starters, we listen to music that is tuned at a higher pitch than the earth tone within which humanity evolved over millennia. Worse, our lives are much more filled with noise (constant sound) than music (intervals of silence and sound). Indeed, to quote Shakespeare's *Macbeth*, our days are often "full of sound and fury, signifying nothing."

We live in a world that suffers from a significant imbalance between sound and silence. It is almost as if we have a terror of silence: We talk on cell phones as we walk down the street. Car radios blare from engine start-up to shutdown. Muzak, rock stations, or talk shows accompany us as we shop. We have the TV, stereo, or radio on while we eat, study, converse with others, or read. Meanwhile, fans, computers, air conditioners, or heaters hum constantly in the background.

What are we so afraid we will hear if we are silent?

The absence of quiet in our lives means that our minds and hearts have become dulled. We can't hear ourselves think, nor can we hear our hearts when they speak to us, nor can we easily hear each other. Moreover, without the restorative power of silence, our bodily systems are bombarded and weakened. Studies have found that significant levels of noise actually increase mortality (for example, in people living near airports). Both chronic and acute noise can kill us. When we cannot fully rest, the health of our bodies, minds, and relationships are adversely affected. Our nervous systems become shot; we behave less civilly to each other. To regain our balance, we need to return regularly to silence. There is no substitute.

Yet, despite the dissonance surrounding us, both you and I remain, throughout our whole lives, one verse in our world's web of song. We are an integral part of the "harmony of the spheres." We are a hologram of the silence that moved to sing the

*Before we make music, music makes us . . . Music's deep structure is identical with the deep structure of all things.*
—George Leonard,
*The Silent Pulse*

whole universe into existence. And when we listen very carefully, when we are quiet for even a few moments, we can begin to hear, unfolding within us, the echo of that very first song.

## Exercises in Silence and Sound

**1. Listening to AUM.** To hear the echo of the original sound of the universe, cup your hands firmly over your ears. Sit quietly. Turn your attention inward, breathe slowly, and listen carefully. Soon you will hear a low, steady hum. This is said to be the sound of creation as it continues to unfold within you.

**2. Hearing the holomovement of silence and sound.** Sit quietly. Listen to all the noise around you. Notice how these sounds arise from, and return to, silence. They are like bubbles rising to the surface of a pool of water. Listen carefully to how each sound is separated from and distinguished from the next one by the stillness that surrounds each of them. Move your attention first to the whole field of sound and then to specific noises. Focus on one sound at a time, then return again to the whole field and choose a different one to focus on. Go slowly back and forth as frequently as you wish.

**3. Gaining strength through silence.** If you find that your energy is low, try a silence break. You and I are besieged by noise all the time. Our ears tend to work overtime, processing the ocean of sound vibration swirling around us. Indeed, many noises are actually harmful to the human body and can cause significant stress and disease.

To increase your overall stamina, find time daily to give your ears a break. For a little bit of time, sit, walk, or eat in silence—turn off the computer, the TV, the stereo or radio, and remove yourself from idle chatter or negative talk. Feel your body completely sink into relaxation. You will increase your vitality whenever you do not have to expend energy to fend off the subtle, deleterious effects of excess noise.

**4. Moving from your I Am to the Whole I AM and back.** Use your breath and/or a simple breath count to first return to your own Core (your individual "I am"). When you feel in balance again, move into an awareness of the larger I AM that surrounds you.

After you listen to the sounds and silence around you for a while, turn your attention back to the quiet, subtle workings of your own body: the soft hum of your breath, the beating of your heart. Just listen to the echo of the holomovement of creation that still pulses within and without you.

# PERSONAL LIFE

◆

*Once you are Real*
*You can't become unreal again.*
*It lasts for always.*
                        —*Margery Williams*, The Velveteen Rabbit

## Becoming Real

By using the Spiral of Synergy, you can make your life more harmonious. You also can become more "real," more genuine, and act more often from your best self. Unfortunately, most of us don't feel we have the time for this process. As a result, we "spin our wheels" or run breathlessly through our days. Instead, we could be using the Spiral of Synergy to maintain our equilibrium—while simultaneously enjoying the journey *and* getting more done!

### Reviewing the Personal Balance Sheet

**1. Take a moment** to revisit the results of your Personal Balance Sheet. Notice which elements you scored as being stronger and weaker. While reading about all the Elements of Success in Part II, you may have already come up with some ideas for improving a weak element and bringing better balance to your personal life. If you haven't already done so, write down these ideas.

**2. Refer to your scores** from the Personal Balance Sheet to find one part of your Balancing Act that you would like to improve. Note it here.

3. Now use the model of the Spiral of Synergy (and all the Elements of Success) to make an integrated plan for improving one aspect of your personal life. Get started by writing a few of your thoughts in the space below, or use a separate piece of paper if you need more room.

The Spiral of Synergy can help you keep your equilibrium as you go through a normal day. Think of it as a way to make your daily life "music." Indeed, you can create harmony in your life as you systematically "sound" every note in the Spiral of Synergy, almost as if you were playing a full chord on a musical instrument. Remembering this process is also a great way to navigate a personal project you're working on. I regularly use this methodology myself and can attest to its helpfulness. As you go through the examples below, you may want to pay special attention to the elements you have already identified as being a bit weak. Over time you can create new habits that provide better balance—and more synergy—in your life.

The Sacred begins and ends all the Spiral of Synergy exercises that follow in *The Balancing Act*. (Again, please define the Sacred in whatever way is most meaningful to you.) Many mythologies from around the world say that, in the beginning of time, humanity was connected to the Sacred by a Tree of Life whose roots and branches linked us to the invisible worlds that existed both Above and Below us.

For instance, in Norse mythology the Yggdrasil was a giant ash tree that stood at the center of the earth in the First Age of the world. Its branches spread over the whole earth, and beneath its roots was a well of wisdom. After an epic battle between good and evil, chaos ensued and paradise was destroyed. However, from deep in the roots of the once magnificent tree, the first man and woman crept out and created a new world from the ashes of the old. The biblical story of the Garden of Eden tells us that the Tree of Life stood at the center of paradise. All was well until Adam and Eve ate from another tree in the garden—the forbidden Tree of Knowledge—and were expelled. In Celtic lore, all trees were considered to be sacred and alive, providing bridges between the gods and humanity. And Siddhartha became the enlight-ened Buddha by sitting under the Bodhi Tree until he felt its energy pulse through him, connecting him to the sky and earth, and removing all sense of separation and suffering.

In many ways, each one of us is like a "tree of life" that can bridge Heaven and Earth. This is particularly true when we stay sufficiently in balance to enliven our daily actions and interactions with our very best selves. The rest of this chapter will provide you with step-by-step ways for doing just that. These techniques range from "quick fixes" for your on-the-go-lifestyle all the way to more detailed, in-depth strategies for helping you transform your life, relationships, and workplace.

Let's begin with the *really* short form. With practice, you can almost instantly touch the Sacred and infuse your next action or interaction with it. This miniexercise can dramatically alter the quality—and your experience—of that next event. Here, then, is the "one minute version" of connecting yourself with the Sacred. I call this Finding the Sweet Spot. Before moving on to your next task, all you have to do is pause for *just one minute.*

- Stay quiet for 15 seconds.

- Then do a 5-second inventory to determine how you feel right now.

- Take 20 seconds to determine what it is about this next task or interaction that could bring you (or someone else) joy, happiness, peace, contentment, or delight. These are internal experiences of touching the Sacred—and the "sweet spot" you're looking for.*

- Relax for the next 15 seconds in that sweet spot. Feel this happiness as if the experience has already happened.

- Express gratitude. (5 seconds)

When this brief exercise is over, you can move forward with a greater sense of equilibrium.

Because the Sacred is the silent source of life and regeneration, resting there for even this one moment can restore you and make your daily balancing act easier. Making this a new habit can completely invigorate your life. It's worth the effort: remember that the Sacred is the holomoving universe that carries within it every possibility you can imagine (and many more) for re-creating your life.

In all the exercises that follow, I use a *circle* at the start of the exercise to symbol-ize the One that you move from (the "Above"). And, I use the *squared circle* at the end

---

* Note: If you come up dry here, neutralize your resistance to this upcoming situation by making it an offering. Realize that this, too, will pass. Often that thought alone will make you feel better.

to symbolize that you've done your part to bring heaven and earth together, and have thereby returned to the Sacred (the "Below"). All the Spiral of Synergy exercises move from the Sacred, through the five elements, and back to the Sacred. This is a natural pathway that has been used throughout the ages to help people just like you and me create a more healthy and joyful life.

In its most basic form, the Spiral of Synergy can be a "quick-and-easy" fifteen-minute methodology for keeping your life in balance. With practice, this spiral path will turn into a well-worn route that you can travel at light speed. The more you do this process, the more automatic the Spiral of Synergy will be for you—and the easier your Balancing Act will become.

## The Basic Spiral of Synergy

| Minutes | Element | Activity |
|---|---|---|
| 1 | | Sit down in a place where you won't be disturbed for the next fifteen minutes. Have a pen and a journal or notebook beside you. |
| 2 | O. Sacred | Sit quietly. Listen to the silence and noises around you. Remember to breathe slowly—starting now, and through all the steps that follow. |
| 2 | 1. Essence | Recall your Core identity and values. |
| 2 | 2. Air | Clear your mind and focus on the question at hand. Write it down. List the relevant information you have. |
| 2 | 3. Fire | Think of possible actions. Write them down. Check those that are most congruent with your personal values, vision, and mission. |
| 2 | 4. Water | Jot down your feelings by each option. Then, of those choices that are most aligned with the other elements, choose the option that your "gut" feels best about. |
| 2 | 5. Earth | Make notes about what you need to do to implement your choice and make it a reality. Write down one concrete goal. Decide on the first step you will take, any resources you need, and when you will start. Make this a promise to yourself. |
| 2 | ⊕. Sacred | Sit quietly. Express gratitude. Breathe. Relax and let go, so you can move on with the rest of your day. |

In all the Spiral of Synergy exercises that follow in this chapter, many details are given for each step in the process. What follows immediately is a comprehensive step-by-step guide for using the Spiral of Synergy to bring greater balance into your daily life so that you can bring all of what you are to whatever you do.

## Using the Spiral of Synergy in Your Personal Balancing Act

O. **The Sacred (Above)**—Before you begin your day, sit quietly for just a few moments. (If you'd prefer, you can also walk in nature or connect to the Sacred in any way that is meaningful to you.)

One of the best ways to start your daily Balancing Act (or to regain your balance if you notice that you've lost your equilibrium) is by sitting still for a moment. Silence is the living, pulsing space that is full of infinite creative possibilities. From this formless beginning point, you can elicit the best possibilities for yourself.

During your first tries, you may feel some agitation as you enter silence. Trust me, it will pass. If you have trouble with this first step, you can use your breath or a breath count to slow you down a bit and move you through your Core into the Sacred. When you have been quiet for a short while, you will feel a point at which you relax on a deep level and "sink" into a peaceful state.

Ask if there is anything you need to know or understand before you move into your day. Listen with your heart. If you hear anything from your "gut" (your internal seat of wisdom), write it down in your daily journal or a separate notebook. This voice is internal and preverbal—it is the language not of the mind but of the soul. It may begin as a gentle whisper or be unmistakably clear. Make notes. At first listening in this way will seem quite odd. Just stay open to the possibility of connection. After a little practice, you will find that simply being still for a few moments quickly connects you with the Source.

In a way that is congruent with your beliefs, ask for grace and guidance as you go through your day. Bless yourself and anyone you are likely to meet. Ask for the best possible outcomes for everyone concerned—your family, friends, or colleagues. You can also "turn over" the day to your understanding of the Sacred and express gratitude at the outset for whatever will happen. This attitude of openness will allow the Sacred to flow easily into and through you, as with any open system.

**Element #1. Essence (Soul)**—Use your breath to calm and center yourself and to make certain you're fully present in that moment. You can also use your breath, whenever you remember to do so, to stay connected to your Core. This is the center point of your Balancing Act, the identity and values you will continually self-reference. Then, no matter what happens, you can remain calm and give of your best self.

During your day, observe from this quiet place exactly what you are feeling and thinking. Notice how you act. Watch what goes on around you. Listen from your heart to what is said, and also to the silence between the words.

Honor everyone you meet. Similarly, honor yourself. Do not allow disrespectful behavior on anyone's part. Remember your values and act from them. If you are "hooked" at any time and thrown off Center (this will happen as surely as night follows day), simply notice and pull yourself back to your Essence as soon as you are able. If you cannot return to your Core and feel that you are about to interact out of fear, anger, or envy, it may be best to remove yourself from the situation until you have regained self-control.

**Element #2. Air (Mind)**—Whenever possible, use the breath to still and focus your mind so that it works like a laser light. Trust yourself to make good decisions; don't fret, second-guess yourself, or worry. Lighten up whenever you notice that you're overly serious, critical, or running negative mental loops.

Allow yourself time to dream. Write down your thoughts and ideas so that you can give them shape later on. When interacting with others, take a moment to think before you speak or ask questions. Also, take some time to think before you answer. (I promise, this will save you a lot of trouble.) Articulate your ideas and opinions as clearly as possible, speaking from your heart. Make certain that whatever you say is consistent with your beliefs and core values. Stay open to learning and changing your mind. Use learned optimism to approach any problems you encounter. If possible, share with others your ideas and visions for the future.

**Element #3. Fire (Will)**—Act with full commitment as you go through your day. Do whatever you do with all your heart. You can even "offer" your actions (like a sacrifice) to your definition of the Sacred so that your personal will is aloigned with Divine will. In deciding what to accomplish or what to do next, recall your purpose in life, your personal mission. Prioritize those actions that would further this mission.

Have the courage to speak about what is important to you. If you have a conflict with someone, surface it as quickly as possible and fight fairly, always maintaining respect for the other person and demanding respect for yourself. Remember that anger is an instinct that can help you define appropriate boundaries and that conflict can be used as an alchemical fire to transform difficult situations and improve your life.

**Element #4. Water (Emotions)**—As you complete your tasks, reflect on what went well and why. In this way, you're more likely to repeat your successes.

Also stay aware of what you are feeling. Occasionally do a quick check-in to name the emotion you're experiencing. When dealing with other people, observe how you feel during and after the interactions. Watch how your energy increases or decreases by being with different individuals. Be sure to use the basics of communication (for example, making "I" statements, listening with complete attention). Wherever possible, engage in real dialogue. Deliberately develop your emotional intelligence. Be kind, considerate, and compassionate as often as you can.

Welcome those you meet; establish community whenever possible. Enjoy some time during the day to be with your friends and family, even if it's just a phone call or an e-mail to check in.

**Element #5. Earth (Body)**—Dig in and do the work that is before you. Decide what tasks need to be done and by when. Implement the things you've learned (i.e., put them to work). Make only the promises that you know you can keep. Spend according to your means. Keep things in order. Maintain a steady pace, taking care not to overly stress or strain yourself. Work productively and efficiently (not necessarily "hard"). Pay attention to the messages of your physical body—take a short break if you feel tired or notice that your neck or back is tightening up. Eat well, take a walk in the fresh air, and indulge your senses in some way. Have at least one point in the day when you're able to say, "It's great to be alive."

⊕. **The Sacred (Below)**—At the day's end, sit again for a few moments in silence. Express gratitude for everything that has happened. You may even want to journal (for example, write down five things you're grateful for from the past twenty-four hours).

Silently thank the Sacred for the opportunity of serving, for everything you've learned, and for how you've been changed. Ask if there is any more you need to know. Listen for an answer. Write down anything you "hear." Again, thank the Sacred. Claim your internal power to bless this day, yourself, and others.

Then let go and drift happily off to sleep. Sink into silence and return peacefully to the One.

## Changing Your Personal Relationship to Work—Making It Sacred

In his classic book *Working*, Studs Terkel asserts: "I think most of us are looking for a calling, not a job. Most of us . . . have jobs that are too small for our spirit. Jobs are not big enough for people."[33]

Terkel wrote *Working* after years of interviewing Americans about the work they do. He concludes that working is about a search for "daily meaning as well as daily bread."[34] We each have a very personal relationship with our job. Sometimes it's a good relationship, sometimes it's a "so-so" relationship, and sometimes it's a love-hate relationship. The problem is that it will be quite difficult for you to experience balance or synergy in your life if you are unhappy at work. Fortunately, you can use everything you've learned so far about the Elements of Success to create or find a career that is a good fit for you—work that you consider sacred.

I am fascinated by those people who still manage to find joy and meaning in their jobs, no matter how "small" they are. One such example is Delores Dante, a waitress for twenty-three years when Terkel interviewed her. I find Delores's story particularly compelling because I have served my own stints as a waitress. It is a difficult and often menial job, physically and mentally demanding. Yet Delores infuses her work with *who she is* and in this way she makes it sacred. Delores says: "I have to be a waitress. How else can I learn about people? How else does the world come to me? I can't go to everyone. So they have to come to me. Everyone wants to eat, everyone has hunger. And I serve them. If they've had a bad day, I nurse them, cajole them. Maybe with coffee I give them a little philosophy. They have cocktails, I give them political science."[35]

I have met many other people who infuse their work with who they are. This includes subway drivers who (by commenting cheerfully on the attractions available at each stop) make jaded New Yorkers smile and converse with each other; cabbies who enjoy talking with their fares; teachers who delight in their students; mothers who love welcoming their children home from school; health-care workers who heal with a warm smile and a gentle touch; receptionists who greet people as if to their own home; musicians who thrill at the beautiful sounds they make; and CEOs who steward their companies with intelligence, care, and fairness.

Terkel says that stories such as Delores's probably say a lot more about the person than the job. I would agree. After all, if a form of work is necessary to the functioning of a society, then it is an integral part of the holographic Whole—and sacred by that definition. That doesn't mean that *you* have to do that work. Your goal always is to find the career that uses your gifts and suits you best.

But sometimes, en route to our perfect job, we have a great deal of learning to do, which often includes trying out many forms of work. This is how we figure out what we do and do not like. It helps to think about what is wrong or right about each job we do. Ask yourself: What can I learn here? What are the lessons for me? Take a look at what beliefs, attitudes, and set of skills got you where you are now. (If you don't like where you are, you may need to retrace your steps mentally so that you don't recreate the same problems in the next setting.) This is one reason the alchemists recommended taking "a long, hard, unblinking look" at yourself. If you are having problems with your career, ask what is in your power to change. This could include work habits, communication skills, or attitudes. Also ask yourself what you need to change, starting now, to find work that is better suited to you.

With these reframing questions, you can make any job (from window washing to waitressing to running your own company) alchemical and transformative. When you do find the career that is right for you, you'll know it by the balance and synergy you experience. It will seem to "hum" for you. Terkel tells the story of Mario Anichini, who worked for twenty-eight years as a butcher, during which time he never felt well. He developed sciatica and an ulcer. Then he switched to being a stonemason, a craft he had studied and loved as a young man in Italy. Mario says, "When I started this business, I became better and better, and I feel good and enjoy myself." His son concurs: "My dad was an old man fifteen, twenty years ago. Today he's a young man."[36] I've witnessed this same kind of transformation countless times as the executives I've coached found their "real work."

You can use the Elemental Circle to make your work sacred. This is a comprehensive list that is infused with information I gained from years of coaching executives in career transition and entrepreneurs in the first stages of establishing their own businesses. You are likely to need several sessions and a separate notebook to complete the steps below. This Spiral of Synergy exercise provides an excellent guide for changing your career or transforming your personal relationship to your current work.

## Using the Spiral of Synergy to Change Your Career

O. **The Sacred (Above)**—Begin by sitting quietly. In this stillness is contained an infinite number of possibilities for your future work, possibilities you may not even know exist.

Remember that you are a part of the Whole, a reflection of the Sacred. You are in this world to do the "Great Work" of which the alchemists speak, that is, to make your life golden. Therefore, it is important that you spend your time and efforts in a way that allows your special gifts to come into the world. Even if your current job situation is uncomfortable, realize that you are now on your way to finding work that is right for you.

After you have been silent for a short time, ask if there is anything you should know before you begin. Listen attentively. Write down anything you "hear." Claim your own internal power to bless your search. Express gratitude for whatever is about to happen. This attitude of openness will allow the Sacred to flow more easily within you.

**Element #1. Essence (Identity)**—At this point, you can revisit your personal identity statement and the core values you listed in chapter one. This is the centerpoint you will self-reference as you look for work that is a good "fit" for who you really are.

If you have not completed that exercise, you can do so now. Or you can proceed by answering questions such as: What's really important to you? What work seems meaningful to you? What have you liked about the jobs you've done to date? Conversely, think about what really bugs you: What can you *not* stand to do? (The inverse of what you really dislike are your values, and I find that people are often more clear about what they dislike in a career than what they do like.)

Your work needs to be congruent with your core identity and values if you are to experience the "bliss" that mythologist Joseph Campbell described. It is most important that you are clear in this matter. Otherwise you will find that no work makes you happy.

**Element #2. Air (Mind)**—Once you are comfortable with your identity statement and list of core values, sit quietly again. Allow yourself to fantasize, to daydream, to envision what the "perfect" career would look like for you. (You may have already completed this task in chapter two. If so, revisit it now. If not, continue with the instructions that follow.)

Sometimes it helps people to first envision what a perfect world would look like, and then think of the work they really want to do within that context. Write down whatever occurs to you. What kind of tasks do you see yourself performing? Where do you live? What is your work environment like? How much time do you spend on the job, with family, with friends, commuting, relaxing, walking in the woods, painting, doing other activities? Write it all down, no matter how futuristic, fantastic, or utterly impossible any of it seems. Better yet, draw it.

This is your ideal, the dream that has been sleeping inside you, probably for some time. To articulate it in this way, to bring it into the light of day, to admit it to yourself, takes courage. Congratulations.

Now refer back to the first Element of Success. How congruent is this vision with your core identity and values? How inspiring or exciting is this vision? Does it contain your hopes for your own future? If so, this is your vision. The next steps in the Spiral of Synergy will help you close the gap between this ideal and your current reality.

Another component of the Air element is to clarify your beliefs, your worldview, your hopes and fears. What do you believe about yourself, your capabilities, your value in the workplace? What do you think is possible in the business world and in working relationships? Do these beliefs support or undermine your vision?

**Element #3. Fire (Will)**—How can you find the ideal career you listed above? In what tangible, specific ways could you contribute to your vision of the world; that is, what could be your piece of this puzzle? This is your personal *mission* in work. (If you have already articulated this in chapter three, you can revisit your mission statement now.)

Write down all the things that set you apart from others. What are your specific "gifts" and talents? What makes you unique? (If you completed this exercise in chapter three, you may want to look at it again with an eye toward finding the career that best suits you.)

What activities do you find energizing? Has any kind of work ever made you want to leap out of bed in the morning? What activities fascinate you so much that you sometimes spend hours doing them, completely losing track of days? And finally, if you were independently wealthy, how would you spend your days? What kind of work would you do even if you did not *have* to work?

You know you've found your personal mission if you feel "on fire." Your task then is to develop a strategy that will help you find or develop this work. You also need to make a firm commitment to yourself to pour your efforts into that goal. Next, arrange your priorities so that you can close the gap between where you are now and where you want to be.

**Element #4. Water (Emotions)**—When you envisioned your future career, with whom were you interacting? Were there many people, or just a few, or were you by yourself? Whom were you serving; that is, who received your product or service? As you design your strategy, determine who would want to receive your services and also who could help you bring your work out into the world.

You can look back to chapter four to note the personal connections you have (or your friends, colleagues, relatives) that might help you secure the work you want to do. If you did not do so then, complete the exercise now. When the time is right, you can meet with your community members, ask for their help, and get their advice, input, and perceptions.

Answer this next question candidly: How well do you work with others? Ask others for their feedback. What is their experience of how well you interact and communicate with them? Ask others for specific feedback about how you can improve your professional relationships. Your real friends can give a wonderful gift by letting you know your communication strengths and weaknesses, including any ways you drive them crazy. With this information, you can improve your emotional intelligence—and your odds of success.

**Element #5. Earth (Body)**—What skills do you have now, and which ones do you need to develop your career? What are your financial resources and needs? Can you meet your needs doing the work you want? If not, can you design a life that allows you to do this as an avocation in addition to your "day job"? If you do not now have the resources or skills you need to qualify for the career you want, what strategy do you need to put into place so that you can have this vocation in the future? How can you move to your goal in small, incremental steps?

When you envisioned your desired life and work, what did the structures in it look like: your home, your neighborhood, your workplace? Did you see yourself sitting at your computer in your own office in a big building in a midsized city or by a country river with your easel and paintbrushes?

How can you structure your days now so that you are able to maintain a better balance in your life? In what ways can you stay physically healthy and strong? How can you change your workplace so that it is more physically beautiful, aesthetically satisfying, safe, and supportive of the tasks you have to accomplish?

⊕. **The Sacred (Below)**—Turn it over. Know that there are unlimited opportunities in the world, an infinite array of ways to live and work. Believe that you've done your part to "draw" the work you're here to do. By using the Elements of Success and the Spiral of Synergy, you have now put in a very clear, focused, better balanced, and unmistakable order to the universe.

Now you need to stay alert for opportunities. They may come in unusual forms. You may be fired from one job so that you can land in a new one. You may need to move to another region of the country to be near your new mate or ailing relatives.

While you are in between what exists now and what is coming into being, learn whatever you can. As the saying goes, "Grow where you are planted." On a regular basis, bless both where you are and where you are going. Be careful to express gratitude for—rather than curse—your current job. Gratitude has a magical way of magnetizing good things to us. Stay confident—and let go. Know that the seeds you have just planted are in an enfolded state and have already begun the holomoving process of unfolding and bearing fruit.

# RELATIONSHIPS

◆

*I love the melody in your voice,*
*The sound of your laughter,*
*The rhythm of your ways,*
*The beating of your heart.*
*You are music to me.*

—John Ortiz, The Tao of Music

## Making Beautiful Music Together

If a relationship is especially wonderful, it is said that these two people make beautiful music together. I think that perhaps, in the best relationships, we hear echoed in each other the same harmony that made the world. We "pulse together"—we are "two hearts that beat as one."

However, sometimes the harmony lasts only a short while. What the Elemental Circle teaches us is that the partnerships most likely to endure are those with a richness in all the Elements of Success.

*One day when a new friend and I were driving a long distance to a conference, I asked how she and her husband first met. I thought they were a lovely couple and very fortunate to have each other. I was stunned when my friend replied, "I saw him for the first time on our wedding day."*

*I almost drove off the road. I had never before met someone whose marriage had been arranged. It seemed to me like something from another century. I pumped her for details—and learned a great deal from that interaction.*

*Neither she nor her future husband was looking to marry. Her parents, however, took it upon themselves to seek a man for her who had deep spiritual values and was exemplary in his conduct. Then they met her husband's parents, who also were in search of an excellent match for their son. Both sets of parents finally prevailed upon their children until these two professional adults relented.*

*However, because these two people were so well matched at the outset (cultural identity, values, spiritual leanings, beliefs), their marriage had a strong foundation, and they were able to grow, through commitment and respect, into love.*

Let me say, before I go any further, that I am a romantic. However, upon reflection I have to admit that any intimate relationship built from the Core (shared values, compatible identity) probably has better odds of succeeding than one that is built upon mutual physical attraction. (For proof, you only need to look at the staggering percentage of Western romance-based marriages that end in divorce.)

I think that any relationship is more likely to be successful when the two people involved (either instinctively or consciously) employ all five Elements of Success. The Elemental Circle can serve as a checklist to help you determine the real health of any friendship or partnership you have. (This is a good time to review your scores on the Balance Sheet for Relationships.) Then you can note in the box below some ideas for bringing better balance into an important relationship.

Even if the relationship you rated is weak in one or several Elements of Success, you probably have gained some good ideas from Part II about how to improve it. Also, you may want to look at your interactions with key people in your life and see if there are any particular elemental patterns that emerge. After all, you are the one constant in this mathematical equation. By working though your issues with others, you will change yourself. From this point on, you can use the Elemental Circle to interact in more balanced ways with everyone you know.

## Reviewing the Balance Sheet for Relationships

**1. Part II** may have already given you some new ideas for attaining better balance in your relationships. If you haven't already done so, write down these ideas.

**2. Refer to your scores** from the Relationship Balance Sheet to find an aspect of a key pertnership that you would like to improve. Note it here.

**3. Now use the model** of the Spiral of Synergy and all the Elements of Success to make an integrated plan for improving your interactions with one important friend, relative, or coworker. Write your thoughts in the space below.

## The Infinite Possibilities of Relationships

There are infinite possibilities in relationships. They are, to quote Meg Wheatley, "quantum." In the best relationships, synergy is created. You and I become more together than we are on our own. We help each other experience the Sacred. The "relationship," after all, is not "you + me." It is the field that exists between us. It is the "+."

As you know all too well, partnerships can be great, good, bad, or ugly. What is amazing to me is that not infrequently they are all of the above; that is, you can pass through every possible parameter of relationship with the very same person. For example, you like your friend today, but yesterday you were really peeved with her. A parent whom you adored as a child and were estranged from as a young adult is now a dear, cherished friend.

I don't mean to be cavalier, but relationships change, just as everything else in life changes. This fact can cause us a great deal of pain. Indeed, many people are thrown completely off balance when a significant relationship shifts. This is one reason it is helpful for us to use the Elements of Success to develop a dynamic balance that keeps us from being tossed around as important people come into—and leave—our lives. I recently learned a wonderful technique that is designed to help people attain this sort of equanimity. It was not easy for me, but I have found it enlightening. Here's how it goes.

---

### Friend, Foe, or Stranger?

1. **Think of three people you know.** First call to mind someone you love, then someone you really dislike, and finally a stranger (someone to whom you feel neutral, perhaps whom you've met only once).

2. **Begin by calling up the feelings,** as clearly as you can, for each of these people in turn: first the dear friend, then your adversary, and finally the stranger.

3. **Now imagine a situation** by which the stranger could turn into a new friend—or conversely, could insult or deeply offend you. Got it? See that stranger first as your friend and then as your foe.

4. **Then move on** by calling your dear friend to mind. Wasn't this person also once a stranger? And could you imagine a situation that would turn the two of you against each other? Bring each of these imagined scenarios clearly to mind.

5. **Lastly, look at your foe.** Was there a time when this person was very close to you? And wasn't he or she also once a stranger? Again, remember these times clearly. Contemplate the shifting sands of relationships.

This exercise gave me an experience of my relationships as shapeshifting prisms in a kaleidoscope. It is disconcerting—but a great way to attain a better perspective on the reality of our interactions. Because the underlying nature of relationships is change, it is not a bad idea to treat everyone in your life with more equanimity. This does *not* mean that you will become indifferent or that you will love anyone less. On the contrary! It just means that you are less likely to cloy to those you love or harbor resentment toward those you dislike. And it also means that you might now look at the strangers you meet as if they could become your new friends.

## Building Good Relationships

You can build better relationships in every part of your life by deliberately including every Element of Success in your interactions. The Spiral of Synergy outline that follows is designed to help you through a critical interaction with a friend who is very important to you. Perhaps there's some strain on this once-excellent relationship, and you'd like to improve things. You can also adapt this exercise for other scenarios; for example, providing a supportive context for a talk with your spouse about finances or child rearing, trying to repair a lover's quarrel, or planning a pivotal meeting with a business colleague. In each case the same fundamental principles apply. And happily, by practicing this process in one arena of your life, you will gain excellent relationship-building skills that you can transfer to every other interaction in your life.

### Using the Spiral of Synergy in Your Relationship Balancing Act

O. **The Sacred (Above)**—Before the interaction, take some time alone to be silent. Because stillness is the space filled with limitless possibilities, you may find inspiration here about how to proceed in a way that will elicit the best outcome for both of you.

Reflect for a moment on the fact that both you and your friend are an integral part of the One. When you have been quiet for a short while, ask the Sacred if there is anything you need to know or understand before you begin. Listen with an open heart. If you "hear" anything, write it down in your journal or a separate notebook.

Silently bless yourself, your friend, and the relationship that exists between you as a way to help you prepare for this meeting. Call upon the Sacred to be with you as you proceed.

If you choose, you can also bless the space in which you will be meeting. You can do this blessing in whatever way is comfortable for you. For example, you can look to the center of the room, then to the four corners, then above and below the center, sending a thought of acknowledgment to each point. Or you can send a prayer into the room.

You also can turn control of the upcoming interaction—and the relationship itself—over to your understanding of the Sacred and express gratitude at the outset for the time you will be spending together.

**Element #1. Essence (Soul)**—Use your breath to calm and center yourself and to make certain you're fully present. Welcome your friend as an honored guest. Remember why you first came together. Make him or her feel comfortable. Allow yourself to see the best part of this person.

Proceed with love and respect, both for your friend and yourself. Use your breath to stay connected to your core indentity and values, so that no matter how the other person acts, you can reference these to stay calm and give your best self to the interaction.

At all times, observe from this quiet place exactly what you are feeling and thinking, and how you are acting. Observe also what seems to be going on for your friend. Listen carefully to all that your friend says and to the silence between the words.

Honor the other person and yourself. Do not allow any disrespectful behavior on anyone's part. Remember your values and act from them. Articulate the values the two of you share. Make this the foundation for your interaction.

If you are "hooked" by old behavioral patterns and thrown off Center, simply notice and bring yourself back. If you cannot return to your Essence and feel yourself interacting in an out-of-balance way from fear, anger, or envy, it may be best to take a time-out and resume your meeting at another time.

**Element #2. Air (Mind)**—Pay attention at all times to your mental dialogue. Use your breath to steady your mind, and keep it focused on the interaction. Articulate the vision and beliefs that the two of you share.

Inquire about the other person's thoughts and opinions on the matter before you. Take time to think before you speak or ask questions. And make sure you pause to think before you answer. This will save you a lot of grief. Clarify your ideas and opinions. Make certain that whatever you say is consistent with your own beliefs and values.

Stay open to learning and changing your mind. Use learned optimism to approach shared problems and resolve them together. Try to share your visions of the best possible outcome.

**Element #3. Fire (Will)**—Recall your shared mission and your purpose in being together. What are you trying to achieve in partnership? What can you do to support and empower each other? Identify the qualities you share, the unique talents that you respect in each other, and also note any differences that may be causing conflict.

Have the courage to speak about what is important to you. Encourage your friend similarly. Identify current obstacles in your shared path. Surface conflict. Allow your anger to show you where your boundaries are protecting you and where they may be unnecessarily getting between the two of you. Make certain you agree (in advance) about how to fight fairly and honestly, while always maintaining respect for each other.

Stay open to the possibility that the relationship may shift its shape as the two of you differentiate, grow, and change.

**Element #4. Water (Emotions)**—Stay aware of your own feelings and those of your friend. Articulate these feelings (when and if appropriate). Make certain you're using the basics of communication; for example, make "I" statements and listen with complete attention. Allow an easy flow between you. Don't try to control or direct the conversation—and don't allow yourself to be bulldozed or bullied, cajoled or manipulated.

Wherever possible, move from discussion into dialogue so that you both can access the deep pool of meaning that lies between you. Allow an ebb and flow of silence and words. Stay aware of your connection to each other, the ways you are the same, your respect for each other, and how you have helped each other become better people.

Clarify what you mean whenever necessary, and reiterate any agreements you come to. Make certain that both parties are truly happy with any decisions you arrive at, and that you're ready to move together to implement them.

**Element #5. Earth (Body)**—Pay attention to any body messages that are being sent. Do you really have agreement? If so, work together to decide how that agreement is to take shape. Determine what tasks need to be done, who will do them, and by when. Decide how you can help each other implement your shared decisions. Be as specific as possible about allocation and use of shared resources.

Make promises that are clear to both parties and that are likely to be kept. Write them down to help with mutual clarity. Make decisions about financial or work division issues. Be certain tasks are divided evenly and in ways that are sustainable; that is, that won't create other problems in the future. Make plans to check in regularly with each other in case someone encounters difficulties and "course corrections" need to be made.

⊕. **The Sacred (Below)**—Express your respect, affection, and gratitude to the person at the conclusion of this meeting. If possible, sit quietly for a moment before moving on. Revisit the fact that both you and your friend are an integral part of the whole.

Silently thank the Sacred for what you learned and for how you have been changed by this interaction. Ask if there is any more you need to know. Listen for an answer. Write down anything you "hear" internally.

Now it is time to first bless, then let go of, this interaction, knowing that you've done your very best for this important relationship.

# LEADERSHIP

*The great leaders are like the best conductors—they reach*
*beyond the notes to reach the magic in the players.*
—Blaine Lee, The Power Principle

## Holding the Sacred Space

Leaders set "the tone" in their communities or workplaces. People listen carefully to see if what they say "sounds true"; if it is sufficiently congruent with their behavior. Managers who are authentic create harmony and trust among the members of their workforce. Those who are not create dissonance and tension throughout the fabric of their system.

Leaders are responsible for determining what the rules are in an organization; for example, how respectfully people are treated. They set the tone for the quality of life in their workplace. By so significantly influencing morale, executives affect even the physical and mental health of their employees!

Whether or not they are aware of doing so, leaders hold "the space" that is known as their workplace systems. They have the ability (and responsibility) to make this space, and the effort expended there, sacred for everyone involved. One of the ways that great leaders accomplish this is by listening carefully to both silence and sound; for example, to what is (and is not) being said by members of the organization.

## The Five Key Components of Leadership

**Element #1. Integrity.** Leads by "being"; is principle centered, honest, and calm. "Walks the talk," has strong guiding values. Is authentic, genuine, "real," and comfortable in his or her own skin. Helps develop and personally reflects the organization's core values and identity.

**Element #2. Inspiration.** Inspires staff; has positive attitude; is open to new ideas. Learns well; is innovative and alert to changing environment. Takes time to think and plan for the future. Has a decent sense of humor and knows how to lighten things up when they get too tense. Articulates the company's vision and keeps it alive in people's minds.

**Element #3. Power.** Aligns, focuses, and prioritizes activities. Clarifies and promotes the organization's mission. Empowers and motivates others. Develops individual talents and helps staff members find their own personal missions within the organization's mission.

**Element #4. Emotional Intelligence.** Knows own self and interacts well with others. Is accessible and empathetic. Has excellent communication skills, listens well, delegates easily, and speaks clearly. Demonstrates genuine care for employees and pays close attention to morale. Makes certain that the organization's communication lines and information flow are excellent.

**Element #5. Management.** Is reliable, solid, and steady. Maintains order, makes realistic goals, is productive. Is competent in own skill areas and delegates to others when subject is not within own area of expertise. Pays close attention to the proper stewarding of all the organization's resources. Ensures the daily implementation of the Five Elements od Success.

One way leaders can "hold the space" for their corporations is by using the Elemental Circle to increase synergy. When I work with most business executives, I use the image of the compass or the baseball diamond to explain how the Elements of Success can help them improve their leadership skills.

By drawing upon all the Elements of Success, managers can attain the mastery they need to do the "Great Work" that will turn into gold for their organizations. Again, it is vital that decision-makers look first to their own internal state, for this determines the quality of their leadership. As John Heider says in the *Tao of Leadership*, "The leaders' personal state of consciousness creates a climate of openness. Center and ground give the leader stability, flexibility, and endurance. Because the leader sees clearly, the leader can shed light on others."[37]

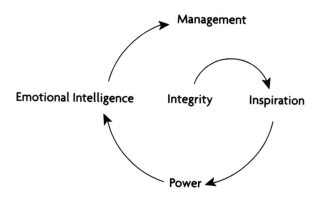

**The Leadership Development Spiral**

## The Maestro or the Duke?

Executives have the responsibility of getting everyone to sing off the same sheet of music, because as we now know, there are infinite possibilities (cacophony or a masterpiece) that can arise when so many people are simultaneously in motion. Management theorist Peter Drucker compared leaders with orchestra conductors who create beautiful music by coordinating their instrumentalists so they stay in dynamic balance and move at exactly the same tempo. (I've seen many organizations in which people acted more like orchestra members who think playing well means beating everybody else to the end of the symphony!) It is helpful to think of the all individual jobs as if they were part of a musical whole. Synergy happens when managers can get all the parts of their systems to work together in a more harmonious way.

John Clarkeson, chairman of the Boston Consulting Group, argues that leaders should consider themselves *jazz improvisors*, rather than orchestra conductors. He states that the major flaw in the analogy of a leader conducting a symphony is that "no one gives the CEO the music he should play!"[38] How true. Clarkeson refers to jazz great Duke Ellington, who would offer an idea to his band, then manage their different talents as they improvised, learned their parts together, and created a magical whole. In a typical jazz ensemble, all the instrumentalists know the standards they will play (i.e., each song's melody, basic harmonies, and rhythm). With these key components aligned, the group's members are free to improvise. They have the autonomy to vary any of the standard's basic components, but they also have to listen very carefully while doing so—staying attentive to, and coordinated with, their colleagues. Leadership is rotated in the jazz ensemble as different instruments are featured. The result of this dynamic collaboration is vital, exciting, vibrant music—and the kind of synergy that is every business leader's dream.

## From Grind to Gold: Using the Spiral of Synergy to Get Great Work Out of Meetings

By using the model of the Spiral of Synergy, managers can conduct meetings so that they are more productive and a better use of everyone's time. Indeed, executives can strike "gold" by facilitating great work from their employees, rather than forcing them to grind out their daily chores.

The list below includes many of the basic principles I have used to facilitate successful work teams. Then it creates "alchemy" by adding some magic to the mix. This exercise is written so that you can use the Elements of Success on your own. However, if you believe the workgroup's members are open to learning about the Spiral of Synergy, you can offer this meeting model so that the whole group can benefit. (The whole-group suggestions are written in italics.)

### Using the Spiral of Synergy to Get Great Work Out of Meetings

O. **The Sacred (Above)**—Arrive early and sit quietly for a few moments before the meeting is to start. Remind yourself that this silence contains all the possibilities that could help you solve the issues you are addressing today, and that a great many of these possibilities have not yet even occurred to you or other team members. The stillness also enfolds all the possible interactions among people who will be attending the meeting.

Request the best possible outcome for all involved. After a few moments, ask the Sacred if there is anything you need to know before beginning the meeting. Listen carefully. Write down anything you "hear" internally. Make notes that will help you prepare for the meeting.

When you enter the meeting room—also a little early—quietly bless it. You can do this blessing in any way that is comfortable for you. For example, you can say a prayer in your tradition, or you can think of the Elements of Success to remind yourself of the gifts of each of the five elements. You can also turn control of the meeting over to your understanding of the Sacred.

Try to arrange the chairs so that they are in a circle. This will allow the group members to more easily see and converse with each other. When the room is prepared, sit quietly and wait for the others. Express your gratitude to the Sacred for whatever is about to happen, and let go of the illusion of control.

Another way of invoking the Whole is to actively share leadership of the group. This can be done by rotating that role or by designating both a team leader and a facilitator to make certain the group continues to balance process and content as it does its work.

*If the whole team chooses to use the Spiral of Synergy process, you can begin the meeting by sitting quietly until all the members signal that they are ready to move on.*

**Element #1. Essence (Integrity)**—Calm and center yourself to make certain you're fully present. Warmly welcome everyone who enters the room. Allow time for people to settle down. (Sometimes it helps everyone to fully "arrive" at a meeting to first take a moment to write down whatever is on their minds. Then they don't have to worry about it during the meeting.) Have at least a five-minute check-in as the first agenda item, so people can connect with each other before starting their work together. (This will make for a much smoother and more effective meeting.) Whenever the group hits a snag, return to your Center, then get the group to stop long enough to solve the problem that has arisen, rather than ignoring it or trying to push on.

*If the team is open to the Spiral of Synergy process, have people articulate their values and the team's identity when they first start working together. Everything you do together needs to be congruent with these values and identity. Moreover, you also need to make sure that the work your team does is congruent with the organization's values and identity; otherwise, your efforts will not be integrated into the larger system.*

**Element #2. Air (Inspiration)**—During the first meeting establish your group's ground rules and operating procedures. (I promise you, these will be important later on.) For each meeting, take time at the outset to plan what you have to accomplish during your time together. Finalize an agenda at the beginning of the meeting, and assign realistic time frames per agenda item. Write these and the ground rules in large print on flip-chart paper so everyone can see them. In this way, the team can stay aligned and keep their shared vision clearly in mind.

For each agenda item, give people time to think before proceeding. (This allows the more introverted people to contribute to the meeting.) Take time to brainstorm in a structured, respectful way so that you can generate new ideas and innovative solutions for old problems. Capture all ideas on flip-chart paper. Make certain everyone has "air time" to articulate thoughts and ideas.

If there is a lot of laughter at your sessions, you are on the right track.

*Surface the groups hopes and fears, then help the group develop a unifying vision of what their work together could be. When that is done, see how this vision fits within the organization's vision.*

**Element #3. Fire (Power)**—Clarify what the group is supposed to achieve. A shared mission will align the group, then galvanize it into action. Determine the objectives of each particular meeting within the context of that mission.

Make certain that team members are empowered to act on behalf of their constituencies; otherwise, everyone will just be wasting time, and that will make them lose their "fire," both on this assignment and on their jobs.

Surface conflict and disagreement. Recall the group's ground rules to insure that fighting is always fair. When the team seems sluggish or confused, dig deeper to discover the real obstacles. Look to specific contributions of all the members of the group. What special abilities do they have? How do these talents—and the individual missions of each person—fit within the charge of the team?

*Help the group develop a specific mission that is achievable. Measure the results of each meeting against that mission to make certain you are staying on track. Recall the mission of your organization, and then see how the team's mission fits within it.*

**Element #4. Water (Emotional Intelligence)**—Pay attention to your own feelings and to the group's "process," i.e., the way people interact and communicate. Make certain that participation is even, that everyone gets the chance to speak, and that no one dominates the group. Do a round-robin technique (everyone takes a turn speaking) when things get out of hand. Make certain communication is clear. Remind group members to make "I" rather than "you" statements. Define what words mean.

Give feedback to each other during the meeting. Be sure that everything that needs to be spoken is articulated. Make decisions by consensus after every aspect of a particular issue has been addressed. (*Consensus* does not mean 100 percent agreement, but rather that everyone agrees sufficiently on a matter to try it.)

Clarify agreements. Evaluate the meeting at its conclusion: What did we do well, and what needs improvement? Use the Myers-Briggs Type Indicator, the Core Type Profile, or other typologies to help individual members gain a better understanding of their own and each other's personality and work style preferences, thereby increasing the group's collective "emotional intelligence."

*How do the relationships within this group fit within organizational relationships? Do you have all the people in this work group that you need to make it successful within the organization? How are communications among members of the team and those outside it? Is information being passed to and from the group in a timely manner?*

**Element #5. Earth (Management)**—Roll up your sleeves and do the work. First, define problems clearly. Then look for root causes before coming with potential solutions to test. Determine small next steps that you can monitor and measure. If the pilot is successful, you can then bring this change to the next appropriate level. (For example, statistical process control techniques such as flow charts and fishbone diagrams or structured brainstorming techniques will get you data you will need to make decisions.) Decide what has to be measured. Help the group access the physical resources that it needs to accomplish its work.

At the end of each meeting, give each other feedback. Evaluate both how the team managed its process and how it completed its tasks (the content of the team's work). Decide what tasks are to be done before the next meeting so that the team can do necessary work in between time. Assign "homework" evenly. Discuss ways to improve the team's processes so you continue to be efficient.

*This is perhaps the easiest element to get everyone to "buy into" and is likely to be done whether or not the Spiral of Synergy is used. However, giving the Earth element its proper context within the Elemental Circle actually increases the odds of getting the results you want.*

⊕. **The Sacred (Below)**—Express gratitude at the end of each session. Thank all the members for their contributions. Silently bless all individuals in the team. You also can thank anyone else who occurs to you; for example, those colleagues outside the meeting who are helping the group accomplish its goals.

Take a moment to sit quietly—this will help you "let go" before you have to move on to the next task. Thank the Sacred for what you learned and how you have been changed by this interaction. Ask if there is anything else you need to know. Listen for an answer. Write down whatever you "hear" that could benefit you, the group, or your organization.

Then take a deep breath to clear your mind, and then move on to the next thing on your agenda.

*You can end the meeting by sitting quietly until people are ready to leave. Ask if anyone has something more to say from this centered place. Make a point of thanking the other team members by acknowledging their special contributions to the team effort.*

# ORGANIZATIONS

◆

## The Elements of Success in Organizational Systems

I have found that the Elemental Circle is an excellent tool for organizational development, strategic planning, and change management. Clearly, the way to develop enduring systemic change in any organization is to use the evolutionary model designed by nature itself for learning, adaptation, balance, and healing—that is, the Elements of Success.

I've observed that many change-management and strategic-planning approaches (even those that claim to be "systemic") rarely address more than a few of the critical Elements of Success. I have used the Elemental Circle as an overlay for more traditional strategic planning models, (to make certain that the organization has comprehensively dealt with all its vital components), and also as the primary strategic planning tool.

## The Five Key Elements of All Systems

1. **Cultural Identity**—Shared core values and identity, the "gravitational center" of organization. Strong ethics and integrity. The "why" of organization's existence, its meaning a strong sense of who we are together, our unique culture, what we're supposed to do, and what we have in common.

2. **Vision**—A clear unifying vision, shared beliefs. Inspiration, hope, optimism regarding the future. Innovation, ability to learn and adapt, and generate new knowledge. Ability to scan the environment for change, clear-sightedness. Clear articulation of shared hopes and fears. Encouragement of good humor and support for positive attitudes.

3. **Mission**—Alignment about shared mission and purpose, ability to prioritize. High level of commitment, energy, pride, and empowerment throughout staff. Direct dealing with conflict. Individual work has meaning within context of whole system.

4. **Interactions**—Good relationships with internal and external customers. Excellent teamwork and communications between individuals and among departments. Ease of information flow. Strong sense of community. High staff morale, general environment of respect and trust.

5. **Structure**—Efficient, effective work processes; strong and flexible organizational structure (formal and informal); supportive policies and procedures. Well-trained management. Sufficient resources (finances and other), good physical working environment.

*I was called in to the Federal Aviation Administration (FAA) to facilitate a strategic planning team that had gotten bogged down. As I presented the traditional (very complicated) strategic planning model to the group, I could see their eyes cross and feel their energy drop.*

*I was losing them. I decided to gamble.*

*This consultation took place when I was first developing the Elements of Success. I asked the team members if they were willing to try another approach—that we would return to the standard methodology at any point they desired. I then drew a circle on a flip chart and explained the Elements of Success to them. They "got it" immediately. It just made sense to them, they said. What's better, they were galvanized into action. I was thrilled.*

*The next day the group arrived at our session with five laptops. They then divided the work assignments by each Element of Success, and began flying though their strategic plan. The plan they produced was nothing short of excellent. Later, the team won an award from the FAA for its exemplary efforts.*

Both individuals and organizations are much more than the sum of their parts. When a system maintains a dynamic balance among the five Elements of Success, it functions as a well-integrated Whole that can grow in more healthy, resilient, and coordinated ways. Any business that ignores (or overemphasizes) any one of these essential parts of itself will quickly go out of balance. This can result in serious malfunctioning when the system is under stress.

The problem is actually rather perverse. Organizations tend, when stressed, to do more and more of what they already do well. The sales force adds more perks for winners of a new, exciting internal competition. The think tank does yet more analysis of the problem. The bureaucracy reorganizes yet again. What was originally a significant problem then becomes an absolute crisis due to the system's out-of-balance response. A good way to avoid this tendency is to use all five Elements of Success to make certain you take a *whole, integrated, and systemic* approach to solving organizational problems.

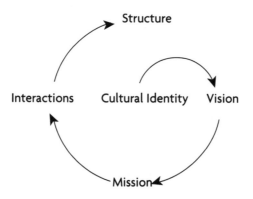

**The Spiral of Synergy for Organizations**

I enjoy illustrating organizational applications of the Elements of Success with one of my all-time favorite movies, *The Blues Brothers*:

1. *The Blues Brothers started on their adventure when they discovered that their old orphanage was going to be closed because it owed back taxes. Because they personally identified with the delinquent boys who needed a good home, they vowed that they would find a way to keep the orphanage open.*

2. *They had no idea how to solve the problem until they "saw the light"; that is, they had a vision while attending a church service.*

3. *When they realized what they could do to save the orphanage (put on a concert), they embarked with great energy on what they referred to as their "mission from God."*

4. *The next step was to find all the members of the old band and persuade them to join this effort (i.e., they had to reestablish the relationships necessary to accomplish their mission).*

5. *Finally the Blues Brothers band put on a concert to a full house, collected the money, and triumphed over many obstacles (including real roadblocks) to pay the back taxes so the orphanage could stay open.*

## Change Management: From the Sacred to the Bottom Line—and Back

So many workplaces are harming themselves by repressing all the talent within. Over time, this has a tendency to adversely affect the bottom line. What amazes me is how difficult this problem is for many leaders: first to see, then to address. Unfortunately, many people think that this is just the way organizations are, and there's nothing they, or anyone else, can do about it. A few others actually take advantage of dysfunctional situations to gain turf or line their own pockets. And still others I've seen are so paradigm-rigid that they cannot adapt to the industry environment that is changing around them. As a result of all these factors, many workplaces are so profoundly out of balance that there is barely "a pulse" detectable in the patient.

But good organizations do exist. And changing systems for the better is definitely possible, particularly if you use the Spiral of Synergy to do so. When I consult with organizations, coach executives, or lecture at universities about the Elements of Success, I sometimes begin with the most visible of the Elements (Earth) and then trace the spiral inward to Essence. Actually, the challenge I often encounter is to convince clients that there is anything more to business than the phenomena they can measure or what they can see with the naked eye. By tracing the evolutionary path inward, however, I often can gently ease people into understanding the ritual role each element plays in the success of their systems.

## Reviewing the Balance Sheet for Organizations

**1. Part II** may have already given you some new ideas for attaining better balance in your organization. If you haven't already done so, write down these ideas.

**2. Refer to your scores** from the Organizational Balance Sheet to find an aspect of your system that you would like to improve.

**3. Now use the model** of the Spiral of Synergy and all the Elements of Success to plan that improvement. Write your thoughts in the space below.

*I was called in to TRANSCOM (in the Department of Defense) to review the strategic plan they had well under way. TRANSCOM's purpose is to coordinate U.S. and Allied troop and relief movements through the world. Here I used the metaphor of the baseball diamond with the officers to make certain that all the Elements of Success were addressed. (I'm not crazy— this was a Warrior organization, after all.)*

*After we were done, the commander who had retained me asked if I would be kind enough to meet with a general and his staff from the Strategic Air Command. (They needed to make certain that their two plans were compatible and well integrated.) I agreed and was escorted to SAC headquarters.*

*While waiting for the general to appear, his staff officers and I began talking. Before I knew it, I was up at the flip chart, explaining the baseball diamond to them. They almost instantly determined the holes in their elaborate plan—and the reasons for them. When the general finally strode in, I suddenly realized that there I was at the front of the room, baton in hand, pointing to a large Elemental Circle. (It was a very funny moment in my career. Fortunately, I did not break into the laughter I felt inside.) The general listened to what his staff and I had to say, nodded, asked a few questions, and agreed with our initial assessment. Then he thanked me and strode out of the room.*

The optimal way to begin the Spiral of Synergy for organizations is to start by invoking the Sacred (because it contains all possibilities) and then move in a spiral fashion through all the Elements of Success, from the most to the least subtle. The inner-to-outward direction of the spiral is important in strategic planning because the tendency in most organizations is to start changes with the Earth element. Managers tend to do a financial analysis, then leap into cutting costs or restructuring the organization as a first (and sometimes only) step. I think that this is a lot like moving furniture around a room or rearranging deck chairs on a sinking ship. This common reflex strategy rarely results in any sustainable change or positive outcome. Worse yet, it can be a deliberate sleight of hand, that is, changing so as *not* to change.

However, I am a pragmatist. If you meet resistance in your organization, just start wherever you can. (For example, if managers think the greatest need is to improve communications, start there, then touch the rest of the bases as you proceed with the strategic effort.) As you proceed with your planning or intervention, use the template of the Elemental Circle to remind you to include all the Elements of Success. Over time, by going back and forth to make adjustments for the integration of all the Elements, you will create balance—and then synergy—in your corporation.

In the exercise below, I describe an integrated systems approach to organizational change efforts and strategic planning. For this example, I have assumed a managerial team whose members:

- are in charge of writing a strategic plan that is designed to create real change in the organization,

- think that the Elements of Success integrated systems approach would be useful, and

- are willing to devote several meetings to this effort.

You may have already completed some of this work in the organizational sections of the five chapters in Part II. If so, please refer to the comprehensive exercises in each relevant chapter as you work your way through the Spiral of Synergy for Organizations. I recommend that you write on newsprint as you go through this exercise, then transcribe the results after each separate work session.

---

## Using the Spiral of Synergy
## for Strategic Planning and Change Management

O. **The Sacred (Above)**—Gather the management team together. If possible, arrange your meeting in a circle, so that everyone can easily see and talk with one another.

Before you begin, have all the team members sit quietly for a few moments and "touch the Sacred" according to their own understanding of it. Realize that infinite (enfolded) possibilities exist here and that your organization has numerous possible solutions to even its most resistant problems. Your task is to create an "open system" that allows these new possibilities to flow more easily into the organization.

Ask the Sacred for the best possible outcome for your organization and everyone within it. Claim your personal power to bless yourself, the other team members, and the whole organization. After you have been still for a few moments, ask internally if there is anything you need to know before the session begins. Listen carefully. Write down what you "hear." Make notes for the meeting. When everyone is ready, move on.

**Element #1. Essence (Cultural Identity)**—In the Center of your organization is its core culture and shared values. The management team needs to make a strong start by examining the subtle but pervasive influences of the organization's culture. *All organizational change efforts must be congruent with (self-reference) the organization's identity if they are to succeed.* Any cookie-cutter strategic planning, change-management, or organizational development efforts will (at best) be just a waste of time, money, and effort or (at worst) create even more problems. This is why the strategic planning team needs to examine every suggestion for change to make certain it is congruent with the system's identity. The team also needs to pay close attention so that it can distinguish the real versus stated values in the organization.

*Please refer to the organizational exercises in chapter one for more detailed instructions on developing this first Element of Success.*

**Element #2. Air (Vision)**—Once the organization's identity, real values, and ethical standards are clarified, the management team can move on to the second Element of Success, Vision. Here the team examines the hopes and fears that are making the rounds in the company. This answers the question, What is the vision we are currently creating? The team also looks at the beliefs that are driving the business, scans the environment for new ideas, and thinks about how the organization has learned, adapted, and changed in the recent past. The strategic planning team may also want to examine how proficient the system is in generating new knowledge or intellectual capital and then decide how to stimulate more revitalizing innovation.

Again, the team needs to discover the real vision and beliefs in the organization. If these are not positive, determine what can be done to define a better shared future. How can the system develop a pervasive attitude of "learned optimism" so that it can create its best possible future?

*Please refer to the organizational exercises in chapter two for more detailed instructions on developing this second Element of Success.*

**Element #3. Fire (Mission)**—Once the team is clear that the organization has an inspiring vision of its future, it will be able to determine its current mission. Does the company's mission align its people and propel them into a course of action that is congruent with its vision and values? If not, what can be done about it? How can the mission align and empower people to do their best work for the organization?

A mission is measurable and doable. The Elements of Success up to this point have served as a vital, life-generating, unifying field (context or foundation) for a strategic plan. Now the team can begin designing an action plan that will set everything into motion. This includes timelines and specific goals that ensure the accomplishment of the mission.

*Please refer to the organizational exercises in chapter three for more detailed instructions on developing this third Element of Success.*

**Element #4. Water (Interactions)**—Next the management team needs to determine *who* is going to do what work. What are the relationships among departments and individuals going to be? How does the team insure proper communication and information flow? Are there any existing barriers among departments or individuals that could sabotage the interactions needed for this effort? If so, what can be done about it? Is any staff training, leadership development, or mediation necessary? The team also needs to clarify who the customers will be for the eventual fruits of its labors—and how these customers will be reached.

*Please refer to the organizational exercises in chapter four for more detailed instructions on developing this fourth Element of Success.*

**Element #5. Earth (Structure)**—Now the point has arrived where the team needs to decide the best structure for implementing the plan and accomplishing its objectives. (It may be wise to start small and "pilot" the suggested solutions so they can be fine-tuned before full implementation.) What design, what vehicle will best support the interactions, mission, vision, and values the team has outlined? What work processes would be most efficient and effective? What financial resources need to be committed to this effort? With that information, a budget needs to be drafted. Feedback systems for monitoring the process and assuring success of the plan must be established. The products and services will need to be tested in an ongoing way for quality and customer satisfaction, then corrected when there are problems.

Make clear assignments so that all necessary tasks can be completed before the next meeting. Schedule the date and time when you'll next work together.

*Please refer to the organizational exercises in chapter five for more detailed instructions on developing this fifth Element of Success.*

⊕. **The Sacred (Below)**—After all the Elements of Success have been addressed in turn, the team can complete the Spiral of Synergy by returning again to the Sacred.

When each session is over, express gratitude to all the team members for their contributions. Then have everyone sit quietly for a moment before rushing on. Thank the Sacred and each other for the revitalized organization that is coming into being. Ask if there is anything more you need to know. Listen. Write down anything you "hear."

Bless yourself, each other, and the whole system of which you are an integral part. Then, take a deep breath and let go of this meeting so that you are able to move on easily to the next task you have to do.

I have used this strategic planning process with many of my consulting clients. In most cases, clients come in with common "presenting problems" such as irregular cash flow, poor teamwork, internal systems that are no longer working well, high turnover, or difficulty in recruiting staff. The Spiral of Synergy process serves as a diagnostic tool to discover the *root causes* of these problems. I invariably find that this cause is further "upstream" elementally (i.e., it originates in a more subtle element). For example, one extended-care nursing facility was beleaguered by recruiting and retention problems. The owners and I started by defining their core identity and values, then worked systematically through all the elements. These people had done their homework, and we were able to move through the process very quickly. They later reported back to me that their staff members seemed galvanized by the new clarity and energy of the owners—and then, "like magic," five new nurses "showed up out of nowhere." As the most skeptical of the three owners said to me—"I don't care how it works. Seeing is believing."

# WORLD

*Awaken and listen, you solitary ones!*
*Winds are coming from the future*
*With mysteriously beating wings,*
*and good news is reaching sensitive ears.*
—*Friedrich Nietzsche*, Thus Spake Zarathustra

## Awaken and Listen

The Elements of Success and Spiral of Synergy outline a natural evolutionary path that can lead you to an experience of greater balance in your life, relationships, and work. These models provide a formula for creating greater unity, not only within yourself and your relationships, but also in the larger web of song of which you are an integral part.

*We devote our veneration*
*To Him*
*Whose voice we hear*
*But whose form no one sees.*
—*from the Rig-Veda*

Harmony, the sages and scientists tell us, is after all, our real nature. Chaos, they tell us, does not really exist. It is "merely a degree of order and harmony which our senses cannot (yet) perceive."[39] The great David Bohm thought music was an excellent metaphor for the "resonance" of the holomoving universe. He referenced the constant motion between tension and harmony in music, adding that, "In listening to music, *one is therefore directly perceiving the implicate order.*"⁴⁰ (Italics his.)

You and I create synergy when we decide to dance with the pulses of tension and harmony, imbalnce and balance, in our lives. But, as you well know, you can't dance well if you're not listening to the music. (To quote the Duke, "It don't mean a thing if it ain't got that swing.") We cooperate in the creation of a more unified world when we "awaken and listen." Then we can better perceive the natural music that exists in the apparent chaos around us and participate in its unfolding.

But how do we arrive at such a peaceful and happy state?

## Creating Harmony in the World

The Upanishads say that "the ear is the way." Today it is the way for you and me to thrive in this In-between. In recent centuries humanity has begun to rely more on seeing than hearing to discover the true nature of the world. Magicians, mystics, and sages, however, have always preferred hearing, because they knew that much of what they saw was an illusion and that much more existed in the world than they could possibly detect with the naked eye.

The difficulty is that today our sense of hearing is being bombarded. Our minds and hearts have been dulled by a constant onslaught of sound. We are living in a state of dissonance. We seem addicted to noise. This makes us increasingly insensitive to the needs of our own body. We do not listen when it screams at us to slow down. And if this is how we treat ourselves, how can we possibly bear to hear about the plight of others—or nature herself?

We have forgotten the "third ear"—the internal ear—that is designed to perceive the guidance whispered to us from the "still, small voice" inside. In turn, this loss prevents us from accessing the wisdom we need to solve our complex shared problems. It is a vicious cycle.

You can cooperate with the natural music that surrounds you by listening—simply by listening. This will help you become more "in tune" so that you can resonate with the exhilarating truth of the underlying, universal order. Then the exquisite overtones of Creation will ring throughout your life and you can reclaim your rightful place in the web of song.

And when you have found your own harmony and balance, you can help me regain mine. It is in this way that, one by one, we hear the undying music of the spheres and join with one another in the Sacred Dance.

◆

# 7

## INCREASING YOUR WEALTH: THE NATURAL LAWS AND FORMS OF PROSPERITY

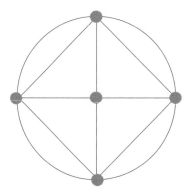

### The Goddess of Prosperity

*Many traditions across the world have deities of prosperity. One such goddess is Lakshmi, the life-sustaining aspect of the triple goddess of birth, life, and death. She is usually pictured as a radiantly beautiful woman, richly attired in the finest silks and jewelry. It is Lakshmi who answers her devotees' prayers for success and prosperity. She even has two extra hands with which she generously bestows the bounty of the universe. In one hand this diety holds a golden flower (for spiritual attainment and beauty), from another hand comes an endless supply of gold coins (material gifts), in the third hand she has a golden book (wisdom), and in her fourth hand she holds a golden weapon (to destroy evil).*

*According to legends, Lakshmi often appears to humans while standing on a lotus, the pure white flower that grows in muddy water. This symbolizes that the bounty of the universe can be found in every part of the world, even in unlikely looking places such as mud, which has the rich nutrients from which life grows. In this way the goddess of prosperity reminds us that we are to live fully in the world, to thrive and blossom wherever we are "planted." Lakshmi represents, and bestows upon us, every conceivable form of wealth: outer and inner, both worldly wealth and liberation.*

*However, she requires that we perform "right action" in order to receive her gifts.
This means appreciating what we already have, treating it with respect, not being
wasteful of our money or skills, giving ourselves fully to our tasks,
and being honest and compassionate in our dealings with others.
When this beneficial bestower of wealth is pleased, our lives can blossom like the
lotus, and we can rest easily, even if muddy waters surround us.[1]*

## Making Your Life Golden

The purpose of *The Balancing Act* is to provide you with practical tools (the Five Elements of Success, the Elemental Circle, and the Spiral of Synergy) that can increase your experience of balance, happiness, and abundance. The primary goal of the Magicians known as alchemists was to change themselves so that "the ordinary (leadlike) level of everyday perception" became "a subtle (goldlike) level of perception";[2] that is, they wanted *to make their lives golden.* In the ancient world, gold was considered to be symbolic of perfection and the divine, primarily because of its color and its association with the sun.[3]

The alchemists' Magnum Opus (*Great Work*) was the connection of their spiritual and physical worlds. The alchemists wanted to create heaven on earth, as represented by the *squared circle* (see cover). Indeed, this is what many of us are still trying to do in our daily Balancing Acts.

Alchemy was thought to be a rainbow that bridged the chasm between earth and heaven, between matter and spirit. The Alchemists' emphasis was on living the holographic connection between the invisible (enfolded) and visible (unfolded) worlds, *not* on making gold. Indeed, adepts were warned that one of the dangers of alchemy was that "like the rainbow, it may appear within reach, only to recede if one chases it merely to find a pot of gold."[4] Similarly, it is not just the pot of gold but rather the complete rainbow of abundance that most of us seek. Gold, then, was a *metaphor* the alchemists used. It was a symbol of the ultimate internal perfection they sought.

Alchemists were master chemists; indeed, alchemy was the forerunner to modern chemistry. The Magicians sought the creative tension (the balance) of combining opposites in many forms: the male and

*We shall understand
the world when
we understand ourselves;
for it and we are inseparable
halves of one whole.
We are children of God,
divine seeds.*

*—Novalis*

female principles, matter and spirit, the visible and the invisible, above and below, inside and outside, heaven and earth.

The alchemists thought of their Great Work as "a way of Life . . . a way *to* Life." They considered life itself to be an alchemical process; that is, life changes us the more fully we engage with it. The trials of life, relationships, and work test and challenge us, putting us through the "fire" until we are transformed. When we bring all the Elements of Success—our soul, mind, will, emotions, and body—to whatever we are doing, we can make it into something golden. *Our lives, then, become the Great Work when we allow ourselves to be transformed by the ongoing process of the Balancing Act.*

The goal of alchemy is to transmute whatever is heavy and leaden into something light, alive, and liberating, which is why its practitioners referred to it as the "redemption of matter." That is, as spirit enters matter, a coupling occurs (symbolized by the sexual union of male and female). This creates a third, new entity (as in the birth of a child). Alchemists contended that if you wanted to unravel the great secrets of life and make your own life golden, you needed to start by taking "a long, hard, unblinking look" at yourself. In this way, they said, you would soon see that the root cause of your problems was "ignorance of that which matters most: one's true self."[5] The alchemists would argue that, to an extent greater than you and I can possibly imagine, we create our own happiness and prosperity in this laboratory we call life!

This last chapter of *The Balancing Act* uses the templates of the five elements, the Elemental Circle, and the Spiral of Synergy to reveal the hidden nature, rules, and forms of wealth. There are many other versions of the "laws" of prosperity. (Some notable ones include *The Dynamic Laws of Prosperity* by Ponder, *Creating Affluence* by Chopra, and *The Seven Laws of Money* by Phillips and Raspbery.) However, the archetypal templates provided by *The Balancing Act* are very easy to remember and therefore to apply. They have the further advantage of integrating the issue of prosperity with everything you've learned so far about creating synergy in your life, relationships, and work. This will make wealth in every form that much easier for you to attain.

## The Natural Laws of Prosperity

The Natural Laws of Prosperity and their corresponding elements are as follows:

O. **The source of all prosperity is an abundant universe** (Sacred—Above).

1. **You are one with the Source** (Essence).

2. **Your mind creates your experience of prosperity or scarcity** (Air).

3. **Wealth requires that you give your talents to the world** (Fire).

4. **Because we are all one, your prosperity is connected to mine** (Water).

5. **Wealth has many forms** (Earth).

⊕. **You can create heaven on earth** (Sacred—Below).

## O. The Source of All Prosperity Is an Abundant Universe (Sacred—Above)

*Observe the wild flowers, how they grow; they do not get tired out,
nor do they sow. But I say to you that not even Solomon with
all of his glory was arrayed like one of them.*

*Now if God clothes in such a fashion the grass of the field . . .
is he not much more mindful of you, O you of little faith?*

*Therefore do not worry or say, What will we eat, or what
will we drink or with what will we be clothed?*

*Your Father in heaven knows that all of these things are also necessary
for you . . . Therefore do not worry about tomorrow,
for tomorrow will look after itself.* [6]

In this quote from the Bible (Matt.: 6:26–34), Christ urges us to place our faith in the natural abundance of the universe. I begin the Natural Laws of Prosperity with the Whole of the outer Circle, which is symbolic of heaven and this macrocosmic universe in which we all live. The Circle represents the implicate (invisible, enfolded, hidden) order of the world. It is the eternal pulsing silence from which everything is created and to which everything returns. Because the Circle is the original unified, complete One, it reminds us that we live in cosmos that contains all the Elements of Success and absolutely every possibility of creation within it. Therefore, because we are an integral part of this seamless Whole, we need not worry about tomorrow.

This macrocosmic universe is an "open system"; indeed, it is the original open system—living, pulsing, constantly creating. When the enfolded/implicate order moves, it becomes unfolded/explicate in all the bounty we see around us. The shamans in the Hawaiian Huna tradition believed that there are no limits in the world and that instead there was both a hidden and a visible order, with a fluid movement between the two. (Sound familiar?)

But, as I look around me at the city, nation, and world I live in, and then contemplate the known universe, with its millions of planets, stars, and galaxies, Creation seems abundant beyond my mind's capacity to comprehend it. (And that doesn't include the infinite "ensemble of possibilities" that is now in the process of shapeshifting from raw unformed energy into matter; that is, currently coming into form!) This ongoing miracle is probably why sages from all times and places agree that the underlying nature of our universe is abundance.

Prosperity in any form exists within a larger *ecosystem* of energy and matter. Interestingly, both *economy* and *ecology* come from the same Greek root *eco*, meaning "house."

*Ecology* is the house of nature within which we all live. Nature is an open system, therefore open systems are necessary to experience nature's abundance. As biology teaches us, open systems create prosperity. Closed systems create entropy, scarcity, and death.

*Economy* is the systematic management of the financial exchange systems in our nation and the world. This includes not only money but also what it represents: our natural resources, our combined talents and creativity, all of which contribute to the prosperity of the Whole. Buckminster Fuller defined the world's assets as consisting of two basic components: physical [energy] and metaphysical [know-how]. He came to two conclusions as he considered the nature of wealth:

1) Humankind is always in the process of becoming more affluent.
2) Our combined activities produce a *synergy* that results in a pattern of economic progress.

Quoting the law of the conservation of energy (which proved that energy can neither be created nor lost) and pointing out that every experiment builds on, or corrects, prior knowledge, Fuller argued that our collective prosperity can only increase; that is, energy cannot decrease and the metaphysical constituent of wealth ("know-how") can only increase. Fuller's conclusion was that "every time we use our wealth it increases."[7] Fuller also criticized the premises upon which our financial systems are built, because they have no way of accounting for *synergy!* He said, "Because our wealth is continually multiplying in vast degree unbeknownst [to] . . . human society, our economic accounting systems are unrealistically identifying wealth only as matter and are entering know-how on the books only as salary liabilities. . . . [Wealth] develops compound interest through *synergy*, which growth is as yet entirely unaccounted anywhere. . . . No value is given for the inventiveness or for the synergistic value given by one product to another . . . whose teamwork produces results of enormous advantage. . . ."[8]

## 1. You Are One with the Source (Essence)

*Do not try to live as if you are separate.*
*You are not.*

*You are of God,*
*part of the Tao.*
*You are within the landscape.*
*You are elements of the seasons.*
*You are of both heaven and earth . . .*

*Hold true to God*
*rest in the Tao,*
*and you will be carried to where the future needs you.*

—*Martin Palmer*[9]

Everything you need is available to you from the Source of abundance. When you connect from your Center to the Sacred, you feel "at one" with the world and experience a golden life. (This message is encoded in the alchemist's icon of gold, which combines the Outer Circle and the mystic Center as One.)

⊙

The Center is your own personal microcosm within the Great Circle's macrocosm. This symbol shows that you can "unfold" the wealth that is now invisibly enfolded in the Source by linking with that bounteous open system from your own Essence.

You will feel disconnected from the Source whenever you are out of balance, off center. This disconnection turns into poverty because you then live in a very limited part of Creation, your own little world of scarcity, worry, and fear. Wealth comes from experiencing yourself as One, an indivisible part of the holographic Whole. When you feel integrated with the Source, life has a magnificent, all-encompassing context and you can experience the Sacred in all the forms of prosperity that surround you.

When you move into the infinite universe of possibilities from your true *identity*, you will be better able to define—and then attract—those forms of wealth that are most valuable to you. What is "of value" to you is determined by your personal identity and core values. For example, a gift of a beautiful antique desk would be of value to you only if you appreciate antiques and have room for it in your house, Alternatively, you could consider it priceless simply because it is from someone you love.

True, there will often be ebbs and flows in your holomoving state of prosperity, much as there are waves on the sea. Yet all you need to remember is that you are an integral part of an abundant world. As such, you have power to draw riches in every form when you stay connected to that Source through your Essence.

Part of the Great Work you and I have to do is to unlock the secrets of prosperity and to use them for the good of all. Part of this process is to discover what it is inside ourselves that holds us back from experiencing the full prosperity that is our true nature. In what way have we become closed systems? How are we not fully participating in the open system of Creation? What beliefs limit us? When we notice an area of our lives in which we are not thriving, when there is a form of wealth we lack, then we can use this feedback from our environment to "take a hard, unblinking look at ourselves." We can treat this temporary deficit as an "irritation of doubt" that invites us to learn and change. Whatever you and I need is available to us. When we experience scarcity, we need only to return to our Essence and contemplate what is holding us back. This learning will then direct us to whatever we are temporarily missing.

What this law of prosperity means is that there is always enough, as long as we do not cut ourselves off from our own infinite supply by envying others, fighting over crumbs, or blaming ourselves or others. Fear, greed, anger, and self-doubt are primary reasons for scarcity. If we stay in any of these states overly long, they can create an unnatural reality by closing us off from our best selves, from others, and from the Whole. They keep us from giving our gifts to the world and from receiving gifts from others. This creates personal and collective poverty.

Unfortunately, the underlying abundant nature of reality is often hidden from us in this constantly shifting In-between era. But despite this illusion, we can draw whatever we need to us by staying centered in our core identity and values. And then, in turn, we will be more able to contribute to the good of the whole. This is the way to prosperity. This is the way to transmute our lives, relationships, and work—and the world around us—into "gold."

## 2. Your Mind Creates Your Experience of Prosperity or Scarcity (Air)

> *Nothing is either good or bad,*
> *but thinking makes it so.*
> —*William Shakespeare*, Hamlet

Your mind has the power to determine whether or not you *experience* the world as abundant. Truly, to quote the Bard, thinking makes it so. Your beliefs determine what you are able to perceive, and that in turn becomes self-fulfilling, creating your own personal reality of prosperity or scarcity.

Indeed, the world we each choose to live in is more "mind *before* matter" than "mind *over* matter." Much as our holomoving world changes from energy into matter and back again, our lives move from belief to "reality," then back again to reinforced belief. In many magical and healing traditions, it is thought that attention directs energy; that is, "energy flows where attention goes."[10] The way this principle works is that each one of us has the option to choose from an infinite number of beliefs. The ones we choose are like slides we put into a slide projector. Once we shine a light (our attention) on these "slides" we will be able to see them as clearly as if they were projected onto a screen.

If what we want already exists in the unfolded order, we will start to notice it where we never did before. For example, if I'm considering buying a certain kind of car, suddenly thereafter I notice that model everywhere I drive. It just seems to pop up out of nowhere. The thoughts you and I have act as catalysts to start the transformation from energy to matter. Depending on the complexity of the thought, this may take some time. But the energy has gone out as directed by our minds. In a very real way, our personal orders have been put into Creation. Self-fulfilling prophesies are already in the making. Or, to paraphrase Shakespeare, thinking *will* make it so.

And this magical process becomes all the more true when we add a great deal of feeling energy to a given thought; that is, when you or I want something so much that we have the *internal experience* that it is already true. This deliberate thought-feeling connection significantly increases the voltage of the light we shine on a "slide," thereby making it all the more likely to come true. So this law of prosperity encourages us not only to think about the life we want to create, but also to go ahead and *experience* it as if it had already happened! Paradoxically, this law contains a kind of "short cut" by which our minds can help us create a more affluent life.

This law of prosperity can be either good news or bad news, depending upon the thoughts and feelings you've been having. For example, when you are afraid that something bad might happen, you are feeding that scenario by giving it so much attention. All thoughts (slides) are the same as far as attention and energy (light in the slide projector) are concerned. It doesn't matter if your mental focus is due to your hopes or fears, love or anger, or whether you are cursing or blessing someone. In all cases, you are giving energy to that mental image and consequently ensuring that it will be projected into some form (manifested into matter) in your life. This phenomenon is like the law of cause and effect. Your thoughts are the cause, and your life, relationships, and work are the effect.

I need to make a distinction here between conscious and unconscious beliefs. The unconscious beliefs you and I have are extremely powerful and deeply ingrained— and usually override our stated, conscious beliefs. For example, we may say we have the power to change our lives, but still act as victims, blaming other people for our difficulties. We may insist that we are strong, independent adults, but find ourselves in dependent, dysfunctional relationships. In these cases, our two belief systems are incompatible. We are sending out contradictory "orders" to the world around us. Taking a hard, unblinking look at what we say versus what we do can help us surface unconscious belief systems, so that they no longer act as an undertow sabotaging our experience of a fully prosperous life.

Your attention will feed whatever your mind lights on. This affects not only you but also (because we are all connected) everyone around you. Indeed, whatever you are thinking about will affect the physical health of the person seated next to you and vice versa. In double-blind studies, a group was directed to concentrate on either positive or negative thoughts while a subject sat behind a screen. Muscle testing (checking the effect of different stimuli on the strength of a given muscle, usually in a person's arm or hand) showed that the subject was weakened by the group's negative thoughts and strengthened by its positive thoughts! The implications for organizations are enormous. (Just think of how general "morale" affects you in the workplace.) Indeed, this kind of thought-feeling "contagion" may be how virtuous cycles gain momentum and how vicious cycles eventually spiral out of control. As individuals or groups, we are either strengthening or weakening ourselves with our own thoughts. We are shining the spotlight of attention on, and therefore feeding, the creative process that will draw the prosperity we hope for—or the scarcity we fear. When it comes to creating prosperity, then, attitude is (if not everything) certainly an indispensable component.

The topic of *money* is one area in which attitudes toward prosperity vary dramatically, all the way from worshipping it to treating it as if it were the root of all evil. Neither attitude is particularly helpful when it comes to enjoying a full-spectrum "portfolio" of wealth. For example, people who think that money corrupts will never be fully prosperous in their work. They will sabotage themselves just as money starts flowing into their lives. Those at the opposite end of the spectrum (who believe that money is the cure for all life's problems) also will never feel rich, because it is impossible ever to have enough money.

Money then is neither good nor evil. By itself, it is neutral. It can best be thought of as an attitudinal *projection test*. The way you spend money reflects what you value and therefore how you are willing to spend your energy, time, and life. It is your attention that activates and enlivens money. In this way, money serves as a magic mirror in which you can see your fears and hopes clearly reflected back to you.

You and I can only access the wealth of this abundant universe if we are able to perceive it. Otherwise, we will starve because we are blind to the feast that surrounds us. We experience poverty when we look at the world through the blinders of limiting beliefs. For example, if racial bigotry or sexism prevents us from seeing the contributions and gifts of others, then we will always be that much poorer.

Another secret to experiencing abundance is to pay attention in the moment. Attention magnifies that moment in our minds, making it bigger somehow, our experience of it more vivid, and our lives richer because of it. We can increase our sense of wealth—instantaneously—by keeping our minds focused on what we are doing *while* we are doing it. Are we tasting the food we're eating, or are we distracted by reading the newspaper? Do we notice the sun flickering through the trees on our way to work, or we are talking on the cell phone or fretting about a project that's due? We lessen our experience of the treasures we already have by a) allowing our minds to wander out of the present into the future or past, or b) doing several things simultaneously (multitasking). To fully prosper, we need to make ourselves a "present" of each moment.

> *Money, which represents the prose of life, and is hardly spoken of in parlors without an apology, is in its effects and laws, as beautiful as roses.*
> —Ralph Waldo Emerson

## 3. Wealth Requires That You Give Your Talents to the World (Fire)

*The biblical Parable of the Talents tells of a master who entrusted his servants to manage his property while he was away. He gave one servant five talents, another two, and the last person, one. Then he left on his journey.*

*The man who had received the five talents traded with them and made five more. The one who had received two made two more in the same way. But the man who had received one talent dug a hole in the ground and hid the money.*

*A long time after, the master returned. The first two servants came forward with what they had earned in his absence. To each of them he said, "Well done . . . you have shown you can be faithful in small things; I will trust you with greater. Come and join in your master's happiness."*

*Then the man who had one talent finally came forward. "Sir," he said, "I heard you were a hard man . . . so I was afraid, and I went off and hid your talent in the ground. Here it is; it was yours, you have it back."*

*But his master replied, " . . . take the talent from him and give it to the man who has the five talents. For to everyone who has will be given more, and he will have more than enough; but from the man who has not, even what he has will be taken away."[11]*

This parable (Matt. 25:14–31) is rich in meaning, for a *talent* is not only "an ancient weight and money unit"; it also is defined as:

- the abilities, powers, and gifts bestowed upon [one], and

- natural endowments—thought of as a divine trust.[12]

Much like the servants in this story, you and I are the *stewards* of our own talents. It is our responsibility to participate fully in the cycle of creating prosperity by using these gifts to take care of ourselves, our dependents, and our world. To bury our talents—to "devalue" them or hold back out of fear or apathy—is to squander the gifts we have been given.

Work is one of the vehicles by which each of us brings our talents into the world. It provides us with the opportunity to use and multiply our talents, thereby increasing our own, our loved ones', our workplace's, and the world's wealth. In many ways, all the different kinds of work we do (whether paid or unpaid) are like the gold coins in this parable; they are gifts with two sides. One side of each coin represents the gift *to* us, the means by which we sustain and cocreate our lives. Work helps us survive. It keeps a roof over our heads, food on the table, and clothes on our children's backs. Sometimes work even helps us thrive, by providing opportunities for us to learn, change, and grow.

The other side of the gold coin represents the gift *from* us, what we return to the Sacred, even in the most menial of tasks. Work is also like the ancient talents in another way: It is the means by which we *invest* in our own and the world's future and how we transform ourselves in the process. Indeed, investing ourselves fully in work creates an alchemical fire, thereby transmuting whatever is mundane into gold.

The fact remains that we all *must* work, one way or the other. To quote the Bible: "By the sweat of your brow shall you toil" (Gen. 3:19). I have heard it argued that this was not really a curse but rather a command that assures us working is the right thing to do, that we are all here to do our part. When we align our personal wills with this natural law of prosperity, we connect with the Whole and experience abundance. Otherwise we separate ourselves from the will of the Source and experience scarcity.

If we resist this law of prosperity in any way (refusing to work, doing a sloppy job, taking shortcuts, shirking our responsibility, climbing over others, grabbing more for ourselves), we primarily harm ourselves. Giving "an honest day's labor for an honest day's pay" is a cocreative process that helps us grow up and take our place within our social system. It helps us move from a childlike state of dependency into an adult state of (physical, financial, psychological) independence and interdependence. It is therefore vital that we don't hold back in any way, that we fully give of ourselves for the good of all. Not only our prosperity, but that of a great many other people depends on our cooperation with this natural law.

To lead a fully prosperous life, you need to make sure that the work you are paid to do does not "consume" you; that is, come with the price tag of losing other forms of wealth, such as your health or time with your loved ones. (This can happen when you lose yourself in your job or, conversely, when your career is such a poor fit that it exhausts you.) The best working experiences, of course, are when we get paid well for doing what we love, in collaboration with people we respect. To discover the vocation that suits you best, ask what makes you happy. What things have you always wanted to do that you put aside and never made time for? What are your special gifts? (You may want to revisit chapter three where you listed these gifts.) Making a living doing the work that suits you best requires a) that you are good at what you want to do (i.e., that you have that particular *talent*), and b) that you are resourceful and creative in finding or making that work.

Author Ursula Le Guin has called work "one of the lasting satisfactions of life." Many of us would have to admit that we would work even if we were millionaires. In fact, a great way to discover what Joseph Campbell called "your bliss" is to decide what you would do even if you won the lottery. You know you're on the right track when you hear yourself say, "I can't believe they pay me for having this much fun."

People work for many reasons: For the satisfaction of a creative and productive endeavor; to have the experience of being with others who share our values; to support our families; and so that we can do our *real* work as artists. We also work so that we feel our lives matter because we have helped to make the world a better place.

Even if you now have a job that is not a good fit for you, you can still employ this natural law of prosperity to make your work a two-way gift. Start by backing up a step in the Spiral of Synergy and deliberately shifting your attitude. Choose some different slides to project your life. For example, you could think of this position as an *apprenticeship*, an opportunity to learn. That attitude will increase the motivation and power you need to do your work well. (It is also likely to have the added benefit of giving you enough energy to move on, rather than stay stuck where you are.)

The only lasting satisfaction of any labor, after all, is your own recognition of a job well done. This attitude toward work is very simple, yet it is alchemical in its effects. It releases a storehouse of fiery energy inside, thereby making your work easy and joyful—a gift freely given.

## 4. Because We Are All One, Your Prosperity Is Connected to Mine (Water)

*Once upon a time, the river and the pond were talking to each other. The pond had long been curious about something.*

*"Why," it asked the river, "do you give your water to the ocean? It's so much bigger than you are. It doesn't need it."*

*The river replied only that it was its nature to do so.*

*So while the river poured itself into the ocean, the pond kept all its water to itself.*

*As the years wore on, the pond stagnated. Finally, it completely dried up. By keeping all the water, it had suffocated not only itself but also all the creatures who lived within it.*

What neither the pond nor the river realized was that the great ocean was the source of wealth for each of them. It supported them invisibly by giving rain to the winds that fed them both. The river was right. It is in our nature (and also in our best interests) to flow continuously. The lesson of the river and the pond is that because you and I are part of the open system that is an indivisible Whole, your prosperity is connected to mine (and vice versa).

This law asks that we completely rethink the true nature of prosperity. Wealth, as it turns out, has little to do with the comparative size of our bank accounts. Rather, our true wealth flows from the ocean of Abundance in which you and I swim daily. This law of prosperity is a big leap from our current dearly held paradigms about individual wealth. It's hard to see this hidden, enfolded reality. But upon reflection most of us realize intuitively that our well-being is interconnected. Giving to others, our communities, and the world takes on new meaning in the light of this natural law of prosperity. It also underscores the assertion from *Tuesdays with Morrie* that "Love is the only rational act."[13]

A better analogy for the real nature of wealth is the image of lighting candles (rather than the traditional metaphor of cutting up pies). After all, one candle can be used to light others. In this way, you and I help each other thrive. In truth, any wealth someone else gains is shared with the Whole when it flows back into the economic system. In this way, it fosters growth elsewhere. This is how the cycling of *your* wealth can increase *my* prosperity (and vice versa). In reality, *more wealth breeds more wealth.*

In contrast, if you and I think that the nature of the world is scarcity, the potential wealth either of us can attain is indeed limited, and we are forced to cut up what we have as if it were a pie. This means that if you get more of the pie, I get less. With this mind-set, I will start competing with you for the pie. You and I may then hoard pie or steal pieces from each other. We also might eat more than we want right now, because we are afraid there won't be any left later on. Before we know it, the whole pie is gone!

Prosperity in every form requires an open-system flow of energy. In fact wealth can be thought of as a flow of energy, shapeshifting into matter and flowing back again into energy. Here's an illustration. The money you earned last week is transformed into a bag of groceries, then into a nice supper, and finally into a healthy body. The next day your well-fed and well-rested body carries you easily through your day on the job. You complete a report by deadline. That work is translated into a paycheck that is deposited in the bank. Then it is turned via a cash machine into the money you put in your pocket, which you use to buy groceries on your way home from work. And on it goes.

As energy, prosperity requires motion, a flow, a change of hands, participation in the larger open system of the "houses" we all share—our ecosystems and economies. Wealth requires you and me to interact in an integrated system of barter and exchange with other people, thus contributing to the synergistic creation of mutual prosperity. Money is worthless when stuffed under the mattress. It is *out of circulation*, no longer a part of the Whole economic system by which it gains a relative value. Money is merely a symbol of worth. Indeed, it is only at the actual point of exchange—when it is flowing—that your money has any real value at all.

The monetary system is not unlike the ocean that fed the river and the pond. It has constantly changing ebbs and flows—and we even call money *currency*. The monetary system's "currents" change as the consensual reality itself shifts, thereby changing the relative value of the dollar, pound, or yen, individual products, commodities, or specific stocks. It is a mistake to think that money, in and of itself, has some kind of solid reality. We can gain a better understanding of money by watching a day of trading at one of the stock exchanges. Here we usually see a frenzy of seemingly unpredictable activity. All its crashing-atoms-style emotion and lack of apparent logic demonstrates the highly energized, *alive* quality of the monetary system. We can also note how individual stocks and national currencies respond within the open system of which they are an integral part, quickly inflating or deflating value, roller-coastering up and down due to industrial, political, or global influences.

As a form of currency, it is in the *nature* of money to flow. The phases of currency are like the flow of a river. Money flows into and through our lives (earnings). If properly diverted, some of it flows into a reservoir for dry periods (savings). Then it flows out (into other forms of wealth; for example, purchases or contributions to the common good). You and I experience prosperity when we have a good flow of currency in our lives; that is, when there is enough money flowing in, enough flowing into reserves, and also enough flowing out to the rest of the economic system.

One currency problem in this In-between is the definition of "enough." We are—personally, nationally, and internationally—accumulating an extraordinary amount of debt. Debt is an unnatural monetary relationship, where more money or resources are flowing out than are flowing in. People in past decades generally saved their money and bought only what they could afford at that time. We, on the other hand, have the "benefit" of credit cards, car loans from the dealer, and instant department store credit, whereby we can simultaneously receive not only instant gratification but also instant debt. Unfortunately, we then have to pay exorbitant interest rates that only put us deeper in the hole. We also are losing our shared wealth and going into deep debt as a world community by spending down rapidly on the earth's total "capital" of natural resources.

I believe that the reason for our debt problems has a lot to do with our out-of-balance lives. We experience anxiety when we feel disconnected from the Source. One common way of trying to fill up this hole inside us is by buying "stuff." But, of course, the hole caused by this kind of disconnection from each other and the Source can never be filled this way. (To quote the old phrase, "Money can't buy you love.") However, purchases do ease our anxiety temporarily and make us feel good at that moment, much as alcoholics drink to dull their minds and relieve emotional pain. Meanwhile, our anxiety continues like a hidden undertow, an additive pattern is established, and we will very soon need to buy more "stuff."

If you, like millions of other people, have a problem with the proper flow of your finances, you may want to ask yourself the following questions:

- How are you spending your time and energy now?

- How could you better "invest" your energy so that it will increase your overall prosperity?

- Which of your talents can you exchange within your economic community for increased prosperity?

- What obstacles (beliefs, emotions, knowledge) should you address to alter the situation?

- What are you now giving back to the system in which you live and work?

- In what ways can you spend your time and energy to rebalance your current money flow?

The answers to these questions usually consist of specific ways you can a) increase the flow in, and b) decrease the flow out. This equation, although quite straightforward, is not always as easy to accomplish as it would appear. To get a better handle on your finances, you might want to consult the following books: *Your Money or Your Life* by Joe Dominguez and Vicki Robin; Suze Orman's *The Nine Steps to Financial Freedom*; or Jerrold Murdis's *How to Get Out of Debt, Stay Out of Debt and Live Prosperously*. You could also engage a financial advisor or debt counselor, or attend a Debtors Anonymous meeting.

When our lives are in balance, we know what "enough" is. We have all the forms of wealth we need. We experience a full, multifaceted, constantly flowing prosperity. It no longer occurs to us to keep up with the Joneses. (Who *are* those people anyway?) When you and I share our values, knowledge, talent, and resources with others in our communities and world, and they with us, our collective wealth is synergistically multiplied. Abundance occurs when energy flows easily into, through, and then out of our lives, back into the universe from whence it came. This is the best of all possible worlds, in which we get to experience the prosperity of the constantly flowing miracles of one thing.

## 5. Wealth Has Many Forms (Earth)

*King Midas simply could not have enough gold. He collected it, he bought it, he stored it. But he never had enough.*

*One day Midas wished out loud that everything he touched would turn to gold. His wish was magically granted. Midas was ecstatic; he went around the castle, turning chairs, walls, statues, fences—everything—into gold. He was so happy that he didn't stop for an instant to think as his youngest daughter, the only creature he truly loved, rushed into his arms.*

*King Midas recoiled in horror as she changed to a lifeless mass of metal. She was gone.*

*The king was inconsolable. Soon thereafter he realized that his own life was at stake. Every time he tried to eat or drink something, it turned into gold. He was about to starve amidst incomparable "wealth."*

*The king was about to despair. He begged, again out loud, to have his daughter and old life back. His wish was granted but under one condition: Midas must give up not only his newfound ability and all the gold he had created with it but also all his prior gold.*

*Without hesitation, Midas agreed.*

The story of King Midas underscores the fact that there are many different forms of wealth in the world. In fact, there are *infinite* forms of prosperity available to us, an ensemble of possibilities in this open system of our abundant universe. However, most of us are like Midas in that we usually equate being "rich" with having lots of money. Buckminster Fuller had a better definition. Wealth, he said, is, "Our organized capability to cope effectively with the environment in sustaining our healthy regeneration and decreasing both the physical and meta-physical restrictions of the forward days of our lives."[14]

Fuller illustrates his definition of prosperity with an example. A billionaire goes on a cruise. He takes all his money, gold, jewelry, art, and other possessions with him. The ship begins to sink; his money is of no use to him now—unless the billionaire can convince someone to give him a life raft in exchange for all his possessions. But who would take money or precious jewels under those conditions? No one—because we all know that the life that pulses through our veins is more valuable than gold. Fuller concludes that wealth is what we have to keep us and those we love alive and happy from this moment forward.

Much as the earth provides infinite diversity in its life forms, there is also great diversity in the natural forms of wealth. (Indeed, I list some of these later in this chapter.) I often ask the executives I coach to analyze their current work situation, or an offer they have for a new job, by defining the different forms of wealth involved. Many have put together spreadsheets in which they analyze the "real" money they make per hour (factoring in commute time and actual hours worked per week). They also examine how the job affects other treasures in their lives—their physical and emotional health, family and personal time, intellectual challenge, supportive workplace culture. In this way, they gain the clarity they need to make decisions that will simultaneously balance their lives and increase their experience of prosperity.

After all, it is not money itself that gives us the most satisfaction. (As Neil Diamond sings, "Money talks, but it can't sing and dance, and it can't walk.") Money, in truth, is just symbolic paper, metal, or an electronic transaction; in other words, a *means* for gaining other forms of wealth. And, as the story of King Midas points out, it is dangerous to confuse the ends with the means. Many of us seek more money when what we really want is security, freedom, beauty, comfort, respect, status, time, or love. It is important for us to first determine what assets we have in our lives and what we are truly lacking. We need to be extremely clear about what would make us feel more prosperous. Then we can focus the light of our attention so that we can increase that particular form of wealth. If we just try to get more money, as a reaction to feeling poor, we will never be happy. Like Midas, we will never have enough of what we really want.

Moreover, if you and I think our personal worth is defined by how much money we make, our position, or what things we own, we are making a potentially tragic mistake. One important distinction between having money and being prosperous is that our financial situation can easily fluctuate from year to year, month to month, or, in the stock market, moment to moment. If you feel defined by these fluctuations, your self-image will suffer from the roller-coaster ride. On the other hand, if you have a better balanced, full-rainbow–spectrum "portfolio" of wealth, you will be quite able to withstand these fluctuations. You will feel more steady, secure, and affluent, whatever your circumstances.

A riveting way to determine which of the many forms of wealth you most value is to review your life from the perspective of your deathbed. This may seem, on the surface, to be a morbid proposal. However, it does serve to clarify things wonderfully: at that last moment, no one is likely to wish that he or she had more money in the bank. We all know this, but this truth rarely results in a shift of our daily priorities. To quote from *Tuesdays with Morrie*, one of the great secrets of life is that "Everyone knows they're going to die, but no one believes it." And Morrie adds, "If we did, we would do things differently."[15]

One way for you to do things differently is to start carving out time for what matters most to you. The majority of people who make short- and long-range plans, tend to focus on improving their work or financial situation (e.g., making career plans that will increase salary, status, or perks). Typically, people do not make balanced plans, for example, to increase time spent with friends, strengthen their health, develop their minds, or nurture their spirits. Therefore, it should come as no surprise to us that, as we climb the "ladder of success," our imbalance only increases. In this way, we actually *decrease* our quality of life and experience of prosperity! The danger is that although we may achieve our stated goals, they include only a few of the many forms of wealth. As Joseph Campbell warned, sometimes we find out too late that our ladder to success has been up against the wrong wall.

Most of us want much more than career or financial success; we want love, good health, secure family lives, and some time to walk quietly in the woods or sit on the beach. But if our planning does not include these things, our attention (and energy) will not feed them. Often those things that matter most to us are inadvertently, unthinkingly, sacrificed along the way. To discover the forms of prosperity we are in the process of creating, we need only look at the way we spend our days and weeks. For example, we may say we value our friends, but how much time do we really spend with them? We may think that our family is our priority, but where do they rank in how we spend our time?

As you look at the many forms of wealth listed later in this chapter, you can think about how balanced and wealthy you truly are. If you want to attain a more diversified portfolio of prosperity, you will need to pay attention to the particular forms of wealth you most value and include them in our planning, from daily goal setting to life planning. (Note: When doing your planning, be sure to let go of the specific form of the results you want by always asking for "this or something better." Sometimes the universe has more to give us in the future than our minds can imagine right now.)

One way to accomplish this kind of balanced portfolio is by getting a coach. Personal coaching is a profession that has grown at an extraordinary rate in recent years; largely, I think, to help people address the imbalances they are experiencing in their lives. I have used one myself. Her name is Lee Estridge, and she has helped me more than I can say in my own personal and professional Balancing Act. On a regular basis Lee urged me to reclarify my life, relationships, and work goals, and then she gently but firmly kept me on track. Having a coach is like having an extra conscience—or a special friend who is completely focused on your well-being.

The richest individuals have a sufficiency of every form of wealth in their lives. This includes physical and emotional health, strong relationships, meaningful work, living in attractive surroundings, and having enough quiet time. However, when we lack one component of prosperity, we can sometimes compensate for it with others. For example, Stephen Hawking (one of the greatest theoretical physicists since Einstein) is confined by Lou Gehrig's disease to a wheelchair. However, his extraordinary intelligence, determined will, and supportive family and community make him very rich. These other forms of wealth, in turn, have allowed him to contribute his genius to the world. Hawking's triumph over his physical limitations reminds me of Jimmy Stewart (in his movie portrayal of Lou Gehrig) shouting to an empty, echoing baseball stadium, "I am the luckiest man in the world!"

This brings me to one other aspect of this law of prosperity. You need to work with what you have. The element of Earth requires each of us to accept and optimize our physical or other limitations. You and I need to care for whatever forms of wealth we've been given. Indeed, dealing with limitations is part of your alchemical work. These resources, these forms of wealth, are the cards you've been dealt. They are the raw material—the matter—that you can transform into gold as you do your Great Work in the world.

## ⊕. You Can Create Heaven on Earth (Sacred—Below)

*There are only two ways to live your life.*
*One is as though nothing is a miracle.*
*The other is as though everything is a miracle.*

—*Albert Einstein*

This last law of prosperity returns us to the Sacred, but this time with a twist. We have combined our human effort with "divine grace" to create the miracle of synergy. We have done our part in the process of cocreation, thereby accomplishing the Great Work of the alchemists. By bringing together heaven and earth, *we have made our lives golden.* This return to the Sacred is symbolized by the squared circle.

We now experience that we are fully part of the miracles of one thing. The above has become the below, and what was outside us we now experience as being within!

Now there is no sense of separation, between us and the Sacred.

In this final law of prosperity, our abundance moves from unfolded to enfolded state, from invisible to visible. There are several ways you and I can participate in this final step of the wealth-creating process:

1. The first is by expressing *gratitude* for all the bounty we have received—and also for all the things that we have *not* received or for what has left us.

2. The second is by *blessing* ourselves, a given situation, others, and the world. We "bless" by claiming responsibility for the divine power that exists within us.

3. The last is by *letting go* of the results of our actions and also any forms of prosperity that leave our lives. This includes releasing any feelings of regret, sadness, or resentment.

The forms of wealth we gain as a result of all our efforts include a *profound equilibrium, equanimity,* and *equipoise*—the end point of *The Balancing Act!* Like an Olympic gymnast who springs off the balance beam, we now land gracefully on both feet and lift our hands triumphantly to the sky. What we experience inside when we achieve this state is unparalleled *freedom, joy,* and *happiness.*

**Gratitude.** Most of us, even if we're relatively affluent, do not experience ourselves as wealthy. This amazes me. For one thing, we tend to take for granted the forms of prosperity we already have. Instead, we focus on what we do not have; that is, what we *want.* (Think for a moment of the dual definition of the word "want." When we say we "want" something, it broadcasts the message throughout our psyche that we lack it. As Neale Donald Walsh recommends in *Conversations with God,* use this word very carefully—and sparingly.)

Many of us live in fear that we will lose what we have. Or we regret what we have lost or what has passed us by. In these ways, we create an inner state of felt poverty. Paradoxically, people who do experience a great loss often wind up feeling more grateful for what they do have, because they have stopped taking that form of wealth for granted. To illustrate why it is wise to be grateful for what we have *not* received, I only have to ask you to remember the things (or relationships or jobs) you once passionately desired. Now think of how much happier you are because you did not get them—or because they left your life! (Most people have only to think of their ex-spouse or a job they were fired from to realize how much better off they are today as a result.)

Our prosperity increases whenever we experience gratitude. Gratitude springs from an understanding of the true nature of wealth. It turns our attention to what we have in the moment, so that we truly experience it. Otherwise, in a very real way, we do not "have" that form of wealth.

Gratitude makes us aware. It wakes us up. It also acts like a magnet. Gratitude actually increases our experience of both internal and external prosperity by opening us up from the inside outward. In this way we become a more alive, vital, open system that can draw the natural abundance of Creation to us. Moreover, gratitude for what we have already received increases our faith and reinforces our learned optimism. This, in turn, increases the likelihood that our future needs will also be met. The Bible hints at this when it says:

> *Ask and ye shall receive.*
> *Seek and ye shall find.*
> *Knock and the door will be opened.*
> —Matt. 7:7

**Blessing.** Our internal Ally, the Magician, encourages us to claim the personal power we have to bless ourselves, others, and our world. Blessing sets a virtuous cycle into motion. We become like a magical Johnny Appleseed, sowing seeds of abundance everywhere we turn our attention.

It is very empowering to make blessing an integral part of your life. Indeed, although quite subtle, blessing is one of the most powerful ways you can actively participate in both increasing your own wealth and establishing heaven on earth.

> *Bless a thing and it will bless you. Curse it and it will curse you.*
> *If you bless a situation, it has no power to hurt you, and even if it is*
> *troublesome for a time, it will gradually fade out, if you sincerely bless it.*
> —*Emmet Fox*

**Letting Go.** When all is said and done, when we have done our part to increase our prosperity, it is time to let go. This is a crucial step. It is an act of faith and trust, a vote of confidence in an abundant universe. It indicates that we know we must make enough space in our lives so that nature, which abhors a vacuum, can fill us up again. As mythologist Joseph Campbell once said, "We must be willing to get rid of the life we've planned, so as to have the life that is waiting for us." Because Creation is much more bountiful than we can possibly imagine, we are unlikely ever to be able to think of all the options available to us. We need to do our part by planning and then letting go to life if we are to experience the full wealth of synergy.

> *With a right intention,*
> *you quietly face the risk of losing the*
> *fruit of your work. With a simple*
> *intention, you renounce the fruit*
> *before you even begin. You no longer*
> *even expect it. Only at this price can*
> *your work also become a prayer.*
> —*Thomas Merton*

Moreover, when we separate our personal

egos from the fruit of our work, letting go of it by giving it up to a higher good, we will be able to do better work overall. With our energy freed up, it is also easier for us to move on to the next task. We're not waiting around for someone to notice or praise us.

Trying to hang on to something, or someone, is evidence that we don't trust the Source to do right by us. Doing what we can to prevent change is like trying to swim straight up a torrential waterfall of grace. By letting go, we turn all our efforts into something much more—a meditation, a service, a prayer.

Letting go allows us to experience freedom and happiness. This is, after all, what each of us is seeking in our own Balancing Acts. With this last natural law of prosperity, we have reached the end of all our striving. Not only have we found the pot of gold at the end of the rainbow, we are enfolded in the rainbow itself. Truly, the Sacred has always been there, patiently waiting for us to realize our true, golden nature.

## The Professor, the Rock Star, and the Natural Laws of Prosperity

As I write the last pages of *The Balancing Act,* U2's lead singer Bono is a few blocks away, delivering the Class Day Address for Harvard's graduating class of 2001. Why an internationally acclaimed rock star was invited to give such a high-profile speech in these hallowed halls provides a brilliant example of how the Natural Laws of Prosperity can work together to increase our collective wealth.

0. **The Source of all prosperity is an abundant universe (Sacred—Above).** Out of all the possible combinations in the world, an American college professor and an Irish rock star formed a remarkable friendship. A few years ago, U2's Bono began studying privately with prominent Harvard economist Jeffrey Sachs, director of the Center for International Development.

1. **You are one with the Source (Essence).** In ways that were obvious only to them, these two men with such distinctly different identities shared many common values. I also think they connected on some level with something (however they defined it) that was larger than either of them and that guided the way they conducted their lives, work, and relationships.

2. **Your mind creates your experience of prosperity or scarcity (Air).** Both men shared an ideal—that the world could significantly reduce its overall poverty. Their vision was to lift the crushing economic burden of debt repayment in Third World countries. They believed that a global shift was possible if enough people challenged the ignorance and indifference that permitted this scarcity to continue.

3. **Wealth requires that you get your talents to the world (Fire).** Sachs and Bono combined their extraordinary talents (and the public platforms afforded them by

these talents) to draw attention to the widening gap between the world's "haves" and the "have-nots." They took to the road and publicized the fact that for every one dollar given in international aid, a shocking nine dollars is returned in debt service. They put their power behind the London-based New Economic Foundation's Jubilee 2000 program, headed by Ann Pettifor. The mission of this organization (now Jubilee +) is to convince the wealthier nations of the world to cancel the unpayable debt of the world's poorest countries.

**4. Because we are all one, your prosperity is connected to mine (Water).** Jubilee + is powerful coalition of many of the world's religious, political, academic, and celebrity leaders who share Sachs's and Bono's desire to relieve the long-standing economic drought in these Third World countries. Their friends in this international effort include Bobby Shriver (who introduced the two), U.S. Treasury Secretary Larry Summers, the Pope, Mohammed Ali, Kwesi Owusu, Liana Cisneros, and countless other influential individuals and organizations throughout the world.

**5. Wealth has many forms (Earth).** One tangible outcome of the combined efforts of all these individuals is that the U.S. Congress was prevailed upon to vote for $435 million worth of international debt relief. This in turn has been leveraged to free up *billions* of dollars worth of debt from other wealthy nations. And, this accumulated money has already been transformed instead into education, health care, housing, and food in Third World countries. As a result, these poorer countries will be better able to take their rightful place in the global economic system.

**⊕. You can create heaven on earth (Sacred—Below).** Clearly, the professor, the rock star—and their many friends—have blessed us all with their generous efforts. Together they have brought more than a little bit of heaven to earth. I know that I am richer because of them.

## The Infinite Forms of Prosperity

You and I live in an abundant universe whose nature is to continuously enfold and unfold infinite forms of prosperity. Not only is there great diversity in the world's many forms of wealth, but all these forms can shapeshift into others. For example,

- your time at work turns into a paycheck that you use to pay the mortgage on your home;

- members of your community lead you to a new job;

- a neighbor to whom you've been kind brings over dinner when you're ill;

- gratitude becomes a gift of flowers.

I remember one of my first lessons as a child in the diversity of wealth. I was listening attentively to my great-uncle, Stephen Kindregan, who was visiting from Athenry in County Galway, Ireland. He declared, "You have nothing if you lose your health." (Of course, I later learned that for centuries the Irish had little else. But back then it made quite an impression on me.)

Listed below are some of the many forms of wealth that contribute to your experience of prosperity. I have grouped them according to the Elemental Circle so that they are easier to remember. Feel free to add any that I may have missed.

| O. **Sacred** (Above) | The Source of abundance; all of Creation<br>Grace<br>Time; eternity<br>Universal wisdom, collective wisdom<br>Awareness that we are all One<br>The gift of Life itself<br>Human dignity and respect<br>Unconditional love<br>The implicate *and* explicate order; an alive universe with infinite possibilities of abundance<br>Deep silence and internal stillness |
|---|---|
| **1. Essence** | An experience of being One with the Source of abundance<br>Touching the Sacred through meditation or prayer<br>The experience of feeling fully alive<br>Contentment; peace, a sense of having enough time<br>Calm, ease, being stress-free<br>A sense of deep security—that you live in a safe, abundant world<br>Feeling of having a "Center" that keeps you in balance<br>Strong personal identity; knowing who you are in the world<br>Clear personal values and strong ethics; integrity; living your values<br>Self-knowledge; being comfortable with yourself ("to thine own self be true")<br>Moments of intuitive knowing ("aha" insights); personal wisdom<br>Sense of individual soul; spiritual health<br>Self-love, respect, and esteem; personal dignity and nobility<br>Having meaningful work that is congruent with your values and identity |
| **2. Air** | Learned knowledge; areas of expertise; excellent education<br>Ability/willingness to learn<br>Optimism, positive attitude; hope |

| | |
|---|---|
| | Good sense of humor<br>Feeling light (not overly serious)<br>Raw intelligence (IQ)<br>Supportive empowering belief system (e.g., belief in yourself, prosperity beliefs)<br>Mental health<br>Work that uses your intelligence, knowledge, competence |
| **3. Fire** | Personal "gifts," i.e., individual talents<br>Strong will; intention; knowing what you want; a sense of direction<br>Personal energy<br>Sense of power and empowerment<br>Focus and discipline in bringing talents and skills to fruition<br>Pride in what you do<br>Ability, willingness, courage to take action<br>Assertiveness in managing conflict<br>Healthy individuation and personal boundaries<br>Understanding of, and belief in, your personal uniqueness and talents<br>Work that uses your personal talents, skills, gifts |
| **4. Water** | Felt connection to the well-being of all other people and creatures<br>"Emotional intelligence"—self-awareness and social skills<br>Friendships and other nurturing personal relationships<br>Supportive family and community<br>Communication skills (active listening; clear speaking; ability to read non-verbal cues)<br>Capacity to love and respect others<br>Compassion; empathy; kindness<br>Ability to both give and receive love; respect for and from others; a feeling of being known and loved<br>The gift of welcoming others and being welcomed<br>A workplace with good morale, excellent communication, supportive colleagues, and teamwork |
| **5. Earth** | Physical aspects of wealth: possessions, cash flow, savings, resources<br>Bodily health<br>The gift of the five senses (ability to hear, see, taste, touch, smell)<br>Attention in the moment to input from the five senses<br>Physical beauty<br>The nourishment of physical touch<br>Physical intimacy, sensuality, and sexuality<br>Ample money for current personal and family needs and savings for future |

| | Safety, comfort, and beauty of physical environments (work, home, other)<br>Regular contact and connection with the earth (being in nature, ability to walk in the woods, or relax on the beach)<br>Positive, supportive work and life habits<br>Social, community, and work infrastructures (e.g., the roads you drive on) that support your personal and professional needs<br>Sufficient structure, infrastructure, and resources to get your work out into the world |
|---|---|
| ⊕. **Sacred** (Below) | Gratitude (for all you do—and do not—have)<br>Willingness to bless yourself and others<br>Happiness; joy; bliss<br>Ability to let go (nonattachment)<br>Equanimity; equilibrium; equipoise (the goal of the Balancing Act)<br>Freedom; liberation |

## Increasing Your Wealth

*I got rhythm*
*I got music,*
*I got my guy,*
*Who could ask*
*for anything more?*
*—George and Ira Gershwin,*
*"I Got Rhythm"*

To stimulate your thinking, and to add some fun to the mix, I've included several boxes below so that you can take stock of the forms of prosperity you have in each element of your Balancing Act. This exercise is meant not only to help clarify the many forms of wealth you already enjoy but also to galvanize you into claiming a full-rainbow–spectrum of prosperity for your life, relationships, and work. Refer to the forms of wealth listed on the preceding pages to do your assessments.

# PERSONAL LIFE

◆

This is a good point at which to do an "accounting" of the forms of prosperity that already exist in your personal life. You can use the boxes below to note the wealth you have now and give yourself a subjective "score" per element. Then you can use the material in the rest of *The Balancing Act* to find ways to increase your overall abundance. Below is an example that was completed by "John Doe."

|  | Forms of Wealth You Now Have | Forms of Wealth You Now Lack | Overall "Score" (0–10) |
|---|---|---|---|
| **0. Sacred** | Gift of life; grace | Stillness; awareness that we are all One | 6 |
| **1. Essence** | Calm most of the time; sense of individual soul | Regular spiritual practice; self-esteem; contentment | 4 |
| **2. Air** | Raw intelligence: willingness to learn new things | "Lightness"; sense of humor (too serious most of the time) | 5 |
| **3. Fire** | Lots of talent (especially mathematics and art) | Work that uses talents; energy, focus, and discipline; belief in my uniqueness; sense of direction | 2 |
| **4. Water** | A good community; supportive friends and family | Sufficient compassion and empathy; felt connection to the well-being of others | 5 |
| **5. Earth** | Physical health; enough money for needs plus retirement; gift of all five senses | Good work habits | 7 |
| **⊕. Sacred** | Ability to let go; happy some of the time | Gratitude; equanimity (not happy enough of the time) | 4 |

John now has a thumbnail sketch he can use to contemplate and better balance his overall wealth portfolio. His own assessment is that he is strongest in Earth and most lacking in Fire. Now he can use this feedback to draw up a strategy that will help him increase the Fire forms of prosperity, while not losing the others he has. (Often, when we try to make improvements in our lives, we inadvertently "throw the baby out with the bath water." For example, John could pay less attention to his community, thereby losing that form of wealth.) With the above assessment, John might also decide to increase his wealth by doing his spiritual practice more regularly, and by adding a very short gratitude practice as an integral part of that set-aside time.

Now, do this for yourself.

|  | Forms of Wealth You Now Have | Forms of Wealth You Now Lack | Overall "Score" (0–10) |
|---|---|---|---|
| O. Sacred |  |  |  |
| 1. Essence |  |  |  |
| 2. Air |  |  |  |
| 3. Fire |  |  |  |
| 4. Water |  |  |  |
| 5. Earth |  |  |  |
| ⊕. Sacred |  |  |  |

## Notes to Yourself

- Areas that are in good shape:

- Areas that need more attention:

- Ideas for increasing prosperity:

- Action plan (use the Natural Laws of Prosperity to increase your personal wealth):

# RELATIONSHIPS

◆

I am always amused that so many of my single friends want to be in an intimate relationship—while so many of my friends who currently have a mate complain that they want out! It is my hope that the following assessment of one important relationship can point to ways you can increase your prosperity in this critical aspect of life. You may want to do this assessment in two parts: the wealth you receive from a particular relationship and the wealth you give in return.

| | Forms of Wealth You Now Receive from the Other Person | Forms of Wealth You Now Give to the Other Person | Overall "Score" (0–10) |
|---|---|---|---|
| O. Sacred | | | |
| 1. Essence | | | |
| 2. Air | | | |
| 3. Fire | | | |
| 4. Water | | | |
| 5. Earth | | | |
| ⊕. Sacred | | | |

## Notes to Yourself

• Areas that are in good shape:

• Areas that need more attention:

• Ideas for increasing prosperity:

• Action plan (use the Natural Laws of Prosperity to increase your relationship wealth):

# LEADERSHIP

◆

You may or may not have a managerial position in your organization. However, both you and I need to exercise leadership if we are to increase our own prosperity and that of the systems of which we are an integral part. If you are in an executive position in your corporation, use the boxes below to assess the resources you now have to do your best work. If you are not, use this material to determine what you need to in order to become a better leader in the future. Again, you may want to do this "accounting" so that you look closely at what you give to your system and how it supports you in return.

|  | Forms of Wealth You Now Receive from Your System | Forms of Wealth You Now Give to Your System | Overall "Score" (0–10) |
|---|---|---|---|
| O. Sacred |  |  |  |
| 1. Essence |  |  |  |
| 2. Air |  |  |  |
| 3. Fire |  |  |  |
| 4. Water |  |  |  |
| 5. Earth |  |  |  |
| ⊕. Sacred |  |  |  |

## Notes to Yourself

- Areas that are in good shape:

- Areas that need more attention:

- Ideas for increasing prosperity:

- Action plan (use the Natural Laws of Prosperity to increase your leadership wealth):

# ORGANIZATION

◆

You can help your organization by accounting for its assets in a more comprehensive way. After all, each form of wealth can change shape and be transformed into bottom-line results. Once you have done the assessment below, decide what you can do to increase your system's success in the future.

You can do this dual assessment in one of several ways. You can determine what forms of wealth your business currently does and does not have. Or you can calculate what you, as a worker, give and receive from the organization. (If you are a leader, this may be redundant with the prior exercise.) Or you can assess the forms of wealth that this system gives to and receives from the world.

|  | Forms of Wealth the Organization Now Has | Forms of Wealth the Organization Now Lacks | Overall "Score" (0–10) |
|---|---|---|---|
| O. Sacred |  |  |  |
| 1. Essence |  |  |  |
| 2. Air |  |  |  |
| 3. Fire |  |  |  |
| 4. Water |  |  |  |
| 5. Earth |  |  |  |
| ⊕. Sacred |  |  |  |

## Notes to Yourself

- Areas that are in good shape:

- Areas that need more attention:

- Ideas for increasing prosperity:

- Action plan (use the Natural Laws of Prosperity to increase your organization's wealth):

# WORLD

◆

Your community, nation, and world are all open systems that, optimally, both support you and are supported by you. You may want to determine the forms of wealth you currently receive from, and give back to, one of these large systems that provide the infrastructure for your life, relationships, and work. Afterward, you can decide the actions you need to take to increase the synergy and prosperity you experience as a part of this Whole.

|  | Forms of Wealth You Now Give to Your Society/World | Forms of Wealth You Now Receive from Your Society/World | Overall "Score" (0–10) |
|---|---|---|---|
| O. Sacred |  |  |  |
| 1. Essence |  |  |  |
| 2. Air |  |  |  |
| 3. Fire |  |  |  |
| 4. Water |  |  |  |
| 5. Earth |  |  |  |
| ⊕. Sacred |  |  |  |

## Notes to Yourself

• Areas that are in good shape:

• Areas that need more attention:

• Ideas for increasing prosperity:

• Action plan (use the Natural Laws of Prosperity to find ways you can increase this large system's wealth):

## Prosperity and the Balancing Act

In concluding *The Balancing Act*, I ask that you think of your life, relationships, and work as alchemical laboratories where you are constantly being transformed. Indeed, one of the greatest gifts of the alchemists may be their worldview that each part of your life is an inseparable part of a whole, seamless fabric.

In many cultures it is the practice to dedicate one day of the week to worship. However, a great secret to creating synergy and gaining prosperity is to make your daily life, interactions, and work an integral part of your spiritual practice. After all, there is no way to separate them! Although this may seem like a daunting prospect at first glance (that we have to be on our best behavior all the time), it actually is quite liberating.

The key to the Balancing Act is integrity, which includes the realization that we are all One, that we are connected to the Sacred, and that all the various aspects of our lives are linked. When we separate work from spirit, home from work, family from coworkers from friends, we fragment ourselves unnecessarily. Although this fragmentation may at first seem to be efficient and timesaving, in the long run it is neither. It winds up costing us our balance.

The alchemists argued that "what is below is like what is above, and that what is above is like what is below, to perpetrate the miracles of one thing." By implementing *The Balancing Act*, you can make your whole life a unified miracle of one thing. Your daily life, including interactions at home and work, will provide you with countless opportunities to practice the concepts you've learned in this book. You have the opportunity to turn your daily Balancing Act into a "palace of mirrors" in which you can see your shortcomings exposed, your temper uncovered, your fears displayed, and your buttons pushed. If you treat every day as a laboratory for learning, your worst and best sides will constantly be exposed for you to witness, study, and improve. It's not always fun, but it's deeply satisfying to live your life in a way that will help you attain mastery in your Balancing Act, create synergy throughout your whole life, and dramatically increase your wealth.

Go for it!

# A Blessing

Dear Reader,

I wish you the very best as you use what you've learned in *The Balancing Act* to make your life golden. I truly hope this book serves as a tool to help you and those who are dear to you.

Because you and I are connected—now more than ever—I invite you to share your thoughts, insights, victories, and obstacles with me. It is one of the great joys of authors to hear from those people who listened, understood, and put their material to good use. After all, it is you who will animate this print on paper by taking it into your own life. Don't be shy! You can contact me by writing to:

sharon@theCorporation.com.

In every aspect of your life, relationships, and work, I wish you balance, harmony, synergy, and joy.

*May you be happy,*
*May there be nothing you lack.*
*May the soft winds of fortune ever be at your back.*
*May you live forever,*
*Yet never grow old.*
*May your children have children whose children you hold.*[16]

Godspeed!
Sharon Seivert

# APPENDIX A

## WORKING FROM YOUR CORE

◆

In *Working from Your Core: Personal and Corporate Wisdom in a World of Change* (Newton, Mass.: Butterworth-Heinemann, 1998), I describe ten "Core Types" and ten "Core Cutures" that have a direct effect on each one of the five Elements of Success, both individually and organizationally. For example, your dominant Core Type influences your personal identity and values, vision and beliefs, what motivates you, how you interact, and your daily habits. Knowing the Core Types and Core Cultures will greatly assist you in your own Balancing Act.

*Working from Your Core* introduces an internal council of advisors who make their home in the human mind and heart (and body, will, and soul). These familiar, colorful characters are human instincts that can serve you in many ways—guiding you to a greater understanding of yourself, colleagues and friends, current and potential customers, neighbors, and the culture of workplace systems. Although *Working from Your Core* focuses on business applications, the material is easily adaptable for personal, home, or social use.

Many organizations (businesses, communities, or families) rise or fall depending upon how people inside them deal with each other. Unfortunately, many otherwise competent workers and leaders encounter—or cause—significant difficulties in their organizations due to their lack of understanding and poorly developed emotional intelligence. *Working from Your Core* allows you to take a clear snapshot of yourself, others, and your company. Then, it provides you with tools and a road map that can lead you to better communications, interactions, and leadership.

*Working from Your Core* does not require you to learn any new material. You already know the Core Types. Indeed, you will find that they are familiar to you as the main characters in stories human beings have told about themselves since the beginning of time. These internal advisors can serve you in a myriad of ways.

## Summary of the Ten Individual Core Types

Each one of the Core Types makes significant contributions to—and has significant difficulties within—the workplace. Because each type has its own special strengths and weaknesses, each is important at different times of our lives. All have gifts that can significantly enrich your life, relationships, and work. This then, is your inner council of advisors. (To obtain your personal Core Type Profile, complete the instrument provided in *Working from Your Core*.)

**Innocent.** The Innocent is the part of us who lives—or believes it is possible to live—in Eden. The Innocent's gift to the world is trust, optimism, belief, and a contentment with life as it is. The Innocent in each of us has a kind of pristine faith, an incorruptibility that others often try to protect. The Innocent's contentment and optimism, however, may be somewhat dependent upon a tendency to denial.

**Orphan.** The Orphan inside us wants to live in a safe world—but feels this is impossible. Orphans feel betrayed, abandoned, prematurely on their own, and powerless to help themselves. They tend to expect the worst and are prone to cynicism, which they may call "realism." However, the Orphan in each of us does help us face the unpleasant aspects of reality. It also reminds us of our interdependence with others and gives us the great gifts of compassion and empathy.

**Seeker.** The Seeker's journey is about identity and finding one's vocation or mission. The Seeker's story usually begins with a feeling of entrapment or restlessness and then a resulting escape—from a relationship, a job, a way of thinking or living. Then comes a solitary journey to find oneself. Seekers travel light (usually alone) and often avoid commitment in one or many parts of their lives.

**Jester.** The internal Jester lightens us up by finding clever, fun ways around obstacles—these can be intellectual, physical, or emotional. At worst, Jesters are irresponsible. At best, Jesters free us from convention to see things afresh. In either case, the Jester always undercuts order—even our own sense of individual identities.

**Caregiver.** The Caregiver is the part of us who tries to make the world a better place. Often, they will even sacrifice their own good for the sake of others. Caregivers are those ordinary individuals who aid others through their genuine selflessness and generosity. At the lowest levels, Caregivers can be manipulative; but at the highest levels, the act of giving is its own reward.

**Warrior.** The standard Warrior story has three principle characters: the Hero, the Villain, and the Victim. The Warrior's gift to each of us is the courage, will, and discipline to confront the enemy—within and without. Warriors are competitive, stoic, and value toughness and team spirit in themselves and in others. Their worst fear is being weak or cowardly.

**Magician.** The internal Magician helps us create what has never been before by opening us up to inspiration and then by manifesting new ideas into concrete reality. The Magician may be an inventor, an artist, or anyone who comes up with a new way of doing things—then makes it happen. Like the ancient alchemists, Magicians strive to transform lesser realities into better realities (symbolized by changing lead into gold).

**Ruler.** The Ruler is the natural leader who establishes and maintains order by taking diverse, seemingly chaotic, elements and making them into a harmonious whole. At worst, the Ruler can be a despot who creates order by subjugation, fear, or exclusion of less desirable elements. At best, the Ruler has the creativity to find the use for all the diversity in the workplace. It is the Ruler within us who understands that we are responsible for both our internal and external realities.

**Lover.** If the Warrior, the Caregiver, and the Magician try to change reality, the Lover in each of us embraces, accepts, and appreciates it. Lovers choose their work because they fall in love with it. At a lower level, the Lover may love only a few people or things; at a higher level, the Lover may love everything that exists. In the workplace, the Lover is associated with passion for what he or she does and for appreciation of self and others.

**Sage.** The Sage's journey requires the ability to let go, to rid the self of attachment to people, things, and ideas. At the lowest level, the Sage has little ability to empathize with ordinary people (loves humanity, but hates people). At the highest level, the Sage loves—but without ego attachment. In the workplace, the Sage may take on an explicit teaching function, may act as an elder statesperson or general advisor, or may choose to retreat to some variety of "ivory tower" for contemplation.

When you have a better idea of which internal advisor is taking the lead—in yourself or others—you will quickly be able to work from your Core in the following ways:

- developing a common language for better communications;

- improving personal mastery and emotional intelligence;

- increasing self-understanding and professional development;

- developing leadership skills and managing difficult employees;

- building teams, resolving conflict, making the most of diversity;

- determining who your individual and corporate customers are, then speaking their preferred language so that you can deliver better service.

Each of these ten cross-cultural models comes in positive and negative, high and low forms. Misunderstandings easily occur among individuals who have different dominant Core Types. This is because the Core Types represent (are codes for) not just behaviors, but whole worldviews. The ten core models of human behavior are not abstract theoretical constructs. They are living, breathing realities.

Indeed, each Core Type influences us to live our lives, and do our work, according to a completely different script. Working from your Core can help you notice these scripts as you watch them being played out daily. You will be able to see the Core Types in others as they walk by you in the hall, or hear which advisor is in charge as someone delivers a presentation at a staff meeting. And as a result, you will interact more effectively and get your ideas across in a way that is easier for others to comprehend.

Sometimes you may find yourself mystified—sometimes downright annoyed—by the differing behavior and ideas of others. Knowing the Core Types will always give you a better chance of understanding what others are thinking and feeling, and why they're acting as they are. This knowledge translates into greater self-awareness and professionalism, less conflict and suffering in the workplace—and better business.

## Summary of the Ten Forms of Organizational Culture

Each of these Core Cultures feels different, responds to change differently, and learns in different ways. In order to make effective and lasting improvements in any workplace (or community or other system), the culture must first be properly understood so that it can be managed successfully. Here then is a summary of the ten Core Cultures. (To obtain your Organizational Culture Profile, complete the instrument provided in *Working from Your Core*.)

**Innocent.** Highly hierarchical and centralized workplaces in which management functions as parents and employees as well-behaved offspring. It also usually provides employees with considerable job security. A well-developed Innocent organization is a pleasant place to work—the environment is full of hope, optimism, and contentment. The least successful are so steeped in tradition and convention that they avoid changes that should be made and may have a tendency toward denial of reality.

**Orphan.** The Orphan organization is a common kind of organizational culture, especially during times of upheaval. It includes many systems that have experienced some "wound" or serious disruption. The most successful Orphan organization is aware of its wound and functions as a "wounded healer" (such as Alcoholics Anonymous or Solidarity). Less well-developed Orphan cultures are those in which both management and employees feel fearful and powerless; this results in a workplace environment that is discouraged, cynical, and distrustful.

**Seeker.** Highly decentralized workplaces that place a primary value on the autonomy of individuals. Professional associations in which colleagues work together-but-separately are typical of this cultural type. The most successful Seeker organizations are peer groups with enough interest in each other's work to keep in regular contact, thereby developing some level of cohesion. The least successful Seeker organizations have such weak centers that they are organizations in name only.

**Jester.** Highly creative, fun organizational environments that value spontaneity and innovation, and that have little tolerance for forms, policies, or bureaucratic procedures. The best Jester cultures are characterized by lightness, having fun even in difficult situations, brainstorming, and maximum creativity. Less well-developed Jester cultures can take shortcuts that result in inferior products, not complete their work by deadline, or use "flim-flam" techniques to sell their products.

**Caregiver.** Workplaces whose purpose is to make life better for, or to take care of, other people, particularly the less fortunate; they are characterized by selflessness and service. In a well-developed Caregiver organization the service performed is its own reward, and the employees themselves are also well taken care of. In a less well-developed Caregiver culture, employees are not paid well and work long hours; this contributes to burnout, low self-esteem, little mutual respect, and high staff turnover.

**Warrior.** Highly competitive businesses that are focused, results oriented, and goal directed. The well-developed Warrior organization expects its employees to function as a winning team, and its rewards are commensurate with results. Values include loyalty, discipline, hard work, and constantly proving oneself. A less well-developed Warrior culture may be inflexible, have too much activity just for activity's sake, and encourage internal competition that undercuts teamwork.

**Magician.** Systems that are highly energized, focused, flexible, innovative, and quick to respond to change. This makes them able to "thrive on chaos" (such as rapidly changing market conditions). A successful Magician organization uses its energy, will, and focus to do its work in the easiest, most efficient ways possible, and it always looks for win/win solutions to problems. A less successful Magician workplace may change too much too fast, burn out its people, or be too "far out" for its time.

**Ruler.** Corporations that are stable, orderly, and function smoothly with timely procedures and policies. They are usually hierarchial and often bureaucratic. Their "currency" is power and prestige. The best Ruler organizations use their power judiciously, treat their staff fairly, and actively seek talent and diversity of all types. The worst Ruler cultures are authoritarian, elitist, intolerant, inflexible, slow to adapt to changing conditions, and clogged by their own bureaucracy.

**Lover.** The Lover workplace is intense, highly energized, and seemingly tireless in its attempts to fulfill its mission. Consensus and harmony are major values. In a well-developed Lover organization there is a shared passion for both the mission and one's coworkers. The atmosphere tingles with positive energy and enjoyment. In a less well-developed Lover system there can be slow decision-making and a deemphasis on the product while staff focus on building consensus and personal relationships.

**Sage.** The Sage culture values quality, competence, planning, analysis, intellectually interesting models, and clear, logical thinking. Its structure will be determined by the organization's mission. It emphasizes fairness, equanimity, and respect, and is intolerant of petty conflicts. A successful Sage workplace is pleasant, calm, easy-going, productive, and seems unflappable, even during times of crisis. The least successful Sage systems are so emotionally detached and analytical that they feel inhuman and are cold, uncaring places to work.

The ten Core Types are universal models that can be easily understood and discussed across corporate lines. In addition to its applications for individuals, the ten forms of organizational culture can be used as a framework to diagnose your workplace. With that point of reference, you can better tailor and optimize the effectiveness of all your change efforts. You can put your knowledge of the ten Core Cultures to excellent use in:

- preparing for successful mergers and acquisitions (a great many fail due to inadequate mutual understanding of the two business cultures);

- resolving departmental conflicts;

- clarifying shared corporate values and core corporate identity;

- developing a strong brand indentity within the industry;

- designing strategic initiatives that are compatible with the organization's Core Culture;

- making certain that the organization's stated mission, vision, values, communications channels, and structure and policies are aligned with the underlying core cultural identity;

- tailoring all change and development efforts by framing them in language that fits the organization's culture;

- addressing the root cause of staff morale issues.

Organizational culture is an invisible, yet extraordinarily powerful force that propels each of us through our work days, affecting our every action, interaction, and decision. Unfortunately, because culture is such an abstract concept to discuss, it has largely been ignored as a factor in the rush of daily decision making. Corporate culture can silently sabotage seemingly rock-solid business deals, transforming them instead into economic disasters.

You can obtain a copy of *Working from Your Core* by ordering directly from Butterworth-Heinemann (Phone 781-904-2500; or write PO Box 4500, Woburn, MA 01801-2041), from your local book store, or from an on-line e-bookstore (amazon.com, bn.com, etc.).

◆

# APPENDIX B

## EMOTIONAL INTELLIGENCE
## AND THE CORE TYPES

◆

*The Balancing Act* requires a great deal of emotional intelligence. (See discussion in Part II, chapter four about this relatively new and exciting field of inquiry.) Below are the primary emotional intelligence testing instruments developed by current leaders in the field and a discussion of how you can use the Core Types to develop your own emotional intelligence.

| Bar-On EQi Test (BO) | Emotional Competence Inventory (ECI) | Multifactor Emotional Intelligence Scale (MEIS) |
|---|---|---|
| 1. **Intrapersonal:** emotional self-awareness, assertiveness, self-regard, self-actualization, independence | 1. **Self-Awareness:** emotional self-awareness, accurate self-assessment, self-confidence | 1. **Identifying Emotions:** the ability to recognize how you and those around you are feeling |
| 2. **Interpersonal:** empathy, the quality of interpersonal relationships, social responsibility | 2. **Self-Management:** self-control, trustworthiness, conscientiousness, adaptability, achievement orientation, initiative | 2. **Using Emotions:** the ability to generate an emotion, and then reason with this emotion |
| 3. **Adaptability:** problem-solving, flexibility, reality testing | 3. **Social Awareness:** empathy, organizational awareness, service orientation | 3. **Understanding Emotions:** the ability to understand complex emotions and emotional "chains," how emotions transition from one stage to another |
| 4. **Stress Management:** ability to handle stress, impulse control | 4. **Social Skills:** developing others, leadership, influence communication, change catalyst, conflict management, building bonds, teamwork, and collaboration | 4. **Managing Emotions:** the ability that allows you to manage emotions in yourself and in others |
| 5. **General Mood:** optimism, overall happiness | | |

# How the Core Types Develop Emotional Intelligence

You can use the Core Types to develop your own emotional intelligence, as indicated below.

**Intrapersonal/Self-Awareness.** Learning the ten Core Types can help us identify what we are feeling, thereby increasing our emotional self-awareness, accurate self-assessment, and eventually, our self-confidence. These ten different energies show up in our body and facial movements, word choice, clothing, dominant emotion, and expressed beliefs about how the world works—thereby giving us very tangible ways to become more astute about what's going on inside us.

**Self-Management.** Knowing the Core Types provides a variety of choices with which to respond to situations and to behave. It is especially helpful in giving us options if we're "stuck." Knowing the Core Types and the options we have to call upon gives us significant self-control and adaptability, and helps us take the initiative in interactions.

**Interpersonal/Social Awareness.** Because all of the Core Types exist in each one of us, they give us empathy, then provide a tangible way to directly relate to other people. First they help us understand the "script" someone else is following. Then we can relate to that aspect of ourselves and connect directly (type to type) to another person. Moreover, because the Core Type system includes a parallel model of organizational culture, it can dramatically increase our awareness and our ability to adapt to and serve our worplaces.

**Social Skills.** Core Types provide techniques for experiencing emotional intelligence in the body. This allows us to better remember and apply emotional intelligence when needed. In particular each Core Type helps us develop our social skills because each has a unique approach to leadership, influence, communication, conflict management, bond building, teamwork, and collaboration. (However, not all are change catalysts.)

**Identifying, Using, Understanding, and Managing Emotions.** These are critical aspects of emotional intelligence, as defined by those researches who first coined the term. All of these functions are facilitated by learning the Core Types. (See table of Core Types and Emotions below.)

**Stress Management and General Mood.** These categories are, I believe, key to personal and professional success. Other researches have documented the phenomenon of "learned optimism" as being a factor that contributes to health and wellness.

## Core Types and Emotions

| Core Type | Emotional Difficulties for Which This Core Type Provides Help | Specific Emotions This Core Type Helps to Access (And Emotional Intelligence Test Item to Which It Relates) |
|---|---|---|
| Innocent | Sadness; depression, hopelessness, fear of abandonment | Optimism (BO5), trust and trustworthiness (ECI2), hope, faith in the goodness of what is right now, delight in small things, cheerfulness, happiness (BO5) |
| Orphan | Lack of connection to others or self; interpersonal naivete | Empathy (ECI3 & BO2), i.e., compassion for those who suffer as you do; awareness of own sadness; doubt, or vulnerability (ECI1); reality-testing (BO3) |
| Seeker | Definition of self versus community or any other "norm"; sense of own uniqueness and special gifts | Independence (BO1); willingness to let go, give up, move on to something else; agitation; restlessness; angst about what is; change catalyst—especially to find meaning (ECI4) |
| Jester | Finding innovative ways out of difficult situations; a key survival tool | Humor for problem solving (BO3); paradigm/ belief flexibility (BO3); adaptability (ECI2); independence (BO1); willingness to take risks and risk being laughed at, looking silly; change catalyst (ECI4)—for the sake of change; enjoyment; pleasure |
| Caregiver | Envy, jealousy; self-absorption; lack of connection to others | Tenderness; willingness to sacrifice and desire to make things better for others— service orientation (ECI3); social responsibility (BO2); conscientiousness (ECI2) |
| Warrior | Confusion, lack of focus; definition of adequate personal boundaries | Willingness to fight for what believe in; anger/rage at enemy; anger/impatience with whiners, losers, or ineptitude; impulse control (BO4); achievement orientation and initiative (ECI3); assertiveness (BO1) |
| Magician | Duality; rigidity of thought; sense of personal powerlessness | Change catalyst (ECI4); adaptable (ECI2 and BO3); sensitive to energy in people and its movement among them; collaboration (ECI4) and peacemaking—ability to see and secure win/win; problem-solving (BO3) |

| Ruler | Bringing life/work/home into order, efficiency—for utilitarian good | Feeling responsible to bring order out of chaos, to make things run smoothly; social responsibility (BO2); conscientiousness (ECI2) |
| --- | --- | --- |
| Lover | No "juice" or vitality in life; boredom | Passion; love of work, person, place, or life; anger/rage of whatever obstructs love object; self-actualization (BO1) |
| Sage | Emotional excess in any direction | Stress management (BO4); dispassion; self-control (ECI2) equipoise; equanimity; balance; calm; peace; quiet joy |

# NOTES

◆

## Welcome!

1. *Webster's Collegiate Dictionary*, 5th Edition (Springfield, Mass.: G. & C. Merriam Co., 1937), 80.

## Part I

1. Richard Erdoes and Alfonso Ortiz, eds., "The Good Twin and the Evil Twin," *American Indian Myths and Legends* (New York: Pantheon Fairy Tale and Folklore Library, 1984), 77, 78.

2. Robert Lawlor, *Sacred Geometry: Philosophy and Practice* (London: Thames and Hudson, 1982), 58.

3. Ibid., 58.

4. J. E. Cirlot, *Dictionary of Symbols*, translated from the Spanish by Jack Sage (New York: Philosophical Library, 1962), 222.

5. Ibid., 122.

6. Ibid., 45.

7. Carol Pearson and Sharon Seivert, *Magic At Work: Camelot, Creative Leadership and Everyday Miracles* (New York: Doubleday/Currency, 1995), 5.

8. Ibid., 5.

9. Fritjof Capra, *The Tao of Physics* (New York: Bantam Books, 1984), 6.

10. Serge Kahili King, *Urban Shaman: A Handbook for Personal and Planetary Transformation Based on the Hawaiian Way of the Adventurer* (New York: Simon and Schuster, 1990), 22.

11. Sharon Seivert, *Working from Your Core: Personal and Corporate Wisdom in a World of Change* (Newton, Mass.: Butterworth-Heinneman, 1998), chapter seven.

12. These two phrases are traditionally used in Wicca affirmations

13. Charles Handy, *The Age of Unreason* (Boston: Harvard Business School Press, 1989), 24.

14. Radcliffe Public Policy Institute, "Life's Work: Generational Attitudes Toward Work and Life Integration" (Cambridge, Mass.: Harris Interactive, 2000). A study funded by Fleet Boston Financial—1008 people were interviewed in the first quarter of 2000.

15. Joe Dominguez and Vicki Robin, *Your Money or Your Life: Transforming Your Relationship with Money and Achieving Financial Independence* (New York: Penguin Books, 1992), 227. The study, done by the Hilton Hotels Corporation in the early 1990s, found that "70% of those earning $30,000 a year or more would give up one day of salary per week for a four-day work week."

16. Ibid., prologue.

17. Maharishi Mahesh Yogi, *Creating an Ideal Society: A Global Undertaking* (Switzerland, New York, India: Maharishi European Research University Press, 1977), 8–9.

# Chapter 1

1.  Bruce Chatwin, *The Songlines* (New York: Penguin Books, 1987), 72, 73.

2.  J. E. Cirlot, *A Dictionary of Symbols*, 91.

3.  Chatwin, *The Songlines*, 72, 73.

4.  Lise Vail, "Spanda: The Vibration of Freedom," *Darshan 73, The Unstuck Sound*: 9.

5.  Michael Dames, *Mythic Ireland* (London: Thames and Hudson, 1992), 194–196.

6.  Deepak Chopra, 3 December 1991, lecture presented in Boston, Mass.

7.  Jonathan Kaufman, "German Workers Accept Offer," *Boston Globe*, 8 May 1992, p. 2.

8.  William Butler Yeats, "The Second Coming," *The Collected Poems of W. B. Yeats* (New York: Macmillan, 1933), 104.

9.  John Heider, "Doing Little," *The Tao of Leadership* (Atlanta: Humanics New Age, 1985), 73.

10. Lorna Catford and Michael Ray, *The Path of the Everyday Hero* (Los Angeles: Jeremy Tarcher, Inc., 1991), 183–184.

11. This self-inquiry technique is a slight modification of a Siddha yoga self-inquiry method taught to me by a teacher in that tradition.

12. Betty J. Eadie, *Embraced by the Light* (New York: Bantam Books, 1992), 42.

13. Al Stillman and Ben Weisman, "When I Am with You" (New York: Johnny Mathis Music, 1957).

14. Mary Walton, *The Deming Management Method* (New York: Perigee Books, 1986), 55.

15. J. E. Cirlot, *A Dictionary of Symbols*, 352.

16. Serge King, "The Way of Adventurer," in Shirley Nicholson's *Shamanism: An Expanded View of Reality* (Wheaton, Ill.: Theosophical Publishing House, 1987), 193.

17. Lawrence M. Miller, *American Spirit: Visions of a New Corporate Culture* (New York: William Morrow and Company, Inc., 1984), 184.

18. Ibid., 184.

19. Margaret J. Wheatley, *Leadership and the New Science: Learning about Organization from an Orderly Universe* (San Franciso: Berrett-Koehler Publishers, 1992), 11.

20. Ibid., 57.

# Chapter 2

1.  George M. Lamsa, trans. (from the Aramaic of the Peshitta), Genesis 1:4–5, *Holy Bible: From the Ancient Eastern Text* (San Francisco: Harper San Francisco, 1968), 7.

2.  Ibid., Genesis 2:7–8, 8.

3.  Tor Norretranders, *The User Illusion: Cutting Consciousness Down to Size*. Translated by Jonathan Sydenham (New York: Viking, 1991, translation copyright 1998). Quotation is from jacket cover.

4.  Robert Ornstein and Paul Ehrlich, *New World, New Mind* (New York: Simon & Schuster, 1989), 217.

5.  Fred Reed and Sharon Seivert, "The Implications of Autonomy for Learning in Organizations," Steven Cavaleri and David Fearon, eds. *Managing in Organizations That Learn* (Cambridge/Oxford: Blackwell Business, 1995), 377–402. This summary is also taken from discussions with coauthor Fred Reed.

6. Lynnette Yount, *Teams Course Instructors Manual* (Arlington, Va.: Lynette Yount Associates), 8–9.

7. Deepak Chopra, *Quantum Healing: The Frontiers of Mind/Body Medicine* (New York: Bantam Books, 1989), 41.

8. Patricia Monaghan, *The Book of Goddesses and Heroines* (St. Paul: Llewellyn Publications, 1990), 18–19.

9. Martin E. P. Seligman, *Learned Optimism: How to Change Your Mind and Your Life* (New York: Pocket Books, 1990, 1998), 15.

10. Ibid., 14.

11. Art McNeil, *The "I" of the Hurricane* (Toronto: Stoddart Publishing Co., 1987), 99.

12. J. E. Cirlot, *A Dictionary of Symbols*, 5–6.

13. Marvin Weisbord, *Productive Workplaces* (San Francisco: Jossey-Bass, 1987), 266–271.

14. W. Edwards Deming, *Quality, Productivity and Competitive Position* (Cambridge, Mass.: MIT Center for Advanced Engineering Study, 1982), 33.

15. Art McNeil, *The "I" of the Hurricane*, 65.

16. Peter Block, *The Empowered Manager: Positive Political Skills at Work* (San Francisco: Jossey-Bass Publishers, 1991), 108.

17. Margaret J. Wheatley, *Leadership and the New Science*, 13.

18. Peter Block, *The Empowered Manager: Positive Political Skills at Work*, 115–122.

19. Robert Ornstein and Paul Ehrlich, *New World, New Mind*, 264, 265, 260.

20. Ibid., 12.

## Chapter 3

1. Harold Fritzsch, *The Creation of Matter: The Universe from Beginning to End* (New York: Basic Books, 1984), 3, 4, 223–225.

2. Joseph Campbell, *The Masks of God: Oriental Mythology* (New York: Penguin Books, 1962), 176.

3. Thom Hartmann, *The Last Hours of Ancient Sunlight* (New York: Harmony Books, 1998, 1999), 109.

4. Ibid., 105.

5. Kenneth Thomas, "Conflict and Conflict Management," *The Handbook of Industrial and Organizational Psychology* (Chicago: Rand McNally, 1976).

6. Thomas F. Crum, *The Magic of Conflict: Turning a Life of Work into a Work of Art* (New York: Simon & Schuster, 1987), 73.

7. Ibid., 15.

8. Mary Walton, *The Deming Management Method*, 94.

9. Art McNeil, *The "I" of the Hurricane*, 15.

10. Doris Gates, *Lord of the Sky—Zeus* (New York: Viking Press, 1972), 20.

11. Edward Tripp, *The Meridian Handbook of Classical Mythology* (New York: Meridian Books/New American Library, 1970), 499–500.

12. Richard Erdoes and Alfonso Ortiz, eds., *American Indian Myths and Legends*, 344.

13. Barbara G. Walker, *The Women's Encyclopedia of Myths and Secrets* (San Francisco: Harper & Row, 1983), 1046.

14. Manuela Dunn Mascetti, *The Song of Eve* (New York: Fireside/Simon & Schuster, 1990), 194.

15. Stephen R. Covey, *The Seven Habits of Highly Effective People* (New York: Simon & Schuster, 1989), 149–154.

16. Steven Cavaleri and Krzysztof Obloj, *Management Systems: A Global Perspective* (Belmont, Calif.: Wadsworth Publishing Company, 1993), 62–65.

17. Edward Tripp, *The Meridian Handbook of Classical Mythology*, 598.

## Chapter 4

1. Barbara G. Walker, *The Women's Encyclopedia of Myths and Secrets*, 489, 490.

2. Margaret Wheatley, *Leadership and the New Science*, 51.

3. Robert Lawlor, *Sacred Geometry: Philosophy and Practice*, 22.

4. J. E. Cirlot, *A Dictionary of Symbols*, 345.

5. Ibid., 490.

6. Barbara G. Walker, *The Women's Encyclopedia of Myths and Secrets*, 490.

7. Daniel Goleman, *Emotional Intelligence* (New York: Bantam Books, 1995), 15–18.

8. Ibid., 312.

9. Ibid., 15–16.

10. Howard Gardner, *Frames of Mind: The Theory of Multiple Intelligences* (New York: Basic Books, 1983).

11. Robert Ornstein and Paul Ehrlich, *New World, New Mind*, 109.

12. The Dalai Lama, *The Power of Compassion* (London: Hammersmith, Thorsons/Harper Collins, 1981), 74.

13. Daniel Goleman, *Emotional Intelligence*, 97.

14. Ibid., 99.

15. Margaret Wheatley, *Leadership and the New Science*, 40.

16. Ibid., 34.

17. Sharon Seivert, Alex Pattakos, Fred Reed, and Steven Cavaleri, "Learning from the Core," *Managing in Organizations That Learn*, 365.

18. Walt Whitman, *The Works of Walt Whitman: The Collected Poetry*, vol. I (New York: Funk and Wagnalls, 1948), 118–19.

19. John Redtail Freesoul, "The Native American Prayer Pipe," *Shamanism: An Expanded View of Reality*, Shirley Nicholson, ed. (Wheaton, Ill.: Theosophical Publishing House, 1987), 207–8.

20. S. L. Bem, "The Measurement of Psychological Androgyny," *Journal of Consulting and Clinical Psychology*, 42 (1974):156–62.

21. Margaret Wheatley, *Leadership and the New Science*, 70.

22. Samuel Taylor Coleridge, "The Rime of the Ancient Mariner." In Robert Shafer, ed., *From Beowulf to Thomas Hardy* (New York: The Odyssey Press, 1940), 337.

23. Peter Block, *The Empowered Manager*, 127.

24. James Gleick, *Chaos: Making a New Science* (New York: Penguin Books, 1987), 8.

# Chapter 5

1.  Joseph Campbell, *The Masks of God: Occidental Mythology*, (New York: Penguin Books, 1991), 153.

2.  Edward Tripp, *The Meridian Handbook of Classical Mythology*, 248.

3.  Barbara G. Walker, *The Women's Encyclopedia of Myths and Secrets*, 263.

4.  Ibid., 264.

5.  Mary Catherine Bateson, *Composing a Life* (New York: Atlantic Monthly Press, 1989), quote from back cover.

6.  Walt Whitman, *The Works of Walt Whitman: The Collected Poetry*, vol. I, 117.

7.  Deepak Chopra, *Quantum Healing* (New York: Bantam Books, 1989, 1990), 49.

8.  Alan Jay Lerner and Frederick Loewe, "Show Me" from *My Fair Lady* (New York: Coward-McCann, 1956).

9.  Deepak Chopra, *Quantum Healing*, 41.

10. Peter M. Senge, *The Fifth Discipline* (New York: Currency/Doubleday, 1990), 341.

11. Steven Cavaleri and Krzysztof Obloj, *Management Systems: A Global Perspective*, 24.

12. Charles Handy, *The Age of Unreason*, chapters 4, 5, and 6.

13. Ibid., 183–184.

14. C. K. Prahalad and Gary Hamel, *The Harvard Business Review*, May–June 1990, 82.

15. Robert Ornstein and Paul Ehrlich, *New World, New Mind*, 45.

16. Thom Hartmann, *The Last Hours of Ancient Sunlight*, 19–20.

17. Ibid., 17–18.

18. Ibid., 76.

19. Ibid., 46.

20. Ibid., 59.

21. Ibid., 46–52.

22. Ibid., 201.

# Chapter 6

1.  Pandit Satyakam Vidyalankar, *English Translation of the Holy Vedas* (Delhi: Clarion Books, 1998).

2.  J. D. Cooper, *An Illustrated Encyclopaedia of Traditional Symbols* (London: Thames and Hudson, 1978), 36.

3.  Richard Erodoes and Alfonso Ortiz, eds., *American Indian Myths and Legends*, 77, 78.

4.  Seivert, *Working from Your Core*.

5.  Ronnie Lessem, *Total Quality Learning* (Cambridge, Mass.: Blackwell Business Books, 1991).

6.  Ibid., 284.

7.  Margaret Wheatley, *Leadership and the New Science*, 94.

8.  Seivert, *Working from Your Core*, 286.

9.  J. D. Cooper, *An Illustrated Encyclopedia of Traditional Symbols*, 32.

10. Erich Jantsch, *The Self-Organizing Universe* (Oxford, England: Pergamon Press, 1980), 1, 7, 10.

11. Michael Talbot, *The Holographic Universe* (New York: HarperPerennial, 1991), 47.

12. Fritjof Capra, *The Tao of Physics* (New York: Shambala/Bantam Books, 1976), 95.

13. Ibid., 6.

14. Stanislas Klossowski de Rola, *Alchemy: The Secret Art* (London: Thames and Hudson, 1973), 48. Quote attributed to Hermes Trismegistus.

15. Ibid., 15.

16. Robert Lawlor, *Sacred Geometry: Philosophy and Practice*, 23.

17. Hans Biederman, *Dictionary of Symbols: Cultural Icons and the Meaning Behind Them* (New York: Meridian Books, 1989), 154.

18. Black Elk, John Gneisenau Neihardt, Vine Deloria Jr., *Black Elk Speaks: Being the Life Story of a Holy Man of the Ogalala Sioux* (Lincoln, Nebr.: University of Nebraska Press, 1961.)

19. J. E. Cirlot, *A Dictionary of Symbols*, 223.

20. William Fix, *Lake of Memory Rising: Return of the Five Ancient Truths at the Heart of Religion* (San Francisco: Council Oaks Books, 2000), 36.

21. Joachim-Ernst Berendt, *The Third Ear: On Listening to the World* (New York: Henry Holt and Company, 1985), 72.

22. J. E. Cirlot, *A Dictionary of Symbols*, 221.

23. J. D. Cooper, *An Illustrated Encylopaedia of Traditional Symbols*, 113.

24. Robert Lawlor, *Sacred Geometry: Philosophy and Practice*, 19, 20.

25. Joachim-Ernst Berendt, *The Third Ear: On Listening to the World*, 104.

26. Ibid., 103.

27. From the introduction to the video *Cymatics III: Bringing Matter to Life and Sound* (Epping, N.H.: MACROmedia, 1986).

28. From the video *Cymatics III: Bringing Matter to Life and Sound*.

29. Jeff Volk, *Of Sound, Mind and Body: Music and Vibrational Healing* (videotape) (St. Petersburg, Fla.: Lumina Productions, 1992).

30. Joachim-Ernst Berendt, *The Third Ear: On Listening to the World*, 102.

31. "Sa" (136 Hz) is considered to be the earth-orbit note, played many octaves higher so that it is audible for human ears. From Joachim-Ernst Berendt, *The Third Ear: On Listening to the World*, 90.

32. Ibid., 90.

33. Studs Terkel, *Working* (New York: Avon Books, 1972), xxix. Quote attributed to Nora Watson.

34. Ibid., xiii.

35. Ibid., 390.

36. Ibid., 704.

37. John Heider, *The Tao of Leadership* (Atlanta: Humanics New Age, 1985), 53.

38. John Clarkeson, "Jazz vs. Symphony," *Perspectives* (Boston: Boston Consulting Group, 1990).

39. Joachim-Ernst Berendt, *The Third Ear: On Listening to the World*, 102.

40. David Bohm, *Wholeness and the Implicate Order* (London and New York: Routledge, 1980), 200.

## Chapter 7

1. "Maha Lakshmi—the Goddess of Prosperity," *Darshan Magazine*, 8–17.

2. Stanislas Klossowski de Rola, *Alchemy: The Secret Art*, 7.

3. Jack Tresidder, *Dictionary of Symbols: An Illustrated Guide to Traditional Images, Icons and Emblems* (San Francisco: Chronicle Books, 1998), 92–93.

4. Stanislas Klossowski de Rola, *Alchemy: The Secret Art*, 7.

5. Ibid., 14.

6. Alexander Jones, ed., *The Jerusalem Bible* (New York: Doubleday & Co., 1966), Matt. 6:26–34.

7. R. Buckminster Fuller, *Operating Manual for Spaceship Earth* (New York: Pocket Books, 1970), 85.

8. Ibid., 86, 87.

9. Elizabeth Roberts and Elias Amidon, ed., *Prayers for a Thousand Years* (San Francisco: Harper, 1999), 80. Poem is by Martin Palmer of the International Consultancy on Religion, Education and Culture, England.

10. Serge Kahili King, *Urban Shaman*, 62.

11. Alexander Jones, ed., *The Jerusalem Bible*, Matt. 25: 14–31.

12. *Webster's Collegiate Dictionary*, 5th Edition (Springfield, Mass.: G. & C. Merriam Co., 1937), 1017.

13. Mitch Albom, *Tuesdays with Morrie* (New York: Doubleday, 1997), 52. Quote is attributed to Levine.

14. R. Buckminster Fuller, *Operating Manual for Spaceship Earth*, 78.

15. Mitch Albom, *Tuesdays with Morrie*, 81.

16. Sharon Seivert, "Kathleen's Blessing," from an unpublished musical play *Acts of God: The Year of Natural Disasters*.

# INDEX

◆

# BOOKS OF RELATED INTEREST

### Creating the Work You Love
Courage, Commitment, and Career
*by Rick Jarow, Ph.D.*

### Enlightened Management
Bringing Buddhist Principles to Work
*by Dona Witten with Akong Tulku Rinpoche*

### Transforming Your Dragons
How to Turn Fear Patterns Into Personal Power
*by José Stevens*

### Financial Success
Harnessing the Power of Creative Thought
*by Wallace D. Wattles*

### Crafting the Soul
Creating Your Life as a Work of Art
*by Rabbi Byron L. Sherwin, Ph.D.*

### Creative Visualization
Using Imagery and Imagination for Self-Transformation
*by Ronald Shone*

### Leading From Within
Martial Arts Skills for Dynamic Business and Management
*by Robert Pater*

### The Spiritual Art of Dialogue
Mastering Communication for Personal Growth,
Relationships, and the Workplace
*by Robert Apatow, Ph.D.*

Inner Traditions • Bear & Company
P.O. Box 388
Rochester, VT 05767
1-800-246-8648
www.InnerTraditions.com

Or contact your local bookseller